MICHELLE SAGARA

CAST IN OBLIVION

mira

mira

Recycling programs
for this product may
not exist in your area.

ISBN-13: 978-0-7783-0784-6

Cast in Oblivion

For questions and comments about the quality of this book, please contact us at CustomerService@Harlequin.com.

BookClubbish.com

Printed in U.S.A.

This is for Chris Szego.

Thank you for almost two decades of bookselling, management and, in the end, friendship—even if I only get to keep one of them, they've all been invaluable.

CAST IN OBLIVION

CHAPTER 1

The Consort was coming to dinner.

Hurried attempts to cancel that dinner—for obvious reasons—met with no resistance. Unfortunately, they met with no response whatsoever. Kaylin had, with Bellusdeo's help, attempted to use the Imperial messenger service to relay news of the cancellation, but to no avail. The Consort was not within the High Halls. Kaylin had no idea where, exactly, the Consort was; she had last seen evidence of her presence in the Hallionne near the West March.

And no one in the High Halls apparently felt up to receiving a message intended for the Consort herself. They were conspicuous in their absence; according to the messenger service, the High Halls were practically empty.

Kaylin had other avenues of approach and, when the messenger service failed, chose to use them. She, unlike most of the mortals or Barrani in the Empire, held the True Names of a number of significant Barrani lords. She started at the bottom.

Ynpharion.

"Kaylin, dear, don't play with your food." Helen's Avatar was not physically in the dining room, but she kept watch over the occupants of the house. The house was her body, after all.

"I'm not playing with it. I'm eating it slowly."

"I've watched you eat slowly," Mandoran said, "and that's not eating. Food is meant to enter your mouth. Which is closed." Before Kaylin could snap at him, he added, "Most of us don't mind if your mouth is closed. You've done nothing but swear all morning. And afternoon. And it's not even your day off."

This was not true. Technically it wasn't *supposed* to be a day off, but she had been given leave to take a few, where "leave" in this case meant Marcus's very rumbly suggestion. Apparently the upper echelons—the Lord of Hawks at the very least—knew about the upcoming dinner, and everyone considered preparation for said dinner to be of vastly more import than catching petty criminals.

Kaylin didn't agree.

She did, however, find it vastly more stressful.

She had been given permission to cancel the dinner. She had not, however, managed to reach the dinner's most important attendee: the Consort. If the Consort showed up at her door on the appointed evening, she was going to be welcomed, and she was going to be fed.

Bellusdeo seemed entirely sanguine about the visit, which Kaylin tried not to resent. Her eyes were slightly orange tinted, but that could also be explained by the presence of close to an extra dozen Barrani beneath Helen's roof. She had expected the visitors—Teela's friends from a very distant childhood—to be vastly more difficult about Dragons in their living space, but the cohort seemed to view Bellusdeo largely through the lens of Mandoran. And when that had become reassuring Kaylin didn't quite know.

They were therefore not worried about Bellusdeo. They

didn't feel she was the biggest danger they currently faced. Since this was more or less true, Kaylin didn't ask; it also seemed rude to ask when Bellusdeo was sitting in the same room. Bellusdeo, however, didn't seem inclined to give the cohort any privacy; if they wanted privacy, they could stay in their own rooms.

Mandoran no longer considered alleviating boredom by heading out into the city streets. He wasn't bored, at the moment. Although the cohort could fall silent without warning, Kaylin was certain that the inside of their heads was one long, continuous argument, the subject of which—or one of the subjects—was the Consort.

Who was coming to dinner.

Sedarias was in favor of the dinner. Annarion and Mandoran were not. It wasn't clear to Kaylin how the rest of the votes were falling, but it didn't matter. Even if they voted universally against the visit, none of them could tell the Consort what to do. Any attempt to do so would probably start the war they had only narrowly averted.

Kaylin, however, was actually angry with the Consort. She wanted an apology from that august personage before she was allowed in the house.

Helen was politic; she had no opinion on the matter one way or another. In those exact words. Multiple times.

The Barrani—with the exception of Teela, also on brief leave of absence and also living in rooms Helen had provided—didn't really consider Kaylin's anger sensible or relevant. Any anger they now felt was pointed at each other and their current disagreements, whatever they were.

Teela *was* angry with the Consort. She was angry with Kaylin. She was angry with Annarion. Since she didn't expect to get any relief from venting that annoyance, she was currently most angry with Tain. Kaylin had suggested—very quietly—that Tain at least head into the Halls of Law for a normal day at work; Tain failed to hear her. Given the superiority of Barrani hearing, Kaylin took the hint.

So: Tain was at the dining room table—a place he frequently avoided—across from Teela, and frankly, given the color of his eyes, he wasn't any happier than his partner.

Bellusdeo was angry with the Emperor, who had strongly suggested that she return to the Imperial Palace for the duration of the cohort's stay, and all but commanded that she at least skip dinner with the Consort. The "all but" was the only reason the Dragon could be mellow, relatively speaking, at meals. Mealtime in the dining room resembled mealtime in the mess hall.

In all, it was easier to deal with criminals than it was to deal with friends. At least for the next few days.

Severn did not appear to be angry with anyone. Which was why he wasn't *at* Kaylin's place, of course.

Kaylin's familiar, perched on her left shoulder, seemed to have recovered from his emergency—and disastrous—trip to the West March; Hope was positively perky and cheerful. This didn't improve Kaylin's mood any.

Ynpharion, I know you're there.

I am currently occupied.

You can talk to the Consort.

Oh?

You can pass on the message.

He radiated frustration through the bond that connected them—a bond he despised and would happily remove. Sadly, the only sure way to remove it was to kill Kaylin. Or himself. And Ynpharion certainly didn't consider his own life to be of so little value.

You fail to understand, and I must assume that failure is deliberate. You may pester me—and do—at your leisure. You hold my name.

She hadn't noticed that Ynpharion failed to pester her in return.

You could prevent that if you had an ounce more will and determination. You do not. The Consort, however, is not as weak as you are, and she does not lack will. She will speak to me when she decides she must; she will allow me to pass on messages that are considered dire emergencies. But even then, she commands me. The discretion is not my own.

But I can't get a message to her any other way!

Ah. And you feel this is somehow some oversight?

She didn't. Not really. But she held on to faint hope.

Ynpharion wasn't big on any hope that wasn't his own or the Consort's. *She will not receive the message no matter how often you send it. No one will accept that message, either. Her orders are quite clear on that subject, and even were they not, the High Lord has made his will known. Anyone fool enough to accept the Imperial message is not long for the Court.*

You invited her to dinner. Live with the consequences. Ynpharion's tone made clear that he wanted Kaylin to go away.

I invited her to dinner, Kaylin said, grinding her teeth because she didn't need to open her mouth to speak to him, *before she attempted to imprison my friends. My home is their home in the immediate future. It would be beyond awkward to have her here now, and I can't even guarantee that it would be safe.*

You can.

No, actually, I can't. If you'd like to haul your butt here and speak to my house in person, you'd understand that. There's some risk, if things aren't handled very, very carefully. The cohort isn't like the rest of the Court. Maybe Hallionne Alsanis could host, but given what almost happened to him, I doubt it.

Then perhaps you could convince your friends to forgo the Test of Name. Should they choose to do so, I am certain the Consort would be willing to alter her plans. If you cannot convince your friends to forgo that test, how can you possibly expect that I, or anyone else, could convince the Consort *to forgo her one opportunity to meet the cohort and assess the threat they pose in person?*

"If you don't stop making that face, we're going to assume Helen's food has been poisoned," Bellusdeo said. "If you honestly feel it will pose that much of a danger, just fail to open the door when she arrives."

The silence around the table was an entirely different silence.

"I have oft wondered," Sedarias said, breaking it, "what form Dragon hospitality might take."

"This is where I live, but it is not my home. I am therefore not free to refuse a guest entry. Were I, I believe I would."

"Liar," Mandoran said quite cheerfully.

"You clearly don't spend enough time with Kaylin when she's in this mood. Satisfying base curiosity is possibly—just possibly—not worth it. As for Dragon hospitality in general, it is, as you suspect, somewhat different. If someone shows up at the heart of my Aerie with no invitation, we do not consider that a visit. We consider it an attack." Her smile had teeth in it. "I'm sure you can imagine the rest."

"I'm not sure I can," Sedarias replied, although she was grinning.

"Dear," Helen's voice said, "I'm not certain the table—or the room—will survive draconic transformation."

"Then let's hope it's not necessary." Bellusdeo was almost golden-eyed as she pushed herself up from the table. "If it makes you feel any better," she said to Kaylin, which was almost a guarantee that whatever followed wouldn't, "the Arkon is *also* coming to dinner."

To Kaylin's surprise, the Imperial messenger service delivered a parcel to her door. In it were two things. The first, a very, very thick pile of papers. The second, a letter written in a bold but tidy hand that made clear that if she lost *this* version of important information, dire consequences would be forthcoming. Given that the letter came from Lord Diarmat, Kaylin was left to imagine what those consequences were.

But she *had* lost the previous packet about the Barrani High Court, somewhere between Evanton's storefront on Elani street and the West March; she'd barely had time to panic about the loss, the threat of the Consort's visit loomed so large.

Mandoran had made his way to the door just as Kaylin was intercepting the package, and stared at it with bright-eyed curiosity. Had it not, in fact, been in Helen's hands, it would likely have been in his. The cohort didn't understand the concept of privacy. No, that was unfair. Teela understood it pretty well.

"What is it?" Mandoran asked, looming over Kaylin's left shoulder.

None of his business. But she could barely think that with a straight face; saying it was out of the question. "The Consort," she said, "is coming to dinner. This is a Dragon's concept of what I need to learn in order not to offend her."

Mandoran eyed the stack dubiously. "Dragons are weird. Sedarias wants to know what's actually in it."

"Exactly what I said." Kaylin exhaled. "Diarmat seems to feel that if I don't understand the political structure of the High Court, I'll cause offense no matter what I do. And this? It's the Dragon Court's understanding of the current hierarchy. A sort of who's who. Or maybe who's trying to kill who."

"You're not going to be surprised when I say she wants to see it, are you?"

"I'm not sure she won't consider it comedy."

"Given her mood? Comedy would be appreciated by the rest of us." He winced. "She's not happy with the available clothing in the house."

"Helen can probably help out with that—but the clothing she makes doesn't tend to stick around beyond the front gates."

"Unless we're eating in the streets, that shouldn't matter." He winced again. "I have to head downstairs."

"Someone other than you getting stuck in the walls?"

"Very funny."

Only after Mandoran had headed downstairs, as he referred to the shifting complex of rooms and stairs that comprised Helen's basement, did Terrano appear. Of the cohort, he was the most silent, the most withdrawn. Allaron, the cohort's giant, and easily the tallest Barrani Kaylin had ever met, usually grabbed him by the shoulder and physically dragged him to wherever the rest of the group was seated. But Terrano couldn't join their internal banter—or internal screaming arguments, which was what Kaylin suspected was more likely—and she knew when Terrano was actually with his friends because they were all forced to speak out loud if they wanted him to hear what they said.

"What is it really?" he asked.

"It really is a document that's supposed to help me navigate the political undercurrents of the High Court. Or at least that's what I was told. I've only managed to look at the first few pages."

"Is a Dragon really coming to dinner?"

"If the Consort is, yes." She exhaled. "We have a Dragon for dinner on most nights."

His expression made clear that he knew this. He was still

far warier of Bellusdeo than any of the rest of the cohort, and it was clear that he found their reaction to Kaylin's housemate confusing. Or wrong.

"The *other* Dragon is called the Arkon. I don't actually know why, so don't ask; he has a perfectly reasonable name, but Bellusdeo is the only person I've heard use it. He's old, he's cranky and he'd prefer to be walled into his library; the only thing that can dig him out of it is a literal fireball. Or Bellusdeo."

"Why is he coming?"

It was her turn to grimace. "Because the Dragon Court doesn't trust my political competence. The Arkon chose to come because Bellusdeo and Lord Diarmat don't get along all that well, and having Lord Diarmat be my supervisor— in my own home—would be a disaster. Worse than a disaster. For me," she added, seeing Terrano's expression. "He's my etiquette teacher."

Terrano laughed; the laughter was brief. "You don't think that's funny."

"No. Then again, I'm the one taking the lessons."

"Doesn't seem to be much of a teacher."

Considering the source, Kaylin almost found this insulting.

As if he could read her thoughts, Terrano shrugged. "I don't have to worry about my manners. There is *no way* I'm coming to dinner if the Consort is here."

Kaylin decided to change the subject. "Mandoran just headed downstairs."

"Someone stuck in a wall?"

"He didn't seem to think it was that funny when I asked, which probably means yes. Or worse," she added. Terrano brightened and drifted—literally—toward the closet that led to the basement.

★ ★ ★

"I'm worried about Terrano," Helen told Kaylin when the door itself had closed.

"Worried for him or worried about what he'll do?"

"He has no intention of harming the Consort. He's less sanguine about the Arkon, but that's because he assumes that the Arkon may attempt to harm him. Or his friends. It is not a concern of mine," she added. "Terrano is…not happy."

"None of the cohort is particularly happy."

Helen nodded. Because a messenger had arrived at the door, she'd brought out her physical Avatar. "I'm not certain we'll be able to keep him." At Kaylin's expression, she added, "Unless he means to harm any of my guests—or you—I'm not equipped to be a prison. And even if I had that inclination, Terrano is unusual enough that I'm not up to that task, not for long. He spent most of his life attempting to escape a Hallionne. What he learned over the centuries in the many attempts, I cannot easily counter.

"His thoughts are generally opaque—but I think that's deliberate. He's not afraid that I'll hear him. Or rather, he's not afraid that I will use what I hear against him. His interaction with Alsanis was extremely unusual, and he thinks of me—in some fashion—as a Hallionne."

"And you're not."

"I am neither as powerful nor as extensive as the Hallionne. I have more autonomy than the Hallionne, which gives me flexibility that is somewhat foreign to Terrano. But no, dear, I'm not worried about that. I do not believe he will intentionally damage me. Sedarias has disentangled herself, and will be joining you shortly."

Kaylin, stack of papers in hand, headed toward the dining room.

★ ★ ★

Sedarias arrived without the rest of the cohort, but was joined by Teela and Tain. Although she was casually dressed—for a Barrani noble—she looked forbiddingly martial; had she shown up in plate armor, Kaylin wasn't certain she'd look any less intimidating.

"Mandoran says you have a mirror here."

"Helen?"

"There is one room in which mirror access is permitted; mirrors do not exist in any of the living quarters."

Teela took a chair and flipped its back toward the table before sitting; she draped both arms across the top of the chair and slouched—elegantly. When she wasn't eating, this was her preferred posture. Tain took a chair and sat in it stiffly, back straight against the chair's frame. This, more than the color of his eyes, made clear that the two were still arguing.

Tain intended to join the cohort in the Test of Name.

Kaylin couldn't, Severn couldn't and Teela couldn't. Nor could Nightshade, Annarion's brother. They had faced the test; they had passed it. The Tower would not allow them to go through the process again.

But when Kaylin had somehow made it to the basement of the High Halls, when she had seen what lay in wait there—and seen, as well, those who were trapped for eternity by its shadows—Evarrim had been there. And Evarrim was demonstrably a Lord of the High Court. If the Tower itself didn't open a figurative door for the supplicants, there *was* another way down.

There had to be. The Consort and the High Lord had been there.

Kaylin wondered how much of this she should tell Teela.

"I think she knows, dear," Helen's now-disembodied voice said.

Teela shot Kaylin a glare of midnight blue. Since Kaylin hadn't said anything, she thought this a tad unfair. "Don't start," the Barrani Hawk said. She looked pointedly at the stack of paper in front of Kaylin.

"You *want* to see paperwork now? Marcus will have a heart attack."

"Marcus doesn't have a heart. Sergeants are required to have them surgically removed. Now, spread them out."

"There's probably nothing here you haven't seen," Kaylin said, although she obeyed Teela's command. There was a *lot* of paper, all of it in High Barrani, a language not known for its precision. Or for its brevity, at any rate. "And even if there is, it's going to take hours—at best—for you to *find* it."

"That," Sedarias interjected, "is why I'm here."

"And no one else?"

"No one else wanted to be in the same room as Teela's foul mood." Elantran still sounded strange, coming from Sedarias, but Sedarias, like the rest of the cohort, used it whenever Kaylin was in the room. It wasn't necessary—Kaylin had a more than passable command of Barrani—but Mandoran had pointed out that there were things one could say in a foreign tongue one wouldn't say in one's mother tongue.

"And you don't care?" Kaylin asked. The papers seemed to be divided into Barrani lines or lineage, and the hierarchical lineage was complicated. Not all of the members of any particular family actually bore the same name—there were alliances and offshoots of the main branches scattered everywhere, and some of the offshoots had roots in more than one significant family. Ugh.

"My mood," Sedarias said with a sweet smile that nonetheless appeared to drip venom, "is equal, at the moment, to Teela's."

"So no one wanted to be in the same room as your mood, either?"

"Got it in one. Hand me that. No, not *that* one, the other one. The small stack under your right hand."

Kaylin's eyes drifted to the top of that small stack; she'd been trying to keep the hierarchical lines together, inasmuch as that was possible. *Mellarionne* was written and underlined three times. The triple underlines seemed to denote important family. Kaylin now classified them as "first rank." Something old and just beneath the High Lord in importance to the Barrani—or at least the Barrani Court. She was pretty certain that Sedarias was of the Mellarionne family line.

"She is, dear," Helen said.

"You know," Sedarias said with a raised, dark brow, "I begin to understand why Mandoran thinks giving Kaylin his name—or *our* names—would be both practical and convenient."

"Oh?" Teela said, because Teela absolutely did not agree.

"Living with Helen is very much like living with the named. There's nothing we think, unless we're very, very careful—" and her tone implied most of the cohort found that impossible "—that she can't have access to if she needs it. Helen pretty much fills that function."

"Helen," Teela pointed out, "is in one location; it is not hard to avoid her, if it becomes necessary."

"And it would be hard to avoid us?"

"The word *hard* implies that it would be possible. I am against it, as you well know."

"She's saying that out loud," Sedarias pointed out as Kaylin passed the intel on Mellarionne across the table, "because she expects that her opinion or her desire carries more weight with you than any of ours."

"You agree with Mandoran?"

"Of course not. But this is possibly the first time I've really considered that he may not be an utter fool in this regard." She had slipped into Barrani.

"Is there anything in there you don't know?"

"Probably most of it," Sedarias replied. The answer surprised Kaylin. "We've been shut away in Alsanis for nine centuries, give or take a few decades. It's only in the past few months that I've been able to cautiously reestablish connections. Most of my early connections are dead now. Some are nonresponsive. I *have* information; I have contacts. But as I'm sure you can imagine, things have changed.

"How much, how markedly, I won't know until we are invited to Court. At this point, we won't be invited to Court unless and until we pass the Test of Name."

"You're certain you'll pass."

"You have doubts?"

About Sedarias? No. Not really.

"This is Dragon intelligence, not Barrani intelligence, but some of the information was clearly gleaned *from* Barrani." Sedarias was frowning. "My brother is An'Mellarionne."

"You were considered the heir?"

"The most likely heir, yes. It is why I was sent to the green. My family was considered bold, at the time; some called us reckless. But it is clear that Mellarionne, at least, survived and thrived. Ah, yes, very bold." She smiled. It was not a kind smile. "I see we survived an attempt to take the High Seat."

Teela frowned. "The Imperial intelligence—"

"It wouldn't have been Imperial intelligence then," Kaylin pointed out. "The Empire didn't exist."

"We don't know when this information was gathered. I highly doubt it was gathered at the time of the attempt."

"You remember it?"

"Clearly." Teela offered nothing else. Kaylin had the suspicion that Teela would offer nothing that was not in the dossier itself.

"Were you involved in it?"

"What does the document say?"

"You were not An'Danelle at the time."

Teela stiffened. "That is not the styling of my court name, as you are well aware."

"It is not a styling," Sedarias said—to Kaylin, who would have edged her way out of the conversation, and the dining room, given half a chance. "It is a statement of fact."

"And perhaps when *you* are An'Mellarionne, you can call my personal choices into question." Ugh. Teela's eyes were definitely a darker shade of blue now.

"And does your line accept the obliteration of *its name?*" Sedarias demanded. It had the sound of an old argument. It was a new argument to Kaylin, who didn't know much about the hierarchy of the Barrani lords. She knew that being a Lord of the High Court meant that you had passed the Test of Name; she knew that the Court in the West March did not *require* that their lords take and pass that test.

The An'Teela, An'Mellarionne, An'Danelle—which she promised herself she would never, ever use—were new to her. But she could read between the lines. If someone was An'Mellarionne—and that someone wasn't Sedarias—it meant they were the head of the family, the first among the Mellarionne kin. Teela was called Teela; sometimes she was called Corporal Danelle. Danelle was her family.

But she was called An'Teela at Court. Kaylin had half wondered what the "An" before her name had signified, but assumed it was a pretentious Barrani styling. And apparently she had been wrong.

No, it seemed to imply that Teela was the head of her line. A line name she did not use. Technically, then, she *was* An'Danelle. And working as an Imperial Hawk. Kaylin understood that every Barrani family of note had a ruler, a leader. It was not that different from mortal, or at least human, families.

But the rest? Had never been relevant. She had a queasy feeling it was *all* going to be relevant soon. And she remembered that the Hawks, or at least the Hawklord, never, ever sent her to site investigations that required diplomacy and tact. Or Diarmat's punishing school of proper etiquette.

Putting Teela's and Sedarias's anger aside, Kaylin took a look at the documents Sedarias hadn't yet demanded.

After perusing too many pages of High Barrani, she realized that she didn't know the families or lines from which most of the cohort came. That was going to have to change.

Sedarias was simple: she was Mellarionne. She wasn't the head of her line, and she intended to change that. She had killed her sister—also not the head of her line, but probably working in league with her brother, who was. Probably. Kaylin had been an only child. Had Kaylin been born Barrani, she'd probably never have longed for siblings.

Annarion... She frowned. She was certain she'd heard his family name at some point, and since that family was the contentious issue between Annarion and his brother, she should remember it. She didn't.

"Solanace," Helen said quietly. "I don't believe he would be discomfited if you knew, or if I reminded you."

"He's not," Sedarias said, although she didn't look up from her reading. "I think Teela has his family's section."

"I do."

"Who's An'Solanace? And are they at Court?"

There was a long silence. It was long enough to be uncomfortable, and no movement punctuated it, which often happened when the cohort discussed an issue *before* someone opened their mouth. No, this was the silence of held breath. She had asked the wrong question.

"It is not the wrong question," Helen said softly. "But, Kaylin, it is at the heart of the conflict between Lord Nightshade and his brother."

"I thought the conflict was that Nightshade abandoned his family—but it was *his family* that kind of threw Annarion away."

"It was the head of his family, yes," Helen agreed. She paused, and silence descended once again. This time, there was more expression in it.

"Maybe I shouldn't have asked."

"It is relevant. And if you read the documents concerning Solanace, you will understand why."

Kaylin held out a hand. Teela, who had the document section, failed to move.

It was, as usual, Mandoran who picked up the broken thread of what had been a very pragmatic conversation until Kaylin's question. Kaylin jumped. Until he spoke, she hadn't realized he'd entered the room. Terrano followed. In ones and twos, so did the rest of the cohort.

The dining room was now a war room, with paper rather than place settings. The color of Barrani eyes was blue.

"Karellan was Annarion's uncle. He was ambitious; he had considerable power of his own. But he was of the line Solanace, and inasmuch as any ambitious man, he served its interests. After all, weakening the line you hope to take over is not doing your future self any favors." This last was said without apparent bitterness.

"Annarion's father died—honorably—during the wars. That's the story we're told. Then again, all deaths are honorable among the Barrani." Terrano snorted. Sedarias looked like she wanted to. Mandoran ignored both, with the ease of long practice. "Nightshade became An'Solanace. There'd be no argument between Annarion and his brother if Nightshade had remained An'Solanace. None. Annarion believed that his brother was the better man in every way. Reckless, yes, but always for a purpose. Annarion would have come home, and he would have been happy. Nightshade would have welcomed him home without hiding a dagger behind his back or a new supply of poison."

Kaylin looked to Annarion, whose head was now bent just enough that she couldn't easily meet his gaze.

"Karellan thought that Nightshade was his superior, as well. He was a better man than his father had been. He had earned one of the three. He was liked and respected. Solanace was Nightshade's far more securely than it had ever been his father's."

Annarion had stiffened. Mandoran now turned to Teela. "You were there for the rest. We weren't. And even now, all we've got is Annarion's anger. Oh, and an earful of Nightshade's, as well."

"If it isn't obvious," Sedarias added before Teela could speak, "we were all shocked by Annarion's anger. We understood that his view of his older brother was possibly not entirely realistic. Annarion has never been as angry, in our years of captivity, as he has been under your roof."

"Because Nightshade is here."

"Because Nightshade is here."

"But... Nightshade became outcaste..."

Teela said, "Yes. He was obsessed with Annarion—with his lost brother. He joined the Arcanum. He left the Arcanum. He traveled. He entered the fiefs—not as fieflord—and returned. He wished to understand the nature of the Hallionne, and also the nature of the green. Some of his travels, some of his research, some of his defiance of the High Lord—the former High Lord—rankled.

"And during the time that he did his research, Karellan remained at home."

"What, exactly, was the pretext made for casting him out?"

"That, sadly, is none of your business. He will not make it clear to even Annarion. Perhaps the Consort can answer your question—but, Kaylin, *do not* ask her at dinner."

Kaylin was silent for a beat, but she wasn't finished. "Fine. So: Annarion is the heir, right. The direct heir."

"He is heir to Solanace, yes. But, Kaylin, he is considered the last of his line."

"But you said his uncle—" Kaylin stopped.

"His uncle is Karellan. When Nightshade was made outcaste, Karellan approached the High Seat and prostrated himself and offered the High Lord of the time the penitence due him for the treachery of Calarnenne—this much was public. But in great sorrow, he offered the High Lord the *existence* of Solanace itself."

Kaylin frowned.

Mandoran said—out loud, "I told you."

Annarion lifted his head, his eyes blue and narrow. "He did not kill what remained of his family; I believe there were two 'accidents,' but the High Lord did not require the death of every member of our family. What he required was the loss of the family name. Karellan, my former uncle, is not An'Solanace. No one is. I am the last of the line who bears that name.

"If the former High Lord ruled the High Court, I would not survive the Test of Name. My uncle is the first of his name; he is Karellan Coravalle. But all of his lands are the ancestral lands of my line."

"What happened to the rest of your line? The other cousins?"

"They relinquished the Solanace name, and joined my uncle. They are Coravalle dependents." His eyes were almost indigo, but that color softened. "Some may have chosen that over death.

"But I did not relinquish my name. I am the last of my line. I *am* Solanace."

And this, she thought, was why his anger at Nightshade was so intense. It wasn't just his own life that he had abandoned in his search for some way to free his younger brother—it was all of their lives. Their history. She frowned. No, she thought, the history was immutable. It existed no matter what.

Teela cleared her throat and lifted her chin, and Annarion cast her a grateful glance. "Karellan has a place of minor import in the High Court. He supported the High Lord of the time in Nightshade's removal, but his influence did not increase; it decreased. Although the gambit was understood by the High Court it was nonetheless distasteful; Solanace was an old lineage, and a worthy one. To enrich himself, Karellan destroyed it."

"I don't understand why he didn't just keep the line."

"Nightshade's removal was political. Had he been hunted as outcaste—had he perished—Karellan would have taken the name. But Nightshade failed to die. If he did not suspect his eventual fate—and I believe he must have been informed of the High Lord's decision before it was handed down publicly— he was nonetheless a power to be reckoned with, on a purely personal level. Those who went to prove themselves against him never returned.

"And eventually he became fieflord, and the High Court could not touch him. We understand the function of the

Towers," she added softly. "And we do not interfere with them."

"But—but—"

"Yes?"

"He can't leave the fief."

"He can, obviously. Has he not visited his brother here?"

"So Karellan was afraid he'd come back."

"So we believe. He wished to—what is the phrase now?—salt the earth? The name An'Solanace had been stripped from him by the High Lord and the High Court, and Karellan relinquished all claim to any such name so as not to be associated with his disgrace. There was, therefore, no Solanace to come home to, because there were none who remained of Solanace.

"But Annarion is Solanace. He has not, and will not, give over that name; he does not intend to be the last of his line.

"Karellan is not Nightshade's equal, but underestimating him at this juncture could prove fatal—to Annarion. Karellan would never be foolish enough to attack Nightshade; he's been bold enough to demand the return of *Meliannos*, Nightshade's sword, but the sword was earned by Nightshade, and he holds it until his death."

"Even if he's outcaste?"

"What would you bet on your chances of retrieving it from him if he doesn't want to return it?" Her question was Barrani; her grin was Hawkish. "But his sword is a bargaining point should he ever wish to return to Court. And you understand why, while he is Lord of Castle Nightshade, he will never surrender it.

"Annarion, however, as Solanace, has the legal right to make claims to the lands which went, wholesale, to Coravalle. And the High Lord that rules *now* would, I believe, have some sympathy. Coravalle supported the previous High Lord, but he did not support the current one, when it appeared there would be contention for the High Seat."

"So...he tried to support the current Lord of the West March?"

"Ah, no. He chose to support a cousin who had a reasonable claim and the right lineage; it was not clear to any observers that either of the two sons of the High Lord would succeed him."

"So how much of a threat is Karellan, then? Or Coravalle? Technically, couldn't Solanace and Coravalle exist side by side if they hashed out the problems with the estate?"

Sedarias snorted, but said nothing out loud. Teela pinched the bridge of her nose.

"Understand that while the Barrani claim power, they seldom allow it to be put to the test in a public venue. In this case, public means, in Elantran, 'where anyone else can observe it.' Karellan is first of his name, but head of what remained of Solanace. He has a daughter, Reyenne; she is his most active agent. There are scattered cousins, lieges. I have not tested myself against Karellan or Reyenne. Nor have they tested themselves against me. Reyenne spent some time within the Arcanum, but did not choose to struggle her way up that hierarchy."

Great. Another Arcanist. But Teela had spent some time in the Arcanum in her distant past, and Teela was her friend. Being an Arcanist, or being a student Arcanist, didn't mean you had to be monstrous. It was just the likely outcome.

"So Annarion is likely to come up against Karellan and Reyenne if he stakes his claim to his family lands."

"Yes. But not only those two; against just two, I don't think he'd have too much difficulty."

"You said we shouldn't underestimate Karellan."

"Yes, I did. But, Kaylin, they will *all* underestimate *us*." Her smile was feline—but the cat it most resembled was Leontine.

CHAPTER 2

Kaylin loved her job. At the moment, surrounded by paper-work and the need to memorize huge chunks of it, she wished she were at the Halls of Law. Or at the foundling hall. Or at the midwives guildhall. Anywhere but here.

She wondered if this was how Marcus felt when he had to deal with reports. Given the stacks of paperwork on *his* desk, this was a comforting thought.

Sadly, Marcus had made clear that she'd be missing chunks of her throat if she showed up at the Halls of Law, and she half suspected that if she did, Clint and Tanner would turn her away, orders being orders, and Kaylin being a private.

She was sick to death of Barrani and in need of a break; the cohort, being Barrani, and being at the center of what was not yet all-out war, weren't. Kaylin soldiered on, mostly keeping her whining on the inside of her head, where only Helen could hear it.

Not just Helen, Ynpharion very helpfully pointed out. *I imagine that anyone listening can hear every word of it. This would include—*

Helen keeps everyone else out. She wondered why Helen didn't keep Ynpharion out. She'd have to ask, but later.

"Ynpharion is, unlike the rest of your nameheld, remarkably up front for a Barrani. He is open in his hostility, open in his disgust. If he is actually capable of manipulation, I have yet to see it. I consider some of his commentary unreasonable, but I consider none of it harmful. And although his opinions are often expressed in the rudest possible way, they are nonetheless occasionally useful."

Meaning that she agreed with them.

"With some of them, yes."

Ynpharion did not find this insulting, which was what Kaylin would have expected. *She keeps the others out?*

"Yes, dear, I do. I will allow Lord Nightshade to speak on occasion, when the discussion might affect his relationship with his brother. I have chosen to keep the Lord of the West March at a distance. If Kaylin wishes to speak with them," she added, her tone changing, "I, of course, allow that."

Everyone was staring at Kaylin. She managed not to say that Helen was talking to Ynpharion, on the very off chance the cohort didn't actually know that he was name-bound. This both surprised and almost pleased Ynpharion, although he thought she was foolishly optimistic.

I admit to surprise at the extent of the reports you've read so far, he said. *And perhaps it justifies your exhaustion. You are only mortal, after all.*

If you don't have anything useful to add, could you just shut up? Kaylin privately disagreed with Helen's opinion. Yes, Ynpharion was rude and openly condescending; yes, it would probably kill him to attempt to be friendly or, gods forbid, charming. And yes, he was never going to stab her in the back. But in her work as a ground Hawk, Kaylin had had people attempt to stab her from the front, and while that hadn't worked out well for them, she didn't see how that was any less dangerous.

That is because you are lowborn and your first response to every-

thing is simple, physical violence. *Were you capable of* any *subtlety at all, you would not be in this position.*

Oh?

"Please don't tell me you're attempting to hold a rational discussion with any of your name-bound," Teela said. When Kaylin turned to look at her, she added, "Your knuckles are white, you are creasing that page and you have all but slammed the side of your fist into the table. Perhaps you wish to take a break?"

"The Consort is coming to dinner," Kaylin replied. "And I think we need to know this stuff."

"It would have been better, by far, if you had learned some of this *stuff*, as you call it, before you extended the invitation."

That, Ynpharion said with enough smug satisfaction it should have been poison, *is exactly what I meant.*

You wanted *me to invite her!*

I wanted you, he said with more obvious irritation, *to notice that that's what the* Lady *wanted.* Annoyance firmly entrenched, he continued. *You know almost nothing about the so-called cohort.*

I know that they were sent—as children—to the green, to witness the regalia. I know that it changed them. I know that they were then jailed in the Hallionne Alsanis for centuries.

Yes, and all of that is almost irrelevant.

She considered asking her house to shut Ynpharion up. She considered it loudly, mentally enunciating each less-than-polite word. Helen, however, did not respond. *Fine. What do you consider relevant?*

You know what happened to them, *but it is irrelevant to the information you have beneath your nose. It is all but irrelevant to most of the High Court. It is* not *irrelevant to the Lady or the High Lord, but most of your political difficulties—*

And by difficulties, you mean assassination attempts?

If the cohort is careless, yes. His tone implied that although this was so obvious it was not worth putting into words, for the sake of the ignorant, he would force himself to do so. *Understand, however, that while being sent to the green, for the children themselves, was an act of sacrifice, it was not without prestige. There were twelve children chosen, twelve sent. There were* many *who sought to add children of their own to that delegation, and in the end, only the families of first rank in the High Court were given permission to do so.*

It was considered a prize, at the time. It was, as most prizes are, contested. You know that the cohort felt discarded. What you fail to understand is that everyone *is expendable. High, low, in between. Everyone is expendable when ambition is involved. Some of the twelve families have retained their positions of political prominence. Some have not.*

Kaylin grimaced. *They were all important at the time?*

Yes. All. The lines still exist; in theory, almost all of the cohort have family to whom they might return. But not all of their families remain powerful. It is possible, should the cohort prove to be powers, *that those of lesser significance might welcome them back without offering them poison at their first meal. But if so, those who desire the* line's *prominence will be fighting internally with those who do not wish to surrender the power they now have. It is better to be ruler of a lesser family than servant in a greater one.*

But if they could use the cohort to gain prominence, they could then dispose of them after the fact.

Ynpharion seemed to approve of this line of thought. *Yes. The possibility of greater personal power in future might stay the hand of the ambitious, and it is entirely possible, even probable, that they might ally themselves with your cause. Or rather, with the cause of the cohort. The possibility of alliance is much higher if the Consort chooses, in the end, to lend her support to the cohort.*

And she can't make that decision until she comes to dinner.

Yes.

What do you think will happen?

I do not know. He was frustrated Ynpharion again. *I do not know the Lady's mind. I know as much as she wishes to share, and unless it has entirely escaped your notice—and given your present guests, one* might *understand how or why—the Barrani are not a "sharing" people. You understand what occupies the Lady's thoughts. You understand that the very nature of the cohort—their uncertain nature—is the reason she has hope for them.*

She hadn't seemed all that hopeful, in the end.

They are a weapon one has seen at a distance, but has never attempted to wield. Had she control of them, had she some lever with which to enforce their obedience, she would not only accept them, but insist on their presence at Court—itself a dangerous move. His tone shifted. *Sedarias is impressive. She would be a valuable leader, should she take the seat that is hers by birthright. But Mellarionne is not an insignificant family; it is of the first rank. And it has had a brittle interaction with the High Lord's family for centuries.*

Kaylin nodded. *If they made a play for the High Seat* and *survived it, they'd have to be politically impressive. What about Annarion's former family? Coravalle?*

It does not have the power or influence it once did.

You...don't approve of what Karellan did, either.

Ynpharion's response was a very grudging no.

"Do either of you have the bit about the Consort's family?"

Both Sedarias and Teela stiffened. It was Teela who replied. "If you can leave the Consort entirely out of your rudimentary grasp of court politics, things will be much safer for all of us."

"But—"

Teela rolled her eyes. They had actually lightened to a blue that implied annoyance; it was a familiar color. "But?"

"Leaving aside the fact that she attempted to ambush us and imprison us all—"

"Imprison *us*," Sedarias said, the correction sharp-voiced and blue-eyed. "Not *you*."

"She's coming here. Given Diarmat's homework—" she jabbed the table with the back end of the stack she was holding "—and the Emperor's very politely worded request that Bellusdeo return to the palace—" at this, Teela winced "—how is this not political? It's apparently the most political thing I've ever done. I've got no way to stay out of politics. Look, I've *tried* to cancel dinner, and she's not answering. I suppose I could slam the door in her face if she shows up—"

"No!" Sedarias all but shouted.

"I'm not *that* stupid."

"And how, exactly, am I expected to know that?" Sedarias dropped the stack of paper that had occupied most of her attention. "In the West March, the Consort made clear—to you—that *you* were not at risk. Instead of accepting her offer of safety, what did you do? You ran across the outlands to the edge of the most feared city in our history—in *any* history!"

"I'm not sure that you could have found what you needed to find without me. You *certainly* couldn't have entered the fief of Tiamaris—and that was my only hope." She hesitated, and then added, "Well, we couldn't have found our way without Bellusdeo, and there was *no way* she was going to accept the Consort's hospitality.

"And if I returned without Bellusdeo, I'd be an ash pile—at best. So I did the only smart thing. It worked, didn't it?"

Mandoran reached across the table and placed a hand over the top of Sedarias's left hand. This made Kaylin wonder if Sedarias were left-handed, but the gesture seemed to be intended to calm or comfort, not to restrain.

"I *know* all of this is above my pay grade," Kaylin continued, gesturing at Diarmat's report. "I'm a *private*. This is probably Hawklord territory. But the Hawklord isn't living with the rest of you. I am. And she's coming here. Because she is, I need to know this stuff. And before you decide what I do, or do not, need to know, consider this: I don't think the way the rest of you do. I don't have your experience. I'm never going to have it. This is my best shot at not screwing things up so profoundly we end up with Barrani war bands laying siege to Helen.

"You guys are Barrani and you remember everything. I can't. *Mortals* can't." She folded her arms and leaned back in her chair, tilting it on two legs. "Because we can't, and because I'm mortal, I have my own ways of hooking things together so they stay in place. Helen?"

Helen had agreed to have an entirely internal Records repository. Kaylin couldn't have an internal *mirror* connection, but Records? For Helen, that was trivial.

"High Lord and Consort."

"Would you like this to be full visuals, dear?"

"Umm, could you maybe make them like little chess pieces? We've got the whole dining room table."

"I could indeed. I'm not certain, however, that a chessboard will have the required room."

"No, but it could be useful. Just...leave the pieces off the board until we start a game?"

In the center of the table, two figurines appeared. They were disturbingly lifelike: a small Consort with her white, white hair, and a rather forbidding High Lord. "Add Lirienne."

Sedarias opened her mouth. Shut it.

"He's Lord of the West March, yes, but he's also a Lord of the High Court, and he's supported his brother and sister throughout both their tenure and his. He feels that the cohort will harm the alliances the High Lord's rule—or at least his own—depends on."

"He is not High Lord."

Ugh. Helen created a figure of Lirienne in spite of Sedarias's objections.

"Okay." Kaylin looked at the documents that, not coincidentally, were now beneath the feet of the Consort. "They're at the top."

"That is not the correct configuration," Sedarias began.

"They're part of the same family, right? Let's just put the family groups up, and then we can start to move them. Somehow."

By the time Kaylin had named each of the twelve families that had offered a child to the green, the table was longer, which was not a bad thing. Nor was it a simple matter to sort out the structure of those twelve lines, because there were more than twelve families involved. Each of the twelve had strong connections with other, theoretically lesser, families.

There was disagreement about how the families should be structured around or against each other. Some of it was because of ego. Some of it was different assessments. And all of the cohort were aware that their centuries of absence meant they were operating on very little information. Or worse, on *Dragon* information, which would have been unthinkable to all of them, had Mandoran and Annarion not lived with Bellusdeo.

The arguments were mostly silent; they broke the surface when Kaylin made a mistake, in one person's opinion or another, and needed to be corrected. Unfortunately for the cohort, or perhaps for Kaylin, most of Kaylin's so-called mistakes were not universally criticized. Sedarias's corrections caused subsequent arguments.

Kaylin forgot why she'd started this exercise by the middle

of it; given that Barrani didn't need sleep, she wasn't certain it was ever going to end.

"Memory," Helen supplied, her voice soft. "You were attempting to demonstrate how you construct memories."

Kaylin listened to the arguments she could hear.

"Mellarionne is almost of equal rank with the High Lord's family. That's not a *guess*, and it is not *sentimental*. It is *fact*."

"Solanace is not first rank," Annarion said. "It is considered of the first rank because it stands—or has stood—so close to the High Lord's family for so long. Even when Mellarionne made its move, Solanace did not intrigue or join them."

"Probably because Mellarionne didn't attempt to negotiate with them directly," Sedarias snapped. "And with the single exception of you, there is no Solanace."

Annarion bristled as Kaylin cringed. "There would be nothing to be gained from such negotiations."

"Solanace has always been the High Lord's lapdog."

Kaylin was certain she had had stupider ideas when interacting with the cohort. At the moment, they failed to come to mind. Karian's line was Reymar; its leader was Illmarin, and Illmarin stood behind—or in chess terms, in front—of Mellarionne. The pieces for Reymar and Mellarionne were, or should have been, faceless, more like chess pieces than the miniature High Lord's family.

They weren't. They had tiny faces and their clothing was distinct and distinctly colored. Illmarin at least appeared to wear a tiara; it was oversized for her small face, something Helen had chosen to do deliberately. The gem in the center was a pale, colorless sparkle. Diamond, then. And: Arcanist.

"Teela?"

Teela lifted her head. She was focused but silent; most of the actual appearances Helen was drawing on came from the memories that Teela had elected to share. It surprised Kaylin.

"She is not directly offering them to me," Helen said. "She is, however, offering them to the cohort, and Mandoran is being fussy."

"How many more Arcanists do we have?" Kaylin asked, squinting. "Umm, Helen, could these be a little bit bigger?"

"They could be life-size, but it would make the dimensions of the current dining room insufficient. Would you prefer that?"

She wouldn't. Helen's compromise: to create each figurine at life-size, and then shrink it to match the growing number of chess pieces. Kaylin wondered why this wasn't done in the Halls of Law almost as a matter of course. She'd have to suggest it. An image of an orange-eyed, exhausted, extremely *cranky* Leontine sergeant came to mind. Yeah. She'd suggest it when all of this had blown over, one way or the other. And maybe, just maybe, if she handled everything properly, she'd finally be a corporal.

"If you are thinking about your possible promotion," Teela said from across a longer table than they'd originally sat at, "I will strangle you."

"No, you won't. Helen won't let you."

"Helen?" Teela said.

Helen chuckled. "I would prevent you from harming Kaylin, as you well know. But I would do it as much for your sake as I would for hers. Sometimes we say things in anger that we wish we could take back. I would class physical harm in the same category. And yes, dear, I realize that was an attempt at humor. Ah, I believe Kaylin has a visitor."

"Are you expecting a visitor?" Teela asked. As her eyes were already blue, they didn't get darker. She did, however, look at the reams of paper and the small army of chess pieces, most of which would no longer fit on a chessboard, given the board's limitation.

"Is it Severn?"

"No, dear. I thought, when he approached the perimeter, that he might be here to speak with Bellusdeo."

Now all of the cohort stiffened. Bellusdeo meant Dragon. Kaylin rose immediately while the room fell into a morbid hush. *Please*, Kaylin thought as she abandoned the dining room. *Please let it not be the Emperor.*

"It's not, dear."

She looked up to see Bellusdeo descending the stairs, her eyes a martial orange. One day soon, she was going to live in a house in which all of the various races did not look so prepared for all-out war.

Lord Emmerian stood in the door. His eyes were an orange-gold; he was wary, but did not expect disaster. Bellusdeo stood to one side of Kaylin, and Kaylin dared a glance at her eyes; they were still orange, but they didn't darken into a redder shade.

He bowed instantly to the Dragon who lived here, and then bowed to Kaylin in quick succession. He carried a case by a worn brass handle, but was otherwise dressed for the palace. As he rose, Helen moved out of the doorway, and he entered the foyer.

"Please," Helen said before Kaylin could come up with an excuse for the mess of the dining room, "this way."

She couldn't *always* be rescued by her house. But the past few days had driven home an important lesson: almost everyone currently living in her house was above her pay grade. And she was going to have to change her responses to match them.

"Teela and Tain haven't changed," Helen said.

"No, but—"

"The only thing that's changed in the recent past is your knowledge of the other parts of their life. The cohort is more of a muddle—but the people you helped to free, with the possible exception of young Terrano—"

"He's not really young," Kaylin said, interrupting. "Where is he?"

"He is in the basement training room."

"Alone?"

"All the rest of the cohort drifted to the dining room." Helen's Avatar winced. "They are arguing about position, rank and general political power now. And even those who have disavowed connection to their family lines are joining in. I really do think you'll appreciate Lord Emmerian's company at the moment." She winced again.

Bellusdeo was not dressed for company from the Imperial Dragon Court. Clothing, however, did not make the Dragon—which was more or less literally true, as adopting draconic form generally destroyed their clothing. She did, however, take a seat in the parlor, and invited Emmerian to do the same. This was technically Kaylin's job.

"I apologize for arriving without notice—or permission," Emmerian said. He set his worn case gently on the nearest flat surface. "The Arkon asked me to visit. He will, of course, leave his library on the evening the Consort arrives for dinner, but—"

"He doesn't like to be far from his hoard."

"No. Emergencies notwithstanding, he is at home there. He would be at peace were it not for the presence of the various librarians, but he has managed to fully train those. It is visitors—"

"Like me?"

Lord Emmerian's smile managed to be apologetic. "I will not apologize for the Arkon. Nor will I speak for him; he is more than capable of speaking for himself."

Bellusdeo snorted. There was smoke. "So you are now running the Arkon's errands."

"Yes." His smile deepened. "I am fond of the Arkon. He was a charismatic figure in my youth."

Kaylin couldn't imagine that.

"Charisma is not about simple appearance," Helen said as she entered the room carrying a large tray.

"No, I know. But...he's fussy, he hates people and every other word that leaves his mouth is a lecture."

"That is an exaggeration," Bellusdeo told her.

"It isn't much of an exaggeration," Emmerian replied. "The Arkon is fond of *you*. He is testier in his interactions with others; *we* are frequently wasting his time."

The gold Dragon's smile deepened, and the last of the orange drained from her eyes. "Did he send you with some protection for me?"

Emmerian nodded. His eyes retained a trace of orange, but this was normal. "I suggested that this was unnecessary, as Helen has befriended you."

"And his response?"

"I hesitate to repeat it in public."

At that, Bellusdeo laughed. It was a low, full laugh. Kaylin wished, in that moment, that the Arkon wasn't ancient. If Bellusdeo had to have children with *someone*, the Arkon seemed to be the Dragon she felt the most affection for.

"Did he mention this to the Emperor?"

"No. He felt that mentioning it to the Emperor would waste both his own and the Emperor's time. And also," Emmerian added softly, "that it would add conflict to his request. He serves—and admires—the Emperor. But he holds you in great affection, and it grieves him to see conflict between you." Before she could speak—and she did open her mouth—he continued. "He understands the root of the conflict, on both sides. But he has hope that, in future, it will pass."

"Am I free to refuse whatever protection he offers?"

"Of course. The Arkon understands that you are not, technically, a Lord of the Court. You are not subject to his commands. He will not stoop to drama; he asks that you consider it, for his sake, not your own. May I?"

Bellusdeo nodded, and Lord Emmerian opened the case.

Kaylin's allergy to magic manifested itself instantly; all of the hair on her arms stood on end. To make matters more interesting, the marks on those arms, hidden by the usual layer of cloth, began to glow brightly enough their outlines could be seen through said cloth.

Bellusdeo noticed, but did not consider the glowing marks to be a sign of imminent danger. She rose, moving to stand beside Emmerian, who remained in his seat.

"He understands that this might seem proprietary," Lord Emmerian said. "And again, only begs you to consider it."

"What were his exact words?"

"Many of his exact words involved instructions to me, and I assure you that the Arkon is not nearly as warmly affectionate when speaking to, or of, me. I had a small accident in his library once and he was only barely persuaded to allow me to extend my existence." This was said with a wry smile.

"Was it like my small accident?" Kaylin asked. She moved—slowly—toward Bellusdeo to see what the Dragons both saw.

"No. Nothing I touched disintegrated. On the other hand, he considered both your age and your mandate—as Chosen—in his response to you."

Kaylin winced.

"I'm not sure I have been fully apprised of an incident involving Kaylin. Or perhaps there are just too many," Bellusdeo added.

"Ask the Arkon—but perhaps inquire when Kaylin is at home and you are at the palace," Emmerian told her. "The Arkon was oft indulgent of the very young."

"I'm *not* very young!" Kaylin objected.

"For a mortal, perhaps not. But were I you, I would not assert your ability to bear the brunt of his anger."

"Is this why he always lectures me?"

"Ah, no. He lectures everyone—mortal or Dragon—with a handful of notable exceptions."

Kaylin looked down. Set in silk in the worn case were two medallions. "Why are there two?"

"One, of course, is for you."

"Look, given what my skin is doing, I'm not going anywhere near it."

"That," Helen said, "is due to the enchantments upon the case itself. I believe you will find the medallions will not exert the same influence when they are removed and the case itself closed. I believe you've worn one of these before."

"I assume you are speaking of Kaylin; I certainly have not," Bellusdeo told the Avatar. "I have not seen this emblem in a long, long time—and the last time, it was not Lannagaros who had the right to use it." She reached out, ran her fingers along the crest at the center of the medallion. Her expression shifted, the corners of her lips turning down, her eyes narrowing not in anger or suspicion, but something that resembled sorrow.

CHAPTER 3

Bellusdeo seemed frozen in place.

Lord Emmerian was watching her, and managed to do it without giving the impression that he was staring, which was a neat trick, given that his eyes hadn't moved. His hands hadn't, either; for one moment, it seemed that he wasn't even breathing. But he did turn as Kaylin shifted in place, his brows rising as if he were asking a question, but without the actual words.

Kaylin bent. "May I?"

Emmerian nodded. "I am aware of your strong reaction to magic, and I apologize for the necessity of the case; the Arkon was only barely willing to trust me. But given your current predicament, I thought it better than his initial suggestion."

"And that?" Bellusdeo interrupted, her expression once again neutral.

"An invitation to attend him in person."

"I'll take the rash," Kaylin said.

Emmerian smiled. His smile had no teeth in it, and his expression implied mild relief when Kaylin's hand hovered over one of the two medallions. It seemed, to her eye, to be very simple; it had a stylized representation of flame at its core but, around it, a whirl of lines that implied wind or air. There were runes carved in a circle around this, and the whole appeared to be made of...stone?

"They both look the same," Kaylin said.

"They are both identical; you may take either one safely. The Arkon felt that you would not be discomfited by the medallion, and the chain that supports it is gold, with a very light enchantment meant to keep the chain in one piece. He gives permission, however, to break that enchantment should it prove necessary for your comfort."

"These are stone?"

Bellusdeo snorted, with smoke. "Yes." Before Kaylin could ask another question, she added, "The Arkon did not make these. They are in his possession, and if you somehow manage to harm or destroy even the one you are holding, I cannot guarantee that you will survive. They are precious to the Arkon."

"They are of value to all of Dragon kind," Emmerian added softly.

"He has chosen to grant them to us, at least for the duration of your dinner."

"At least" implied longer. Kaylin, however, now looked at the stone medallion in her hand with more visceral dread. "How old are these?"

"They are from the first Aerie," Bellusdeo replied. "Not *my* first Aerie, but *the* first Aerie. It is long gone—it was long gone by the time of the Arkon's birth. This is what remains of it: this, and its like. Destroy it, and it will not be remade."

"I don't think I can wear this," Kaylin said, handing the medallion to Emmerian.

"Kaylin, dear, may I speak to you?"

Emmerian failed to notice the hand that Kaylin had thrust beneath his chin. Kaylin glanced at her house, and then nodded. It was very seldom that Helen wanted privacy, and she suspected that the privacy involved comments about either Emmerian or Bellusdeo.

"Bellusdeo has not been commanded to wear the Arkon's medallion." This wasn't news to Kaylin. "You, however, have."

"What?"

"Bellusdeo has been given a choice. She is not a Lord of the Dragon Court; she has not sworn personal loyalty to the Emperor. Regardless, I believe the Emperor believes—correctly—that a command will be met with both anger and resentment. She was once ruler, as he now is; she will weigh the dinner and its possible outcomes."

"And my anger and resentment would be pointless."

"You are a Hawk, and you are sworn to serve the Imperial Laws. He is the man to whom the Lord of Hawks reports. He is therefore your commanding officer, at a great remove. You have been given an order."

"Why didn't Emmerian just say that, then?"

"I believe he did not say it because Bellusdeo was present."

"But he's not telling her what to do, just me."

"Yes. But, Kaylin, Bellusdeo is very sensitive when it comes to Imperial commands or demands. The offer itself might move her—she is fond of the Arkon. Commanding you, however, is likely to annoy her. She is protective of you because she no longer has a kingdom or an empire to govern. And you find yourself in the middle of so much trouble, it has comforted her to be so." At Kaylin's expression, Helen sighed. "You give her something to do that doesn't feel trivial. You're Chosen. She has great respect for that, and the Emperor appears to have none.

"If Lord Emmerian is to tell you that you have no choice unless you wish to disobey a direct order…"

"Oh. I get it. And he wants me to wear this without having to give me those orders."

"Yes. I believe it is very important to the Arkon—but that is just a guess, and at that, it is Lord Emmerian's guess. And frankly, if you wear it, Bellusdeo is far less likely to argue or resent its presence around her own neck." Helen smiled. "I like Bellusdeo. I wish for her to be happy; she is not happy now, and I do not believe she believes that happiness exists for her.

"The Arkon would *ask*, no more. Lord Diarmat would demand. The Emperor would command."

"But he didn't."

"No. He didn't. But command is his nature."

"And Sanabalis?"

"I have not met him, and have only your impressions to go by; I am not therefore certain what he would do. But Lord Emmerian has chosen the best approach. To offer, and to wait."

"And my best approach?"

"To do what you would otherwise be ordered to do, but gracefully. Not for your own sake, of course, but for hers."

Kaylin cursed—quietly—and slid the uncomfortable gold chain around her neck. It was cold, and it was itchy. "Helen—"

"Yes, I can remove the enchantment. But I cannot do it *well*. I think you might ask Teela for help. Or perhaps Lord Emmerian himself. It is a minor magic."

Lord Emmerian did, as Helen suggested, have the ability to remove the enchantment. So did Bellusdeo, and in the end, although Emmerian offered, Bellusdeo took the gold chain in hand, and Bellusdeo removed the protection. It made no immediate difference to the look of the chain, nor did it make any difference to its weight—which was not insubstantial. This was not meant to be hidden.

"I wore something like this the first time I had to visit the High Halls," Kaylin said.

"I assure you, you wore *nothing* like this," Bellusdeo said.

"Well, it came from Sanabalis—uh, Lord Sanabalis, but it was sort of similar."

The two Dragons exchanged a telling glance.

"And it was actually useful, unlike most jewelry."

Lord Emmerian rose and bowed to Bellusdeo; Kaylin suspected it was because he was fighting to keep his smile from becoming all-out laughter. Bellusdeo, however, didn't bother. She laughed. "There are subtle uses for much jewelry, and the tiaras of the Arcanum are, as you said, actually useful to their wearers. But...yes, most jewelry is a statement, a bit of color." She was wearing the medallion, but it had not left her palm. "Lord Emmerian, I thank you. You are a Lord of the Dragon Court, and it cannot be often that you are sent as an errand runner."

"Far more often than you think," Emmerian replied. "But I understand the purpose of the errands I am asked to run, and in the end feel that they are necessary."

Kaylin attempted to imagine Diarmat running errands, and failed spectacularly.

"Yes, perhaps. If Lannagaros was not to deliver these in person, they could not simply be handed to the Imperial messenger service. He trusts you," she added.

"Yes. But, Bellusdeo, he trusts every member of the Dragon Court. It is a small Court, smaller even than the smallest of Flights during the ancient wars, but given the nature of the Emperor's hoard, those who comprise the Court must be trustworthy. Arguments cannot be resolved in the manner of old; it would destroy or damage what he has built.

"And what you," he added softly, turning to Kaylin, "and your mortal kin have built."

Bellusdeo said something; it was lost to a roar of pure rage.

Helen's Avatar froze as she abandoned it. Abandoning it, on the other hand, meant that the *whole* of her house's attention was focused elsewhere. Bellusdeo all but ran toward the dining room; Kaylin followed.

Or she would have followed, but Emmerian grabbed her arm.

"I'll be safe."

"It's not your safety that I wish to speak of. I wish to extend my gratitude."

She blinked.

"Thank you for accepting the Arkon's gift. Thank you for allowing Bellusdeo to likewise accept what otherwise might be almost humiliating for her."

"Not humiliating. She *likes* the Arkon."

His expression shifted. "Yes. She does. But she was Emperor, in her world. It was hers to protect, to safeguard, to fight for. She failed. It is gone. She has been reduced, here and now, to someone who can no longer do any of the things for which she trained. She protects *you*, Chosen. She is still searching for a different life on which to build."

Kaylin frowned, her brow furrowing. After a long pause, she looked up at Emmerian. "Does the Emperor consider the palace guard to be an embarrassment?"

"No, of course not."

"The mostly human, very mortal palace guard?"

Lord Emmerian's brows rose slightly, as did the corner of his lips. "No."

"Then Bellusdeo shouldn't consider the protection offered by those who are somehow weaker embarrassing."

"And if we all managed to do what we logically should, the world—all worlds—would be a different place." He bowed deeply. "I will see myself out if you wish to investigate."

When Kaylin managed to get to the dining room, it was silent.

It wasn't empty—but half of the cohort was missing. She cringed. "Training room?" she asked her absent house, without much hope.

"There was a stability problem," Helen replied. Although she had a deadpan voice, this was a dead giveaway; the more neutral Helen sounded, the more frantic she was.

"'Frantic' is harsh. The word you want is *concerned*."

"What happened?"

"Tain joined the group and they were forced, for reasons of consideration, to have their arguments verbally."

Ugh. Annarion and Nightshade had only *barely* stopped having their "verbal" arguments.

"What?" Mandoran said. He looked queasy, almost hungover. "You didn't expect that with all of us under the same roof it'd get *quieter*?" He rolled his very blue eyes. Kaylin was almost surprised to see that he was still in the dining room. So was Annarion, but where Mandoran's skin was a shade of yellow-green, Annarion's was chalky.

Tain, the reason the cohort had become deliberately vocal, was no longer *in* the room.

To one side of the table, obviously separate from what remained of the cohort, sat Terrano. His eyes were black, all pupil, but otherwise he appeared to be a normal, if dejected, Barrani youth. Allaron, the giant, sat beside Terrano, but his attention was turned to Torrisant and Serralyn.

The rest of the cohort was absent. Kaylin silently counted by name: *Karian, Eddorian, Valliant, Fallessian, Sedarias. Teela.* Teela. "Helen?"

"There has been some dissolution; some of the cohort let their emotions get the better of them. They are contained, at the moment, but it is surprisingly difficult."

"Worse than Mandoran?"

Mandoran snorted.

"Mandoran has never been difficult to contain," Helen replied. "He is very difficult to *cage*, but he is more or less in control of his actions."

This time, it was Terrano who snorted.

Mandoran glared at the side of his face.

Bellusdeo, Kaylin noted, had arrived in the dining room, but she hadn't taken a seat. "Lord Emmerian has departed?"

Kaylin nodded.

"I'm sorry," Helen said, her voice at its most gentle—which was also, oddly enough, her most intractable, "but Teela has asked that Bellusdeo remain in the dining room with the rest of her friends. I think she believes it will keep them calmer."

"Why?" Kaylin demanded. "It's not like they're not already screaming at each other on the insides of their heads."

"They are guests when outsiders are present."

Bellusdeo snorted. "At this point, we're hardly outsiders." She folded her arms.

"I haven't noticed that Teela is in the dining room," Kaylin pointed out. "I'll pull her out if she's caught in the same mess as last time."

"And I'll go with her," Bellusdeo added.

Allaron rose, as well. Unseated, he towered. His eyes were blue, but they weren't as dark as Annarion's. Teela did not ask Helen to keep Allaron at the table as he joined Kaylin.

★ ★ ★

"What were you arguing about?" Kaylin asked as they headed toward the kitchen and the closet with the actual descending stairs.

"What *weren't* they arguing about?" Allaron's Elantran was as good as Mandoran's, but at this point, Kaylin expected that.

"They?"

"Allaron doesn't generally argue," Terrano said.

Kaylin jumped; Terrano wasn't small for a Barrani, and until he'd spoken she hadn't been aware that he'd joined them.

"No?"

Allaron shook his head. "At my size, you don't." Kaylin had always envied people of Allaron's stature. "At your height, at your size, you're not a threat. You might annoy people; you won't terrify them. If you're angry, people don't immediately assume that you're going to hurt them. They probably won't immediately assume you can." He held up a hand as Kaylin opened her mouth. "I'm not questioning your ability to hurt someone. I'm fairly certain you've killed men in your time. But your casual anger doesn't cause fear.

"The Barrani don't like fear. Some will start a fight to prove they don't have any—fear, that is. And some will hide the fear, but…there's constant, quiet anxiety. I try to sit, if I don't want to cause pressure, but because of my size, I learned—early—to control myself and to choose my words with care."

"So did I."

"You learned to avoid causing offense around people who had more power. I learned to avoid causing anxiety in people who had less. It became second nature."

Terrano was frowning. Helen repeated Allaron's words in Barrani, and he snorted.

"I didn't mind causing anxiety in armed people who were

trying to remove my limbs. We're not talking battlefield etiquette here. And Teela doesn't think the argument is worth repeating."

"To me, right?"

"Yes. Tain was present, and he heard it all. I don't know why she bothers, though. Mandoran will say something sooner or later."

"So…the people who are in the training room didn't deliberately lose cohesion."

"No."

"And they dragged Teela in?"

"Yes. Teela did not lose cohesion—as you put it—of her own volition. I believe she finds it very disorienting."

"And none of the rest of you do."

"Not in the same way, no."

Kaylin cursed in Aerian, which the cohort was less likely to know. "You guys do realize that the Consort is coming to dinner, right? This is *exactly* what she's going to be afraid of."

"You've been attempting to cancel that dinner."

"Of course I have!"

"Teela suggests you keep trying."

The first thing Kaylin saw as they finished their crowded descent was Tain's back. He stood in front of an open door, arms by his sides. It was a readied stance, but he carried no weapons. The first thing she heard was a very chilly Teela, although she hadn't reached the door itself to peer through.

"I asked you to remain upstairs."

Tain didn't bother to reply, and at that point, Kaylin was almost directly behind him.

People were more or less in their regular shapes and sizes. They were, to a Barrani, blue-eyed, and Karian was quivering with indignation—or with the attempt to actually maintain a physical form. Kaylin wasn't certain which. Terrano whistled, and the whole of the cohort beyond the now-open door turned to glare at him.

He deserved the glare; his smile was beyond cheeky. Kaylin was clearly not the only person to feel this way; Allaron cuffed him on the head. This made Kaylin smile, but inwardly; she could remember Marcus doing the same to her, back in the day. She had watched his first wife send the cublings rolling; they curled into literal fur balls, and when they came to a stop, unfurled, exposing their stomachs, which she then nuzzled. It was the same kind of smack.

Terrano was never going to expose his stomach, though. "You are all *hopeless*," he told Sedarias. Kaylin, frankly, would have gone for a different target.

Eddorian, Valliant, Fallessian and Sedarias turned to glare at him; Karian still seemed to be concentrating. Teela turned to glare at Tain. Bellusdeo cleared her throat. The miasma of anger and hostility froze instantly; even Terrano tensed. The only people who didn't were Teela and Tain.

Having a group mind clearly didn't confer actual, physical experience. Kaylin was pretty certain Mandoran wouldn't have tensed, either. Oh, he'd've been thinking—but he'd have been thinking of a clever rejoinder, a way to tease the Dragon, to score a point.

"Yes," Helen said. "He would. But although he won't come out and say it, he's quite fond of Bellusdeo. He was far less comfortable about having Tain come to stay. Ah, apologies," she added, her voice indicating a blush her face usually wouldn't. "I forget myself."

Teela snorted. The rest of the cohort seemed to accept that the apology was genuine.

It was Kaylin who pushed past Tain to enter the room

first, although Bellusdeo was not far behind. Tain stepped to the side to get out of the Dragon's way. "What happened?"

"As Helen has no doubt informed you," Sedarias replied in stiff High Barrani, "our discussion involved some heated disagreement."

"Did one of you try to kill another one of you?"

"The word you want is *punch*," Helen said.

At Kaylin's expression, Sedarias snorted. "Please do not tell me you have never experienced the desire to punch Teela."

"I've never been a great liar, so I'm not going to bother. I wasn't ever stupid enough to try, if that helps."

"You did try to change the lock on your apartment door, that I recall."

"I was tired of getting pushed out of bed whenever you were bored!" The lock change had resulted in a door that couldn't be locked, an angry landlord and Caitlin fielding questions, demands, carpenters and locksmiths.

Terrano snickered. "You broke her door?"

"I thought the door was stuck. It was an aged building with warped, creaking floors, and warped shutters over small windows."

It was Tain who coughed this time. Teela shrugged. "It's not like she didn't give us a standing invitation. And keys, at least to the first door."

Kaylin thought Terrano's understanding of Elantran had improved markedly. "No," Helen said quietly. "I am translating for him. I sometimes forget to do it quietly."

"Quietly?"

"I am capable of speaking to one person, and one alone— but it uses different muscles, and more power, and it requires the creation of a small, contained space. I explained this to Terrano, and he was willing to allow this. I haven't tried to do this for you."

"Sometimes it would be helpful."

"Yes."

"But?"

"But," Helen agreed. "This house is your house. To isolate you within your own house is obviously something I *am* capable of—but it is best left for emergencies. To do this for you—as opposed to your guests—I would be cutting you off from the rest of the space that comprises me. It would make functioning as a house much more difficult."

"You know," Karian said, apparently to the room at large, "it would be helpful to the rest of us if you'd just return to us."

Terrano stiffened. Allaron dropped a hand on Terrano's shoulder, but before he could speak—and Allaron wasn't one for a lot of words—Mandoran materialized. He put a hand on the shoulder Allaron's wasn't occupying. "Walls?" he asked.

Terrano slowly unclenched. "You know—you guys can't do this anywhere but here. Not until you're good enough at it."

"Which in some people's cases will be never." At Kaylin's expression, Mandoran added, "We can speak to each other. We can think at each other. We can share information so easily, information is central, like your Records, but contained to us. But there was a reason Terrano was the first—and the only—one of us to escape the Hallionne. I was close, I swear it."

Terrano nodded. "You'd have been able to join me if you hadn't been so lazy. You didn't *want* it enough."

Mandoran ignored this. "We're *not* one person. We're a dozen people, give or take, with access to the *same* knowledge. But we have different strengths and different weaknesses. And different tempers. Look, you know True Names, right?" He winced; no doubt Teela, Sedarias, or both, were telling him not to say that where anyone else could hear it. "But you're not the people whose names you know. If you knew them for centuries—if you could imagine knowing them for centuries— would you become those people?"

The thought of becoming Ynpharion made her grimace. "No."

"It's the same with us. We're all still ourselves. It didn't surprise you to know that Annarion and I are completely different. You didn't expect us to be the same person."

"That's because I live with you."

"Yes. You'll get more of an idea of what we're like when you live with the rest of them, too."

Kaylin looked around the training room.

"This isn't the first time someone's been shunted to this damn room." He spoke with a broad grin, since the person who had most often been shunted here was Annarion. "It won't be the last."

"There's a big difference."

"Well, yes, there are more of us—"

"The Consort is coming to dinner."

Teela was green. She looked queasy, her eyes underlined by dark, dark circles. Taking her life in her hands, Kaylin turned to the Barrani Hawk that was part of the cohort. "You couldn't unconsciously lose cohesion—not like Annarion does. This is twice in less than a week. Why are *you* doing this?"

When Teela failed to answer, Tain cleared his throat. He would never have dared to ask the question Kaylin had just asked, but he wanted the answer. He wanted it badly.

Teela didn't answer. None of the cohort did. Mandoran took a step back and Kaylin grabbed his arm before he dispersed through the nearest wall.

It was Bellusdeo who broke the awkward silence that had enfolded them all; she roared. Kaylin nearly jumped out of her own skin; so did Terrano. The rest of the gathered co-hort were still.

"If you are going to interrupt other people's conversa-tion with your arguments," the gold Dragon then said in a much more normal voice, "I suggest you at least *practice* to get it right. If you manage a genuine roar, you could prob-ably blame the expression of rage on me, even if I'm not the actual source." She smiled. There was teeth in it. "There has to be some advantage to living with Dragons, hmm?" To Kaylin, she said, "I'm going upstairs. I have a sick headache, and if I hear another half-hearted roar like the first one, ev-eryone in this house is going to know what an angry Dragon *really* sounds like."

"I think she does have a headache," Kaylin offered when even the echoes of Bellusdeo's heavier-than-necessary steps had died away. Kaylin was well on the way to a headache herself, because Bellusdeo had used full Dragon volume, and had given her no time to attempt to plug her ears.

It had, on the other hand, had an effect on the cohort. Terrano relaxed—marginally—when Bellusdeo left, but the rest of the cohort looked slightly embarrassed. Which was better than fire and fury.

"Did you guys always argue like this?" Kaylin asked them.

"'Like this' has different meanings," Sedarias replied.

"That's a yes," Terrano added, weathering Sedarias's result-ing glare. "It didn't *matter*. And it doesn't really matter here, either. Helen contains them, just as Alsanis did. We didn't have to worry about the harm we were doing to the environ-ment, and we weren't actively *harming* each other. We were... trying to be more emphatic. To make our points more clear."

"I fail to see how turning into splashes of badly matching color is going to make anything more clear."

"That's because you have terrible vision, and that's all you're capable of perceiving. That is *not* what they were doing."

"Could you join them?"

"Thanks, I spent centuries doing exactly that, and it's the one thing I *do not* miss."

Kaylin laughed. So did Mandoran. Sedarias, notably, did not. "We communicate that way when in states of emotional duress."

Kaylin nodded, biting back a sarcastic comment.

"It is our way of making clear exactly what we mean, and why; it's a way of emphasizing our personal contexts."

That was so not what it looked like to Kaylin; it seemed more an attempt to overwhelm anyone else's. She also kept this to herself. "If you're finished, we've got a ton of paperwork to get through."

"Serralyn is reading it now," Sedarias replied. She seemed to redden. "And you are correct. We don't have time for this."

"Can you promise that you won't do this—won't come even close to *considering* it—while we have guests?"

"I can."

"Can you do it so the promise actually has real meaning?"

Sedarias's smile was chilly. "Yes, I can. You, however, cannot."

The marks on Kaylin's arms began to glow as Kaylin once again forced herself not to respond. Sadly, the marks were visible. Spoken words would probably have been better, even if they were snappish and sarcastic. "I'm not doing that on purpose," she told the cohort.

The cohort, and Tain, were now staring at Sedarias, not Kaylin, even though Kaylin was the one with the glowing arms.

"Sedarias, dear," Helen said, breaking a silence that had begun to stretch out to encompass everything, "I believe that

Kaylin's marks—and she really isn't controlling what they currently do in any conscious fashion—disagree with that assessment. But I also think that the question she asked—not so much about oaths or promises, as about controlling the *expression* of your tempers—is the necessary question.

"It is *not* anger, fury, fear or any other emotion that defines you here. It is how well you control them. They are yours; they do not belong to anyone else. You will have your own priorities. Of course you will. But you cannot force others to adopt them."

Mandoran coughed.

"Yes, dear," Helen replied, although he hadn't spoken. "I suppose that *is* one definition of power. But those people—the ones you do not destroy in your rage—do not adopt your priorities; they live in your shadows instead. They live in fear of you. And I don't think I need to tell you that while I have no control over what occurs outside of my boundaries, I will not allow fear to be the fulcrum by which the people in this house move others.

"If for no other reason, Kaylin is my lord, in more archaic terms. And that is *not* what Kaylin wants from a home." Helen's Avatar turned to Sedarias. "Kaylin can, I believe, enforce a binding oath. It would harm her to do so and I will therefore ask that she refrain."

"How would it harm her?" Sedarias demanded.

"How would it harm me?" Kaylin said. The words overlapped, which was always a bit embarrassing.

Helen's Avatar frowned, her obsidian glance moving between the Barrani and the Hawk. It was therefore Mandoran who answered, although he glared at Teela as if demanding she do it first. "You force a binding oath on someone you don't trust. The Barrani don't trust easily, if ever. Had the High Court chosen to send us, as adults, to the *regalia*, we wouldn't be here now. We would never have taken the risks we took back then. We wouldn't know each other's names. Look—you trust Teela, right?"

Kaylin nodded. "With my life."

"With your keys?"

"That's different."

He laughed. "You trust her, though."

"Of course I do. She's a Hawk." Kaylin could practically hear Tain rolling his eyes beside her.

"Would you ask her to swear a binding oath?"

"Why?"

Mandoran now rolled his eyes. "That's not an answer. Would you ask Teela to swear a binding oath?"

"Well, what exactly *is* a binding oath?"

He glanced at Sedarias with a very *I told you so* expression. "A binding oath enforces penalties should the person who has voluntarily entered into it break that oath. In some cases, and depending on the oath itself, it can kill." He spoke Barrani. High Barrani. The language the Imperial Laws were written in. "Would you make that demand, if you could?"

"I trust her. If she promises to do something—"

"You cannot know all of a person's intent, all of their concerns, all of the fears and duties that press down upon them. You cannot know all of their motivations, and assigning your motivations *to* them, while comforting, is generally unwise. If Teela, for reasons that you did not know, were to break her word, and the cost of doing so would kill her, would you force this on her?"

"No!"

"Mandoran," Teela said out loud. "That is quite enough."

But Helen said, "I believe you should allow him to finish."

"You are Kaylin's home," Teela said, never moving her eyes

from Mandoran. "I'm her friend. And I am doing Mandoran the kindness of offering a distinct warning."

Tain tensed. Glancing at him, Kaylin saw his eyes change shade—they'd been blue to start with, and they became midnight blue. Oh. She was tired, she was stressed out, she was terrified about the consequences of the Consort's arrival, she was worried for the entire cohort—except maybe Mandoran at the moment, because she wanted to strangle him—and the anxieties had made her stupid.

She moved her gaze from Tain to Teela, whose eyes were *also* midnight blue; the Barrani Hawk who was also Lord of the High Court and one of the bearers of the three dragonslayers was vibrating in place. Almost literally.

"Teela, the argument you guys were having?"

Teela failed to hear her, which was always deliberate. But she was looking at Sedarias. Allaron moved to stand almost in front of Kaylin, and when Kaylin tried to push him out of the way, he failed to budge. At all.

"Was it about *me*?"

CHAPTER 4

Teela didn't answer. Neither did anyone else—not even Helen. There was a strain in the wake of the question that made the answer perfectly clear. Not everyone in the training room had been in agreement.

"What, exactly, were you arguing about? Is it something I did?"

"No," Teela said. It was a snap of ice, a single word that implied death.

Kaylin exhaled slowly. The cohort—or those trapped here—had fully reassumed their physical forms, their Barrani identities, and she didn't want to cause a repeat of the argument, which was clearly only finished for now. "Fine. We've got stacks of political fieldwork to read, and a Consort who, you may have forgotten, is going to descend on this house tomorrow.

"I can't—or won't," she added, looking at her arms, which were still glowing, "force a binding oath on anyone. Helen wouldn't like it—and to be fair, neither would I. But if this happens again, if it happens one more time, I'm going to refuse to let the Consort in when she does show up at the door.

"I'll refuse to let the Arkon in, as well."

"That would be politically very unwise," Sedarias said, her tone only marginally less icy than Teela's had been. "For you."

Kaylin shrugged. "It's not my life's goal to become a powerful, political figure."

"You are a Lord of the High Court."

"On paper, yes. But what can they do to me? Toss me out?" Kaylin shrugged. "I can't be made outcaste by the Barrani. I could possibly be made outcaste by the Human Caste Court, but our Court doesn't work the way yours does. The Human Caste Court—the lords who comprise it—would have to know who I am. Even if they did, I'd have to accept the designation. And I wouldn't. I'd invoke the law; I wouldn't just sit around waiting to be kicked while *they* attempted to invoke laws of exemption.

"Shutting the door in the Consort's face wouldn't harm *me*. But letting her in without some kind of guarantee from the rest of you would possibly harm *either* her or *you*." She folded her arms, adopting a Leontine maternal posture.

The silence extended for a while. Kaylin was issuing a threat, of a kind. Sedarias did not like to be threatened. But she did exhale—heavily—before she nodded. "Very well. Inasmuch as I can, I will give you my word that I will not… descend to this level of argument again."

"Look—I don't care if you're screaming your lungs out at each other. I've spent what feels like months being woken up every night because Annarion and his brother are arguing. Just…not this. This—and your immediate and unexplained disappearance when Helen chooses to invoke the safety of the training room—will be major trouble."

Sedarias's nod was even stiffer than her previous words, but she did give it. Largely because she was practical, Kaylin thought. She couldn't argue against any of what Kaylin had said, because the facts were the facts.

"People can argue against facts," Helen said quietly. "And frequently in your history, they have."

Yes, Kaylin thought with just a bit of embarrassment, but not *Sedarias*.

Sedarias bowed to Helen's Avatar. It was a stiff, perfectly correct bow. "Thank you," she said, as if the bow hadn't said enough. "We are in your care, Helen. We will struggle to be worthy of it."

Mandoran's jaw dropped, but it remained attached to his face, and after a moment, he closed his mouth. Sedarias walked stiffly through the door to return to the dining room, and the rest of the cohort trailed after her. To Kaylin's surprise, Teela was first in line. Mandoran would have been second, but Kaylin hadn't let go of his arm, and had no intention of doing so.

She would have shooed Terrano up the stairs, but he lingered, as if waiting for the distance between him and the rest of his friends to grow.

"All right, spill."

Or as if waiting for Mandoran's discomfort. It was Terrano that Mandoran glared at, but that was fair; only Terrano was grinning.

"Why are you asking *me*?"

"Because you're going to let it slip sometime. Look—she's right, and you know it. You guys can't do this anywhere near the Consort. You can't do it anywhere near the High Halls. There's a *reason* I didn't want to come here. Too many people. Too narrow a space to live—to truly *live*—in. But this is what you chose. You wanted to come home—but you're going to destroy your home without even noticing it if you can't..." Terrano stopped. Shrugged. "Doesn't your mouth get tired?" The latter was a genuine question.

"Not mine," Mandoran replied, his expression changing. He exhaled. Loosely clasping his hands behind his back, he looked up the stairs, which were now empty. "Yeah," he said. "They were arguing about you."

"I can—"

"It's not about what you're going to do. Or not going to do. It's not *really* about your survival. I mean, yes, Teela is worried, and yes, she's angry. She feels you'll be dead in a couple of eye-blinks, and we could wait because *we* have forever. She likes you, you know?"

Kaylin nodded, but cringed. She knew it, yes. But stated that way it was embarrassing somehow.

"She's lived in this world—this place that Terrano finds so narrow—for way longer than we have. We were born in it. We woke to it. We followed the rules of it—and of the powerful above us. But we did that for a tiny fraction of our lives. She did it for all of hers. So she's seen the powerful rise—and fall. She's seen mortals, watched them age, watched them go from weakness to strength to weakness again, like the resonant wave of a struck bell.

"She knows you're mortal. She knows you're going to die. Mostly, she doesn't think about it, unless she feels you're taking stupid, unnecessary risks." He flashed a grin. "Which these days is all the time. But she feels that this isn't about you being stupid—this risk is about *us* being impatient. She thinks we're not ready for the test.

"And, Kaylin, we *aren't* ready. But Annarion is going to go, anyway. And if he goes, we're going to go."

"They're fighting because Teela wants them to wait."

It was, oddly enough, Terrano who snorted; Mandoran still looked uneasy. Terrano had not been part of the unspoken argument, although he'd certainly heard whatever was said in the dining room. "I forgot. Sometimes Mandoran makes the attempt to tell us things, but just doesn't get to the heart of the problem."

"Lazy, remember?" Mandoran replied. "She's not one of us."

"Neither am I, anymore."

Mandoran flinched. "You are," he said softly.

"I was," Terrano continued. "I was part of you. I was part of you for longer than Teela. But I can't hear any of you now. I don't know what you're saying to each other." He exhaled again, which was a neat trick, because he hadn't apparently inhaled first. "In theory, they're fighting because Teela wants them to wait. Frankly, I'd guess half of them want to wait. The arguments make clear that they don't have the self-control to hold things together in a meaningful way. Literally." To Kaylin, he said, "You know that we mostly consider ourselves thrown away. Our lives were put on the line for a gamble. The gamble failed.

"You know that we exchanged True Names—which would have been unthinkable had we remained at home, had we not been considered expendable. We were a bit young, a bit raw, excited, terrified or heartbroken. All of those." He shrugged; clearly he was not comfortable exposing this, although it was all well-known to Kaylin. "We only had each other.

"We promised that we would have each other—but we're Barrani."

Kaylin thought about this for a moment, looking at her feet. "So…what you're saying is that you only had each other, and in some way, the promise was that you would only *ever* have each other?"

Terrano nodded.

Mandoran looked highly uncomfortable. "Not in so many words," he murmured.

But Kaylin now understood. "Sedarias is mad because in asking you all to wait, it's like Teela is choosing *me* over the rest of you. Did she say that?"

"No, of course not," Terrano replied. "But she doesn't *have to say it*. They understand it all, anyway. Sedarias feels betrayed. She won't blame you," he added quickly. "It's not your fault. You can't betray Sedarias in the way any of the rest of them can."

"Will you stop talking about us as 'them'?" Mandoran snapped.

Kaylin privately agreed with Mandoran, but then again, she could. "But she *can* blame Teela."

Mandoran nodded.

"And you?"

"I'm staying out of it. So is Annarion. Annarion understands why Teela wants him to wait. His brother wants him to wait a few centuries, as well—probably not for the same reasons. If Nightshade could tell Annarion that he is doing his level best to be reinstated in the High Court, Annarion *might* wait. But Nightshade won't make that promise.

"We've both lived with you. We've spent time with Helen. We sort of understand why Teela likes you, and no, we don't feel betrayed. I *get* why Teela worries. You're even more reckless than Terrano was, back in the day. I've been dragged into the weirdest things because apparently worry is contagious.

"But—mortal or no—you've survived. Teela thinks it's luck. Maybe it is. Annarion and I believe you'll continue to survive. Teela is less certain. But we don't feel that Teela has to ignore you or abandon you."

"And Sedarias does."

"No—look, it's like Joey and his cat. If you were all trapped in a fire, he'd save the cat first."

"You've heard about his cat?"

"Everyone in the office hears about his cat, and I've been in the office. People who have cats are fine with it. They get it. They understand. People who don't are mystified. Why would a dumb animal be more important than another human being?"

"So I'm the dumb animal in this analogy."

"Yeah, sorry."

Kaylin shrugged. "I'd probably be more insulted, but Teela is Joey in this analogy, so I'm in good company."

"We're trying to explain," Mandoran continued. "And if you could get the Consort to reschedule for a month from now, I think it'd all settle down."

"I've been trying."

"We know that, too." He met, and held, her gaze. "Tell me, honestly, do you think the Consort is right to fear us?"

Kaylin didn't answer.

The cohort decided to work in shifts. Teela, blue-eyed and rigid, nonetheless provided most of the practical resources as they attempted to confirm some of the Imperial observations. Kaylin expected that Teela would know everything the report contained, but was wrong. She knew most of it, but sometimes what she knew overlapped Diarmat's knowledge in a way that made her eyes narrow.

Terrano was conscripted by Helen, to Kaylin's mild surprise. The reason the cohort worked over the documents in shifts was because they were down in the training room, also in shifts. Terrano was teaching. Or supervising, as Helen was teaching. Teela, however, joined them in their rotating shifts.

Kaylin wasn't certain how she felt about that. No, she kind of was certain: she didn't like it.

"Why, dear?" Helen asked. Of course Helen asked.

She couldn't answer her house without sounding like a petulant, insecure child. She knew that. But at the end of a day that had been way too long, when she was getting ready to fall face-first into bed, Helen asked again, and this time she could answer. Because this time, the only witness was

Helen, who heard everything she ever thought while she was at home, but liked her in spite of that.

"It isn't in spite of it," Helen said softly.

"If you know, why do you want me to say it?"

"Because sometimes saying it—where only you can hear it, but forcing yourself to find the actual words—is helpful. Or at least it has been for some of my tenants. Not all of them, of course; all of you are different individuals. But some found it helpful—almost as if saying it out loud was an exorcism. It released the words instead of allowing them to remain trapped in their thoughts, wearing deeper and deeper grooves."

This sounded like garbage to Kaylin, but she trusted Helen.

"Teela's my friend," she said. "She's Barrani. She's part of the Hawks. She's...mine." And even saying it out loud, she thought: *I'm an idiot*. She didn't own Teela. She didn't own the Halls of Law. She didn't own any Hawk but herself. "She has history with the cohort. They all know her True Name. I don't. And I'm never going to. And I know she worries about me. I know she cares about me."

"She loves you, dear."

Kaylin couldn't bring herself to say *that* out loud. "But."

"But?"

"She trusted them so completely she gave them her name. Her True Name. For Barrani, that's closer than family. That's closer than friends. That's closer than anything. I mean— I don't think Barrani parents tell their own children their True Names.

"I'm afraid of losing her. She's known them for *centuries*. She's known me for seven years. Almost eight. It's a huge part of my life, but to her? To them? It's nothing. And when she— when she disappears like that, when she...disincorporates... I'm afraid part of her won't come back, because they've always been so important to her. I'm just a newcomer."

"Do you believe that?"

"Believe what? It's a fact, Helen. Facts exist all on their own."

"Yes, they do. It's a fact that they know her True Name. It's a fact that they've been an important part of her life since they first came together. And it's a fact that their absence was as large a part of her life as their presence was. But when they were shut up in Hallionne Alsanis, she wasn't there. She couldn't hear them and couldn't reach them. They've spent less physical time with her than you have. If you can believe that they're that important—and yes, I won't argue it—on the strength of so little time, believe that you are as important."

"She doesn't trust me the same way."

"Perhaps not. But, Kaylin?"

"What?"

"Neither do you."

The fact that Barrani didn't need sleep was driven home by the dining room first thing in the morning—or Kaylin's version of morning. Sleep had proved elusive, even in the face of exhaustion; Kaylin had had hangovers that still felt more cheery and energetic.

The whole of the cohort was arrayed in the dining room when she reached it; papers were spread, admittedly in tidier piles, before them. Tain was reading, Teela was reading and Bellusdeo was reading. Even Maggaron had joined them, but Bellusdeo's companion appeared to be concentrating on food, not Imperial words.

Kaylin had no hope of reading and absorbing all of Diarmat's report. She focused on the section involving Sedarias's line—Mellarionne—and its various allies and enemies. That, and the High Lord's alliances. Mellarionne did not support the High Lord, but had made a kind of peace with the Lord of the West March. She glanced at the Solanace details. Clearly Dragons considered the lineage important; all of the information about Coravalle was in the Solanace briefing. Coravalle supported both the High Lord and his brother, but that support might be imperiled if Annarion took—and passed— the Test of Name.

Annarion had not surrendered the family name. In theory, if he had the power, he could lay claim to the lands of Solanace, which were now entirely under the banner of Coravalle. He had not been declared outcaste—an oversight. He'd been presumed irrelevant, as good as dead.

She could imagine the pressure placed on the High Lord; the High Lord could not forbid Annarion the test unless Annarion were declared outcaste. If Annarion could be made outcaste, that was the thin edge of the wedge; all of the cohort was likely to follow, except perhaps Eddorian, whose vastly diminished brother remained in the West March.

The cohort, on the other hand, would absorb—were absorbing as food appeared—everything Diarmat had offered to Kaylin. And it seemed that Bellusdeo would, as well, although her absorption of written High Barrani came with greater effort. Thus, the advantage of not needing sleep, although Dragons used the word *sleep* in an entirely different way.

But at least this morning the cohort seemed to be calmer. There were blue eyes among the bunch—but even those had a hint of green in them. Whatever they'd decided, the task of absorbing and evaluating all of the third-party information had become their priority.

"Is the Consort's dinner today?" Mandoran asked. Sedarias glared at him.

Yes, Ynpharion replied.

"Helen, can you do something about our clothing?" Sedarias glared at her sleeve.

"Of course. But…prior experience suggests that you may be required to leave me at very short notice."

"Can you visually alter more practical clothing?"

"It is harder than creating clothing the normal way," was Helen's doubtful reply. "But I will do what I can. I think, perhaps, the creation of jewelry and accessories might add a touch of the class you desire; their absence in an emergency will not be as dire. It is also likely that the Consort will not be convinced by simple illusion."

"I was hoping for more complex illusion," Sedarias admitted. "We can possibly create clothing of our own—"

"That will not be necessary," Kaylin's house said before Sedarias could finish. "To do so would be to alter what is effectively your skin."

"It's worked for my people for the entirety of their existence," Bellusdeo said cheerfully. Bellusdeo was smiling, golden-eyed, but she had said those words deliberately. It wasn't a challenge, but it was a way of causing a knee-jerk revulsion in Barrani accustomed to thinking of Dragons as the enemy. What Dragons did, they would not do.

She glanced at Mandoran, and reconsidered. What Dragons did, *most* of them wouldn't do.

To Kaylin's mild surprise, Terrano had joined the group activity, although his reading contribution wouldn't immediately be added to the group's store of knowledge. Allaron still loomed over him, like a friendly giant, ready to grab the nearest limb should Terrano choose to flee.

Kaylin wore the pendant that Emmerian had brought for her. She was afraid to lose it, although Helen usually knew where she'd put things down.

"Yes, I do. You have a visitor," Helen added.

"Severn?"

"Yes. He's almost at the door."

Kaylin rose, although Helen was perfectly capable of letting Severn in and telling him—helpfully—where to go.

"That bad?" Severn asked when the door opened and he got a face full of morning Kaylin.

"Probably worse. Well, yesterday was. Today—knock wood—hasn't been so bad. But it's early."

"Another argument?"

Kaylin nodded. "Another argument, another dissolution of physical form. Right now, though, we're reading Diarmat's various reports about parts of the Barrani High Court and their political interactions."

Severn whistled. "Not light reading."

"No—but oddly boring in places. You want in?"

He smiled.

"You don't think those reports are going to tell you anything you need to know."

"I'm aware of the Barrani High Court and the families that comprise it in its current composition."

Sometimes Severn's answers were doors or windows, things that could be opened and looked through. Sometimes they were walls. This was a wall. As if to emphasize this, Severn said, "I've brought clothing suitable for dinner—is there somewhere I should leave it?"

"In your room, dear."

Kaylin did not point out that Severn didn't have a room, because obviously he now did.

"He could leave things in your room, if you'd prefer?" Helen asked.

Did she? And even if she did, did he? "No, it's fine. Is it upstairs in the main hall with the rest of our rooms?"

"Yes—it's the door with the wolf mark."

"If it makes you feel better," Severn said as he headed toward the stairs, "I'm not Teela or Tain. I'm not moving in."

"They're not here permanently, either. You might as well stay while they do."

He stilled. "You think you need the support?"

"I've got Helen for support. But...company that understands where *I'm* coming from might be nice."

After breakfast, Kaylin was assailed with a completely unfamiliar thought: she owed Diarmat an apology. She'd thought him the most condescending, harsh teacher she'd ever have the misfortune of meeting. He now had competition.

Sedarias was a ferocious drillmaster. When learning weapons, Kaylin was fine with bruises and the occasional sprained wrist or ankle. Etiquette on the Sedarias scale was like being screamed at by sergeants, but worse; there was no opportunity to alleviate any of the resulting humiliation and resentment by trying to beat another enterprising trainee in the drill yard.

Bellusdeo, however, didn't find Sedarias nearly as annoying as Diarmat. Kaylin couldn't understand why, but thought, less than charitably, it was because Sedarias was only raking *Kaylin* across the figurative coals. To be slightly fair, it wasn't only Kaylin. Mandoran and Terrano also came in for a fair amount of heat and invective, and Sedarias had astonishingly *good* Leontine pronunciation.

"Look, the Consort knows what Kaylin's like," Mandoran finally said when they started hour two—or eighty, in subjective time. "By all accounts, she accepts it. Kaylin's only mortal; she can use that to her advantage."

"And so will the Consort," Sedarias practically spit. "She will use every *possible* weakness to her advantage. Imagine that she's decided against us. She might approach the Halls of Law or the Human Caste Court in her offense. And *even if* she does not choose to do so, it puts the option in her hands.

"As for *you*, what was that? What *exactly* was that? The Consort is the most elevated of all ranks—did you think you were going to *shake her hand*?"

Kaylin had survived her early life by causing as little offense as she possibly could. Invisibility was a state she'd desired. She'd survived her later life because she was a Hawk and she had friends. She could survive *now* because she had Helen—a home of her own, pretty much until death. At this very moment she was trying to hold on to all three of these experiences because the desire to either shout at Sedarias— or strangle her—was becoming harder and harder to resist.

Helen didn't intervene, which made clear that she didn't consider Sedarias's lessons dangerous. Or possibly that she agreed.

I certainly do, Ynpharion said. She would have raged— silently—at him because he was a safe target, but his internal voice held no smugness, no sense of the usual superiority. He was worried. He was worried for the Consort, not for Kaylin, of course—but he considered Sedarias's manner and instruction to be utterly necessary.

She wondered what it must have been like to be raised as Barrani, and swallowed.

I survived. But, Kaylin, I would not have survived were I as ill-mannered as you. The Consort is indulgent because you are mortal. Or perhaps because you are Chosen. It signifies little to the Court; her indulgence of a beloved cat would be considered similar. You are not, and will never be, what Sedarias is desperately trying to make you. But if the Consort is indulgent, she is the only one.

What do you mean you wouldn't have survived?

I would have been considered a black stain upon the whole of my family. In order to remove that stain, they would have removed me.

If your Helen permits, I will attempt to offer advice when the Consort arrives.

And if the Consort permits?

And if the Consort permits. There was a flicker of doubt in the words that she very seldom heard from Ynpharion.

You think she won't?

I think, if your concern is the welfare of the people you have chosen to befriend, you must *obey Sedarias in matters of deportment.*

By dinner, the cohort had finished with Diarmat's report. It had caused some argument and some disagreement. Teela's actual, centuries-long experience was given more weight by the cohort than the documents offered by the Imperial service, but Teela was willing to trust the Imperial service's observations. This clearly rankled the cohort, but not Kaylin; it was a Hawk's view. Tain said almost nothing, although he looked with interest through the reports about Teela's family, Danelle.

He, like Kaylin, needed to read everything on his own; he was not part of the cohort, and did not have access to their memories or their perceptions.

Serralyn, for instance, had read maybe a third of the reports. She hadn't involved herself in the argument that Helen had chosen to relocate. Or at least, she'd kept her interaction to words that Kaylin couldn't hear. Karian, of those involved in the argument, had become the most silent, the most withdrawn.

What this meant in practical terms, however, was that he was now glued to Serralyn's side, eyes closed, head flopped on her shoulder and the back of her neck. She didn't appear to notice.

No, Kaylin thought, that wasn't true. She did notice, but it was so natural to her it required no response. Marcus's kits had been like this when they were young—piles of interconnected fur of different shades, breathing evenly together, as if they shared a single set of lungs.

The only time Serralyn looked up was when Terrano shifted in place and the chair made the faintest of noises. She didn't speak. Her glance returned to the written High Barrani in her hands. But Allaron sighed, gathered the documents he appeared to have barely started and dragged Terrano toward where Serralyn was sitting.

"Helen?" Allaron said.

"I feel it best to maintain a table," Helen replied. "The documents in question are of some value to Lord Diarmat and, as much as they can be, should be handled with care. But let me alter the dining room slightly to better suit your needs."

Terrano was flushed. He glared at Allaron and attempted to remove the hand on his upper arm. It was like trying to move rock. Kaylin knew Terrano could escape if he really wanted to.

"It is not actually that simple," Helen said in a gentle voice. "Not where Allaron is concerned."

"Because he's larger and stronger?"

Helen smiled. "It's because he's stronger, yes—but his size has nothing to do with it. If he must be characterized at all in regard to his position within the cohort, he's the anchor. He's the foundation, the stability."

Mr. Stability dragged Terrano to where Karian and Serralyn were now sitting—Helen had literally moved them to an enlarged corner of the room in which a carpet and several pillows and throws had been haphazardly dropped.

"You can't help us by reading this," Allaron told Terrano.

"It's useless to me," was Terrano's mutinous reply.

"It's not useless to the rest of us. And neither are you. You've been gone too long. Now sit down and let the rest of us expire from boredom." He dropped Terrano more or less in Karian's lap, and Karian opened one eye—the left eye—and then wrapped an arm around Terrano before Terrano could pick himself up.

"You're warm," he said.

Terrano grimaced. "Karian—"

"You can get away from me, yes. But look at where Allaron is sitting." On the floor, documents moved as his hands moved. Right beside Terrano.

Terrano's spine stiffened, as did his expression, but there was something in that expression that made Kaylin look away. When she looked back, that spine seemed to melt; for the first time, he folded himself into members of his cohort. To outside eyes, he seemed to be at home there.

She didn't understand Terrano. She thought she never would. What they wanted for him, he was afraid to want. But it was what she had wanted, for so long, for herself.

"Here," Sedarias said, lifting a slender sheaf of papers. "This will be our biggest problem."

CHAPTER 5

Kaylin, Severn and Tain turned immediately in the direction of Sedarias's voice; she held up one slender sheaf of papers in completely steady hands. Her eyes were a blaze of Barrani blue.

"Sedarias believes that Mellarionne is always the greatest threat," Valliant said. His expression made clear that he didn't agree with this assessment, but wasn't willing to voice more of an argument where strangers might hear it.

"Mellarionne is in conflict with the High Lord's house," Kaylin said. "I mean, at least according to the documents about Mellarionne."

"Every house is in conflict with every other house," Sedarias replied. She was *trying* not to sound dismissive, but her early lessons about deportment still clung to her tone. "But when you returned from the West March the first time, Mellarionne began to make more conciliatory moves. Or at least the lower echelons of Mellarionne's related allies. They don't approach the Consort directly, of course; they don't approach the High Lord directly. They *can* approach the Lord of the West March. It's taken time to build a reasonable base of power in the West

March because the West March has been considered far less politically relevant.

"But given the presence of my sister there, that is clearly no longer the case." She glanced, briefly, at Eddorian, which was clearly done for the benefit of outsiders; the cohort hadn't moved. "Gennave has supported Mellarionne, but not in an obvious way. Eddorian's sister is An'Gennave. Gennave is not beloved of the High Lord's house. There has been very little movement on the part of Gennave since your first trip to the green; the loss of Iberrienne was costly. Iberrienne was the conduit through which Gennave could make contact with the Arcanum's more private members; it was through the Arcanum—the Imperial service theorizes—that Iberrienne made contact with the humans, some of who…" She stopped.

"Some of who?"

"It is not relevant to the Consort and her arrival."

"It's relevant—it might be relevant—to anything that comes after. Can I see that?"

"There's not much more." Sedarias exhaled. "Fine. At least one of the men who frequently entertained Iberrienne is a lord of the Human Caste Court. A wealthy lord, by Imperial standards."

"That means money," Tain helpfully added. "The Barrani concept of wealth is broader and more complex; I imagine that the draconian concept is similar to ours, as well."

"Don't look at me," Bellusdeo said. "Wealth in my world, by the end, was measured in armies and their martial prowess."

"It was that way for us, as well," Serralyn surprised Kaylin by saying. "During the wars in which we were…empowered. But the wars have passed; we learned martial arts—sword, bow, pole-arm—but they are no longer so highly prized as they were. Perhaps that will change in future; perhaps it will not. If Gennave was their contact—"

"They weren't the only contact," Eddorian finally said. "You remember—"

"I admit I could not decipher much of what Iberrienne said," Sedarias said, as if the admission pained her. "And at the time, I did not think it entirely relevant." Her look soured further, so the cohort was probably talking among itself again.

"Sedarias," Helen said softly, "I have prepared some jewelry for the dinner tonight. I am uncertain what is acceptable to Barrani at this time, and wish to consult with you in the parlor."

Sedarias looked as if she would dismiss this request out of hand. Instead, she took one long breath and rose from her chair, setting the documents she was holding on the tabletop. Everyone watched her go.

It was Eddorian, usually silent, who spoke—but only after Sedarias was no longer in the room. Why, Kaylin didn't know. It wasn't as if the cohort were any good at keeping things to themselves, with the exception of Teela, who had had centuries of practice.

"Sedarias was the bloodline heir. She was considered the member of Mellarionne with the greatest potential for power."

Kaylin knew this already, but nodded, anyway, an indication that she was listening and she wanted the rest.

"Do you think she was surprised to find her sister within Alsanis's core?"

"She didn't look surprised."

"No. Because she wasn't. Her sister had tried to kill her before we were ever sent to the green. Her sister tried to be nominated to go in Sedarias's stead—it was the only time in their mutual history her sister spoke up about how talented, how important, how *necessary*, Sedarias was to the family. There was no love between them, and no admiration; the only time Sedarias might depend on that sister for support might be if the family home were attacked by the Dragon Flights. It's just as likely that her sister would kill her and blame it on the Dragons, though."

"Eddorian," Valliant said, his tone forbidding.

Mandoran snorted. "Let him finish."

"If Sedarias wanted this known, she'd say it herself."

"If Sedarias didn't want it known, she wouldn't have left. She doesn't want to feel public humiliation or pain—but she doesn't care if Kaylin knows. Teela already knows, and Tain is practically oath-bound."

"And the other mortal?"

"Severn's the same, only he serves Lord Kaylin."

Kaylin tried very hard not to grimace at the use of the courtesy title.

"Sedarias accepts you. Mostly," Eddorian added, "because of you two." Although he was looking at Mandoran, he included Annarion in this. "She's willing to trust only us, but you both trust this house, and this house is Kaylin's. It's why she's willing to accept a Dragon." He looked to Valliant, who gave a very reluctant nod.

"Iberrienne isn't like Calarnenne—Nightshade. Neither is my sister. Their actions didn't get them forcibly removed from the High Court by the previous lord. But...when Iberrienne was offered a chance to rescue me—his perception—he took it. He took it instantly." Voice lower, he added, "It destroyed him."

Silence.

Mandoran picked up the thread. "Annarion's brother never stopped looking for some way to save Annarion. Eddorian's brother sacrificed himself to save Eddorian."

"And Sedarias's sibling tried to kill her."

"Her sister, yes—but she doesn't doubt that her brother

was behind it, in the end. And frankly, neither does Teela, which is probably more important, given Teela's long-term experience with the Court and its politics." Mandoran grimaced after a pause; clearly someone was telling him to shut up. Luckily—unluckily?—Mandoran had never been moved by attempts to silence him. "It's hard for Sedarias. So far, none of our families have cared enough to spend the resources attempting to murder any of the rest of us, and some demonstrably spent those resources for the opposite reason: to liberate us. I think it's likely that we'll come under fire at some point, but the stakes aren't as high for our families. Yet.

"She's one of us. She'd never hurt us unless she had no other choice—and frankly, I can't imagine a Sedarias so cornered that she had no other choice. But she didn't pay attention to Iberrienne because he was no longer a threat. She doesn't understand Eddorian's guilt or his concern. She doesn't understand Annarion's attachment to Nightshade, and *really* doesn't understand why Annarion's so angry with his brother.

"And none of us who do understand it can explain it to her. I mean, she knows what we know if she bothers to look— but she can't quite take it in and make it her own, because she's never had what they've had, and she never will. The best chance of peace or survival she has lies in the deaths of her immediate family—those that survive."

"But…"

It was Terrano whose eyes narrowed. Allaron's arm tightened; Terrano was watching the conversation, as such, from the floor. "What now?" He was annoyed. He was, Kaylin thought, angry at Mandoran and Eddorian for telling Kaylin—an outsider—anything that revealed a vulnerability.

He couldn't stop them; he didn't even seem to be surprised that he couldn't. But he wouldn't be, would he?

"If she didn't *want* what they had—what you had," Kaylin added, glancing at Eddorian, "she would never have suggested the giving of the names. She would never have tried to build the cohort into the family that *wouldn't* betray her, wouldn't try to kill her when it was convenient."

"Exactly," Terrano snapped.

Eddorian and Mandoran exchanged a glance. Eddorian shrugged. It was a fief shrug.

"Yes and no," Mandoran then said. "Look—I don't understand Nightshade at all. I do understand Iberrienne at least. He believed that his brother was out of his reach. Out of *all* reach. Only when Terrano appeared before him did that change. But when it did change, he wanted two things: power, and his brother back. Because if he had power, he'd likely have his brother. If he didn't? Well, it's not like much would change. He'd still be more powerful.

"That's what good families are like, at Court. Nightshade would have been considered a sentimental fool—at best. If you'd offered him power *or* his brother, and he believed that you could give him the latter, he would have chosen his brother without pause. That is not what Mellarionne is like. It's not what Sedarias would have been, had she become An'Mellarionne."

"Is it what she'll become if she is?"

Silence.

Terrano said, "She only cares about those who went to the green. You two—papers."

"And you're going to sit around uselessly sulking?" Eddorian demanded.

Terrano's grin was genuine. "There has to be *some* advantage to being on the outside."

Allaron growled. Serralyn cuffed the top of Terrano's head, which took real flexibility.

The cohort had decided that they would allow Helen to create jewelry and outer layers of clothing that were appropriately formal. Their ideas of appropriately formal caused Tain to leave the room—but Tain's eyes were a blue-green and the left corner of his mouth was twitching with the attempt to contain hilarity.

Apparently, the fashion of the highborn Barrani Court was similar to the fashion in the highborn Human Caste Court; it changed for no discernible reason whatsoever, and the changes appeared to be important to the people who followed them. Kaylin personally thought the Leontines far more practical but, as she lacked the fur and the fangs, attempted to keep out of sight of rich mortals.

Teela had a few things to say about fashion at Court. Sedarias didn't appear to like them. Serralyn didn't care. Fallessian did. Allaron, to Kaylin's surprise, did. This started an entirely different argument, but most of that was silent, and Kaylin felt she didn't *need* to know anything about Barrani fashion in the long-ago Court that had sentenced the young cohort to possible death.

"I'm not certain that the Consort will recognize that style of dress," Helen offered to apparent silence. "Are you certain?"

Kaylin glanced at Severn and mouthed the words *formal dress*, raising eyebrows.

"I brought mine."

Kaylin only had one dress that Helen considered good enough for important guests.

"All guests are important, dear," Helen said.

"Fine. For people who can fire me or turn me to ash. Better?"

"Only slightly. But yes. I think you could use a bath and some time to prepare yourself to greet your guests. That is what Teela and her friends will be doing."

Kaylin found the heat of the bath soothing. Also, the privacy. Teela didn't join her because Teela had her own bath. Kaylin's personal rooms didn't contain a bath like this; it wouldn't have fit, for one. To reach the room, Kaylin had to enter the joint hall. Helen had offered, more than once, to redesign Kaylin's rooms, but the alternative—something that resembled rooms to be found in the Halls of Law—didn't please her, either. Kaylin therefore had creaky floors of plain, if somewhat worn, wood.

Small and squawky sat on top of Kaylin's damp hair. He had been so quiet during the day Kaylin had almost forgotten he was there. "He has been watching," Helen said, voice grave. "He understands the shape of the spaces both Annarion and Mandoran occupy; he understands how those shapes distend or break when they're upset. But the rest of Teela's friends are relative strangers, and he does not have the same experience with them. Before you ask, Annarion and Mandoran are not the same; there are subtle differences between the ways they enter spaces that other Barrani cannot.

"He is also somewhat concerned about Terrano. If the rest of the cohort loses control and…spreads?"

Squawk.

"Spreads, Terrano doesn't. He can be emotional; he can be upset. But he doesn't cross boundaries that exist for the others. He chooses which side of the boundary he wants to stand on. He has more control of his form and its dissolution; he has more control of his appearance in the less visible planes. I'm surprised he stays. But he has not breached my borders. He does not sneak out and return."

"He couldn't."

"Actually, I believe he could. He is a danger, but... I do not consider him a threat. I can hear some of what he's thinking, but I am also certain that I cannot hear most of it. What I hear, he chooses to share. No, that's not quite right. What I hear is what he considers speech; what I do not hear is what he considers thought. I cannot hear the latter unless he chooses to share it."

Squawk.

"Teela can keep her thoughts to herself; so can Lord Nightshade, unless he is too angry."

"And the rest of the cohort?"

"Mandoran doesn't try. Annarion tries only when it concerns his family—but his brother's visits destroy those attempts each time. But the others? Yes, they try. I'm not at all offended; I'm not at all concerned. They do not know me. Mandoran and Annarion have reason to trust me, and the cohort knows those reasons—but knowing that someone is trustworthy is merely one step in the building of a relationship of any kind."

Kaylin's hands had now become pleasantly wrinkled in that waterlogged way they did when she'd been sitting far too long in a bath. She rose, water dripping down her body; the familiar rose with her, but avoided the toweling that implied vigorous drying was about to start.

"I don't understand why Terrano can't hear the rest of the cohort."

"He doesn't have a name anymore. The word that was given him, the word that allowed him to wake, to come to life, is no longer at his core."

"But he didn't need that in the Hallionne, did he?"

"I would argue—and this would be a guess, not a statement of practical fact—that they all lacked names. If you recall, you told me you had to give them back their names, and they had to take them, in order to leave the green the way their ancient kin have always left it."

"Alsanis kept their names. Maybe because they were trapped there, they still had some connection to them. I gave them back the names I found within Alsanis. That's it."

Kaylin, drier, donned a robe and headed back to her own room and the white dress that was no doubt waiting there. And shoes.

"But... I don't have a True Name, and I can hear the people whose names I do hold."

"You do have a name, Kaylin."

"I don't have a name that's essential or necessary. I was alive just fine without it."

"I believe that it helps."

Kaylin frowned. "I didn't take a name for Severn. Severn can hear me."

Helen nodded. It was not in any way helpful or informative.

"Please just tell me what you're thinking."

"It is not fact, but theory; it is not something I am certain is useful."

"I listen to a lot of facts that are completely useless. I'm *asking* for your opinion."

"Very well. You are Chosen. You have been Chosen since you were eleven or twelve. The marks that cover a large portion of your body are True Words. I believe your ability to hold, to hear and to contain the True Names you've taken or received resides in the power of those marks. It takes a certain amount of power to speak a name. Not to speak a social variant, but the name itself."

"Severn can speak mine."

"Can he? Has he truly tried?"

"Yes. Once."

Silence. Kaylin held up a hand, although Helen did not seem immediately intent on breaking it. "He tried once, and then was angry enough at himself for even trying that he wouldn't speak normally—to me—for days. It was awful. I barely noticed the attempt."

"You did notice."

"Yes—but, Helen, if I had been Severn, if he'd been in my position, I'd've done the same thing. I'd've tried. And if I think I'd've done what he did, I can't be angry about it."

"He shouldn't have tried."

"No, probably not. But I shouldn't be late, shouldn't swear when dealing with the public and shouldn't damage regulation wear. I also shouldn't take shortcuts through private homes when I'm in pursuit of people, and I definitely shouldn't accidentally knock Margot's damn sign over when I'm in a foul mood. If I have to be angry about every mistake someone makes, wouldn't I have to start with me and work outward?"

"I think those are minor indulgences in comparison."

"They are. And we weren't talking about that; we were talking about the fact that Severn can hear me and can speak to me, and *he* doesn't have a name." She didn't want Helen to be angry at Severn. She didn't want Helen to judge him. Kaylin could fight her own battles, and Severn had done nothing to harm Helen, ever.

"I am not an expert on the Chosen," Helen finally said. "I am only an expert about my tenants, and each tenant was individual. But in your case, I believe that the power that binds you to each other, and the power that is given to Severn, comes *from* you. He could make the attempt to use the name because you understood, on some subconscious level, that that's how True Names work.

"Terrano, however, is not Chosen. Without the name he chose to abandon, he doesn't have the link to the rest of his friends. And no," she said before Kaylin could ask, "I do not believe that you could, with your powers, rebuild that bridge. You don't understand how to use the powers you have. Ah, no. You understand how to use them in certain ways. Your healing magic comes from the marks. But you have never deliberately attempted to experiment with the powers those marks might otherwise grant."

"This is why I'm taking magic lessons."

"I note that you have not had an actual class with Lord Sanabalis in some time."

"Diarmat thought etiquette was more important."

"And it is just possible that tonight you will be able to evaluate that for yourself. Ah, but before the guest of honor arrives, I believe you have other guests. Don't forget," she added, "to wear the medallion the Arkon sent you."

What Kaylin liked about this particular dress—which was white and loose and elegant—was its practicality. It had been magically made by something that might have been elemental. It did not tear. It did not catch on anything. It did not impede movement—she could run in an all-out sprint and it didn't get under her feet or force her to shorten her stride.

What she hated about it was the fact that it was so revealing. Her arms were mostly bare, as was part of her back. She'd spent all of her adult life in long-sleeve shirts or dresses, attempting to hide the marks that adorned over half of her body. This dress did not achieve that concealment in the same way. Helen had offered to make adjustments the last time Kaylin had worn it, but adjustments could not, in the end, be made.

The alternative, which Kaylin did accept, was a jacket that was extremely soft and comfortable, but which *did* catch on things like doors. It was a lovely black—Kaylin's favorite color for clothing because it was practical—but Helen made clear that the minute Kaylin stepped beyond the gates at the front of the house, the jacket would disintegrate or vanish.

Kaylin had arranged the medallion so that it was, if not prominent, then at least obvious; she had Helen knot the chain at her neck so the medallion itself rested between her collarbones. Helen didn't approve, but didn't offer to shorten the chain instead of knotting it.

"Are you ready?" Helen asked softly. Any attempt to create jewelry for Kaylin had met with sullen resentment; Kaylin wore only one ring—but to the Consort, that ring would be significant. It had been given to Kaylin by the Lord of the West March, and it declared Kaylin family.

No. Kyuthe. Ynpharion corrected her with a touch of anxiety.

Is she on her way? It's way too early for her to be on her way.

She is preparing, just as you are.

"The first of your guests has arrived," Helen added.

Kaylin almost shrieked. "Dinner's two hours away!"

"Yes."

The first of the guests, as Helen had cheerfully pointed out, were actually the first and second. The door opened on the Arkon and Lord Emmerian. Kaylin hadn't come up with an invitation list; there was already enough panic and stress about dinner, and since she'd spent most of her time leading up to it attempting to cancel, this made sense. But she didn't remember Emmerian's name being mentioned at all.

Bellusdeo was still in her room, as were the rest of the cohort; Tain was nowhere in sight.

Severn, however, appeared at the top of the stairs. He, like Kaylin, was dressed for a formal dinner, but unlike Kaylin, his clothing suited him.

"Kaylin," Helen said, catching Kaylin's attention and dragging it away from a formal, well-turned-out Severn. "Your guests."

Kaylin grimaced, but managed to realign the shape of her mouth so it looked like she was smiling. The Arkon grimaced in return, which meant she hadn't been entirely successful. She then stepped out of the doorway and allowed both men to enter. Lord Emmerian swept her a perfect but elegant bow. The Arkon didn't bother.

"At my age," he said, "some gestures are considered too taxing."

The familiar on Kaylin's shoulder snorted. Dragons did age, but not the way mortals did; age was considered a sign of strength. That the Arkon had chosen to adopt age as an appearance did not, in fact, mean that something as simple as a bow was beyond his elderly bones.

"If you would care to come this way," Helen said when Kaylin failed to immediately remember what she was supposed to do as hostess. "You are early, but we are of course delighted to have you."

The Arkon accepted.

Lord Emmerian, however, did not—not immediately.

"Yes, of course," Helen said, although neither of the Dragons had spoken. "There are some doors that will remain closed for the entirety of dinner, but if you require entrance for your peace of mind, I will return shortly to supervise. The guest rooms, however, are entirely off-limits."

"Understood," Emmerian replied. "Perhaps the corporal will join me?"

"That is, of course, up to the corporal. Severn?"

Severn bowed—to Emmerian. There was no hint at all that he found the task of escorting a member of the Dragon Court annoying. He probably didn't. But he moved quietly, certainly, and he led Lord Emmerian to Helen's dining room.

Probably, Kaylin reflected, to get him out of the foyer before Bellusdeo came down the stairs.

"Yes," Helen said quietly. "It is only natural that the Arkon have an escort, and you are not fond of the palace guard he might otherwise bring. But Bellusdeo can be sensitive about the Dragon Court. Bellusdeo will join the Arkon in the parlor."

The parlor was a much larger room than it had been the previous day; it was as large—and as richly appointed—as it had been on the night the Emperor had come to dinner. On that night, Lord Emmerian had not come to do a security sweep of the building first.

"Lord Kaylin," the Arkon said as Kaylin hovered near a chair.

Kaylin bowed.

The Arkon waved a hand. "That is not necessary until Emmerian returns—and possibly not even then. Unless you are doing it to annoy Bellusdeo."

"I never try to annoy her."

"Ah, forgive me. I meant, of course, the annoyance of the *necessity* of you, personally, doing so. She is not here, regardless; the gesture is therefore wasted." Helen offered the Arkon a drink; a small amount of amber liquid swirled in the curve of the glass. He raised his brows, both white, both bushy.

"You are very well supplied," he told the Avatar of Kaylin's home.

"It was one of my functions. I am not, however, permitted to harm the guests, and you are a guest."

"Even were you, I have confidence in Lord Kaylin. And, Lord Kaylin? You will cease that cringe."

"I wasn't cringing."

"You cringe every time someone uses the title you have *earned* in the Barrani High Court. Tonight, however, you will hear it when you are addressed. To grimace in that fashion might imply that you hold the title itself in some disdain—and I assure you that is politically unwise."

It was going to be a long damn evening.

By the time Lord Emmerian and Severn returned to the parlor, Bellusdeo had joined the Arkon. *She* didn't bother to use a formal title to address Kaylin, and the Arkon didn't bother to correct her. Of course not.

"You are expecting the Consort, and only the Consort?"

"I highly doubt the High Lord is going to just walk in off the street with no notice," Kaylin replied.

"I assume you did not invite him."

"Well, no."

"Very well. The Consort will arrive. Her escort?"

"Escort?"

Ynpharion screamed in the back of Kaylin's head. He had otherwise been silent, but given the presence of Dragons, Kaylin wasn't certain how much he could now see or hear; she trusted Helen's discretion in what she allowed. *She will have personal guards. Does the Emperor travel without them?*

Kaylin decided not to answer that question, given the tension between the Emperor and the High Court at the moment. "Helen, if the Consort arrives with her personal guards, what do we do with the guards?"

"They, like me, will be expected to do their duty while the Consort socializes. They will not, of course, be serving—but they will likely occupy positions near the doors." To Emmerian, she said, "The Consort's full escort will not be entering the house proper; they will be arrayed just outside of the grounds."

Kaylin wondered whether or not she would be hemmed in by escorts if she were ever rich enough, important enough. She didn't like the thought. In her universe, until relatively recently, power simply meant the freedom to do what she wanted, without fear. She was beginning to understand in a very visceral way that what changed with enough power was the *nature* of the fear.

That, and the number of rules that had to be followed or someone would take offense.

She could tell a Hawk to drop dead on a bad day, and they'd be fine with it tomorrow, with one or two notable exceptions. She could have a bad hair day, a bad clothing day—some encounters damaged clothing and parts of actual body, as well—could come in with dust or dirt under her fingernails, was not judged by the jewelry she wore. She didn't have to somehow stand up as the epitome of…something. Just the law.

Kaylin was used to being judged, although she resented it when it was safe to do so. But to be judged for things that made no sense and seemed unnecessary both flustered and annoyed her. She was taking a test that she couldn't afford to fail, and she realized that two days was not nearly enough time to truly study for it.

"You can afford to fail this one, dear," Helen said quietly.

"I'm not the one who'll pay for my failure."

"No. That is, unfortunately, one of the disadvantages of

power. People with less immediate power are likely to bear the consequences."

"I would not say the cohort is without power," Bellusdeo said in the same subdued tone that Helen had used. It implied that she agreed with Helen, but that she felt obliged to defend Kaylin. Oddly, this made Kaylin feel worse, not better.

The Arkon cleared his throat, the way thunderclouds rumbled.

"We have something to discuss before the most significant of your guests arrive."

CHAPTER 6

Lord Emmerian did not take a seat; he chose to stand by the entrance to the parlor, his arms folded. Bellusdeo nodded in his direction, but didn't otherwise greet him.

"I will not ask you for precise, arcane explanations of what occurred when you traveled to the West March without notice. Nor will I ask you all that occurred in your absence. I have spoken with Bellusdeo, and believe her explanations would be more academically satisfying.

"This is not a matter of the academic. The Hallionne Alsanis was compromised."

Kaylin nodded.

"In theory the first breach occurred some months ago, by one of your current guests."

Kaylin's nod was slower to come, and vastly more troubled.

"You trust that guest."

"Yes."

"Helen, do you feel that you are capable of containing him, should the need arise?"

"I am uncertain," Helen replied.

"Very well. None of the rest of your guests achieved the… freedom that Terrano did."

Kaylin shot Bellusdeo a look. It bounced off her profile. "No."

"Do not make that face. I am not concerned with the possible actions of your guests—or rather, not their intentional actions. But the recent difficulty in the West March could not be laid at the feet of those guests. The Hallionne Alsanis was breached—without his knowledge—from the outside. It is just possible that, were it not for your interference, or the interference of your guests, the attackers would now control the Hallionne."

"Terrano thinks that unlikely," Helen told the Arkon.

"Oh?"

"Apologies. While we have not had this discussion in your presence, Arkon, we have discussed it, and at some length. Some of the concepts cannot be easily explained to Kaylin, and it was judged too risky to demonstrate. But the rest of the guests understand viscerally now. They will be watching and listening in ways they were not while in the West March. They understand how they were trapped, how that pocket space was created, and by what. I do not think the same trap will work again."

"It is not the trap itself, with all due respect, but the possibility of attack."

"Yes. I believe Lord Emmerian has done a comprehensive examination of the rooms which will be in use."

The Arkon exhaled a steady stream of smoke, his eye color deepening to orange.

"Lord Kaylin's guests have, as you suspect, no love of Dragons. They are, however, honorable in the ways of their kin. They owe Bellusdeo their lives. She fought to protect and defend them. They will make no attempt to harm her and, indeed, would risk much to save her—although, of course, that will not be necessary."

"The Emperor remains at odds with the High Halls."

"Because of the misunderstanding caused by Lord Kaylin's familiar," Helen said.

"Ah. Yes." A beat of silence. "I am not a terribly political creature, as you must be aware. But, Helen, none of my kin are naturally political. Politics among my kin generally involved fire, flight and death. The Emperor is capable of subtlety when he is not enraged.

"Unfortunately, he remains very, very angry. We must be grateful that Bellusdeo is not."

Kaylin snorted. "She wasn't angry when it *did* happen. She thought they were *clever.*"

"And they were," Bellusdeo said, smiling.

"The High Lord has been stiff in his interactions with the Imperial Court; he cannot afford to capitulate to Imperial demands. His tenure is too new, too vulnerable. I believe," he added with just a hint of question, "you have been provided with the relevant information. You understand that should *anything* go wrong this evening, it will deepen the rift between the two Courts, possibly irrevocably."

"The Barrani won't harm the Consort."

"It would not be the first time that this particular set of Barrani have tried."

"That was—" Kaylin snapped her jaws together to prevent words from escaping. What she thought was: *So did Ynpharion, and he's now one of the Consort's closest personal attendants.* But... that was information the Dragon Court didn't need, if they didn't already have it.

Ynpharion said nothing, although she was suddenly certain he'd heard that thought. There was nothing he could say. But if he could be accepted, so could the cohort.

"They won't try now. They'll never try again while they have any control over their own actions. I'd bet my life on it."

"I am happy to hear you say that," the Arkon replied.

Bellusdeo stiffened instantly.

"Because in some fashion, Lord Kaylin, you *are*." He lifted a hand in Bellusdeo's direction, possibly to forestall either words or fire, her eyes were so close to red. "The misunderstanding that occurred in the West March involved Lord Kaylin's familiar. Do you understand? Any difficulty that occurs within Lord Kaylin's home will be one misunderstanding, one coincidence, too many. The Barrani who are in conflict with both their own High Court and the Eternal Emperor will seize upon that. Should the Consort come to harm here, it will be laid at your feet. It might end all hostilities between the Emperor and the High Court—"

"Over my dead body," Bellusdeo said, her voice a rumble of Dragon thunder.

"—but that is not an advantage to Elantra, as you must suspect. The Consort is not as secure in her seat as you believe. There are Consort candidates waiting in the wings, some of whom have passed almost all of the tests.

"And one is of Mellarionne."

"I don't think that was in the dossier Diarmat gave me."

"It is a recent development. It was difficult to confirm."

"Look—I *tried* to cancel the dinner. I tried every possible avenue available to anyone!"

"Understood. All I hope you take out of this experience in the future is some measure of control over whether or not you extend an invitation at all." He turned to Helen. "I have questions of a more technical nature, if you are free to respond."

"I am free to respond, but also free to choose not to do so."

"Understood, again." The Arkon pushed himself out of his chair. "Is there another room in which we may have this discussion?"

"It requires your native tongue?"

"Some of it, yes."

"Very well. Please follow me."

The Arkon followed the Avatar, which left a large conversational hole in the room. Emmerian, however, filled it. "You understand the difficulty," he said to Bellusdeo.

"You are concerned that the spies just beyond the grounds and in all directions are not an actual danger."

"Yes. To be honest, the method of your return to Elantra has...increased the uncertainty. It has long been understood among Immortals that the portal paths exist between the Hallionne. You did not traverse those paths; there is no such path that leads to Elantra."

"There is," Kaylin said.

"I assure you—"

"If I understand anything about Shadow and the heart of the fiefs, there is. But it leads through *Ravellon*. All things apparently did, once."

"And telling the Emperor that you followed the path to *Ravellon* is unlikely to induce the calm for which you hope."

"I don't want calm based on ignorance. We had help, in the outlands. We had the Hallionne Bertolle's brothers. They wouldn't go near *Ravellon*—but we could see it. In a plane in which there were almost no physical markers, no geography, *Ravellon* looked like a...city."

"You are straying from the topic at hand."

"Look, Emmerian—Lord Emmerian," she added when Helen cleared her now-absent throat, "I obviously don't understand the topic at hand. I'm a private. I'm a Hawk. Tell me what you're worried about without all the indirection."

"As you wish. If the Barrani can enter the heart of Hallionne without the Hallionne's knowledge, they might just as easily enter Helen in the same fashion. If Mellarionne is involved, it would be an *advantage* to their line to assassinate the Consort. You would bear the blame, but it would also fall upon your various friends. And Mellarionne's candidate would be vastly more important, vastly more significant, than she might otherwise be. She has come far in the testing, and if the Consort dies here, it will be imperative that she be brought up to speed.

"She will replace the Consort, and the High Court will agree because otherwise none of the children will awaken."

"Look—I'm not supposed to be talking about this, but I *highly doubt* that the Mellarionne candidate would be able to pass the final test if that was the case. And frankly, passing the milestones in between is hand-waving. It's meaningless. Only the final test counts. If she does pass that last test, she's not going to be a good little pawn in Mellarionne's bid for the seat."

"And you are so certain of that? Lord Kaylin—Kaylin if you prefer and until the Consort arrives—*if* Mellarionne's various kin have become adept at fooling the Hallionne, at hiding their intent, why do you feel that such a woman would not pass the tests devised by some ancient and unknown magic?

"We are not currently afraid that your guests will attempt to harm the Consort. The Consort does not fear that, either—or she would not have accepted your invitation. But harm can come from many sources, and information is not currently being easily passed between the Dragon Court and the High Halls."

Ah, Ynpharion said. *Now I understand.*

Is it true? Does Mellarionne have a candidate who's almost there?

I do not know. But I will ask.

So. What everyone was afraid of was pretty simple: Barrani would try to kill the Consort, and blame it on the cohort—which would almost certainly result in the entire lot being made outcaste. If they couldn't make that stick—if the Consort was harmed but didn't die—they could try to pin it on the Dragons, because at the moment, there were three of them under Kaylin's roof. They wouldn't need something like actual proof, either.

The Emperor was already almost enraged at what had happened in the West March. He didn't *want* a war between the Dragon Court and the High Halls—it would destroy the city, probably literally. Kaylin was certain that the current High Lord didn't want that, either. But Mellarionne? Mellarionne could use the political tension and the history of the two peoples as a goad to supporters. It was all just ugly.

And she'd invited the Consort.

It pains me greatly to offer you any support whatsoever at this time, Ynpharion said, *but you didn't so much invite her as accede to her very, very obvious desire.*

Did she answer?

No, Lord Kaylin, she did not. What conversation you've had that I can share, I have been asked to share. "Ask," in this case, had a very different weight for Ynpharion than it would for any other Barrani lord, because the Consort had his name. *I hope you understand what she desires from the cohort, as you call them. It is only because of that desire that she is willing to take this risk—but she will not be turned away from it. The High Lord has tried. The Lord of the West March has tried. No others among the Court have any chance of success where these two failed.*

And now, he added, *you are almost out of time. The Consort is leaving her quarters.*

The Arkon returned with Helen, and once again resumed his seat, pausing only to speak a few quiet words to Emmerian, who remained by the door. Kaylin, who hadn't heard the draconian, wondered why Helen hadn't shut Annarion and Nightshade in the same damn room during the endless nights of argument.

The Consort did not arrive before the cohort began to trickle into the parlor. Teela came first. Kaylin had seen Teela in formal court dress before, but it never really got old. She wore a dress of emerald silk—at least Kaylin thought it must be silk—with full, long skirts, and a neckline that was cut in a way that suggested it was meant to set off the emerald necklace that lay flat against her skin. Her hair had been drawn up and away from her back; it was piled on her head, and it glittered, implying either nets or jewelry embedded in its curled, glossy strands.

To Kaylin's utter surprise, Teela wore a circlet of gold that housed an emerald, as well. Her eyes were a martial blue. The lines of the dress did not imply armor, but she wore a sword, as well. Kaylin didn't ask if the sword was significant; she already knew the answer.

None of Teela's clothing, jewelry or weaponry had been created by Helen. Tain was not far behind, and his eyes were bluer. He wore a green that mirrored Teela's, but no jewelry; he did have a sword, as well. The whole impression he gave was shadowed by Teela's. Kaylin liked his boots, though.

Teela bowed to the Arkon, who rose when she entered the parlor. "An'Teela," he said.

"Arkon. It is a pleasure to see you outside of the Imperial Library."

"I wish I could say it is a pleasure to *be* outside of my own domain. In general, I leave it only during times of possible war."

Teela's eyes lightened a shade; there was more green in them. Bellusdeo also relaxed. She eyed the sword that Teela bore, but made no comment about it.

"It is a gesture of respect," Helen said, which caused the people in the room to look in Kaylin's direction. "Were Lord Nightshade present, he would no doubt likewise be so armed."

"How is it respectful to carry a sword that was created—successfully—to kill Dragons?"

The Arkon chuckled. To Helen, he said, "The battles that shaped Kaylin's life are not the battles that shaped either of our people, and on surface appearance, she might be forgiven for confusion." To Kaylin, he said, "The wearing of the sword implies that I am a dangerous man, a worthy opponent, instead of a toothless, ancient Dragon."

"You are hardly toothless, Lannagaros."

The Arkon smiled. His eyes were almost pure gold. Bellusdeo's were the orange-gold that implied caution in a dangerous setting. A backward glance at Emmerian surprised Kaylin; his eyes were lighter than even the Arkon's.

Sedarias arrived with Terrano, although Allaron was not far behind. As Teela was, she was robed in a deep emerald green; her jewelry was different. Rings bound her hands almost ostentatiously, and the necklace she wore was not all pendant; it had a pendant but the chain that bore it was heavy and appeared to be etched or carved in a pattern.

Allaron and Terrano also wore the same green.

In fact, as the cohort came into the parlor in a procession, it was clear that they were all wearing the same colors. Kaylin had assumed that they'd wear colors associated with their family lines, which *might* help her remember which lines those were. No. They wore green. And it came to her slowly that she had seen that green before, and had, in fact, worn it herself on the road to the West March, because a closet had appeared in her room, and she'd been fool enough to open it.

They meant to make a statement.

Severn and Kaylin didn't fit that statement in any way, which was probably for the best. She wondered what it had cost to get Tain to join in, but didn't ask.

"White suits you," Sedarias said in her critical drillmaster tone. "It is the Consort's color. Not her line's, but her own. Had you not chosen the white, I would have asked you to consider it. It will be a reminder of your value to our people, rather than the lesser consideration of friendship." The last word was uttered as if she'd meant to say *enmity* instead.

Terrano was the only member of the cohort who did not wear jewelry. He was finely dressed, but Kaylin suspected he'd agreed in the vain hope that he'd blend in. His eyes were blue, but it was an odd shade—light, for the Barrani. He was also the only member of the cohort who looked visibly uncomfortable. Whatever Sedarias had said—and probably was still saying—to the rest had made a visible impact. They were tall, they were straight, they were elegant; they appeared to be almost at ease.

But it was an ease accomplished only by those to whom power was so familiar it was like air. Kaylin often had to temper her resentment of the Barrani: they were eternal, immortal, unafraid of the Ferals and the smaller Shadows that sometimes escaped *Ravellon*. They didn't have to worry about exhaustion or starvation. They seemed, if she didn't engage her brain, to have no worries at all. But Sedarias's sister had tried to kill her. Immortality was no protection against hatred or ambition.

The truth didn't make Kaylin feel less self-conscious. Mandoran smiled at her. Smiled; it wasn't his usual grin. But it implied that his usual grin was lurking just beneath this polished, perfect surface. She exhaled and nodded.

"Are you ready?" She spoke softly.

All eyes turned to her then.

"Because I think the Consort is almost here."

"Is Emmerian just going to stand by the door all evening?"

"Yes. He is not present as a Lord of the Dragon Court; he is here as a guard. I believe he intends to be roughly where the

Consort's guards will be. It is a pity," Helen added, her voice softening, "that the Arkon does not often leave his library."

"You like him."

"Yes, but so do you. He has made one or two suggestions about security that I find intriguing, and he understands the ancient variant of what you now call mirrors and mirror networks. He does not lay any blame for the current situation at your feet, and I consider this quite broad-minded of him."

"I didn't choose to go to the West March—the elemental water did that for me."

"It would have caused much less difficulty if Bellusdeo had not accompanied you to the Keeper's garden. Bellusdeo, however, is aware of this."

Kaylin came to stand beside the door. "I kind of wish I'd invited Nightshade," she finally said.

"He is outcaste."

"I know. But the Consort likes him, and fails to treat him as social poison."

"Yes—but at the moment, the High Court is embroiled in politics, some of which involve the designation of outcaste. It would have been difficult." She stepped to one side of the closed doors. "And Annarion is still easily upset in his brother's presence. They have both become better at controlling their expression of hurt or anger, but it is always there. Tonight I believe there will be enough internal conflict."

"Aren't you worried?"

"Of course I'm worried. It's what I do. But I understand what the Consort hopes the cohort can achieve, and I believe you understand it, as well."

Kaylin nodded. She exhaled a few inches of height, shook herself and attempted to rearrange her neck and shoulders so that no hint of possible slouch remained.

Helen opened the door while Kaylin stood almost at attention, uncertain of what to expect, but aware that bad handling of those expectations could lead to ugliness that was *definitely* above her pay grade. When she'd first attached herself to the Hawks—without actually being one—she had resented people who told her what to do. In the seven years since, she'd come to not only appreciate the chain of command, but rely on it. Probably because she knew how to do her job, in all of its many variations.

This was not her job, but she was expected to do it well, regardless.

The Consort was revealed by the slow opening of the doors, and Kaylin felt the tension leave her spine.

"Kaylin, you look lovely," the Consort said. Her eyes were as green as any Barrani eyes had been in the past few days, and she wore not the complicated style of outmoded court dress, or even modern court dress, but the white that she wore daily. Her hair was not a mass of braids and combs and jewels; it fell straight down her back. At that back were two—only two—Barrani guards. Kaylin was very surprised to recognize one of them: Ynpharion. The other, she wasn't certain she'd met, and if she had, they hadn't exchanged more than two words, but given Ynpharion's presence, she guessed that he was also a Lord of the High Court.

Ynpharion's eyes, on the other hand, were a deep, deep blue.

Of course they are, he snapped.

Why are there only two of you?

It will amuse you to know that she brought us because the High Lord was willing to accede to your obvious desire to cancel this dinner if she would not agree to guards. We are her compromise, and may I just say that I feel that the High Lord was not emphatic enough? There are six guards stationed at the gatehouse. They will enter the grounds if required.

Ynpharion almost never criticized the Consort; Kaylin was shocked. She hoped her momentarily frozen expression had at least paused on a smile.

Helen gently nudged her back to reality, or at least out of the doorway. The Consort, almost unadorned, entered. Only when her attendants had also crossed the threshold did she frown. It was a thoughtful frown.

"That amulet," she began.

Kaylin had forgotten she was wearing it. A better person would have taken no pleasure whatsoever from Ynpharion's internal shriek of pure frustration, and maybe in the future, Kaylin would become that better person. "It's the Arkon's."

"I see."

"Have you seen it before? Or seen one like it?"

"It has been seen in our history," the Consort replied. "And its likeness painted. It will not come as a surprise to you that it has never been seen on a mortal. And it has never been seen—by my kin—outside of battle."

Kaylin cleared her throat. "I guess I should warn you that the Arkon is actually present."

The Consort's eyes shifted to an almost draconian gold. "The Arkon is *here*?"

"Yes. Bellusdeo was given permission to join us with the understanding that she would not be isolated." Kaylin spoke in High Barrani. It was the language of diplomacy, which was why she found it so hard to maintain.

The gold made way for green again, but the green was luminous.

"Kaylin is fond of the Lady," Helen said, reducing the practical value of silence to zero. "And the Lady is *my* guest. No harm will come to her that she does not inflict—instantly—upon herself." The Avatar's High Barrani was chilly; it was a tone Kaylin almost never heard Helen use.

And, because people were strange, it seemed to comfort Ynpharion. Kaylin was never, ever going to understand him.

The Consort grabbed Kaylin's right arm. "Please—let's join them." She spoke Elantran. Her expression was almost exuberant; it made Kaylin feel old.

Green eyes encountered a field of emerald green as Kaylin led the Consort to the parlor; she couldn't retrieve her arm and half suspected that the Consort knew she wanted to be anywhere else. And in any other clothing. But when the Consort had fully entered the room, she did disengage.

Kaylin immediately began introductions, starting with the oldest person present, who had risen from his chair as if to remind Kaylin that introductions were necessary. "Arkon," she said, "may I introduce you to the Consort?"

He bowed, Barrani-style. The Consort returned that bow, but she held it longer, and when she rose, her eyes were bright. Kaylin was half-afraid she would run across the room and take the Arkon's hands, which annoyed Ynpharion; his expression remained composed bland. She did not introduce Emmerian, but Emmerian had made clear that he, like Ynpharion, was here to work. He was a guard, and guards didn't get named in front of the actual guests; they were like armor or weapons. Or like the armor or weapons Kaylin carried; Teela's weapon had a name.

Kaylin didn't know what it was.

Ynpharion was now so heavily on alert he didn't supply the name, either. It was clear to the visitors that Emmerian was a Dragon, and there were no Dragons who were not Lords of the Dragon Court, with the possible exception of Bellusdeo.

You're a Lord of the High Court and you're here as a guard. Why should Dragons be any different? They're here for precisely the same reason you are.

He didn't answer, which was just as well. Kaylin had no difficulty introducing Bellusdeo, whose presence also seemed to delight the Consort.

When it came to the cohort, however, they both stiffened. The choice of emerald green had seemed a little too political to Kaylin; it seemed a *lot* too political now. But she hadn't argued against it—her ears were still ringing with Sedarias's etiquette criticisms—and therefore accepted the awkward that followed. What she was *really* afraid of was Sedarias's judgment. While Diarmat had the louder voice and the more imperious tone, he wasn't actually *at* any of the occasions in which she tried to apply his lessons. Sedarias was.

While her expression was elegant, genial, even welcoming, her eyes were the same shade of blue as Ynpharion's. She was, however, perfect in her response; her bow was the correct depth, and it lasted the correct length of time; she did not wait to rise, but did not offer insult by shortening the gesture.

The Consort remained standing while Kaylin cycled through each member of the cohort. She started with Sedarias, and ended with Annarion. Terrano was the most awkward, because he *looked* like what he really wanted to do was throw himself at her feet and spend the rest of the evening on the ground. He could no longer hear Sedarias—or any of the rest of his kin— and had to settle with a muted clearing of throat on the part of the woman who led the cohort in most things.

He bowed instead, but even that was awkward; he held the bow for far too long, and did not rise until the Consort bid him do so.

The only other awkward introduction was Tain's, and it was awkward because Tain's chosen form of address? "Corporal Korrin."

It was his rank in the Hawks. Sedarias felt it entirely inappropriate; being introduced as Tain of Korrin would have been acceptable. His response still rankled some of the cohort; he was proud of the rank of corporal. This implied many, many things, and Kaylin, too busy with panic, had failed to consider all of them.

Until, again, now.

This was going to have to stop. It was *her* house. She had some say in what occurred beneath her own roof. She had been afraid that she didn't understand enough to be able to make smart decisions—but that was ignorance, and ignorance could be changed.

"May I offer you a drink?" she asked.

The Consort smiled. "I'm most curious about what the Arkon is drinking."

"It is meant for Dragons," Helen said. "Mortals would consider it poison. I am less certain about the effect on Barrani, as none of my Barrani guests have expressed a desire to try."

"Then perhaps I will not—not while I am here. If it disagrees with me, it might cause difficulties that I do not intend." She smiled at the Avatar, and Kaylin remembered that the Hallionne all adored the Consort. "There will, no doubt, be difficulties that arise out of my own hopes and fears, and they will be more than enough."

A chair moved—untouched—to the Consort's back, and the Consort sat. It was not a throne, of course; it was a chair, and even if it was a very fine, very expensive-looking chair, all of Kaylin's guests—the seated ones, at any rate—occupied chairs its equal.

Ynpharion and the unnamed Barrani lord chosen to accompany him took up positions by the parlor door, which caused a minor—and nonvocal—negotiation with the Dragon who was also in that position. In the end, the Barrani guards chose to stand side by side to the right of the doors as one entered, and Emmerian stood to the left.

Silence descended on the room, and Kaylin's stomach clenched. If it continued for much longer, it was Kaylin's responsibility to break it—pleasantly, in a way that implied delight and contained almost no information beyond that.

The Consort came to her rescue before she could take up the most nerve-racking of her duties. "I cannot help but notice that you have chosen the colors that you wear without regard to your familial lines."

"We are none of us, save only Teela, the rulers of our lines." It was Sedarias who replied. Of course it was. "We are not yet Lords of the High Court, and while it is true that our families have their colors, it might be considered presumptuous for those who are not of sufficient rank to wear those colors in the presence of the Consort."

"Oh?" The Consort smiled; her eyes tinted slightly toward the blue, but only slightly. "Considered presumptuous by who?"

Be wary, Ynpharion told Kaylin, his interior voice sharp.

CHAPTER 7

Sedarias clearly did not need Ynpharion's warning. She fell silent for a beat longer than necessary. But she didn't look away from the Consort's friendly gaze.

It was Teela who spoke—but that made sense. Of the assembled Barrani guests, only Teela and the Consort had taken the Test of Name and passed it. "We are aware that the simple color of clothing is unlikely to cause you mortal offense. Mortal offense, however, has clearly been taken—or perhaps an attempt has been made to express it—by those intimately acquainted with our blood kin.

"We have returned from the green; we wish to return to our families. As you have experienced yourself just scant days past—and I admit I am impressed by the speed with which you returned to Elantra—some of those families are less sanguine about our return." Teela's eyes were blue. Her voice was cool but pleasant; it was a wall, not a weapon. "Designating a person outcaste requires the involvement of the High Lord—and his explicit agreement. Disowning a person does not.

"It would be politically difficult to disown only one of us. In one or two cases, I expect that the heads of lines are interested in the return of their long-forgotten kin."

"Those cases coinciding with a lack of competition for the seat?"

Teela nodded, expression grave. "Or perhaps those whose families have declined in influence in power."

The Consort inclined her head. "They will have to meet your friends in person, because they will require a pretext; to disown them for fear of their essential nature would give rise to difficulties for those whose families wish to embrace their lost kin." Ynpharion was surprised by her response. Surprised and instantly ill at ease.

"But you and your friends—children trapped, until very recently, in the Hallionne Alsanis—are not my kin as kin is reckoned among our kind. I am not the High Lord; I am the Lady, the guardian of the Lake. My purpose has not been political, to the benefit of our race. If you decline to wear the colors of your lines because it might be considered presumptuous, I must ask: by who? For it seems to me your action implies that I answer to—that I will answer to—any of the High Court. For a purely personal visit."

"And it seems to us," Teela countered, "that you intend us to believe that your visit will be considered purely personal. We are willing to lend credence to your personal preferences in this regard; you wished to visit Lord Kaylin, and she wished to offer you her hospitality. But you must be aware that there are Barrani guards lining the perimeter of this property, and those guards—"

"None have been given permission to accompany me into Lord Kaylin's home. My guards are personally loyal to me; they have no other allegiance."

Which meant, Kaylin thought, that the second, unknown guard was almost certainly name-bound, as Ynpharion was.

"What I do not choose to divulge, they will not divulge." The Consort's eyes remained primarily green, but she adopted

Teela's tone. "I am observed, yes. I have been observed by less-than-friendly eyes from the moment I embarked upon the many tests that lead, in the end, to the Lake.

"But Bellusdeo is likewise observed, and she is considered above suspicion."

Mandoran coughed.

"You disagree?" the Consort asked, looking quizzical.

"She's a Dragon."

"She is. But so, too, the Emperor to whom we have all sworn allegiance. All," she added, "who become Lords of the High Court." Her gaze swiveled to Kaylin. "Is that not so?"

"Mortals aren't required to swear personal oaths of allegiance," Kaylin replied. "Or at least not mortals like me or Severn. I haven't been asked to swear an oath since passing the Tower's test."

"You are a Hawk; perhaps he considers the oaths required upon joining the Hawks to be sufficient."

Kaylin shook her head. "The oath Hawks swear isn't to the Emperor, personally. It is to the laws that the Emperor devised. We're not soldiers. If, for instance, the Emperor personally commanded that we murder civilians, we're honor-bound to refuse. He cannot order us to break the laws that we've sworn to uphold."

"Lord Severn?"

"I have sworn an oath of personal fealty to the Emperor. The same oath has not been asked of Lord Kaylin or any of the Hawks."

The Consort inclined her head and turned her attention, once again, to Teela. "A meeting with those who have yet to undertake the Test of Name is, by its very nature, considered personal; momentous events cannot be decided by the powerless."

"We are hardly powerless," Terrano snapped. His eyes were

a disturbing shade of blue—disturbing because it was not the blue Barrani eyes normally adopted.

"Indeed. But your power is an unknown quantity. Because it is unknown, a polite fiction has developed: you remain young, frozen in time, and you are not therefore to be more feared than any of our young." She smiled, the curve of her lips almost Leontine in nature, which, given lack of fangs, was as disturbing as Terrano's momentary loss of control. "Are any of you hungry?"

It was the question Kaylin or Helen should have asked, but unless Kaylin was interrogating a criminal, she didn't think to ask questions when she already knew the answer.

"I find that I have not yet regained my full appetite. The journey from the West March was arduous." The statement invited response, but no one offered, and the cohort's eyes had become a uniform blue. To Kaylin's relief, that included Terrano.

The Consort gazed at them all. "You have come to us in a time of instability. My brother, the High Lord, is newly come to the High Seat, and as is common in our history, his rule is contested. Up to this point, that contest has been a matter for the Barrani High Court and its dependencies.

"Bellusdeo's presence in the West March was a target of opportunity. It was not an opportunity that the High Lord would take, but it fuels his opposition. They feel that Bellusdeo is significant enough that invoking her, accusing her, might drive the Emperor into a corner."

It was Kaylin who snorted this time. "Because the smart thing to do with a Dragon is corner him."

"I did not say they were wise," the Consort replied. "But the young who have no experience of war know only two things: its reported glory and the desire to avenge historical deaths, historical wrongs. We lost much, in the war. But," she added before anyone could speak, "so, too, the Dragons. Do you understand the mode of thought?"

Silence.

This time, it was Kaylin who answered. "Yes. Right now there are only six active Dragons. Some of the Dragons who fought in the wars sleep; most are dead. But for centuries now there's been no chance that the Dragons will increase in number. And the Barrani can, and have. If Bellusdeo had died during the last assassination attempt, I think things would have been quiet again. She didn't.

"And that means those who want—or dream—of ruling this particular empire are looking at an increase in the Dragon population in the near future. So…it's now or never."

"We would, of course, prefer never." It was Teela who spoke. "Unlike some of the younger members of the Court, I did fight in those wars. I was respected far and wide for my courage, my bravery, my…*glory*." Kaylin had heard her curse in a tone that was vastly more respectful.

"You bear one of the three," the Consort replied.

"And I do not intend to surrender it while this conflict brews."

"And after?" When Teela failed to reply, the Consort smiled. "Even so. Calarnenne gained prestige during the wars; he, too, carries one of the three, and he, too, will not be parted from it save by his death. His death would be vastly more difficult to achieve than even yours. And no, Annarion, your brother is not at risk. He is lord of one of the Towers, and his role is essential. You wish to take the Solanace seat that you feel he abandoned.

"He did not abandon it. He was driven from it by my grandfather. But, Annarion, you must know: you are the last of your name. Although your ancestral lands exist, although they are claimed and protected, they are not now known as *of*

Solanace. If you wish peace with your kin, you might adopt the name Coravalle."

"I am Solanace."

"Yes. You are. If you are made outcaste, Solanace will die. It was thought dead before Lord Kaylin found you all in the green. But Solanace was more than a name, and everything about the family you knew is now in the hands of Coravalle. Coravalle is not ancient; it does not have the history of Solanace. Your uncle must have feared your brother beyond all reasonable measure."

Annarion did not reply.

Helen did. "If you are not hungry, dinner can be modified into lighter fare; it can be served later; it can be missed entirely. I do not believe anyone in this room has much of an appetite at the moment. Except possibly Kaylin."

In the end, the Consort requested light refreshments, a light meal; she also asked that Helen offer that slighter meal in less a confined, restricted space. Helen glanced at Kaylin—which, as it wasn't necessary, was probably done to make a point—and Kaylin immediately gave permission; she was curious to see what Helen would now consider appropriate.

Sedarias made a decision, and asked that she be excused; that her mode of attire was not appropriate for a casual, informal space. She did not ask on behalf of the cohort, and the cohort was scattershot in their attempt to do the same; some asked, and some fled the parlor.

Terrano would have stayed, but Allaron, at some unheard command, almost literally dragged him out of the room, leaving only the Dragons, the mortals and the Consort.

"You like these people," the Consort said, turning to Kaylin.

"I consider three of them friends, and I consider the rest family to those three friends. Bellusdeo is also a friend; she came first, and she has every right to be here. Mandoran and Annarion like her, and I expect, with time, the others will like her, as well. So far none of the guests have tried to kill her, and she has not tried to reduce any of them to ash."

"Do you trust them?"

"Yes."

"Would you trust them were Helen not your home?"

"Yes."

"Lord Kaylin—"

Kaylin held up a hand, palm out. "Look—can we just stop with that? If Helen is making a casual room for us and everyone else understands that means they can ditch the fancy, uncomfortable clothing, can we ditch the fancy, uncomfortable titles?"

To her side, Kaylin heard a slight cough, and froze.

The Arkon was, of course, in the room. She was so so so grateful that Diarmat was not. Bellusdeo's face was turned slightly to the side, probably to hide her eye color or her expression.

"I am willing to 'ditch,' as you put it, the fancy, uncomfortable title. I will apologize to you for your...discomfort... in the outlands, and I swear to you that I did not intend to harm any of An'Teela's friends. But I understand as much of their nature as the Hallionne Alsanis was willing to explain, and some containment *is* required. Helen is a reasonable containment only so long as the cohort wishes to be contained."

Helen didn't argue.

Ynpharion was profoundly shocked and outraged. He was also worried. Very worried.

"Yes, dear," Helen said quietly. Her house's eyes were not quite their usual brown. "He is worried because the Consort does not tender apology to mortals or Dragons. Ever. If she is willing to do so—if she is willing to publicly debase herself—it means she intends none of you to survive.

"He is wrong. The Consort does not intend to destroy you; she has, in the past, greatly desired to strangle you—but so have Teela and Tain. Nor does she intend to destroy the cohort—at least not in the foreseeable future.

"She does wish to spend some time in discussion with the Arkon, but the reasons are not political. Ah. Before you answer me, I have taken some caution to say this only to you—which is perhaps why the color of my eyes is flickering."

"Kaylin?" the Consort then prompted.

Wary now, Kaylin nodded. "I know what you're afraid of. And yes, I was lying. If it weren't for Helen, I'd be a lot more terrified. But I'm not watching my back. I'm certain they're not plotting to kill me or rob me or head out into the streets to destroy my city and break all the laws."

"And if I invited them to the High Halls?"

"No." Kaylin folded her arms.

"No?"

"I trust that you wouldn't harm them." This was true. "But I do not trust that that's true of anyone else in the High Halls. If you've spoken to Alsanis—and I don't doubt that you have—you understand the material risks."

"They will need to come to the High Halls to undertake the Test of Name."

Kaylin nodded.

"They cannot arrive in the High Halls with a Dragon escort." She then turned to Bellusdeo. "You have my profound gratitude, for what little it is worth. Understand that among my people, one must volunteer to become Consort, to become the mother of our race. We are tried and we are culled. The culling is not particularly compassionate; the trials kill many.

"But for all that, we have choice. The very first test was to make that choice. It was what my family wanted, of course. It was what my mother had chosen. It has a prestige and an import to the Barrani that no other title can grant. I didn't understand that it was a test until I saw how many failed it. But that single test took no lives, not directly. Those who could not answer affirmatively were simply turned away.

"You, however, have not taken that test. You have not been asked to choose your fate; you have not been asked to become what you must become if your race is to have a future."

"Do not pity me." Bellusdeo's eyes were orange.

"I do not." The Consort bowed her head for one long beat. When she lifted it, her eyes were blue. "I will never attempt to harm you, who are the mother of her future race, as I am the mother of mine. I swear it, and will swear it, under any oath-binding you wish to demand. I will allow none of my kin to harm you, where I have prior knowledge. I will not allow—"

"No," Teela said, stepping into the room. She was wearing a loose shift that would not be at home in the Halls of Law, but would not be at home at Court, either. The color was, however, the same green. "You will not involve yourself further. The matter of a Dragon's attack in the West March is a matter of and for the High Court, and, my Lady, you are of the High Court because of your import to the *Barrani*. Not to the wars they hope to start, not to the politics they play."

Ynpharion had withdrawn completely. Teela's words barely penetrated the surface of his mind; it had grown almost numb with outrage and disbelief. Helen did not need to tell Kaylin that the Consort did not offer to make a binding oath, and the Barrani lords did not tell the Consort what to do. But she couldn't feel Ynpharion's outrage as her own; it was no part of how she viewed the Consort.

And how did she, in the end, view the Consort? One part terror, one part longing, one part confusion. This was the woman who had left her kneeling for the entirety of a Barrani dinner, while everyone else got to eat. *But she didn't make me kneel; I did that.* This was the woman who had openly hugged her in the Barrani Court, whose eyes showed unfettered delight at the approach of a mortal, grubby Hawk. This was the woman who had been willing to doom what remained of the *Norannir* race because to allow them into the city was also to court the awareness of the Devourer.

And the Devourer destroyed worlds.

This was the woman who had offered them all the safety of the Hallionne—but had intended to build that Hallionne into yet another prison for the cohort that Kaylin had been brought to the West March to rescue.

"Were you, dear?" Helen asked, her eyes a misty gray.

She managed to bite down on an answer that would make no sense—or that she hoped would make no sense—to her guests. She *had* rescued the cohort. But the elemental water had sent her to the West March because of the great danger the water felt—a danger Kaylin did not and could not perceive in the same way. What if the water meant the cohort itself was the danger? That the cohort was the terrible *wrongness* in the fabric of the world?

She remembered the first time Mandoran had visited the Keeper's garden, then. She remembered the water's reaction to Mandoran; it had attempted to drown him, and the agitation of the water had flooded the entirety of Evanton's house— outside of the theoretical containment of the garden itself.

What if?

The Consort was afraid of what the cohort might become when faced with the Adversary beneath the High Halls. She was afraid that they could fail that test, and become the agents that the Shadow needed to destroy...everything, really. And Kaylin could admit, with growing unease, that the fear was grounded in fact.

It wasn't about intention; Kaylin believed viscerally that the cohort would never willingly harm the Barrani or her city.

"But Terrano almost did," Helen said softly.

"That was before!" Kaylin cringed as every set of eyes in the room swiveled toward her. She also reddened.

The Consort, however, did not seem surprised. The Arkon's eyes were gold-orange. Bellusdeo had raised one brow, but no one spoke.

"Why don't you go and change, as well," Helen said. "The Consort is already attired for a more casual setting, as is the Arkon. Bellusdeo?"

"If things become...difficult...most of the clothing I wear is irrelevant," the Dragon replied, smiling. It was a very Leontine smile.

"Of course, dear," Helen replied. "Kaylin?"

"Is it Terrano you're afraid of?" Kaylin demanded when she was in the safety of her own room.

"I am not afraid of any of them," Helen replied. "And no. I trust his intent. The only family Terrano is willing to acknowledge is the cohort itself. He will do nothing—at all—to harm them, and this is the life they have chosen. In his fashion, he will help them while he remains.

"But, Kaylin, I've told you before that my ability to contain the full cohort is suspect. If they desire their freedom, I cannot become their cage. I am not what the Hallionne Alsanis was. My imperatives not to harm my guests reside entirely in you. I am more flexible than the Hallionne; I have more choice than they have. But I have attachments, as well. I know there are things you could never accept, never live with. But I also know that there are things *I* could never accept or live with. The ability to live with tenants such as you is the murky combination of those two points.

"But I choose tenants based on compatibility. I desire to be certain things—for myself. But I am what I was made to be. I have more choice than other similar buildings—and at some cost, some injury. I do not desire to be what I am not. I do not desire to have your ability to walk through the city streets. Sometimes I envy it. But I *am* a building. And that is neither here nor there. If the cohort becomes too unstable, too dangerous to contain, I will eject them."

"But—"

"Too dangerous, in this case, involves your safety. I understand that that decision will be costly; I understand that it could break the trust that we've developed. It is the fear of breaking that trust that is difficult for me, because I can clearly see the possible necessity, and you...won't."

Kaylin chose a black shirt, black pants; she considered daggers part of informal wear, but decided that that was possibly *too* informal. She didn't change her hair, though; it would have taken too long.

"And if I asked you not to?"

Helen didn't answer. But then again, she didn't need to answer. Kaylin's shoulders slumped, and the small Dragon crooned in her ear.

"The rest of your guests have assembled," Helen said, which was a signal to move. "What I want you to understand is that intention is not necessary to cause harm. The farmer whose wagon hits a child running across the street did not set out to injure children, but the injury exists, regardless."

"And what I need you to understand," Kaylin replied, "is that the farmer can't stop driving his wagon, even if that injury is a result of the driving. He didn't mean to hurt the child. Yes, lack of intention doesn't guarantee that no one gets hurt—I know that. But the fear of harm caused by even lack of intention can't stop the farmer from coming to market. He'll starve. I'm not afraid that they'll deliberately hurt me, or us. I understand that they *can*. But Teela could pretty much kill me anytime she wanted to."

"Not while she's here."

Kaylin snorted. "I'm not always here, Helen. If I'm afraid of anything bad that can happen to me while I'm not here, and I stay here, protected by you, for the rest of my life, what will my life mean?"

"What does life mean, outside of that?"

Kaylin *really* wanted her tabard at this specific moment. And because she did, it appeared. "I don't know. I don't have a good answer for that. Right now, I want to be able to help the midwives when they have an emergency. I want to be a Hawk because the law is better on this side of the Ablayne than it is across the bridge. I want friends I can trust, and I want friends who can trust me. I want to be more reliable.

"And that's not really an answer, is it?" She opened her door and stepped into the hall. "I did a lot of harm, in the fiefs. I know *why* I did it. I know where it came from. I needed to survive, and everything was stronger than I was. I didn't learn to lie—but I learned to hide. I learned to run. I learned to steal, and eventually to kill. I *hated it*. If I could change it all, I would. I can't, so I have to accept it. I did terrible things. But I can *stop* doing terrible things. It doesn't change what I did in the past, because nothing will.

"And if I did all those things, I can't just judge people who are doing awful things. I can try to stop them. They're not better than me. They're not worse than me. They're...just people, often making choices because they're too terrified to really think about them. I make better choices now because I don't let fear make decisions for me."

"No?"

"Okay, I *try* not to let fear make decisions for me. Sometimes I have to choose between different fears, which, ugh."

"Down to the end of the hall," Helen said.

"And I understand the Consort's fears. But... I can't think of people I don't know the same way she can. To her, the potential Barrani, and the Barrani in general, have the same value, the same weight. To me...they don't. I try to protect what's in front of my face. I don't have any other way."

"The *Norannir* weren't in front of your face, though, and they were the strongest disagreement you've had with the Consort to date."

"It was a metaphor, Helen."

"Yes, dear, but I'm not certain it was a very *good* one."

Kaylin had seen this room before; Helen had brought them here on Kaylin's first night. It was a dining table set beneath a mostly open sky; the sky was an early evening, and the sun hadn't fully set. It was striking.

The Barrani seemed far more at home beneath open skies than they had in the parlor, with the exception of the guards. Of course, that might have something to do with the way they were now dressed. The almost militant consistency of a sea of emerald green had given way to other colors, and the clothing styles were not meant for Court; they weren't meant to impress. They had chosen to be as formal as the Consort herself, although Kaylin noted that most of the hairstyles—which looked sculpted—had remained in place. The time taken to recover from that hair would have been too demanding.

She noted that some of the cohort had relaxed enough that they were, once again, in physical contact—not the Leontine variant of stacked bodies and piles of fur, but they were holding hands or rubbing shoulders. In Allaron's case, though, it was probably because he was literally Terrano's physical anchor.

Only when Kaylin took her seat at the table did the Consort speak. Of the Barrani assembled, she was most like Teela, who retained the inviolability of physical space.

"I admit I don't always understand your version of casual, comfortable clothing."

Kaylin blinked.

"Tabards such as that aren't normally worn to dinner among your people, are they?"

"Helen and I were having a discussion, and the tabard..." Kaylin trailed off, reddening. "No, not normally. Helen?" The tabard faded. Kaylin then drew breath. She glanced at the two seated Dragons, at the cohort and then, for longer, at Severn, who gave her a very small nod. She took the conversation in both hands. "I think we need to talk about why you're here."

Everyone at the table stiffened, except Severn and the Arkon; the Arkon, however, raised a brow at Kaylin, and began to rearrange his beard.

The Consort met and held Kaylin's gaze for a long, agonizing breath. She, too, inclined her head. "Very well." Her posture changed, her expression hardened and the natural green of her eyes lost ground to Barrani blue.

"An'Teela understands my concerns, as do Lord Kaylin and Lord Severn. My guards—both of my guards—are Lords of the High Court; it might surprise you to know that all of the guards assigned to me by the High Lord are Lords of the Court." She spoke to the cohort at large, although her body was turned toward Sedarias.

"It is the custom of our people to assign only those who

have become Lords of the High Court as heads of families. Those who have taken and passed that test understand why. It is also forbidden to discuss the test and its nature with any who have not passed it. And again, to those who have done so, the reasoning for that decision is clear. Is that not so?" She asked the question of Teela.

Teela nodded; her eyes were martial blue.

"I will not ask if you have discussed the Test of Name with your friends; I will assume that the answer is no."

"She has not," Sedarias said quietly. "She has merely advised—heavily—that we abandon the attempt for the time being."

"To your friends, then, the Test of Name is a matter of hierarchical significance. If the Test of Name is not pursued, options are limited. I believe—" and now she definitely addressed Sedarias "—you intend to challenge the current An'Mellarionne for the title, and if you have not passed that test, such a challenge cannot be issued.

"You understand that those who fail the Test of Name never emerge. You assume, half correctly, that they perish—and that has long been the way of our kind, by necessity: the strong survive. The weak die.

"You therefore think—all of you who are willing to take that test—that the worst you face is death. You are…flexible…in ways that most of our kin are not; you believe that the death that you face is trivial in comparison to the other challenges you have faced in your life.

"You are wrong."

CHAPTER 8

Ynpharion was rigid, both physically and mentally. So, too, the second guard who had been chosen to accompany the Consort. Teela was not.

Kaylin knew what lived beneath the High Halls; she had been told that it was the reason the High Halls existed in the first place. It was almost certainly the reason they had been left standing during the wars that had so damaged the Dragons. She understood the relevance of the Test of Name; those who had passed it had proved themselves immune to the corruption of the thing that was caged beneath the Tower that offered the test.

She didn't understand the Tower itself; she didn't understand the words that the Tower seemed to choose for each of the Barrani who ventured into it. And she didn't understand the grim silence that enfolded the actual test. If humans had been the test-takers, there would be guides on how to win—probably sold for ridiculous amounts of money on Elani street, and probably full of lies.

Regardless, the need for secrecy, the silence—those were foreign. The Tower wasn't personal; speaking of what occurred at its base didn't seem to be exposing personal vulnerabilities, especially since the only people who *could* speak had already passed the test.

But she wasn't Barrani, and clearly the customs of Barrani were the ones that mattered here—which made sense. It was Barrani who faced the Test of Name; Kaylin had faced it half by accident. Neither Kaylin nor Severn had lives that required True Names. Their essential selves on some level could not be rewritten or corrupted—not the way Barrani names could.

"Will you speak of the test we face?" Sedarias asked.

The Consort did not answer the question. But she did reply. "There are those among my kin who would ask that you not take the test. There are those among the Arcanum who consider it far too risky—to us, to the High Halls, to the Empire. And the fate of the Empire, ruled even by Dragons, is of relevance to us all." She inhaled slowly, as if measuring words. "The fieflords—or those with whom I have contact—are likewise concerned, but their concern is far more visceral." Turning to Annarion, she said, "I believe you know what your brother's concerns are, but he has not made clear to you what the root of that concern is, because he does not speak of the test he faced so long ago."

Annarion nodded. Mention of Nightshade had caused his lips to thin, his eyes to narrow.

"He wishes you to wait."

"And you, Lady?" Sedarias asked.

"I am less certain, as must be obvious. I have concerns. Those concerns have not been lessened by discussion with the Hallionne Alsanis; rather, they have increased. What I see as a concern, he sees as a distinct possibility—but even he cannot predict what that would mean for us. You are not, due to the interference of the green and the travails of your long captivity, what I am. You are not what An'Teela is. It is possible that An'Teela has the capacity to become what you currently are—but until very recently that would not have numbered among her ambitions.

"An'Teela is no longer considered ambitious, at Court. She has joined the Hawks. She enforces Imperial Law. She has evinced no desire to increase her holdings or the holdings of her line—she does not even style herself An'Danelle, as is both her right and her duty. She has earned the respect of even her enemies, and she carries one of the three."

"But so does Nightshade," Kaylin pointed out.

The Consort smiled. "Indeed he does."

"Wouldn't everything be simpler—at least for Annarion—if Lord Calarnenne could be repatriated?"

"No. Annarion would not take the title in that case—but Solanace has all but ceased to exist. Calarnenne could not do what would be necessary in order to reconstitute his family—not while retaining control of the fief itself. And you understand, perhaps better than most seated here, the necessity of that control. Your presence excepted, Bellusdeo."

"Such Towers, as you call them, did not exist in my world—and yes, had they, I believe things would have been different. We would not, however, have allowed the Towers to so randomly choose their stewards."

"They are not stewards," the Consort replied, her voice gentle and respectful, even if the words themselves were contradictory. "They are captains. They are meant to give orders when battle is joined. The Towers are very like the Hallionne, but with strikingly different mandates. Helen, if I understand correctly, chose Kaylin."

"You are correct," Helen said.

"Could you have been persuaded to accept a tenant chosen by an external council?"

"If the tenant was the person I would have chosen, yes. The fact that an external council suggested it would not sway my opinion in either direction. But, as you suspect, if that person was not a tenant I would choose, then no."

"And if they were installed here, regardless?"

A beat of silence. "I do not believe they would remain."

"Would you kill them?"

"No."

"Then you differ from the Towers in that regard. Not all who enter escape. Not all who enter desire command. Even if they do, they must pass the test set by each Tower. It is not dissimilar, in the end, from the Test of Name—not in theory. You know what occurs when the Towers are bereft of their captains."

Kaylin nodded.

"I have never entered one of the seven Towers. I have heard reports from those who have; I have spoken—as you must suspect—with Calarnenne."

Ynpharion was not happy. Of course he wasn't. Nightshade was outcaste. The Consort was arguably the most important person in the whole of the Barrani Court.

Arguably?

Fine. Most important. Is that better?

It has the advantage, was the acid reply, *of being accurate. He is outcaste. The two should never meet. Nightshade should never darken her presence with his until and unless he recovers from his disgrace.* His tone made clear that there was no way, in his opinion, to recover from that disgrace. Reinstatement did not wipe the slate clean.

"Calarnenne therefore understands the concerns—and, to put baldly, the fears—of the High Court.

"But he understands my hope, as well. And it is hope, not fear, that has brought me here. Fear," she continued when no one spoke into the long pause left in the wake of that last sentence, "made me attempt to cage you all. I did not then—and do not now—intend you harm."

"You don't expect us to trust you," Sedarias said.

"No. But here, it is not your trust that is the issue. Helen?"

"Kaylin was hurt, and because she was hurt, she was angry. But, as you suspect, Kaylin desires trust. She believes you."

The Consort nodded. No trace of a smile remained on her face, and only the barest hint of green in eyes that were usually the deepest of green in the Barrani High Court. "I don't expect trust, Sedarias. Not without some sign of vulnerability or weakness on my part. And that, I believe, I can give you."

She turned then to the Arkon. "We have not had the opportunity to speak, I in my court, and you in yours. And in earlier years, when we were not so confined by our choices and our callings, all speech was the screed of war, of domination. But as you are guest here, and as you are learned, I invite your opinions."

"I have little to offer; the matters of the Barrani High Court are not an area of my expertise."

"No, of course not. No more are the matters of the Dragon Court mine, and even were Dragons my area of study, the Imperial Court is not like the Flights of old."

"You are aware that certain members of your Court are calling for war?" the Arkon asked. He sounded far more amused than Kaylin felt—and she was certain she thought it was hilarious compared to the Emperor.

"Ah, indeed. But the members of the Court are not the High Lord, and the High Lord has not declared war; nor does he have any intention of doing so. There may, however, be extensive use of the laws of exemption in the next few months."

Kaylin stiffened. So did the rest of the Hawks, although Tain was the only one who looked disgusted.

"We have been petitioned," she continued, "by Barrani lords of the low Courts of the West March, to have certain members of your cohort declared outcaste."

This was clearly no surprise to Sedarias. A rumble of expression passed through the cohort; only Teela seemed immune to it. Teela, however, was An'Teela.

"It would resolve some political issues, but not in a fashion that would promote long-term stability in the High Court. There would be immediate advantage, but only that. And," she continued, lifting a hand, "it is not what I personally desire."

"You are not High Lord, Lady."

"No, indeed. High Lord is a political position. It is not mine. But you have heard rumors about the High Lord, his brother and his sister, surely?"

Sedarias said, "Which of the dozens would be relevant here?"

Ynpharion was, predictably, annoyed. But annoyance was the new calm, at least for Ynpharion.

"My brothers had no intention of contesting the rule of the High Court. My oldest brother, the heir, intended to take the throne if he was capable of ruling; my younger brother pledged to support him—and meant it. Had things devolved into the more traditional method of determining a ruler, I would have been the Lady, but I would have refused, outright, to become the Consort. I— What is the word? Ah. Love. I love both of my brothers.

"And they, of course, return that. We are not like your cohort; we do not have your experience to mold and shape us. Our experiences nonetheless have. For better or worse, my desire in this particular case carries a great deal of weight. As outcastes, you would, of course, be forbidden the High Halls. You would be forbidden a great deal. I imagine that

Lord Kaylin would ignore any such decision; she is mortal. She would, herself, be warned or cautioned, and she would, perhaps with effort, ignore all such warnings. She would, herself, become outcaste.

"This would not, of course, have much obvious effect on Lord Kaylin's life. But An'Teela would almost certainly join her."

All eyes became a martial blue in an instant, except for Teela's. Sedarias, however, did not look surprised. None of them did.

"The decision is not mine to make; it is merely mine to argue, one way or the other. If outcaste, you would, in theory, be forbidden the Hallionne, as well—and I do not believe that Alsanis would be of a mind to obey our laws in this particular case. But Calarnenne was accepted—even welcomed—into the Hallionne, and the polite fiction for his presence was his role as Teller in the *regalia*. The green chose."

And the green couldn't be made outcaste.

"Alsanis has only very recently been allowed to converse with outsiders through anything other than his dreams. Yet if you reached him, I am certain you would be welcome. He would, once again, be isolated—and that isolation would afford him no protection against the type of attack to which he almost succumbed."

Terrano cleared his throat. Loudly. Allaron swiveled toward him; Kaylin couldn't see Allaron's expression, but could guess.

The Consort, however, turned to Terrano. "Yes?"

"I was wondering if we could dispense with the subtle threats."

"Do you consider my words threats of any kind? If so, I apologize for my clumsiness. Or perhaps Sedarias will explain that they are not threats; they are observations."

Terrano snorted. "Then perhaps you'd care to dispense with the observations. We may have been locked inside a Hallionne for almost the entirety of our existence, but we understand the consequences that arise from being made outcaste."

"And perhaps, dear," Helen said before the Consort could reply, if she intended to reply at all, "you might make an effort to be polite. And *please* do not say she started it. She has made every effort to accommodate our rather unusual household."

Terrano bristled, but shut his mouth. Kaylin imagined there would be words after the Consort had left. She hoped they wouldn't reach the level of Nightshade-Annarion "discussions."

"We apologize for Terrano," Sedarias said, which didn't improve Terrano's mood. "We none of us have spent time at Court in recent centuries, and our communications with each other have been, as you must imagine, less formal. While we are, of course, accustomed to long discussions which involve threat assessments, we have never imagined that one of the participants in those discussions would be the Consort."

"I would be pleased—indeed, gratified—if perhaps we could pursue the type of discussion to which you *are* accustomed," the Consort replied.

Ynpharion was now so tense he would have snapped in half if forced to bend.

What Kaylin found odd was the presence of the Arkon. Bellusdeo was so much part of her daily life by this point, even the cohort had adapted to her draconic presence with astonishing speed. The Arkon, however, was not Bellusdeo; he didn't live in this house and would probably burn it down if any attempt were made to force him to do so. He was one of the few people Kaylin thought had a chance—no matter how tiny—of succeeding.

As if he could hear Kaylin's thoughts—and Teela generally told Kaylin never to play cards because her expressions were not terribly opaque—the Arkon rose.

"I do not wish to trouble you if the nature of your discussions is purely caste-court-based. I am certain that anything sensitive would best be divulged in the company of your peers—and I am Arkon, of the last of the Dragon Flights; in no wise, except perhaps on the field of ancient battles, would I be considered a peer."

"I have already said," the Consort replied without leaving her chair, "that I would consider your advice and your thoughts on the matter I am about to discuss invaluable. It may be that those thoughts and that knowledge will alter possible future plans. Please—I did not expect to find you here, but I consider it an act of fate. A kind fate."

"What possible expertise do you expect that I possess?" His eyes were almost gold; he truly considered this to be a Barrani problem, which might have some academic—or prurient—amusement value, but did not constitute an emergency.

"Ancient magics that once either contained or created the Shadows."

His eyes remained gold, but there were stronger hints of orange in them. Bellusdeo, however, slid straight into full-on orange.

"I am unaware of how much is understood by the Eternal Emperor. I believe the basics must have been made clear in the negotiations that followed the end of the final war; I believe it is the reason the capital of the Barrani is considered Elantra—a city overrun otherwise by every conceivable race. In any other circumstance, both the Dragons and the Barrani would expect to relocate. Even when the High Halls came under attack, it was the Dragon Court that came to our aid, and we do not consider ourselves part of the Emperor's hoard."

The Arkon said nothing, but he did smile. It was the type

of smile, to Kaylin's surprise, that he offered Bellusdeo; he'd certainly never smiled at Kaylin like that. But Kaylin was a private, a Hawk. Bellusdeo and the Consort were, as the Consort had pointed out, the respective mothers of their race; they were their races' futures.

"Very well, Lady," the Arkon said, executing a bow that would have made even Diarmat proud. "I am honored by your trust, if somewhat surprised by it."

Not, judging from Mandoran's expression—before he shuttered it—as much as the cohort themselves were.

The Consort turned to Kaylin. "Lord Kaylin, you are mortal and, by the strict rule of our ancient laws, a Lord of the Court. Nonetheless, I wish you to now discuss what you observed when you undertook—and passed—the Test of Name."

There was a beat of silence.

It was filled by Teela. "No."

Kaylin turned to Teela—it was easier to meet her gaze, even blue as it was. "It makes sense," she said. "I'm mortal. I'm human. No one expects me to follow the etiquette of a Court I don't even understand. It wouldn't come as a surprise to anyone, given how much Barrani look down on the rest of us, if I talked. I was never told not to speak about what I witnessed."

"And yet you haven't spoken of it. Why?"

"Because it involves—" She snapped her jaw shut. It involved the High Lord. It involved the former Consort—the High Lord's mother. It involved the failure of the most highly placed person at Court. Kaylin wasn't a complete fool; had she been, she would never have survived Barren. No one at her level talked about the weaknesses or foibles of people who could crush her like an ant.

Yes, in theory, laws existed to prevent that. But laws existed to prevent murders, too, and they still happened.

"Exactly," Teela snapped, sounding more like a sergeant than the corporal she was.

"You understand," Kaylin said to the Consort, "that the laws don't work that way? If you tell *me* to break the law, and you have a reasonable chance of expecting obedience, you're complicit in the breaking."

"If the laws you imply I would be breaking were meant for Elantrans, that would be true," was the serene reply. "It is also true that the request—and it is a request, An'Teela, a preference, not a command—can be considered insulting."

"At best," Teela snapped. "And if you have a preference, Lady, so do I. I ask Lord Kaylin to consider her own interests and her own safety before acceding to what *is*, no matter how prettily worded, an insult."

To Kaylin's surprise, Ynpharion agreed. With Teela.

"You are the only person present at the table who might understand what I hope to achieve," the Consort said. "Leaving aside Lord Kaylin, of course, who will understand both what I hope to achieve, and the very visceral desire that it *be* achieved at all. And you will not have a hand in it, in the end; it is with your friends, none of whom have faced the Test of Name—and all that that implies—that all hope lies."

"And you will not speak of it?"

"No. And, An'Teela, neither will you."

Kaylin cringed. Because that? *That* was a command. The silence that followed was an angry one. Kaylin rushed in to fill it, which caused Tain—and only Tain—to wince. Severn's expression was neutral and impassive.

"They're going to need you. You're the head of your line. You're a Lord of the High Court and you have an almost impeccable history. As far as I can tell, your enemies are mostly dead. No one is going to challenge you for whatever it is you hold. You're powerful *enough* that you can be an Imperial Hawk. While the cohort is struggling politically, you are the *only* member who can anchor them."

"You think she hasn't spoken of the Test of Name?" Terrano asked. Terrano, the only person who couldn't actually hear Teela when she chose to speak privately through the bond of True Names.

"I'm sure she hasn't," Kaylin answered, because she was. Kaylin knew that she herself would have talked, but she wasn't Teela.

Sedarias nodded, grim now. "She has argued consistently against any of us making the attempt to pass that test at this time. She has, however, given us no concrete reasons." And clearly, this lack of reason was not to Sedarias's liking. "In the absence of concrete reasons, we have attempted to theorize."

"Of course," the Consort replied, as if this were only to be expected. Then again, it was Sedarias speaking, so it probably was. She turned, once again, to Kaylin.

And Kaylin turned, internally, to Ynpharion.

Why, he demanded, *do you seek my counsel in this?*

Because you don't like it, either.

I dislike almost everything you do.

No, you dislike almost everything I am. *But where the Consort is concerned, you've mostly given grudging approval. You didn't want her here. I didn't want her here. Neither of us had any choice.*

I am not the master here. Neither, he added, in case it wasn't obvious to someone as ignorant as Kaylin, *are you.*

Yes, but I think I know why she's willing to take the risk on the cohort. I think I know what she wants to achieve from all of this. It's not about politics—it's about the names.

It is too much of a risk.

Me talking? Or what she hopes the cohort might *achieve?*

Both. An'Teela will be angry, and An'Teela is—and has been for centuries—a force to be reckoned with. Only desultory attempts have been made against her life in the past hundred of your years. If you do as the Lady has requested, An'Teela will not be angry with you—she will be furious with the Lady. And that, too, is a risk.

What would you do if you were me?

A brief flit of *suicide* came and went. To Kaylin's surprise, Ynpharion was trying to be polite. *I would do as the Lady requested*, he finally said. *But I would do it because the Lady requested it of me. I would do it, even were I not name-bound—and, Lord Kaylin, although I do not wish to add pressure to any decision you make, there is probably a reason that her two attendants are Lords of the Court.*

Is he also like you are? Is he name-bound?

Ynpharion did not answer, not directly. *Do not give me your pity.* This was icier than any of his prior words. *Do you not understand the honor of my position? I will serve as the Lady desires. I will be of use to her. If I die in pursuit of that, my death will have meaning.*

But Ynpharion was bound to Kaylin because he had, like many Barrani, attempted to divest himself of the shackles of having a True Name. Somehow. Kaylin wasn't clear on what he had attempted, and wasn't clear how it was sold to him, how it was supposed to work. He had certainly been able to voluntarily alter his form, because he hadn't looked anything like a Barrani when they'd crossed paths.

My life had no meaning, he said. *It had no meaning. There was power, and the pursuit of power; there was a certainty of my own insignificance because I had achieved no power of note. My service would not have been offered, because I was too lowborn, too insignificant. To approach the Lady would have been impossible in any but a ceremonial, perfunctory way.*

She's not like that.

She is part of the High Court, arguably second only to the High Lord. She behaves differently, yes—but she has the comfort and security of her position in which to push boundaries of behavior. Most of us do not—and will not—have that. And that is not the point. Were she to command me, I would do what she desires. She has not done so, yet. Were I you? I would do what she desires.

But, Chosen, he continued, *I am not you. Were I to do what she asks of you, I would not earn the anger of An'Teela. And if you do what the Consort requests, the Lady will earn that anger. I do not believe An'Teela will hold disobedience against you. She seems almost to expect it.*

So...you would do what the Consort wants?

I would, were I you. But were I you, I would have the same concerns as the Consort, and in this, I do not. The names of the lost are the names of the weak; they are those who were easily influenced, and therefore easily corrupted. Such names, such people, weaken the race, and the Shadows loom above us all as a threat that can even be the bridge to end wars.

Kaylin's smidgen of sympathy for Ynpharion guttered instantly.

We cannot afford that weakness, Ynpharion continued. *Ask your friend, the Dragon. Ask what the cost of that weakness was.*

So. You think it's too much of a risk, but you would do it, anyway.

Silence.

Severn said nothing, loudly. No other voices were present, and Kaylin did not want to reach out to Nightshade to ask.

What the Consort wanted, Kaylin wanted: to open the gates of the hell in which the ghosts of the dead remained trapped for eternity. To free them. They might not want it for the same reason—but Kaylin knew that both the High Lord and the Consort could hear the wails of the damned in the private quarters above the shadowed cavern in which their enemy lay, and had lain for centuries, feeding on the Barrani.

It had almost killed her to hear it once.

She understood what Ynpharion was afraid of. She understood that Teela was also afraid of it; thought that Bellusdeo might, if push came to shove, agree with Ynpharion, a thought that pleased neither her nor the Barrani in question.

She rose.

Teela's expression hardened, but Kaylin shook her head, both mutinously and apologetically. "I'm not a real member of the High Court," she told the Barrani Hawk. "I understand why you don't want it to be me who does this. But someone is going to do it tonight, and… I believe what the Consort believes."

"No one is going to do this tonight if you don't," Teela said in Elantran.

And the Consort—also in Elantran—said, "There is a reason that I have only two guards with me today. Lord Kaylin is correct. If she won't or can't, one of my personal guards will step forward to do so. What I want is what Kaylin wants— but I don't believe we have a hope of success if the cohort doesn't understand what they might face."

"I can talk about it," Kaylin continued, her voice soft and even pleading. "It doesn't matter to me if I'm tossed out of the High Court—I'm a figurehead member with no standing. I get nothing out of it but humiliation at the office. It's not going to make or break my life or my future."

"You cannot know that," Teela said softly. She glanced at Tain. Tain said *nothing*. "Kitling—"

"They're going to take the test." Kaylin folded her arms. "They're at risk. We're *all* at risk. And since they're going anyway, we need to tell them what we know—and frankly, I know almost nothing. I mean, I can't believe that parents don't tell their children before they face the test, Barrani law or custom notwithstanding. It must be a polite fiction that no one talks."

You are so mortal, Ynpharion said.

"Barrani lie all the time. They play at games of politics as if there's an assassination scorecard. You think they're honest about this?"

So very, very mortal.

"The reason there's a Test of Name at all is because there's a powerful Shadow trapped at the base of the High Halls."

CHAPTER 9

Kaylin, born—as far as she knew—in the fief of Nightshade, didn't believe that life was fair. It wasn't. She knew it. But if life wasn't fair, she reserved the right to *whine* about it. She resented the fact that she was risking Teela's wrath—or worse, disappointment—solely to protect Ynpharion, a Barrani who hated and despised her.

Not only that, but he wouldn't—and didn't—appreciate the effort; it was likely to lower his general opinion of her, although on most days that was probably impossible.

You continually surprise me, he said, his tone confirming her suspicions. *I am not your friend. I am not An'Teela's friend. If you died and your knowledge of my name therefore died with you, I would be a happy man. We can, however, discuss this later if you insist; the Consort is waiting.*

The Consort wasn't the only one. All eyes had swiveled toward Kaylin, and while Kaylin was human enough to want attention, this was not the kind of attention she sometimes craved. She'd had nightmares like this—but, on the bright side, at least she was still wearing clothing.

"We have designations for Shadows as they escape *Ravellon*. The Ferals, for instance. But dangerous Shadow—"

"It is *all* dangerous," Bellusdeo said. Her eyes were an orange-red. The Arkon's, however, remained an orange-gold.

"We call those one-offs. It means," Kaylin added, "unique. Something we haven't encountered before. There are Records in the Halls of Law, but our beat isn't expected to cover the Shadows, so there are large gaps in our knowledge."

"Canyons are not generally considered gaps," Bellusdeo said.

"Bellusdeo," the Arkon said quietly. "If we are to lament our ignorance about Shadow, we might be here all year. Please. Allow Lord Kaylin to continue."

Kaylin nodded to both Dragons. "The Shadow beneath the High Halls is unique. I'm not Barrani. I came to the High Halls because Teela— Oh, never mind. I was at the High Halls for reasons that had nothing to do with the Test of Name."

"And you just stumbled into it?" Mandoran asked. Terrano's expression was one of open disbelief—not so much at the facts, because he accepted those, as at Kaylin herself.

"More or less. Look—no one told me that the Tower and the Test of Name were so crucial to the Barrani. I knew nothing about it. Racial integration classes don't cover Barrani minutiae."

"Minutiae." That was Sedarias.

"Mostly the Barrani aren't our problem, speaking as a Hawk. If the Barrani break laws—no, sorry, *when* the Barrani break laws and the Hawks catch even the slightest wind of it—the lawbreakers wind up dead, on our doorstep. The Barrani High Court says 'laws of exemption' more often than it says anything else when dealing with the Halls of Law." She grimaced. "Sorry. I didn't know that I was taking an incredibly important test at the time."

"What, exactly, did you think you were doing?"

Kaylin realized then that this was going to be an even worse conversation than she'd imagined. "Getting lost?"

"I begin to understand why Teela worries so much about you, even if you *are* Chosen. I will endeavor to listen without comment going forward."

Terrano snorted.

"The Tower offers a word—or at least it offered me a word."

"And that word?"

"It apparently differs depending on who enters the Tower, and I don't think it really matters. There are two levels of test that the Tower offers. I think it's a space not unlike the Hallionne, but far more limited in scope. What I saw, what Severn saw, is not what you'll see. Direction shifts; architecture shifts. I *think* we're moving through the same space, but we don't perceive it the same way."

"What I saw..." She shook her head.

"What Lord Kaylin encountered for the early part of her test was not something any of you will encounter," the Consort said firmly. And forbiddingly.

"We don't *know* that," Kaylin said.

"*We* don't, no. I do. Your task was similar, in the end, to my final test. More than that, Lord Kaylin, you will not say."

"So...you want me to break the unwritten law and talk about what I saw, but not all of it, and only the relevant parts."

"That is how we always discuss matters of import," the Consort replied. Her tone was cool; her eyes had shaded to blue.

"Fine. We were—Severn and I—trying to get out of the Tower. As far as I can tell, no matter what else the Tower does or does not do, there's only one way out, and the Shadow sits in front of it." She inhaled, held breath for a few long seconds and exhaled, trying to loosen the line of her shoulders, which had bunched up almost to her ears.

"I had a medallion given to me by Sanabalis." At the Arkon's wince, she quickly said, "Lord Sanabalis. It's not this one," she added.

"I should hope not," the Arkon said, his voice as chilly as the Consort's, his eyes more orange.

"It helped. But the Shadow is…" She fell silent. "I can only tell you what I saw and what I heard. The Shadow exists at the base of the Tower—and my guess is that anyone who makes it that far sees the same thing, in the end. But…"

Teela had folded her arms; her lips were one thin, compressed line.

"But every single person who has ever taken—and failed—that test remains *with* the Shadow itself. The Shadow speaks, and its voice is…compelling. It doesn't look human, doesn't look Barrani."

"Are they alive?" Annarion asked. Of course it was Annarion. "Alive?"

"Those that failed the test. Are they alive, somehow?"

Kaylin shook her head. "I don't think so. But they're not absent, either. They have voices, and…" She swallowed. "I don't know if Barrani have any concept of heaven or hell. But they don't really need it, when they have that Shadow sitting in wait. If the Barrani who are trapped there—and have been for centuries, as far as I can tell—aren't dead, they're still somehow *aware*. And they've been in a hell of that Shadow's devising since the moment they failed the test." She swallowed and looked to the Consort, who nodded.

"The High Lord and the Lady hear their cries. They can hear them from the moment they ascend to the seats of the High Court. They know what the High Halls jails."

"It is the most difficult part of the burden of rulership," the Consort said quietly.

"The reminder of failure?" Sedarias asked.

"Were they truly dead," the Consort continued, as if Sedarias had not spoken, "it would not be so disturbing. But their names—all of their names—are forever lost to us. They do not and have not returned to the Lake, which gives rise to Barrani life. And while the Shadow remains, they will not."

The Arkon rumbled. Literally. The entire table seemed to shake.

Bellusdeo immediately turned to him. "What do you know of this, Lannagaros?"

"You are aware—more than any of us—of the Shadows at war. You are aware of the cost of loss. Historically, our peoples have been enemies, and the result of that enmity has been disastrous. But it is nothing to the cost of the war with Shadows. There is no end to the battle; there is no peace that endures.

"The High Halls has not always been the seat of Barrani power—Barrani government, if you will. But the building itself has been some part of what has now become Elantra for almost as long as the wars between our kind existed."

The Consort raised a brow.

"I do not know what your history documents, Lady, and I do not know if our suppositions have been shared. I will not, however, stoop to say that they are inaccurate."

She inclined her chin, looking—suddenly—every inch an empress. She said nothing, however.

"But it is our belief that the first of the wars that encompassed all of our kind started, in the end, because of that Shadow. It has long attempted to prey upon our two peoples, with greater and lesser success, but it was not contained in the same fashion it is now contained. The end of the first war saw an end to the Shadow's freedom to move, but the current containment saw the destruction of most of the building that preceded the High Halls."

Helen said, "Only the Tower remains."

Everyone in the room turned toward the Avatar, who actually seemed to redden. "It is not well-known, Arkon. And my own history, my own records of that time, were much damaged in the interim." She didn't say by who, but it was irrelevant to most of them. Not to Kaylin, who would not otherwise be living here. "It was understood that the building itself reorganized the power inherent in its structure to contain the Shadow. Entry was not forbidden, but the Tower itself could not prevent its prisoner from harming those who did enter."

"Was it a building like you?" Kaylin asked.

"Inasmuch as sentient buildings are like a race, yes—but you have come to understand that while we share some functionality, we are all individuals. It is not unlike the mobile races; they share the general conditions of their race, but are otherwise unique." She turned to the Arkon and the Consort. "My apologies for interrupting."

"If all interruptions were so relevant," the Arkon said in his grave voice, "I would welcome interruption. For my own part, feel free to interrupt if you feel you have any information that we lack." His tone made clear that he was certain she did.

"It is not always clear to me when information is relevant; I have been mistaken in the past."

"I am willing to trust your instincts. I will take no offense at all at any interruption."

Kaylin tried not to grind her teeth.

"I am not in my library, Private. Nor am I immersed in somewhat delicate experiments. I am a guest here; the scope of my responsibilities while I am within your domicile are largely social."

This caused the Consort to chuckle. "I feel that Lord Kaylin visits you more frequently than she visits the High Halls."

"To both of our regrets, I am sure."

The cohort relaxed slightly. Ynpharion, however, did not, and Kaylin chose—for reasons that weren't clear even to her—to take her cues from Ynpharion.

"Yes. But we have interrupted Lord Kaylin." Or from the Consort, as it happened.

Kaylin cleared her throat. "The Shadow beneath the High Halls can take the names of those who fail the test. I don't know how. I don't understand the mechanism. But… It doesn't *destroy* the names. If the names were consumed, the Consort wouldn't be here."

"I might well be," the Consort replied, although technically Kaylin hadn't directed the comment at her. "Anything that destroys those names lessens the future possibility of my people. It depletes the Lake. But it is my belief that you are correct. The words are not consumed; they are contained. They are caged.

"But they are not always caged. Although we have been limited in our studies and our research—for obvious reasons— it has become clear that at least in one or two cases the Shadow allows its victim to leave. The victim is, in effect, name-bound. The control is not perfect, but the influence itself appears to be strong. I believe the Shadow is substantially different from us; its attempts to exert control are not successful because of that large difference."

"You mean it doesn't fully understand people."

"Yes. It doesn't understand our limitations. Some of its commands—and this is entirely theoretical—instruct the name-bound to do things that cannot be done. By us."

Teela was now the color of wax. The rest of the cohort, buoyed by the typical arrogance of Barrani, were not. But they were quieter now, as they considered the relevance of the Consort's words.

Kaylin did so, as well. Mandoran and Annarion could already do things that Barrani—and mortals like Kaylin—couldn't.

Her familiar, draped around her shoulders like an afterthought, lifted his head and squawked relatively quietly in her ear.

"Fine. And other mortals who aren't Chosen. Better?"

The familiar made a whiffling noise and lowered his head again. After yawning.

"Attempts to destroy the Shadow—and perhaps Shadows similar to it—failed in the past. We have historical records of some of those attempts, and I am certain that the Dragons retain some, as well. But it is our—no, *my*—belief that the reason those attempts were failures was the nature of that Shadow itself. What we can destroy is physical; it is the portion of Shadow that exists where we exist—possibly in order to interact with us, to entrap us.

"Kaylin—Lord Kaylin—has entertained, as a guest, a Shadow."

Kaylin hesitated. Everyone noticed. To Helen, she said, "I think she means Gilbert."

"She does, although she was not aware of his name. And yes, Lady, Gilbert was a guest, but only briefly."

"Did you understand his thoughts?"

"Yes."

"All of them?"

"All that I could hear, yes. There were some things that he could not explain to Kaylin—but I could not explain them, either. Nor do I think they were relevant."

"And could you explain them to Annarion or Mandoran?"

That was the heart of the question that the Consort had come to ask. Helen did not reply. Not directly. But after a moment, she said, "You might ask Spike."

Kaylin had forgotten about Spike. To be fair to herself, Spike had only been in residence for a few days, and the time had been extremely stressful. The cause of the stress—if one didn't count the cohort, and as they were guests, Kaylin was trying hard not to—sat at the open-air table, beneath an early evening sky.

"Who is...Spike?" the Consort asked.

Bellusdeo exhaled a small amount of smoke—which caused an immediate ripple to pass through the cohort and the two Barrani guards. The Consort, however, didn't appear to notice. "You forgot about Spike," the gold Dragon said in Elantran.

"I was kind of busy," Kaylin replied. "Helen, where *is* Spike?"

"He is... I'm not sure what the correct Elantran word would be. Meditating? Studying? He is, however, in his room. His room is not in the regular hallway, which would not be entirely comfortable for him. Should I ask him to join us?"

"You already have the familiar," the Consort said before Kaylin could answer. "And were we to assess danger—to any of us—by competence or ability, I would venture to say that the familiar is the largest threat your home currently contains."

The little egotist sat up on Kaylin's shoulder and all but preened.

"If Helen is willing to allow Spike to live here as a guest, I assume that she is confident that she can keep all of the rest of your guests safe. Regardless, I confess I am curious. Who is Spike? Or perhaps the better question would be, what is Spike?"

"Yes," Kaylin said to Helen. "If he's willing to join us."

"He will be willing to join you," Helen replied. "You offered him your blood and he has used it to form an attachment."

"That isn't, for the record, what 'form an attachment' usually means," Teela told Kaylin's house.

"No?"

"No."

"I believe he will concern himself in matters of both information and Kaylin's safety; I believe that he worries that she will *not* be safe. I am unable to see how this differs from other attachments."

"Is Spike a he?" Kaylin asked.

"I don't believe Spike understands the nature of gender. If you would prefer, I can call Spike 'she.'" Helen's eyes went to obsidian, the pupils spreading to cover the entirety of her eyes. "Spike asks what 'he' or 'she' means."

"Never mind. I'm not touching that one. Will Spike speak with us? I think it might be easier in the long run. Umm, and can you apologize for me?"

"For what?"

"For forgetting him."

"Spike," Kaylin said to the Consort, "is a Shadow."

Bellusdeo snorted more smoke.

"He came from *Ravellon*."

Every person in the room who didn't know about Spike stiffened, except the Consort.

"He was taken out of *Ravellon* by a Barrani lord; he could not leave the containment himself."

The Consort was now as stiff as the Arkon, and both of

their eyes indicated worry: blue and orange. For some reason, Kaylin disliked orange in the Arkon's eyes, although she saw it so often in Bellusdeo's it might as well have been gold. Small and squawky shifted position on her shoulder, sitting up straight on the left one, although his tail wrapped around the back of her neck and dangled over the right one.

"A Barrani lord—you imply he is a member of the High Court by use of title—walked into *Ravellon* and left with a Shadow?"

Kaylin nodded. "I'm sorry—I meant to tell you, but later, when I could make more sense of it." Or, more precisely, identify that lord.

"And instead you spent your time trying to cancel dinner."

Kaylin was certain she was now red to the tops of her ears. "You know why," she replied, trying not to sound defensive.

The Consort, however, nodded. "Yes."

"For our part," Sedarias said, "we take no offense, given our very recent history." She failed to look at Terrano. Terrano said nothing. "And we were somewhat alarmed at Lord Kaylin's choice to retreat when we learned of your offer."

"She is not what we are," the Consort replied. "In her two decades of life, she has not seen enough betrayal—or Barrani alliances—to understand when, and where, things become personal. She considers you family to people she has accepted as friends—but friends incur responsibility as well as affection."

"That is possibly why the Barrani themselves have so few of them."

The Consort inclined her head. "Even so." Her eyes, however, remained blue. "You do not seem surprised at the mention of this Spike."

"No. We encountered him in our time in the West March— or rather, the time that overlapped with Lord Kaylin's unintentional visit. Given the events of that time, I confess that Bellusdeo seemed the far greater threat."

This caused the Consort's eyes to lighten. It also caused Bellusdeo's eyes to lose their red tinge. "I believe the Dragons would consider Shadow to be the greater threat, especially Bellusdeo."

"We were not given the leisure to discuss what constituted the greater threat. At the time, the answer would have been our own kin."

The Consort nodded again, grimmer now. It wasn't that Kaylin hadn't seen that expression on the Consort's face before—she had. But on the Consort's face, it somehow looked wrong to Kaylin, and possibly always would. She gave herself a mental kick. The Consort had been willing— was even now willing—to throw Ynpharion, or perhaps his companion guard, to the figurative wolves if Kaylin was unwilling to give her what she needed.

She was warmer and more welcoming than the Barrani she granted life, yes. But she was not mortal, not human; she was not a mother in the idealized sense of the word. Kaylin's memory made a mother an ideal, a thing yearned for that was no longer possible to have.

She needed to stop that. One of her earliest lessons as a Hawk had been to "See what's actually in front of you. Not what you're afraid of. Not what you want to see. But what's actually there." With added Barrani words. She looked at Teela as memory poked her.

Teela was watching the Consort.

A series of clicks and loud, grinding whirs announced the presence of Spike. Emmerian, Ynpharion and the nameless Barrani guard stiffened, but while the Barrani hands slid to sword hilts, Emmerian's reaction was largely contained to eyes that were almost blood red. Kaylin had seen that color before, but never in Emmerian's eyes.

Kaylin stood immediately and held out her left hand. Spike—adorned with the jutting, sharp points that justified his name—flew lazily across the air and landed in her palm. She couldn't close that hand without bleeding, and didn't try.

"This," she said to the Consort and the Arkon, "is Spike."

"If you will forgive me?" the Arkon asked. The question made no sense until he opened his mouth. Since Kaylin only had one free hand—unless she wanted to jam Spike into her left ear—she caught native Dragon at full volume. Then again, Dragons only really had one volume.

The Barrani present had far too much dignity to even attempt to cover their ears. So did Severn.

Spike clicked; the spikes that surrounded him depressed and shifted. He was answering the Arkon, and the Arkon's expression—one of ferocious concentration—implied that the Arkon could, with effort, understand the response.

"Where," the Arkon asked, his gaze not moving from the creature in Kaylin's hand, "did you find him?"

"I told you—"

"Never mind. It was not an actual question. Do you understand what he is?"

"He's better than portable Records."

"Pardon?"

"He's like Records, but less intrusive. If you can make clear what you want to see, he can show you the information he has—it takes longer than the mirrors we generally use, but it's easier to examine."

"I feel it is a benefit to you that you have no gods," the Arkon replied. "Because gods in general are not fond of blasphemy."

"You know what Spike is?"

"If my suspicions are correct," he replied with no doubt about those suspicions in his tone, "he is an historian."

"You don't seem to be worried by the fact that he's Shadow."

"No."

"Why?" Bellusdeo asked.

"Because he is clearly attached to Kaylin. How and why, I am as yet uncertain, but Kaylin is not at risk."

"Because she's at home?"

The Arkon shook his head. "Look at her marks."

To Kaylin's eye, the more visible marks remained determinedly black-gray, the color she associated with quiet.

Spike clicked a few more times, his visible body undergoing small, popping contortions as spikes protruded and retreated in something that looked almost like a pattern.

The Consort's eyes remained blue, but she lifted them from Kaylin's hand—and Spike—to Kaylin's face. "Please. I look forward to your explanation."

Kaylin almost punted the question to Severn, because Severn seemed to have recognized the Barrani lord in question. She didn't. Instead, she said, "Spike, can you show the Lady the man who entered *Ravellon* and carried you out?"

"Yes," Spike replied in perfect, if somewhat flat, Elantran.

Kaylin stepped away from the table as the air just above her plate began to thicken with silver-gray fog. "Maybe not at the table."

"Helen has been teaching me," Spike said, "about your furniture and how you view the world. It is enlightening, but extremely frustrating."

"Yeah, I hear that a lot. Except not about furniture."

Ynpharion.

Silence.

You must have seen Spike. We were in contact while I was in the West March.

The contact was very intermittent, Ynpharion replied, his words almost as flat as Spike's. In Ynpharion's case, that meant something.

Did you know?

She could feel his sudden frustration and disgust. *No*, he said, his internal voice acid. *I'm stupid and unobservant.*

After this is all over, you and I are going to have a long talk.

Wonderful. Might I remind you that you need to survive?

Right. She cleared her throat, but it wasn't necessary; the Consort was no longer watching Kaylin. She wasn't watching Spike, either. She was looking at the man, in his nondescript clothing, none of which was suitable for Court. He wore a hood, but the hood itself gathered around his neck; his face was exposed.

This time, when Spike began to build a setting around the man, it was clearer. Helen had obviously been successful in her attempts to teach him about normal perception—or at least normal for Elantrans.

"When did this occur?" the Consort asked.

Spike was silent.

"Please answer the Consort," Kaylin told him.

"Apologies. Your concept of time is difficult and narrow. It is not my intent to remain silent."

He began to speak in whirs, and after a lot of them, Helen said, "If I may translate, I believe this occurred before Kaylin's visit to the West March."

"By how much?"

"According to Spike, very close to the same time." Helen's answer was hesitant. "Spike's 'very close' could vary, in my opinion, by years."

"But not by decades or centuries?"

"Perhaps the outside of a decade. Not centuries, however."

"I believe it would have been more recent," Sedarias said

quietly. She did not look to, or otherwise implicate, Terrano. "And Spike said or implied that he—Spike—had been ordered to attend the man who came to collect him."

"By who?"

"Someone or something in *Ravellon*. He doesn't give it a name—and if he could, I wouldn't suggest using it, regardless. You believe that this man is somehow implicated in the task you wish us to perform if you believe it will not destroy the High Halls."

"You were always said to be the best of your kin," the Consort replied, confirming Sedarias's suspicion. "Do you know who this man is?"

"No. I do not believe he was alive—or at Court—when I was sent to the green, and my information since our return has been somewhat fractured."

"You believe that this man's breach of the fief barriers was recent. Perhaps this has something to do with the attempts of your comrade—" and here she definitely pinpointed Terrano "—to persuade Alsanis to release you all?"

"All prisoners with power will eventually be free," Sedarias replied, no hint of repentance in her voice.

"Yes. I hold nothing done in pursuit of your own freedom against you. Nor do I expect that my attempt to...weight the import of the task I hope to set you in my own favor will be held against me."

"We are not Lord Kaylin," Sedarias replied. "Very well. The effort to create the gaps in Alsanis's attention that would allow us to finally slip free were not the efforts of a day, a month or even a simple year. You know that we eventually approached Lord Iberrienne."

"I know of the fate of Iberrienne. It is why my brother has acceded to my request not to cast him out of the Court. Alsanis cradles him, but feels that there is very little that might restore Iberrienne to...what he once was."

Eddorian stiffened.

"It is not a threat," the Consort said quietly. "Iberrienne is safe. But his acts broke many of our laws with regard to the one enemy that unites all of our peoples. Some of his kin have attempted to visit him while he resides within Al-sanis," she added.

Sedarias frowned. "They have not."

"I misspeak," the Consort replied. "They petitioned Al-sanis for permission to visit. Their petitions were refused."

Eddorian opened his mouth. Eddorian shut his mouth. It was clear from his expression—for one, he now had one—that he wanted to say something; it was clear from the tension of the cohort that the argument that was now taking place—in relative silence—was intense.

The silence stretched, Spike's image of the Barrani lord momentarily forgotten.

Kaylin knew how to break that silence.

"Is that wise, dear?" Helen said softly. But not, apparently, silently.

Kaylin shrugged, a fief shrug. "All of this is going to have to come out, anyway. I think," she continued, "that while the cohort's interference in the High Court and its politics opened new doors to trouble, the potential for that trouble already existed. It's just that now it has an outlet."

The Consort turned to her. The whole cohort did.

"The cohort was aiming at the green, at the power of the *regalia*. They wanted to—" she stopped herself and corrected the direction the unfortunate sentence was taking "—be free. To do that, they were willing to throw away almost every-thing else.

"But they had allies. Some of those allies were mortals who

want immortality—and why, I don't understand. There isn't a single story about the attempt to gain eternity, such as it is, that *ever* works out well for us—"

Teela coughed.

"Right. Sorry. They had mortal allies—probably because of the money. They had Arcanists as allies, because: Arcanists. For activities that had the potential to end a race—mine, in case you've forgotten—it seemed almost normal.

"I think some of Terrano's allies weren't Arcanists searching for power or mortals searching for immortality."

The Consort was now utterly still; even the movement of breath had deserted her.

"I think some of those allies have already been somehow bound to the service of the creature beneath the High Halls and, even now, do its bidding."

CHAPTER 10

It was Ynpharion who broke the silence—but only Kaylin's. Everyone else appeared to be holding their breaths.

What are you doing? he demanded.

I don't know how much of the West March you actually eavesdropped on. Eavespeeped? Is that a word? She really needed to become a better person. In a situation as grim as this one was becoming, enjoying Ynpharion's outrage was just too petty. On the other hand, there didn't seem to be a lot to enjoy in the immediate future, otherwise. *But Spike's arrival— from* Ravellon, *a place he can't in theory leave, was a big red flag. The Barrani lord in question—and the Consort seemed to recognize him—entered* Ravellon. *He clearly entered through the fiefs, and it's just possible he was allowed to do so. I'm certain he didn't enter through Tiamaris or Nightshade, and Severn seems to think it was Candallar. It might* have *been Farlonne, which is rumored to be another Barrani fief.*

She exhaled and, opening her mouth, repeated everything she had just said to Ynpharion.

"Why do you assume that the point of entry was defined by the race of the fieflord?" the Consort—quite reasonably—

asked. "Not all of the people involved with the attempt to free the cohort were Barrani."

Kaylin nodded. She'd had the same thoughts. "The Barrani lord in question seemed to be walking through Candallar streets. We know that the geography of both *Ravellon* and the borders between fiefs can vary greatly from moment to moment, but the fiefs themselves don't. Spike?"

Spike hummed. Sadly, it was a beehive hum, not a melody.

"You recognize these streets?" The Consort's voice was thin.

"Not personally, no," Kaylin replied.

"And Halls of Law Records detail them correctly enough?" Kaylin fell silent.

"No," Severn said. "I recognize them. The Imperial Records display of fief streets is more complete—but it is also classified. The last thing the Emperor wants is to provide a physical map of the fiefs for those who believe themselves treasure hunters."

Kaylin stared at the side of his face. Who in the hells would think they could find *treasure* in the fiefs? Then again, the whole "do not enter, death here" sign would probably irritate certain people enough that they'd turn it into a test of courage, because that's what people were like.

"And you believe that this man entered the fiefs through Candallar?"

"I have no idea where he entered the fiefs. Spike was not with him at the time, and therefore does not have a visual display of his entry. What he has is a display of his exit."

"Spike," Kaylin said quietly.

Spike dutifully began to re-create the Barrani lord's exit from *Ravellon*.

"Can you tell us," Kaylin continued, "why you met the man?"

"I was ordered to go to where he would be."

"By who?"

Spike's answer was a sound, a physical sensation, a burst of lurid color. He could see—somehow, since he didn't appear to *have* eyes—that Kaylin didn't understand the reply, and tried again.

Helen stopped him from making any more attempts. "My apologies," she said to the guests.

But Terrano's face was twisted in a ferocious frown. He was concentrating very hard and, at Helen's apology, lifted a hand as if to wave her words away. Helen looked to Kaylin, and Kaylin managed to stop herself from shrugging.

Spike, however, did not repeat himself.

The Consort, blue-eyed and as steely as Sedarias at her worst, said, "Why are you certain that the intrusion into the fiefs is so intimately involved with the failure of the Test of Name?"

That was the question, wasn't it? "I'm not."

"You don't speak with any lack of certainty."

"No. But… I've learned with time to trust my instincts. I think that the Shadow beneath the High Halls was contained because of the danger it posed—but I think that Shadow poses a threat that is linked, always, to *Ravellon* in some fashion or another.

"We know that the Dragon outcaste lives within *Ravellon*—and we know he can leave it as he desires. The Towers don't seem to acknowledge him."

"I do not believe he is working at the behest of the Shadows," Bellusdeo unexpectedly said.

"I don't think he's working at the *command* of the Shadows," Kaylin countered. "But he's home there, and that has to mean something. He uses shadow as power. He has his own goals. But power comes from somewhere, always."

"And you somehow think that that power is sentient?"

"Why wouldn't it be? Fire is sentient if you summon too much of it. Same with the rest of the elements. The reason fire magic is difficult isn't the summoning—it's the control of what's summoned. But the fire has will and desire of its own."

"Mostly to burn everything in its path, yes."

"I don't think Shadow is different. I mean, it doesn't want to burn everything in its path, but it has sentience and will of its own. I just think it's more subtle. And the more power you summon, the more that sentience grows."

The Consort's nod was grave; it wasn't final. "Arcanists have attempted, for some time, to draw power from Shadow; it was originally intended to weaken the enemy. This does not immediately lead to the enemy beneath the High Halls."

Kaylin glanced at Spike. "From what Spike said after we freed him—"

"Freed?"

"He was operating under compulsion. I'd imagine it's very much like what you can do with True Names if you hold them and you have more power."

Spike whirred. "It is not."

"What's the difference?"

"It is complete, Chosen. What those with enough strength can do is retain their memory and sanity; the whole of their being is otherwise some part of the thing that controls them. Your Dragon outcaste is not Shadow by nature; he is flexible in some fashion. He is named, but his name is complex and difficult; some parts of it have been massaged, but the whole has proved resistant to the extreme changes that would other-wise occur. And he has power of his own."

"You have power."

"I have a power you do not have, yes. And in the layers between states, that power is greater than yours; you are wed to your world and your physical presence in it. It is both a strength and a weakness. Helen might be able to explain it; I am…learning…but it is difficult to communicate clearly.

"The Shadow that rules exists in the heart of *Ravellon*, which exists in all spaces. You saw it in what you call the outlands or the portal paths. You see it here. You would see it were you to make the trek to a different world. It is the anchor that binds all things together."

"But why?"

"Why?"

"Why is *Ravellon* the anchor that seems to tie everything together? Why do we even need an anchor?"

The question confused Spike, to judge by the noise he emitted. It also confused Helen, or appeared to confuse her.

"It is confusing," Helen admitted. "Neither Spike nor I fully understand your question. There has always been a point of continuity—perhaps that's a better word than 'anchor'— and reality of many kinds have drifted around that center. When you have a stack of papers and an open window, it is likely that the papers will be blown about the room. If those papers were given you by Lord Diarmat, you would wish to prevent that, yes? *Ravellon* is the spike that is driven through those papers—each in their correct order—that prevents that drift.

"There is, of course, no Lord Diarmat, and perhaps that was an unnecessary part of the analogy. But if those papers, in total, have a meaning, that meaning might be lost or fractured should they be disordered. *Ravellon* was considered the heart of all worlds—and peoples of various races and various worlds could overlap there without harm.

"That changed," Helen continued. "You know this. Shadow gained a foothold in *Ravellon*. We do not know why or how. There are discussions—or were—about the Ancients, the Lords of Law, the Lords of Chaos. We feel that these are inexact terms, at best."

"They are inexact," the Arkon said quietly. His expression was strikingly similar, at the moment, to Terrano's. "We have stories of the beginning of worlds—but those are gleaned from the ancient Keepers in their discussions with the elements they make a home for in their gardens. And many of those distant, unknown worlds were not unknown to *Ravellon*. I do not believe any worlds exist which did not have doors that lead to *Ravellon*; any attempt to remove those doors, to remove access to *Ravellon*, have not met with success. And sometimes the failures have been catastrophic.

"We do not know why. But *Ravellon* was built as it was by beings who left no records that we could read. Perhaps Spike could, if he could access them, but I do not believe he could impart that information to those of us who might be likely to know of it. Ask why *Ravellon*, but ask, as well, why mountains or rivers or Dragons. Why Barrani. Why mortals in all their different compositions. Why birth, in fact, when birth seems messy and leads, often, to death. There are too many things about life itself that make so little sense there are no reasonable answers. At least not to an old and exacting scholar like myself.

"What is of interest to me is Spike's contention that there is *one* lord, or one ruler."

Spike whirred. Helen's eyes turned obsidian, as they did when she was concentrating; having eyes that appeared normal apparently required a good deal of effort, and her eyes were often the first thing that shifted when her thoughts were turned in a different direction.

"Not here," Helen finally said. "And not now. I will entertain the possibility when we do not have guests to endanger."

Spike continued to whir and click. More disturbingly, Helen

joined him. The familiar on Kaylin's shoulder squawked. To the familiar, Helen said, "Are you certain?"

Squawk.

"Is it possible," the Consort finally said, "that the Shadowlord of whom they speak could be in control of Spike but not in control of the man who retrieved him?"

Kaylin thought about it. "Yes, I think it's possible."

"You do not think it's probable."

"I think there are two possibilities. One: the man in question is like the Dragon outcaste. He believes on some level that he is master of his own fate. *If* that were true, he wouldn't be involved with, or beholden to, the creature beneath the High Halls. But he wouldn't be the first person to—" And here, she stopped. There were some things it was not safe to know, let alone discuss. She started again, and stopped because mentioning Iberrienne in front of Eddorian, his brother, caused the latter pain.

"Sorry. Two: he failed the Test of Name, but could withstand the touch of the creature beneath the High Halls; he left the Tower having, in theory, passed that test. If it's the latter, and if Spike is right—or if he's saying what he means in a language most of the rest of us can understand—the creature beneath the High Halls is, in some way, in league with the Shadowlord, if that's what you want to call him. Or her. Or them. Whatever."

"That is incorrect," Spike then said.

"Which part?"

"Shadowlord. That is—" Squawk. "Ah. Apologies. I find your language inexact and frustrating. I have now absorbed the entire lexicon, but it is extremely difficult to match it to actual meaning. Your peoples use the same words to mean entirely different things. I do not see how you communicate clearly. At all." This was more than Spike generally managed to say.

"Is Dragon any better?"

The Arkon cleared his throat. Loudly. "Perhaps you will attempt to focus on the very serious topic at hand. You may interrogate him about the inferiority or superiority of other languages at a different time."

Kaylin turned toward the Arkon. "If it's easier for Spike—"

"It is not easier, and the only people who would understand a majority of what was said if it were are Dragons. We are guests. I have a multitude of questions I wish to ask Spike, and if I, a guest, refrain, you have a duty as host to do so, as well."

Right. Kaylin reddened, but one glance at Bellusdeo made clear that the Arkon was the only thing in the room that could lighten the color of her eyes at all.

She exhaled. "So what you're saying," she said to Spike, "is the creature in the High Halls is in league with the ruler at the heart of *Ravellon*."

"I do not believe that is what I am saying," Spike replied.

Kaylin wanted to be closer to a wall so she could pound her head into it. She managed not to shriek in frustration and considered that an etiquette win.

"I am of *Ravellon*," Spike continued. "And I am no longer entrapped. Because of you, Lord Kaylin."

"I am not..." She exhaled. "So you're saying whatever is at the base of the High Halls is, or could be, like you? That it's not entrapped or enslaved?"

"It is difficult for the ruler at the heart of *Ravellon* to enslave your kind. They do not generally survive the attempt."

"Do you mean it is difficult to enslave mortals?" the Consort asked. "Or do you refer to any of us?"

"To me, you all seem similar," Spike admitted. "But no, in this case, I meant mortals."

"Because we don't have words at our core."

"Because you lack True Words, yes. Some of the words can sustain life even under the weight of Shadow—but not many, not when the words are singular or less innately attuned."

"Can you tell, by looking?"

"Of course not. No more can the Shadow at the heart of *Ravellon*. But *Ravellon* is contained, if imperfectly. I do not know what lives at the base of the Tower you have referenced. But there were, in *Ravellon*, those with a sensitivity to the language of the Ancients, and a mastery of its speech."

"Before or after the Shadow consumed *Ravellon*?"

"Both before and after," Spike replied, the words almost tentative.

"And those could see the True Words at the core of the Barrani and the Dragons?"

"Not as such, and not immediately. But they understood the tone and the feel of the words; they understood the... attenuated vibrations, and therefore found it easier to convince those who held those words to surrender them."

"What did they look like?" Kaylin asked.

Helen immediately raised a hand. "Do not attempt to answer that question," she all but snapped. "My apologies," she added to the guests. "But Spike's attempts to answer questions sometimes cause difficulty. I do not think it will cause harm, but I cannot be certain."

Fair enough. "Spike, would you recognize a significant Shadow if you could only perceive what we perceive?"

"I am uncertain."

"Perhaps," the Consort said quietly, "I may be able to help. I assure you," she added to Helen, "that any attempt I make will not cause the disturbance—the unintentional disturbance— that Spike might."

Helen said nothing.

★ ★ ★

The Consort closed her eyes.

Ynpharion was grim, but silent; his Lady occupied the whole of his attention. He watched, discomfort and anger blending as the Consort lifted both hands and placed them, palms down, on the table. The dishes that had, moments before, decorated her place setting vanished; nothing remained between her palms and the polished, gleaming wood.

"Lady," Teela said, her voice sharpened to an almost lethal point.

The Consort wasn't listening. As she concentrated, Kaylin's skin began to tingle. It went straight from tingling—which was slightly uncomfortable—to pain. In that moment, Kaylin remembered that the Consort, like many of her Barrani compatriots, was a mage. If her magic was odd and not immediately identifiable, it was nonetheless of a kind that made Kaylin's magical allergies, as she called them, flare.

Above the tabletop, hovering inches from her hands, an image began to form. As if the Consort had summoned a Records mirror, it began in a whorl of fog and smoke, but that amorphous cloud began to condense and, as it did, to harden into an actual, visual image.

Kaylin was certain that there were things she would never forget, but memory at a distance was not as visceral as memory aided by images she could no longer clearly recall. And she recognized this one, understood Teela's sharp tone and held her breath.

The cavernous roof opened first, as if the image itself needed to be contained, the lines of a cage drawn first. No one spoke; nothing but breathing could be heard, and most of the cohort, as Kaylin, appeared to be holding their collective breath.

Beneath the uneven surface of rock, lit only by torches, figures emerged.

★ ★ ★

To anyone raised in the fiefs, these figures were familiar nightmares: Ferals. They took the form of dogs—giant, dark dogs with faces full of fangs that made their heads seem slightly unbalanced. They formed slowly, the hints of their bodies a tangle of dark smoke that solidified as she watched. At their bristling backs, she could see other shadows embroiled in the darkness, waiting their turn—as if the Ferals were heralds.

She knew what would follow. She knew what she'd seen.

But she was wrong. The shadows behind the Ferals didn't immediately merge; nothing bearing the face and form of a Barrani man came to greet them. She said, "There's a bridge," half speaking to herself. The Consort's illusion shifted, pulling back as Records mirrors could, to reveal the bridge of which Kaylin had spoken.

All of the Shadows were on the far side. The Ferals. The mass behind them, waiting to take shape and form. Kaylin had seen the first of the forms offered: that of a Barrani man. And she had seen— Oh. The Consort hadn't finished. Sweat beaded her brow now, and her lips were thinned as if with pain. As if? No, Kaylin thought, there *was* pain. It wasn't physical, but for someone like the Consort, that might have been easier.

The dead, in lighter fog, lighter smoke, began to fill the cavern on the other side of the bridge. The light in the darkness was contained entirely in them, and shed by them: they were pale, luminous, ghostly. And they were all Barrani.

Someone's breath came out like a cut of sound, the swing of a blade.

The Consort did not speak. Kaylin did. "They're all still there—everyone who failed the Test of Name. They died," she added, as if it were necessary. When she'd seen them, it almost had been; they had seemed so full of pain, of fear, of life. "They were bound by their names, and whatever it is that lies at the base of the High Halls holds those names; none have returned to the Lake. None have been returned to the Barrani."

"All of the dead are there?" It was Sedarias who asked.

"All of the dead who chose to take the Tower's test—and failed."

"And what *is* at the heart of the Tower?"

The Consort had not spoken a word; the whole of her reply was contained in the images she had set in motion. The shadows at the back of the Ferals shifted and twisted, and in the end, they disgorged the perfect image of a Barrani man. A man Kaylin recognized.

Teela stiffened. Severn stilled. Ynpharion's voice froze— it shouldn't have been audible, but was, anyway. Kaylin was certain that the second guard felt exactly as Ynpharion did. They were seeing the current High Lord. The man who had been called the Lord of the Green, and would be called that until an heir to the High Seat was born.

No one else appeared to recognize him.

He wore a cape of black, but the hood rested around his shoulders, and although his lips moved, the Consort didn't add sound to the image she had dredged out of perfect, Barrani memory.

"Spike?"

Spike was whirring, but there were no accompanying clicking noises.

The image of the Barrani High Lord shifted, the darkness of shadow melting in place. Shadow accreted and re-formed, becoming something far larger than a single man. This, too, Kaylin had seen, what felt years ago, and in a foreign country. She lost sight of Ferals, lost sight of the dead—but it had never been the sight of them that had haunted her. Just the echoing sound of their voices, the cries of the damned.

What emerged, at last, from the darkness was a Shadow that resembled a Dragon's form—but only skeletally. It had the head, the jaws, the neck; it had similar limbs and ebon claws. Absent were the wings, but even had they been present, it wouldn't have made the creature seem less monstrous; it was the eyes. It had a multitude of eyes that opened at asymmetrical places across the whole of its face, and one eye that opened, larger than the rest, at the center of its chest.

She could see the physicality of a roar when the creature opened its jaws, and she could see a tongue that was more disturbing than anything else about it; it seemed to be almost a fully formed humanoid, but glistening and wet.

Spike began to click, the noise becoming high-pitched as it was joined by a whirring whine.

"Spike wishes to ask if both the former and the latter forms are adopted by the same creature."

Kaylin nodded.

Whir, click, whir.

"Have you seen the Shadow adopt other forms?"

"It can adopt other forms," Kaylin said.

Whir. Click click click. "Lady," Helen then said, "Spike asks—if it is possible—that you show him any other forms the Shadow itself might have adopted. Spike understands that you are drawing from your personal experience—and explaining what 'personal experience' means is difficult—but asks if the forms are confined to these two for that reason."

"He used the larger one to attack us. I mean to physically attack us," Kaylin said when the Consort failed to answer.

"The Consort," Helen then said, "does not believe that other forms have been used in her presence. Or rather, that forms other than the larger one and a selection of Barrani appearances have been used. It is of note that when he attacked the High Seat itself, he chose—or was perhaps confined to—a Barrani appearance."

Silence fell.

This time, it was the Arkon who broke it. "I understand now why an unfortunate, noisy fate chose me as one of your guests for the evening." He nodded to Helen. "I cannot speak for the Consort, and I cannot speak for the Barrani High Court. But the Dragon Court has long known what lies beneath the High Halls.

"I am the oldest member of the Dragon Court, and my interest has long been in antiquities and history." He then turned to Kaylin. No, not Kaylin, Spike, who now rested in a vibrating whir in her hand. He then rose and bowed to the Consort. "Lady, if you will, I will require the table and space at which to work. What you have presented is, no doubt, helpful to the young men and women who have gathered beneath Lord Kaylin's roof, but what I will present may be of aid to Spike. I do not believe he has enough information; if he has suspicions, perhaps I may clarify them for him."

The Consort nodded and the image that rested above her hands dispersed. Plates did not return, but a tall glass did, and she clasped it in both of her hands. The surface of the water trembled. To Kaylin's eye, the Consort was slightly off color; she looked exhausted. Perfect, but exhausted.

The Arkon then began.

He didn't put his hands on the table; he didn't otherwise murmur or cast, as the Consort had done. Kaylin's skin was almost numb at this point, but she flinched as a new wave of different pain ran across it, raising goose bumps. In the early years, she had assumed that all magic had this effect; her experience in the past year had made it clear that only certain types caused pain.

Beside her ear, her familiar squawked. It wasn't the angry variety; it was, for the familiar, almost quiet.

"Yes," the Arkon replied. "And for your information, there is no record that indicates that previous Chosen were afflicted with the same sensitivity to magic. Lord Kaylin is not the only mortal to be Chosen, but mortals who bore those marks were rare, and little remains of their history. Lord Kaylin does not consider use of magic in such circumstances to be a threat or a danger." He did not look up as he rumbled—and he did rumble; his voice had taken on the cadence and depth of his race, although—thank whichever gods were listening—not the volume.

Bellusdeo was leaning into the table now, her hands gripping its edge, knuckles white. Her eyes were red-orange, but anyone who lived with the Dragon expected that, since the discussion had moved to Shadow, and was likely to remain there for some time.

The Arkon's image did not start out as moving fog or smoke. It started, suddenly, in flame, a bonfire of orange, yellow and red, with a heart of white. It was the heart that gave way first, as something began to unfurl in its center.

"This," the Arkon said, and he had no difficulty adding words to the emerging images, unlike the Consort, "was at the height of the war, the first war. Geographically, you are unlikely to recognize it; it is much changed from what you will see. Much changed."

Kaylin expected to see forest. Or fields. Or something primitive. "Is it where Elantra was built?"

The Arkon failed to answer.

The heart of the fire widened; the last of the bracketing flames died away, as if starved of fuel. What remained, now, was a spire of stone that rose far above even the Towers in the fiefs. It might have looked small, but at its base was a building that looked almost like a fairy-tale palace; the walls were a gray-white that glistened, and colored windows were evenly spaced along portions of the visible wall.

"Do you recognize it?" the Arkon asked.

Kaylin started to answer, but the question wasn't aimed at her, and she fell silent.

"I do," the Consort replied. "But only from images and paintings that survive the war. The building...did not."

"You believe that the Dragon Flights destroyed it."

"And you do not?"

"No. But I know what did. And if the palace itself was a gutted ruin by the end of that war, the Tower remained."

"It was once like I was," Helen replied softly. "With different imperatives."

"You know of this."

"I know only what I was told. I am not very mobile."

"And who told you?"

"The Sorcerer for whom I was a partial residence."

"Now, watch," the Arkon said. And in the distance, approaching that palace in an almost synchronized beat of wings, came Dragons.

CHAPTER 11

The Dragons grew larger as Kaylin obeyed the Arkon's command. She had heard of Dragon Flights, but had never seen one in action. She had seen Dragons in combat—the entire Imperial Court had taken to the skies when the High Halls had come under attack by the ancient version of Barrani—and had thought she understood what the term meant.

But watching these Dragons flying in formation made a lie of that. There was a cohesion to their flight patterns, a power to their movement and a far greater uniformity of color than there had been any other time she had seen a Dragon adopt its draconic form. They weren't wearing uniforms or armor—Dragons didn't need either—but might as well have been.

What the Dragon Flights gave her was a sense of the size of the palace. She had always thought the High Halls immense; the ceilings towered, where there were ceilings, and the halls themselves were—at least near the front—wide enough for an army to march through. They were modest in comparison to this.

"Is there more than one Flight?" she asked, frowning.

"There are four," the Arkon replied. "There were not four by the end of this battle."

Ynpharion's distress had lessened. He, like the Consort, Teela or anyone else in this room with the exception of the Arkon—and Helen—had not been alive at the time of this battle. He was now watching the Arkon's magical display with an interest, a curiosity, that was very unlike him.

"Which Flight was yours?" Kaylin asked.

The Arkon, once again, did not answer. Bellusdeo, however, snorted smoke. Kaylin shut up.

As the Dragons approached the palace Tower, their forces split, the flight formation shifting as they veered to either side. The Arkon had not chosen to grace his images with sound, but as the Dragons opened their jaws, she could almost hear the thunder of their war cries.

From the ground—it must have been from the ground—lightning struck that living cloud.

The image once again shifted, but the Dragons did not diminish in size; instead, the whole of the moving display expanded to rest above the entirety of the dining room table. Lightning struck again, and this time, one set of wings stuttered, causing a gap in the flight formation that broke the illusion of invulnerability, of death on wings.

Kaylin could now see the army that claimed the ground. She could see the moment lightning leaped from within its far more numerous ranks and took to sky, to targets that were so large they should have been easy to hit.

That is the High Lord's banner, Ynpharion said. *There, in the center of the formation.*

There were a *lot* of banners in that field of armored men.

Kaylin flinched. *Did the High Lord survive?*

Silence. She took that as a no. Maybe, on balance, this history lesson of the Arkon's was not the best idea for a mixed dinner.

"It is not the war itself that he is attempting to show us,"

Helen replied. Given the brief movement of gazes, Helen hadn't taken any care to keep this from the ears of her guests. "And no, the High Lord of the time did not survive this battle. But, Kaylin, I believe the Arkon is attempting to show the destruction of the palace, rather than the death of the High Lord."

"They are linked," the Arkon said. "Ah, now. Look."

Kaylin did, but what she saw was flame, fire, lightning and a vortex of wind—visible because it made such a dent in the formation of the aerial attackers. These were elemental attacks.

"Where were you?" Kaylin asked.

"I am going to bite you if you continue to interrupt," Bellusdeo snapped. "He is obviously flying in from the opposite direction; this would be the view he would have had at the time."

If it had been obvious, Kaylin wouldn't have asked. She did shut up, though.

Lightning. Fire. Arrows that glittered too brightly in the cloudy skies. Wind. No water that she could see, and the Barrani weren't stupid enough to attempt to summon fire. But there was something on that field that rose like lightning but did not flash the same color, the same bright, harsh visual spear.

"What," the Consort said softly, seeing what Kaylin saw, and marking it in the same way, "was that?"

The Arkon nodded with approval, and Kaylin wished she'd asked the question first, since the ones she had asked so far clearly weren't the right ones.

"In the noise and the clamor of battle, it is seldom that we have the time to observe or communicate what we've seen. It is not," he added softly, "what every combatant on that field saw."

"You were not Arkon then."

"No. But it is because of my peculiar magical sensibilities that I was, in the end, selected to become so. Kaylin?"

"Yes," she said, almost curt. "I've seen that before. It's... not quite Shadow; I think that would have been obvious to most observers. But...it's got a distinctly purple-gray hue."

The Arkon nodded. "I do not know what history tells the Barrani of that battle, but given the existence of the second war, I can guess."

"We did not start that war," the Consort said quietly.

"I will not argue that point; I will simply say, Consort, that neither did we. And perhaps, with this hint—ah, see, again—you might understand how both your position and my position could be true."

She was white; it was not a good color. Her eyes were a midnight blue, a martial blue.

"But even that, Lady, is not the point of this exercise." The perspective shifted, and shifted again; Kaylin could now see the wings to either side of the viewpoint that must, as Bellusdeo had said, have been the Arkon's. In color, they were a slate blue, trending to something brighter.

Dragon wings obscured the view of the grounded Barrani—but even thinking that, Kaylin realized that not all of the Barrani were grounded. Some were mounted. A small handful. None of their mounts were creatures that Kaylin had seen before. But their shapes were much harder to define; they seemed blurry, as if they—and they alone—were being seen through fingerprint-smeared glass.

Bellusdeo's eyes—when Kaylin glanced at the golden Dragon—were red. Blood red. She was vibrating. And as if he could hear that vibration, Maggaron, her personal Ascendant, came bursting through doors that appeared to be made of evening sky.

This caught the Arkon's attention, but did not destroy his magic; instead, all of the moving images froze in place as the ancient Dragon looked up to meet the black of *Norannir* anger. Or fear.

Bellusdeo was out of her seat before Kaylin had finished blinking. She stepped in front of Maggaron—probably the only person in the room who could make her look truly tiny—and placed a hand firmly in the center of his chest. He then staggered back, regaining certain footing a distance of three yards from that hand. Kaylin hadn't even seen her push.

She spoke a language that Kaylin didn't understand; Helen didn't bother to step in with a translation, either. But the *Norannir* eyes slowly regained their resting color, and although Maggaron didn't slouch, he lost the appearance of height as he calmed down. He then looked up, to see the entire assembly around the open-air dining table, and blanched.

His first attempt at an apology was a stammer in his native tongue. His second attempt was a stammer in Elantran.

A very large chair appeared at the table, and Maggaron looked—pathetically—at Helen, who said nothing. Bellusdeo, however, caught him by the wrist and dragged him to that chair, and this time, Kaylin did see the Dragon exert herself. "My apologies for the interruption," she said, a hint of a smile at play around her lips, her eyes more orange than they'd been since the first mention of Shadow. "It was entirely my fault. Maggaron is somewhat sensitive to my moods."

"Which is why he's usually smart enough to stay well away from them," Mandoran added, ostensibly to the rest of the table.

A wave of chuckles cut the tension as Bellusdeo turned

once again to the Arkon. "My apologies for the interruption," she said in her sweetest voice. "Please, continue. I am sure this is educational in many ways for all of us."

The Arkon nodded. His eyes remained orange, but there was another shade entwined with it, possibly silver. The large image that took up most of the table, including the new spot that had been opened up for Maggaron, began to move once again.

Kaylin watched as the lightning that had shot up from the ground began to shift and change. It was no longer a flash of power; it was slower, its reach extending so the witnesses could see its full trajectory. It was, after all, what the Dragon who had not yet been made Arkon—and one day, Kaylin would have to ask him exactly what that title meant—was searching for. There. There it was.

"Records, enlarge," she said, and then flushed.

The Arkon didn't apparently notice, and regardless, the image didn't alter to accommodate her command. She wasn't looking at Records. "Yes," he said quietly. "You note the difference in that spell."

She did, although the mage in question wasn't the only one on the ground—there appeared to be several, surrounded by armored men. But one man stood out, although it took her a moment to realize why: there was a subtle fuzziness about his image. She could see his armor clearly, could see a tabard—but didn't know enough, even with the recent studying, to place it—could see the sword that he held in one outstretched hand.

It was the sword, she thought. There was something wrong with the sword. It was limned in a barely visible, almost purple haze—a fog. The man who carried it was Barrani; he had the long, flowing hair. But the hair moved in a wind that seemed counter to the wind that moved through his defenders.

"Who was he?" she asked.

It was Sedarias who answered. "The Lord of Brennaire. What the High Lord did during the attack on the High Halls was of lesser power than what the High Lord did in that first war. Now stop interrupting."

She hadn't been talking at the time, but Kaylin didn't point this out. Instead, she watched. She could see a stillness envelop the field; even the banners paused in motion, flattening as if they had been cut off from all source of wind. She saw fire splash like liquid twenty feet above the army's head.

And she saw a Brennaire Arcanist turn toward the High Lord from whom the stillness seemed to radiate. Kaylin moved—or started to move—and Severn caught her arm. Her arm was glowing—or rather, the marks that adorned it were; they could be seen beneath the fabric of her shirt.

She almost smacked herself. This had happened centuries ago. It couldn't be made to unhappen. There was nothing she could personally do for the Barrani or the Dragons of that time—and given their attitudes toward humans back in those days, did she really *want* to?

The Consort watched. All of the Barrani cohort did. Teela's knuckles were white.

The Arcanist's tiara was a glow of white fire across his brow; she couldn't see the color of his eyes. Even had the image been larger, they would have been hard to see: he was blurring as she watched, his form both distinct and hard to pin down.

"Arkon," the Consort said, her voice far sharper than usual. Sharper, harder, tinged with something that might have been fear.

He didn't appear to hear her. Brennaire's Arcanist turned toward the High Lord in the center of the formation; he lifted both hands and his arms seemed to shimmer as fire sprang instantly from his fingertips.

There was an outer barrier. Kaylin understood, as that fire traveled—instantly obliterating a line of soldiers that stood between Brennaire's banner and the High Lord—that the shield was immobile; the High Lord had placed it above the bulk of the army. He had not expected fire from within. Not now. Even if politics among the Barrani were death games, no Barrani would play those games at this time; the cost would be incalculable.

It was, Ynpharion said. His interior voice was quiet, leached of its usual condescension.

The fire did not immediately destroy the High Lord. But the barrier above the army faltered, and Dragon fire rained down upon those who had sheltered beneath it. In ones and twos across that field she could see pockets of resistance spring up, places the Dragon fire couldn't reach.

But the Dragons didn't contain their attack to aerial maneuvers. She could see that the Arkon—and the Flight he was part of—was rapidly approaching the ground. Not all of the Flights descended—some remained above. The constant rain of fire didn't hurt the Dragons, and never had. The same couldn't be said for the Barrani.

The High Lord staggered; his cape was ash, and some good part of his hair; his face was ruddy, reddened, and he'd lost his eyebrows. He had not lost his bearing. He understood that the blow that had crippled his defenses—ah, no, *their* defenses—had come from within. Kaylin could see the expression and the certainty clearly. He gestured, lifted his horn, blew it; Kaylin couldn't hear the notes, but didn't need to hear them.

The Brennaire banner flapped wildly in a wind that moved nothing else; it whitened suddenly, becoming a flare so bright Kaylin had to squint. That white light spread in a burst of something that nonetheless resembled flame. The flame rose, and at its heart, Kaylin could see Shadow.

Spike said, "Yes."

Kaylin gave herself a mental shake, and tried to remember the reason the Arkon was offering this information. Her familiar squawked—quietly, for him, which implied that he wasn't angry—and Spike's conversation devolved into something not quite designed for human ears. Judging from the expressions on Bellusdeo's and the Consort's faces, it wasn't meant for Immortal ears, either.

As usual, Helen was the bridge. "Spike says that the Arcanist in question was, in whole or in part, in the thrall of the Shadow. He believes, given the casual use of magic—"

"Casual?"

"—that the Shadow was present in person, if that is an adequate description. If, however, he was, there would be more evidence, more magic, involved." She hesitated, and then said, "He does not believe the Dragons were enspelled. They are fundamentally different in the ways they come of age, and it is more difficult to alter them. Perhaps *corrupt* is a better word. He does believe, however, that were the Dragons to be in close and steady contact with this particular Shadow, it would be possible."

Kaylin thought of Makkuron, the Dragon outcaste.

The Arkon folded his hands together, and as he did, the large magical image folded into nothing.

Ynpharion wasn't happy. From the looks of it, neither were the Consort or the cohort.

"My apologies," he said, as if any of them had spoken out loud. "But it is taxing, and I am old."

Bellusdeo snorted. No one else did.

"I wished to have Spike's opinion. And now I do. Your history will tell you that in that battle, the palace was almost destroyed. By us," he added, as if it were necessary—and given what they'd witnessed, it probably was. "But I believe that not to be the case. The building itself retreated into its core, where its roots and power were strongest. In that retreat, it captured the creature that had been controlling Brennaire.

"I am less certain of how, but I believe the High Lord was instrumental in the defeat and containment. I wasn't as familiar with the modes of Barrani magic as I now am."

The Consort's eyes narrowed. "And you will claim that you had nothing to do with that entrapment?"

The Arkon's eyes shaded toward their more natural gold; there was a tinge of orange in them. "No, I will make no such claim. Our people are not at war, and I would offer no pretext for war where none is needed."

"Might I remind you," Bellusdeo said, voice dry enough to catch fire with just the tiniest of sparks, "that the Barrani have all but declared war?"

"A small band of rabble-rousers who have never seen war have attempted to make noise, yes," the Arkon replied. "But the weight of the High Lord—and his Consort—are not behind those noises, and the Emperor does not consider the war band to *be* a delegation from the High Court."

"And for that, you have our gratitude," the Consort said gravely. Her eyes, unlike the Arkon's, had not shaded back to green. "You believe that the creature contained beneath— and by—the Tower was responsible for the war."

"Yes. But that is conjecture. Our information sources, for reasons that must be clear, are scant; while we have our spies, they are not necessarily numerous, and they are not always reliable. Your spies have more flexibility within the Imperial Palace." He lifted a hand and added, "The conjecture is all but irrelevant. The war is in the past; it is done. We cannot return to the past to change its outcome. Nor can we change the facts of the second and third wars. We cannot take back the harm that was done on both sides.

"We have the future, and it has not yet been fixed or decided. I apologize if my recollections have caused you—any of you—pain or discomfort. They were meant for Spike, and Spike's assessment. They are neither a declaration of innocence or an accusation. Not all of those who died on the field died at the hands of Shadow. In fact, I would say that most did not." He then turned toward Kaylin.

No, she thought, toward Spike. "You have spoken of *Ravellon* and its lord. And you believe you have recognized the Shadow that I showed you—the Shadow that is now contained beneath the High Halls."

Spike whirred for a long moment. "Yes," he finally said. "From the evidence presented, I believe I can identify what you now face. More information is required for certainty, but the probability is high."

"Then tell us—or have Helen translate if you cannot— what we, or what Lord Kaylin's friends, will face."

He whirred and clicked in response, and Helen's eyes— still obsidian—widened. They widened enough that they no longer looked human or mortal.

"Spike understands why the Tower withdrew from the rest of the palace; he is surprised and uneasy because in his estimation, containment of this Shadow is...never certain. And yet, he has existed beneath the High Halls for centuries. The containment occurred after the first war?" she asked the Arkon.

"To our knowledge, yes. The Consort would likely have better and more accurate information."

"The loss of the palace shown in the Arkon's visual reenactment occurred after the first war. The current High Halls was built over a number of decades in the aftermath of that loss. The Tower, and its test, have existed since that time."

Ynpharion was *not* happy.

"Were the historical reasons for that alteration preserved?"

"No. Very few who survived that war frequent the Court—but as you must suspect, it is not the Barrani way to share secrets or information. Not when they pose a threat to us. And as you said, many of the greatest harms done to either Dragon or Barrani were done *by* Dragon and Barrani. We are both peoples with long memories and an ability to bring a plan to fruition over the passage of centuries."

The Consort glanced at the Arkon, and then turned fully to face Sedarias. It was why she had come, after all.

"Alsanis said that you are—all of you, with the exception of An'Teela—much altered by the green and captivity within the Hallionne." Kaylin expected Sedarias to interrupt her, and was slightly surprised when Sedarias waited, as if knowing more would come. "He does not fully understand what lies beneath the High Halls—but his understanding is at least equal to the Arkon's in this regard.

"He understands what happens to those of us who face the creature and falter: we die, but we continue; our names do not return to the Lake. He does not know if that would happen to you; he believes your reliance on the True Names that woke you as infants is now vanishingly small. He implied that only one of your number chose to shed his name—to leave it behind. He is not certain what you could or would become should the creature at the base of the High Halls overwhelm you—but he fears the possible consequences."

"Then why are you here?" It was Terrano who asked. Terrano who had shed his name and reached for a much wider universe than Kaylin could—or would ever be able to—perceive.

"Because he also believed that you might have the resilience to face, fight and destroy that Shadow." She hesitated for the first time. "He is fond of you. All of you, but especially Terrano, who he called the most troublesome, difficult, truculent— Ah, apologies, Terrano. I forget myself."

Like hells.

Teela's gaze had sharpened to a knife's edge; her eyes were midnight-blue slits. "Lady," she said, the address loaded with courtly respect. Kaylin couldn't quite understand how that level of formality could be considered far worse than cursing, but apparently it was, at least to the Barrani.

"An'Teela," the Consort replied, returning formality for formality.

"Alsanis suggested that the timing for a possible attempt of such a dangerous mission was fortuitous."

"Indeed."

Tain had tensed. Bellusdeo, accustomed to Teela, was now sitting in a way that implied "at attention" was the new informal posture.

"Did he perhaps suggest that the timing was critical because the Chosen was taken, by the water, to the West March?"

"Yes."

CHAPTER 12

For one long moment there was nowhere else Kaylin would not rather be. She knew that Teela's argument with the cohort involved her; knew that Teela had almost demanded that they wait the pathetic handful of decades allotted to the merely mortal, because Kaylin was mortal, and Teela didn't want Kaylin put at risk.

No one spoke; the Consort's reply seemed to echo in the stillness.

Kaylin cleared her throat. As host, she knew it was her responsibility to smooth over difficulties between guests. *Why* it was her responsibility remained a mystery; her current guests were so far above her pay grade it made etiquette seem like suicide.

"I've already taken the Tower's test," she now said. "I can't go with the cohort."

"You cannot take their test, no," the Consort agreed. "But you must have seen for yourself that those who *have* passed the test can find their way to the heart of the prison. I have been there. Lord Evarrim met you there, as did my father." She hesitated, and then exhaled. "Lord Andellen found you, when you came to attend An'Teela—and with him was a man who had not taken, or passed, that test. The Tower will allow you to pass through to its depths without exacting any further measures to determine your fitness.

"You could not accompany the cohort, no. But you could be where the danger is greatest when they arrived to face it. I am certain An'Teela has every intention of doing the same."

So much for breaking the tension. And since that had failed, she surrendered. "Why does Alsanis think I'll make a difference?"

"Because you are Chosen."

"Does he even understand what that means?"

The Consort smiled. "No. To Alsanis, to the Hallionne and possibly even to Helen, the marks of the Chosen have a weight, a possibility, a suggestion of power, that is almost miraculous. Alsanis understands that you do not believe this; he has hope that as you grow in wisdom, you will grow into the power granted you. He believes that that power was granted for a reason."

"Did he happen to share what the reason is?"

"No. And although it might surprise you, I did press him for an answer I could understand. It is possible Helen could hear what I could not hear, that she could somehow translate his response in a fashion that would make sense to us."

Kaylin turned to Helen, whose eyes still took up way too much of her facial real estate.

"The marks of the Chosen exist," Helen finally said, "across many states. Kaylin is unaware of most of those states—but I believe she has moved between them before. The transition—for Kaylin—is painless; she is only barely aware that a transition has been made. I believe she sees and experiences these changes as if there had been no shift at all.

"The cohort is less unaware—with the possible exception

of Teela. But Kaylin's marks are an anchor, and the cohort does not have that anchor."

"They have their names," Kaylin pointed out.

"Yes. But you are aware that their attachment to name— and form—remains tenuous. They have come home, in a fashion—but, Kaylin, if you returned to your childhood home, do you think you would immediately be comfortable there?"

"That's different."

"Oh?"

"My home was in the fiefs."

"You would not see your home in the same way," Helen continued. "You *could* live there; I am not denying it. You would have a far greater chance of survival as you are now. But in some fashion what *was* home is no longer home. The cohort, with the exception of Teela and Terrano, have chosen to come home. But they are still in the process of attempting to acclimatize themselves to the reality, rather than the memory.

"Very well," she added, although no one had spoken but Kaylin. The whole of her demeanor changed; her eyes once again became almost normal eyes, at least in shape. "As you must have suspected, the cohort—"

"We'll speak for ourselves," Sedarias said in Elantran. "But to be honest, Helen, no one has much of an appetite, and I think the surroundings should reflect what this dinner actually is."

Before Sedarias had finished speaking, the surroundings did shift. Gone was the evening sky; above them now was a roof of carved Barrani stone. It was high, and it was detailed, although Kaylin had to squint to see some of it.

This was a war room.

They were still seated at a table, but it was not a dining

table; it was a large, long oval, and across its surface was a map. Or maps. One was of Elantra as a whole. The other, Kaylin didn't recognize immediately. She didn't like maps much, and had learned to read them because everyone else referred to them when bringing up Records.

It's the High Halls, Severn said quietly.

"You wish us to enter the Tower; you wish us to confront— and possibly destroy—the creature for which the Tower serves as prison."

The Consort nodded.

"We will accept your request. We desire to take the Test of Name—and in order to achieve your goals, we must be allowed to take it."

Since the Consort had said this wasn't factually true, Kaylin hesitated. But she realized as she shut her mouth that this was the opening of negotiations.

"You are no doubt aware that there are members of your Court—some highly placed—that do not wish us to be given that opportunity." As a nod to the Consort's previous information, she added, "And while you have said it is *possible* that we could venture into the prison without taking and passing the test, it is highly unlikely that we could do so as outcastes.

"If we are to do as you ask—if we are to attempt what no other member of your Court has attempted—we will do so as Barrani. Not as outcastes or fugitives. We will not avail ourselves of entrances that are secret and known to few; we will enter the Tower as any supplicant enters it."

"Can you guarantee that you will make that attempt?" the Consort countered. "Once you are there, once you have embarked upon that test, can you guarantee that you will confront and attempt to destroy the Shadow? As you have pointed out, many of our kin have taken that test, and none have directly succeeded in harming the Shadow—or freeing the trapped."

Annarion stood. "Yes."

Kaylin didn't doubt it. Sedarias might be political, but Annarion, while perfectly mannered when he wasn't talking to his brother, was not. Not in the same way. She could easily imagine that he'd try—but he'd try, regardless. It was probably why she liked him.

"Will you swear binding oaths?"

"Yes."

"Will *you*?" Sedarias countered.

Ynpharion was, predictably, outraged. Kaylin thought it unfair—the Consort had asked first, after all. *She is the Consort. She is the heart of our future. They are—* He stopped himself, mostly because Kaylin wasn't as good at controlling her expression as he was.

The Consort said, "If you demanded it, I would. But I would swear only to do my utmost to make certain that none of you could be made outcaste."

"And what does that amount to?"

Ynpharion, on the other hand, didn't have as much facial control as he thought he did.

"A fair question," the Consort replied. Her eyes were blue. The question might have been fair, but it didn't make her any happier. "I am Consort. I occupy one of the two High Seats. How much weight do you think my word carries?

"I have come to dinner. I have spoken with you all. I can return to the High Court and confirm that you are, indeed, Barrani, not something monstrous or dangerous; that you are like An'Teela, who has—in terms of martial prowess— almost no equal.

"Or I could go back to Court to confirm our unspoken fears: that you are other, you are corrupted, you are a threat to the Barrani. If, upon my return to that Court, I offer the latter opinion, you will never face the Tower as Barrani. You will never be Lords of the Court."

The wisdom of threatening the cohort, however obliquely, was highly questionable. Kaylin managed to keep this to herself. There was something about Sedarias that had snapped into place; she was, for the first time, at home.

"If we are never to be Lords of the Court," she replied, her eyes a blue-green at odds with her expression, "we will never encounter your enemy. We will not enter the High Halls; if you return with the latter report, we will be outcaste, all of us. That is not, of course, our desire. You have your duties and responsibilities—to all of the Barrani—and we have ours, to our families, our history.

"We have no desire to interfere with, or denigrate, your duties. We are all aware of your import to the Barrani. Nor do we have any desire to remain sundered from our homes. You did not breathe life into us—but your predecessors did.

"But we have our own—smaller—duties and responsibilities. And we're not about to turn and walk away from them. Even if you tell us it's for the betterment of our race, we don't choose to accept that. You know what we want."

"I do now," the Consort replied, and her eyes, like Sedarias's, lightened, shading toward the green that was their primary color. "Over the course of the evening, I have come to understand that you are not one mind, not one being; you are Barrani, with the variety of individual reactions that any such gathering of our kin might contain. You were the only one of the twelve chosen to go to the green who was designated as the probable heir of your line."

Sedarias nodded.

"I will swear a blood oath, a binding oath, if it will put you at ease. I will ask that you swear the same, because I require it. And because we are in Lord Kaylin's home, I will be honest—

and honesty has often been very poorly respected among our kin. I understand why you are feared. I understand the reasons that your presence at the heart of our ancient stronghold might break far more things than they fix. I understand that not all of the voices raised in concern are raised for purely political reasons.

"In other circumstances, my voice might join those who speak against you. There has been much made of time, in those heated sessions; they wish you to live among the Barrani while they gauge the actual dangers you present. And this is wise; time will often tell.

"But Lord Kaylin is mortal. The time they wish to take—the cautious, perhaps necessary time—will see her years dwindle. Given her remarkable lack of caution in the face of her own ignorance, those years might be far fewer than the expected mortal tally.

"I cannot afford the time, and it is time you yourselves are unwilling to grant." She then turned, not to Kaylin or Sedarias, but to the Arkon. "I am not a scholar of note. I studied only those things that interested me, and in the end, very little interested me for long; I wearied of the lessons that history taught, and I wearied of the conclusions that seemed to be drawn from those lessons by those who were considered much more focused, much more intelligent, than I.

"Even so, I understand that knowledge is necessary, that the wisdom that comes from experience must at least be respected. None here—not even myself—have your breadth of knowledge and experience. If you speak against this, I will be forced to listen."

"I will not force you to listen," the Arkon said; his smile—and his eye color—implied that she had amused him. "Although I have come with my own guard, I do not believe any attempt at coercion would be met with tolerance from the two you yourself have brought. That young man has eyes that are almost—but not quite—black. I believe you have alarmed him."

Kaylin did not snicker, but that took effort. Ynpharion was embarrassed, because the Arkon was, of course, referring to him.

"And starting a battle of that nature while under Helen's protection would be very, very poor behavior for anyone she consents to receive as a guest."

"Thank you, Arkon," Helen said.

"You have given me little time to consider the ramifications of the problem for which you seek my counsel."

This time it was Bellusdeo who snorted. There was smoke in it. This seemed to amuse the Arkon, as well. Whatever had caused his shift in eye color had subsided. "Lannagaros, honestly, you are dissembling."

"Is he?" the Consort asked. Her eyes were still martial, but the line of her shoulders was once again fluid and graceful.

"He accepted the invitation to dinner because I was to be present and I desired it."

"I will, with a few exceptions, grant Bellusdeo anything she desires."

"And she knows it?"

"And yes, she knows it. I am considered far too indulgent—it is one advantage of old age. I am allowed to be."

"She is likewise allowed to be critical?"

"If there is affection in it, yes. But, Lady, so are you. You are allowed a much wider range of emotional expression than any other member of the High Court. You are indulged. It is why no mention is made of her use of a name that is no longer relevant." There was a subtle warning in this that even Kaylin couldn't miss.

Then it isn't subtle, Ynpharion snapped. He was still smarting.

"She knows that I have considered all information that has

been presented to me, as I always do before I venture out of my humble abode."

This caused Kaylin's snort to join Bellusdeo's. The Consort, however, was polite.

"My initial position would match more closely the High Court's. Time—and caution—are critical. For our peoples, the passage of time—a paltry century—should not be telling. But your people, being far more numerous, tend to play games in which survival is not guaranteed; there is a risk to the cohort should they take that time. I am certain they understand this, and I will not insult your intelligence; I'm certain you do, as well.

"If they intend to make their home the Barrani High Court, they will be familiar with those dangers. Time, therefore, is irrelevant. The next decade, however, will intensify those games, regardless of the outcome of the Test of Name. There are three elements that come into play now. One, you've already mentioned: Lord Kaylin. I will agree that she is reckless—even for a mortal, she is young, and mortals who survive do gain wisdom at an astonishing rate.

"The second, linked to Lord Kaylin, is her familiar. While he is willing to converse, he does so in a limited and unpredictable way. With his aid, Lord Kaylin is capable of perceiving things that you or I would have difficulty perceiving without great effort and exertion. And the third, which I did not expect, and have not fully factored in, is Spike.

"I now understand what is at stake for you. What you have shared with me—and I believe it to be the truth, given Lord Kaylin's excessively open reactions—the Imperial Court did not fully comprehend. I believe that there is some merit to taking the risk at this present time."

"If you wanted a short answer," Bellusdeo added, "you've asked the wrong person."

"I would ask him many other questions, and listen to his lengthy response, were I in a position to do so. I envy you," she added, her voice softening in such a natural way Kaylin believed her. "But especially at this time, interaction with the Imperial Court would cause difficulties for the High Lord.

"My presence here has caused political waves—but given the war band and the possible attack, by Dragon, in the West March, waves are the order of the day. You believe that I am correct?"

"I believe that this may be the best chance you have."

"And our chances of success?"

Before the Arkon could answer, Annarion did. "*Our* chances of success. Not yours. You have played your part here—and played it well, if perhaps unconventionally. But you are not coming with us."

"You do not seek, surely, to give me orders?" Her words were cool; her tone was warm. She looked at Annarion in the same way she sometimes looked at Kaylin, and Kaylin realized, with some chagrin, that it was because she thought of them both as children.

It's taken you this long to realize that?

"Lady," Annarion said, bowing. "You have said that you are the mother of our race. We will—should we survive—bring our children to you. Without your presence, they will not wake."

"No. Without the presence of the Consort, without the presence of someone to whom the Lake speaks, they will not wake. But I am not the first, and I will not be the last."

"You are too important to risk," he insisted.

"And do you all feel that way?"

Silence. Kaylin realized, belatedly, that this was a test—

of Annarion, of his honesty. And Annarion was honest. He didn't answer.

"I don't," Sedarias said, speaking in Elantran, as if this were a test of her, as well. Kaylin couldn't decide whether or not she had failed it or passed it; Annarion and Sedarias were not the same people, and the tests they faced would be different. Ynpharion considered it a decided fail, however. "As you must have inferred. I don't believe that we will be able to accomplish what you require without some interference from you."

"And you say this as a member of Mellarionne?"

Sedarias's smile was sharp, edged, infinitely unkind. "So you *have* heard."

"Of course I have. I am not concerned, however, with the Mellarionne candidate. You could never pass the final, and most determined, of the Lake's tests. Nor, I believe, can she. You fail to understand the nature of the Lake, and its sentience; you therefore fail to understand the nature of the Consorts. I have no children, but in the future, I will. And yet, even if some terrible fate were to befall me, if someone could pass that final test, I would have an heir. An heir that would be true to the responsibility that has devoured the whole of my life and thought. There is *peace* in it, Sedarias. I do not fear being irrelevant.

"Should the Mellarionne candidate pass, I would feel *gratitude*, not political tension. Families push their daughters— their competent, powerful daughters—into taking the tests of the Lake. They do it constantly. They see the position of Consort, and they see the tangible political benefit; they may even believe that the Consorts will choose only names of great power and significance when bestowing those names upon the chosen, favored few—those favored being, of course, of the line that birthed the Consort.

"History could teach them better lessons, had they the will to learn them. No one who could use the position in that fashion would ever be granted the position. Daughters of the powerful *have* become consort, or heir, throughout our history—and yet, they have failed to become pawns of the families to whom they were birthed. If your candidate succeeds, so, too, will she."

"But there is no heir," Annarion continued, dogged now. "The High Lord himself would surely forbid it."

At this, her eyes did darken, although her lips turned up in a smile. "He would not dare."

Ynpharion wasn't shocked; he was chagrined. He didn't condescend to confirm the Consort's opinion, but it was clear that he agreed with her assessment.

"You are perhaps laboring under a misconception," she continued when no one spoke. "You are responsible for your choice. You can elect to take the Test of Name and face what waits below the Tower. Or you can refrain. You cannot make choices for me; nor can you direct my actions in this regard. I have assessed the risks I am willing to take, and the choice of those risks resides entirely with me. As do the consequences. No blame or guilt accrues to you—to any of you—should you deign to fulfill my request."

"Of course," Sedarias said, inclining her head. Annarion looked far less accepting. "You are Consort; we are not even Lords of the Court. In no wise would we be up to a task that was beyond your reach." She looked at the maps that were laid across the table. "Shall we now discuss what you feel we need to know?"

"And your oath?" the Consort asked.

"If you feel it necessary, we will undertake that oath and its ceremony when we arrive at the High Halls. I do not believe Helen is equipped to perform it."

"It is not," Helen said quietly, "an oath one would demand of anyone invited as a guest." Which was not entirely agreement. "If it is acceptable to you, I will have food brought in and placed on the sideboard; you may eat in a way that does not disturb either your maps or your discussion. It is not a formal dinner, and for that, I apologize, but I feel that some food is necessary."

"Your hospitality is not in question," the Consort replied, "and it will receive no complaints."

The rest of the meal—such as it was—involved maps and discussions about the nature of Shadow, and the possible nature of the one that existed at the base of the High Halls.

Spike was a ball of nerves. While he was reasonably certain he knew who—or what—that Shadow was, he was not *entirely* certain, and the thought that everyone present intended to stake their lives on what was, in part, his opinion appeared to be giving him hives.

Helen did make changes to the room to accommodate what she called a sideboard; food appeared as if by magic, because it *was* magic. Plates and smaller standing tables also materialized, and if the furniture itself hadn't been so perfect, Kaylin might have been in the Halls of Law at the height of planning an action that involved the full force.

Even with the topic of discussion—and there was no secondary topic—Kaylin felt far more relaxed than she had while considering the Consort's visit; it was far less stressful, somehow, than the Emperor's had been. This work, even dressed up as it was, was work that she knew.

Spike was less sanguine. She didn't know what he'd done for a living—and the idea that Shadows had to do *something* for a living was a new and foreign one to her—but clearly, it hadn't been police work. Maybe his entire existence had been bound up in being portable Records; maybe his function was to be what memory crystals—those expensive and magical intrusions that were costly, and therefore, thank whatever gods existed, rare—were to the Hawks.

Her entire arm felt numb because Spike was vibrating so much while sitting in place. She thought it was nerves until she glanced in Helen's direction. Helen was rigid. She might have been made of stone.

"Helen?"

"Spike's concerns are twofold," Helen said, although Kaylin hadn't had time to frame a question. "You are right; he is concerned that you are making a plan of action based in part on his information, which is not one hundred percent correct. But that is the lesser concern."

Everyone poring over maps and discussing dates of arrival froze and looked up. Everyone except the Arkon, who would have no role to play; the Arkon had never fully taken his eyes off Helen.

"What's his major concern?"

"That he is, in fact, correct in his assumption."

"He's afraid he's right?"

"Yes. I have been attempting to explain this evening's discussion. Spike's understanding of politics—of living politics—is, of course, in keeping with his personal experience."

"Meaning none of this makes any sense to him."

"He can understand that there are variances in your positions—he sensed conflict clearly—but cannot understand why; the two positions, in his view, are so remarkably close together they should engender no difficulties." Helen's smile was brief and wry.

"He probably can't see much difference between the Barrani and the Dragons."

"He does see qualitative differences between the two species. Races," she added, grimacing slightly. "But they are very like the difference between types of grass to Spike—and in this analogy, Spike is *not* a gardener. He sees that you are, effectively, planted in the same soil, and you require the same sustenance—water, sunlight. I have attempted to explain the concept of weeds, but that has not gone well. It is all weeds, to Spike. He now wishes to know why some plants are desirable and others are not."

"Well, I'm kind of with Spike there. Except for poison ivy. And the things with the sharp thorns. Oh, and the things with the burrs that you can't get out of your hair."

Helen lifted a hand, and Kaylin stopped. "If you continue in this vein, Spike will fall back to cataloging your various complaints, and while he is likely to ask you questions, I feel it would be best to have that conversation later. Spike's concerns about the present situation are far more pressing."

"To Spike?"

"Yes, even to Spike." Helen paused, and then added, "Because they are pressing concerns to you, and he is attached to you until you detach him."

"I can leave him here when we go to the Halls."

Both Spike and Helen said "No" at the same time; Spike's contained more outrage. It was clear from Sedarias's expression that she felt the same as Spike. But Sedarias had seen Spike in the outlands; she'd seen the form he'd taken—and if he now fit in the palm of Kaylin's hand, albeit not entirely comfortably, she couldn't have lifted or moved him then.

He had agreed to serve Kaylin, in some fashion. She didn't entirely understand why.

"You will need help," Spike said. "You will need all the help you can get. Is that the right phrase?"

"It's the right phrase," Kaylin replied, although she suspected he was speaking to Helen. "Fine. Spike is very concerned and I'm not leaving him here. But if I take him to the High Halls, he's likely to cause concern to the Barrani Court."

"He will not cause as much concern as your familiar does and has," the Consort pointed out. "And I imagine asking you to—"

The familiar in question squawked in pure outrage.

"—leave him behind will be singularly ineffective."

"Well, it's different. Hope's not worried."

Helen's brows rose. "Is that what you truly believe?"

The Arkon cleared his throat. Loudly. "I would appreciate two things," he said as he rose.

The Consort was instantly attentive. "And those?"

"That you give me some warning before you depart," he replied. "And that Bellusdeo not be involved in any of your plans."

"It's *Shadow*." Bellusdeo almost spit the words out in fury. Clearly being left behind rather than charging into the Barrani version of hell was an outrageous suggestion to many of the people present. Kaylin, who had spent the formative years of her early life hiding from Ferals, didn't viscerally understand why.

"Bellusdeo's presence at Court would cause a very unfortunate stir. And given the current tensions between the Court and the Emperor, I would consider her lack of presence a necessity. I will not, of course, be present. If I can find information that might be of aid to you, I will pass it on through the private. But I will need at least three days."

"I will give you two weeks. I would give you more time, but two weeks is all we will have before things become fractious." The Consort's voice was firm.

He frowned.

"It is better," she said in the sweetest of voices, "to beg forgiveness than to ask permission, no?"

CHAPTER 13

"Of course the High Lord knows!" Sedarias said, six days later, while a tense cohort was considering—rather than eating— breakfast.

She and the cohort were grouped in the dining room, which once again looked like a posher version of the mess halls, because the tabletop here didn't have names or curses carved into its surface.

Helen had given up on chairs for the cohort and instead created long benches so they could huddle together without chair arms getting in the way. Placing chairs on either side of the benches would have been awkward, so everyone got a bit of bench at breakfast.

Severn was now living under the same roof as everyone else. Kaylin realized that she often thought about him as if he were Barrani: he didn't appear to need sleep, or at least didn't suffer visibly from lack of it. Kaylin did, and she looked very much like she'd spent the entire evening at either the found-ling hall or the guild of midwives; there were circles under her eyes. There were circles *under* the circles. She looked like she had a hangover.

But the house hadn't gotten any quieter since that dinner.

The departure of the Consort, which had come as a bit of relief to Kaylin, had not come as a relief to the cohort. They'd become grimmer and far more determined—which, at least in Sedarias's case, Kaylin would have bet a lot of money against being possible.

Bellusdeo—who was not allowed by specific agreement to accompany Kaylin and Severn—was very much an integral part of what Kaylin dubbed the council of war. And she suited it. Kaylin understood that the Dragon had once ruled a world—or its shrinking remnants. She had never doubted it. But seeing her with the Barrani cohort—and with Sedarias in particular—drove that point home.

Bellusdeo had come alive. Kaylin had seen her fight, but the draconic form didn't quite have the flexibility to express subtle emotions—at least not to those who weren't Dragons themselves. All of the Dragon's ferocity had been brought to the literal table. She took in everything, and when she did, she asked questions that were just shy of demands. She spoke as if she owned the table, the room and the battle itself.

While this was a surprise to Kaylin, what shocked her was Sedarias's reaction. A woman who was raised to rule a Barrani family that was, by implication, one of the most treacherous, deadly of houses took the questions that were almost demands, and focused her energy not on defending her turf, but on actually answering them.

Bellusdeo insisted that the reports Diarmat had given Kaylin be brought to her, and she read them with care. This occasioned even more questions—and as the cohort had not lived through most of the actual history the Imperial service had preserved, it should have been difficult to answer any of them. Sedarias, however, made the attempt.

It was Teela who provided most of the actual answers, and when she couldn't, Ynpharion did.

"Teela, did you or do you recognize the man in Spike's replay?"

Teela nodded. Every eye in the room swiveled toward the Barrani Hawk. Terrano was the only member present who didn't seem annoyed.

"Kaylin has guessed that the Adversary beneath the High Halls is actively involved with the Barrani and certain members of its Court," Teela said. "But I am not so certain. I believe it *is* possible—but I believe that most of the Barrani who came into contact with Terrano might be moved to interact with Shadow for their own purposes.

"No one who passed the test of the Tower would instantly believe that they could somehow ally themselves with the creature and come out on top. This allows for only two possibilities. There are Shadows with whom certain Barrani have clearly interacted, or the creature beneath the High Halls has finally discovered how to take a name without destroying its vessel."

"The man is a new Lord of the Court?" Kaylin then asked.

"He is newer, yes."

There were things Kaylin was not allowed to speak about. One of them was the current High Lord and his history with that very test—because he had failed it. He had failed it, and were it not for the interference of his mother, he would have joined the rest of those who had failed. She had hidden her actions, just as she had hidden the truth about her son's failure. But that failure had happened centuries ago.

What if…what if in the intervening time, the Shadow itself had become more cautious, more subtle? What if—in seeing the almost-enslaved heir to the High Seat—he had begun to understand that he could somehow take the name and force the Barrani to do his bidding, to be his eyes, to reach into the world that the Tower separated him from?

"How does it take the names?" she suddenly asked.

Everyone turned toward her. Terrano snorted. "How did *you* take them?"

"I didn't—they were given to me."

Not all of them, was Ynpharion's acid reply.

I wasn't going to tell them that.

Oh? Why? You don't want them to know that you've practically enslaved another person?

You were trying to kill me at the time, and frankly, if there was any way to dump knowledge of a name—other than suicide—I'd do it in a heartbeat. But he was right. To Kaylin, it *was* a type of enslavement. And she'd done it. He hadn't offered her the name; she'd taken it because she could see it so clearly.

"Kaylin?"

"I'm being reminded of something I'd rather not be reminded about. Names, and the taking of names. I mean, Barrani True Names."

Sedarias, blue-eyed, turned to Kaylin. The cohort now watched with interest. "When you look at me, can you see my name?"

"No. Hope?"

The familiar lifted a wing and laid it—far more gently than usual—across her eyes. The answer, however, was still no.

"You've *handled* our names, but you can't see them?"

Kaylin shook her head.

"Since you are so terrible at lying, I believe you. And I better understand why the Consort considers you an emergency replacement. You conveyed our names—returned them to us—and yet you do not remember them, and made no attempt to bind us with them."

"I—"

"Yes?"

"I thought they had to be given."

"In theory, they do. In practice? Barrani can be forced, on pain of death, to 'give' their names. It is like any other application of power."

"It's worse."

"Agreed, but it's a matter of degree. Terrano says you've taken names in a different fashion?"

Bellusdeo, however, said, "Do you know my name?"

Kaylin shook her head.

"You've seen the whole of it. You've practically *seen it built*." This caused the entire cohort to look toward Bellusdeo in something that might have been surprise—or shock. The Dragon noted the attention and shrugged—it was a decent variant of a fief shrug, too. "It saved my life."

Kaylin nodded again, a little bobble of motion that went on a bit too long.

You see? Ynpharion said, sounding both smug and irritated, which was his usual voice. *Ask yourself how you took my name. The how is probably very relevant to your immediate future well-being.*

Why are you telling me this now?

Because the Consort holds my name, and if she cannot divest you of it, she is far more powerful, her will more steady, than you will ever be.

So you're safe with her?

His laughter was hollow but genuine. *No. I am far less safe with her than I would be with you. You will die in a handful of decades even if I lift no hand to hasten your departure. But I serve the Lady with everything that I am—and I offered her the name. It was my choice. And now,* he continued, the pride of that truth fading, *she is willing to take the risk of facing what the High Halls imprisons. And what we know about the creature is...almost nothing. If answering the question that you yourself posed is even slightly relevant, answer it. For her sake.*

But Kaylin didn't have an answer. "Is there some way to make people offer you their name besides threats of death?"

Ynpharion snorted on the inside of her head. *Coward.*

Spike, however, said, "Yes."

"How?" Kaylin said, latching on to Spike.

Spike whirred, clicking so much Kaylin thought he'd fall apart in her hand.

"Spike is attempting to explain what—or who—he believes the imprisoned Shadow to be. Your experience in the High Halls was unique, which is to be expected; you are mortal and your existence does not depend on the blood of the Ancients. I cannot therefore speak to anyone else's experience. Teela?"

Teela's lips were thinned enough they were practically invisible.

"Ah, forgive me," Helen then said before Teela could answer. Not that she was going to, in Kaylin's opinion. "Spike says I am incorrect; he believes the experience was different for Kaylin not because she's mortal, but because she's Chosen."

"Why?" Sedarias asked. Her voice overlapped Bellusdeo's.

The question did not make sense to Spike, judging by his vibration. Helen's expression shifted into one of focused concentration. Apparently, her familiar also had opinions; she lifted one hand to cup the ear closest to his squawky little mouth.

The group gathered around the table waited for the outcome of the conversation—except for Terrano, whose brow was practically folding in half as he concentrated.

"You can understand them?" Kaylin asked, which caused the frown to deepen, and added lines of extreme frustration to an already creased expression.

"Not easily, no. But if I work at it—which is impossible when someone is babbling at me—I can catch the gist of it."

Kaylin was not the only person who was babbling in very short order. "Who taught you this? How did you learn?" Bellusdeo demanded. Hers was the loudest voice, although it wasn't the only one; no one else had that thunderous rumble that implied imminent earthquake.

"No one taught me," Terrano snapped. "I *listened*. Which, can I point out, is impossible right now?"

"Helen will tell us what was said. She'll probably tell us more than you could if you were allowed to 'listen,' as you call it." The gold Dragon folded her arms. "The rest of the cohort don't hear what you hear."

"They would if they bothered."

"We wouldn't," Sedarias said.

Mandoran, however, lifted a hand. "I might. I can hear noise in the background; it sounds mostly like buzzing. There's a strange pitch to it. But we're kind of wandering far afield here. What we need to know is how Kaylin can take a name that isn't offered."

"What we need to know," Bellusdeo shot back, "is that you—all of you—can walk slightly inverted roads without being afflicted by the Shadow's control. And Terrano has walked farthest, longest. If I infer correctly, he's probably a large part of the reason the High Court is now embroiled in Shadow arts, and possibly under Shadow control."

"You say 'Shadow' as if it's one thing," Terrano replied. "It's not. Spike is Shadow. No, never mind. Sedarias is Barrani. I'm Barrani. The Consort is Barrani. Annarion is Barrani. How are we all one mind, one thing? Sedarias's sister was Barrani. She tried to kill Sedarias. The Shadow is like us. Some of the things that exist in the layers outside of the one Kaylin lives in are like Spike—they're bound. They're trapped.

"And some of the Shadows are like fire or water—they can be summoned, they can be invoked. They give power the way controlling fire does—if you mess up, you die."

"That is not all they are capable of," Bellusdeo said, her expression cold, her voice the heart of fire. "I've experienced what happens when people are not cautious. I've seen a world die. You do not want that to happen here."

"I don't want it to happen anywhere," Terrano reasonably pointed out. It wasn't the time for reason, though—not given Bellusdeo's eye color.

Sedarias was easily as unamused as Bellusdeo. Mandoran, however, was not; he looked uneasy, but made no attempt to ditch the meeting he'd contributed very little to.

"It is everywhere," Spike said, his voice quieter, his body almost—for Spike—motionless. "Because *Ravellon* is every-where."

"Are you everywhere?" Kaylin asked.

"I am here."

"Yes, but…where is here, to you?"

"You're confusing him, dear," Helen said. "But his an-swer is largely correct. He is not *Ravellon*. He does not exist in many places at once. He occupies spaces you cannot per-ceive, but they are all here." She paused. It was a thinking pause. "Think of a small hole in a wall. You can see very lit-tle through it from where you stand—but you do not doubt that what you see is only a part of what could be seen, if you were on the other side of that wall. What you see of Spike is the eye through that keyhole. What I see is what you might see if you were on my side of the wall."

"And the cohort?"

"It varies. They are standing by a window in the same wall.

They can, with a little effort, find and look through a window. You can't, in this analogy. You're too short. Terrano, on the other hand, is standing in the doorway."

"And Spike can see what I see?"

"Yes. He can see what you see. He can see what you can't see. For Spike, the wall in this analogy doesn't exist. His difficulty is comprehending what you yourself can or cannot see. He understands that there is a wall, a separation, but the wall is entirely invisible to him. He sees that you are Chosen. You understand that that's what you're *called* by people who see or recognize the marks. But it's as if the sign of the Chosen is attached in its entirety to the back of your head. It's there, it's real, but you can't, without effort or the right equipment—mirrors, for instance—see it yourself.

"He understands that you do not perceive what he perceives. And in his stay here, he has begun to painstakingly construct a sense of where the walls in my analogy are. But it is imperfect; it is hard not to see something when it is staring you in the face. To be fair to you, he doesn't understand exactly how you perceive him, either. My attempt to explain has fallen short several times. Spike, in his fashion, is learning what the cohort is learning: how to exist in your world. But Spike doesn't have even their experience as a guide."

"And this is relevant to all of the questions asked."

"Good. I was wondering," Teela said. Her eyes were a shade of blue-green that was almost normal. "Not that I don't enjoy watching Kaylin splutter on occasion, but Bellusdeo is definitely getting irritated."

This was true, except for the "getting" part, which implied a change of state. Bellusdeo had been sharp as a perfect blade all morning.

"Spike assumes that because you are Chosen, you can see what he calls living names, and what you call True Names."

Everyone was now staring at Spike. This included Kaylin.

"I have tried to explain that he is mistaken, but Terrano isn't as certain."

"Terrano was talking?"

"He was speaking to us, yes. He is not *good* at it—"

"Thanks."

"—but his sense of what you can or cannot see is not my sense of it; I know what you know, and act on that. Spike's contention is that True Names are True Words."

"Because they are," Kaylin said, nodding.

"He does not see the base difference between them."

"True Names are necessary—"

"But, Kaylin, they aren't. He cannot see those words in Terrano, and Terrano is demonstrably alive. He can't see them in Severn, either."

"Severn's mortal, like me."

"Very unlike you, in Spike's opinion. Regardless, he believes that you can see the names if you try. And so we come back to the question of how you took Ynpharion's name."

Teela said nothing, loudly. The cohort said nothing verbal, but their eyes darkened to a man.

"Yes, I knew," Teela said, out loud.

Sedarias frowned and turned to Kaylin. "Did you inform Spike of this?"

"Not intentionally. But I don't intentionally inform Helen of anything, either—she can hear what I'm thinking."

"Given your facial expressions, one doesn't need to be able to read thoughts to know what you're thinking," Sedarias snapped. "Can you see our names now?"

"No."

Spike whirred.

"I don't understand the taking of names. I don't understand how I hold them. I don't understand why, when I hear the name Calarnenne spoken, it's just another word." She stiffened.

"It's all right—we all know about that," Sedarias said. "If not for that, I'm not sure Annarion wouldn't have killed his brother by now." At Kaylin's expression, she said, "He marked you. It is a claim of ownership. But he also gave you—voluntarily—a power over him that might be unique."

"The first time I heard him called by that name, I froze. When *I* use the name, he hears me. Helen stops most of the flow of information when I'm at home, but out in the world, she can't. I could see his name. The first time he showed it to me, I could *hear it* as if it were spoken. I kind of assumed that that's how True Names functioned." She was silent for a bit. Glancing at Bellusdeo, she squared her shoulders and continued.

"I could see the outcaste Dragon's name in the same way. I assume—and assumed—that I could see it because he wanted me to attempt to *say it*. But I couldn't. I couldn't hear all of it; I could study it for a year, and I'm not sure I'd see it all, either, it's so large."

Spike began to clatter.

"But I didn't think it was safe—for me—to even try. I figured if he showed me his name and I tried, the loser, in the end, would be me."

"And if his name had been simpler? If his name had been like the names you do hold?"

"I don't know what I would have done. It wasn't, though."

Mandoran broke out laughing. Terrano turned to him and said, "Share."

"Someone who I will not name out loud is wondering if Kaylin ever plans anything. What she said, however, was, *Does she think at all?*"

She felt Severn's amusement; there was so much affection in it she almost couldn't find it annoying. "She does think," he offered.

"You could say that with more conviction," was Sedarias's sharp reply.

You really could.

His smile widened, and even if it was at her expense, she felt herself relax. She liked—had always liked—his smile.

Bellusdeo was fuming, or at least exhaling streams of smoke. Her eyes had lost a bit of red.

"What do you think? I think he did it on purpose, and I didn't want to play that game."

"I think," Bellusdeo said, breaking a piece off the dining room table so absentmindedly she reminded Kaylin of Marcus, "that if the outcaste were going to play that game, the correct person to play it with would have been me."

"Did he ever?"

"Never."

"You don't think he did it on purpose?"

"I don't know. Do you always see his name on the rare occasion you do see him?"

"I didn't see it in the Aerie. I don't—for obvious reasons—see him often. I'd be just as happy never to see him again. I'd like not to be ash. Or Shadow."

Bellusdeo said, "This is going almost, but not quite, nowhere. Look at me."

She already was.

"Dear," Helen began.

"I'm asking it," Bellusdeo countered. "Demanding it. It is not an invasion of my privacy and it is not a threat. Kaylin walked through *your* words. She saw them. She *repaired* them. And, Helen? She did that for me, as well. I'd ask her to look at someone else, but I can't guarantee that they wouldn't feel threatened. I can guarantee that, regardless of outcome, I won't. If it weren't for her interference, I wouldn't be here, and I wouldn't be whole."

Helen bowed her head. Spike whirred. The familiar squawked—but this squawk seemed to be aimed at Bellusdeo.

"Unless you can answer the question, this is the most practical option. Ynpharion is not present, and in general, he is somewhat hostile to Kaylin, which makes sense. But Ynpharion was attempting to kill Kaylin, and if I understand what actually happened—and I understand only as much as Kaylin does—Ynpharion was not in his Barrani form at that time."

Ynpharion was silent, but she could now feel him as a pressure somewhere behind her eyes.

"No. He wasn't."

"Why do you feel this is necessary?" Helen's Avatar stepped firmly between Kaylin and her view of Bellusdeo.

"Why do you feel it's putting Kaylin at risk?"

Helen is not wrong, Ynpharion said.

Bellusdeo is never going to hurt me.

No. But Bellusdeo is not the only person present. You understand that what I did—what I believed I was doing—was attempting to be free of the constraints of my race? That I, who felt powerless, wanted to feel powerful? I had lived my life behind the lines prescribed for me by circumstances of birth, and I was given the opportunity to change it. He said this with a lifetime's worth of bitterness. Or several lifetimes, from Kaylin's perspective.

And you feel you were lied to?

Yes. Pause. *Yes and no. I did feel free. I did feel unconstrained, unconfined. It quieted those fears.*

But?

Those were not the only fears, Chosen. She stiffened in surprise; Ynpharion almost sounded respectful. This annoyed him enough that he descended into his usual tone. *You have your very odd family—and I will call it that, because your ties seem to be inexplicably ties of kinship. You have your fears. They are not what mine were, but they are constant and solid, the little voices that eat away at you when you have time to stop and think. Which is probably why you don't do it often.*

Gee, thanks.

If, one day, someone offered you power—

No one offered me these marks.

—and that power alleviated all of the fears which have caused so much pain, you might feel relief or even joy at the lack of a fear that has been a constant. But what if, in that reckless, heedless joy, you accidentally destroy your family?

No answer.

Yes, exactly. What I saw was only the immediate end to a specific pain. I did not see—did not even look—at the other costs. And those costs, were I to have suffered them, would cause a pain far, far greater than the fear it alleviated. That fear, in large part, is due to the nature of our names. If you could see a name—just by looking intently—and could take that name and use it as a way to control the person who both owns and is owned by it…

Fear.

Yes. Think of what I became in order to be free, in part, of that fear.

These people aren't you.

No. They willingly took that risk with each other—but they did it when they were children. And children often do not survive to become adults because they make foolish decisions like theirs. But they do not consider you a threat; inasmuch as they can trust outsiders, they trust you. That has been made easier because of your mortality. Even the marks of the Chosen do not elevate you, in their eyes.

And this will.

And this will.

She glanced at Bellusdeo. *Doesn't matter. They're visitors. Bellusdeo actually lives here.*

And that therefore gives her the right to command you?

Kaylin shrugged. *It's not really a command—it just sounds like one. And yeah, it gives her the right to ask.*

Why, exactly?

"I think Ynpharion is correct," Helen said.

Kaylin stared at her back. "I get that. But I think Bellusdeo is also right."

"If you are concerned…" Bellusdeo began.

"I am not concerned that Kaylin will harm you. Nor am I concerned that you will feel threatened enough to subsequently harm her. But this is not an ability that anyone should have—"

"The Shadow at the base of the High Halls *does*," Bellusdeo countered.

"If he had that, every single Barrani that faces him would fail the test. I do not believe it is the same at all."

"And you're afraid that Kaylin can read True Names?"

"Helen," Kaylin said quietly, "let me try."

In the back of her head, Ynpharion was outraged. *I am grateful that you did not attempt this parlor trick in the presence of the Lady.*

The Lady, Kaylin shot back, *knows that I can see names—at least when they're not in use. I've seen the Lake. I've taken words from it.*

Helen very reluctantly moved out of the way.

True Names were like architecture. Kaylin thought that as she remembered Bellusdeo's name. She had stood almost *inside* the rune, walled in by its lines and curves and dots. She had not attempted to say the name; she hadn't attempted to memorize it. But she'd touched it, and that touch had not felt in any way metaphorical.

She'd taken the names of the cohort from the heart of Alsanis; they had been smaller than even the individual marks on her arms. She had carried them as if they were fragile and precious—but again, she could not remember what they were. The thought of attempting to invoke them, to say them out loud, hadn't really occurred to her.

But it wouldn't. Had their names been written in Elantran—or even Barrani—she might have done so without a second thought. But she couldn't read the true tongue. She could only rarely divine meaning—and to do that, she had to *work*. Even working, she mostly failed. She had a glimmer of understanding on occasion; she'd had that when she repaired Helen during the first night's attack on her house.

But Helen's internal words weren't a name. They were a paragraph, or several paragraphs, and likely written in language to make lawyers and bureaucrats green with envy. If Helen had a name through which she could be controlled—but no. She didn't. She destroyed that part of herself long ago, in order to finally be able to make her own choices.

And maybe, Kaylin thought, that's what Ynpharion had wanted. Maybe she'd make the same decision if she could be controlled or commanded in the same fashion. And maybe, in making that attempt, she'd break something of import, too. It was hard to see clearly when you were thrashing and struggling. You didn't even need a True Name for that to be true.

She took a deep breath, and the familiar on her shoulder sighed—it was a bored, weary sigh—and folded himself across her shoulders, his tail drooping. Mandoran snickered. No one else did.

Terrano, however, had turned toward Kaylin and was watching her intently.

She looked at Bellusdeo. Small and squawky did not lift his translucent wing to cover her eyes; he was bored, he clearly thought this was stupid and he had no intention of joining in. The Dragon met her gaze; her eyes were orange, but it was a lighter orange. She was cautious. She was also, judging by her expression, slightly amused.

She saw Bellusdeo every day. Multiple times. Even when attempting to avoid her. When she looked at the Dragon now, she saw...Bellusdeo. She seemed more militant here, but this was a war room for all intents and purposes.

Kaylin understood this because, as a Hawk, many of the strategic discussions that took place in the office were similar, but on a much smaller scale.

Terrano sat up straight, shifting instantly into a warier position. It wasn't necessary; Kaylin could see that the marks on her arms were glowing. It was a faint light, but it was distinctly golden, even beneath the layer of cloth that in theory kept the marks away from prying eyes.

Bellusdeo lifted a brow. "I really wish I had thought to do this when Lannagaros was present."

"I'm really glad you didn't."

"He has the breadth of experience to—"

"Trying to concentrate here. Thinking about cranky Dragons may relax you, but I'm not you." Kaylin forced the image of the Arkon out of her thoughts, which took effort it shouldn't have. The light on her arms—and probably the rest of her body—brightened. Exhaling, she closed her eyes.

No one told her that she couldn't see with her eyes closed.

She saw her own marks first; she saw them clearly. They did not appear to be attached to her, because they were no longer flat. Closed eyes didn't dim their radiance. She could see the shapes, could see the simplicity of some of them, the complexity of others. She had no idea if the dimensionality changed them in any way. She wasn't Barrani or Dragon; her memory for things that weren't trying to kill her or eat her wasn't nearly as good.

Looking away from the marks wasn't difficult, but her eyes—well, her metaphorical eyes, at any rate—had to adjust to the lack of any other light. No, wait, there was light. It was a similar color, but fainter; it felt vaguely familiar, although she couldn't immediately pinpoint its source.

Kaylin wanted to shriek in frustration at her lack of information, and almost did. But the light in the distance had begun to resolve itself. She watched as it grew brighter, wondering if Bellusdeo had moved, or if she had walked through a table to reach the Dragon. Neither were entirely relevant, though.

"Yes," she said quietly. "I can see your name."

CHAPTER 14

In the silence that followed her pronouncement, Kaylin could hear nothing. No one appeared to be breathing. She opened her eyes.

The marks on her skin had, apparently, deserted that skin; they had seeped up, through the cover of sleeves or legs or hair, and they now floated around her, as if they were a very inadequate cocoon. They were golden, glowing. If she could have read them, they might have told her a story.

Like, say, the story of whatever the hells the Chosen was supposed to be doing with them. She looked past this shield of words to Bellusdeo, who had not moved, but did indeed appear to be breathing. She could see the Dragon. She could not see the name at all.

"Can you hear it?" Bellusdeo asked. "Why are you making that face?"

"I can't see it anymore."

"You can't see it?"

"I *did*. But... I can't see it now."

"So...you can only see it with your eyes closed?" Mandoran asked, leaning back on his chair, his arms folded, one brow cocked. "Can you see mine?"

Sedarias lifted a hand, palm flat, and turned toward Mandoran.

"What? I'm not scared, either way. If it were up to me,
I'd've given Kaylin my name just for the ease of communication. If she knows it, we're going to be in much better shape if
we need to reach her. Mirrors apparently work at the bottom
of the Tower, but I doubt we're going to have one on hand."

Bellusdeo snorted. "Try it again with your eyes open."

"I'm trying," Kaylin replied; she was also trying not to
grind her teeth. "But I only see you."

"Fine. Did you see Ynpharion's name with your eyes
closed?"

"No."

But Helen said, "Yes."

"I'm inclined to go with Helen's opinion," Mandoran said.

"My eyes were *not* closed then."

"You close your eyes frequently when trying to separate
a word from the rest of the visual noise," Helen pointed out.
"You've always been able to see the words when your eyes
are closed."

Kaylin nodded, the frown deepening. For the first time
since the dinner, she really wished the Arkon were here. "I
just assumed that was the way True Words worked."

"And you do not often look at people with your eyes
closed."

"No—that would be a bit counterintuitive. But my eyes
weren't closed when I took that name. If I'd closed them, I'd've
probably lost half my throat. They were open."

Helen's silence lasted too long.

Mandoran exhaled and righted himself on the chair, which
he then abandoned. "You know you're not quite like the rest
of the mortals, right?"

"I have the marks."

"It's probably the marks, yes. But it doesn't really matter why. You're not like other mortals, in the same way we're not like other Barrani."

"Hello? I don't try to walk through walls and get stuck there—among other things." She avoided looking at Annarion.

"You don't get stuck in them, no. But, Kaylin, you *do* walk through walls. You're better at it than I am."

She stared at him, only barely remembering to close her mouth.

"You don't think that's what you're doing?" It was his turn to stare.

"I can't walk through walls."

"It is not," Helen said, coming to someone's rescue, whether Kaylin's or Mandoran's wasn't clear, "what she perceives, no."

"What does she think she's doing, then?"

"Stepping into an entirely different reality. Her perception of herself doesn't change. Her perception of her solidity remains largely the same. Her perception of you—or Annarion, although I believe this would be true of any of the cohort—is more accurate. But to Kaylin she remains herself no matter how much the world around her shifts."

"When I closed my eyes just now, did I disappear?" Kaylin demanded—of Mandoran.

The answer was clearly no, so he didn't bother giving it. "You've taken someone's name before. What did you *think* you were doing?"

"Surviving."

"Surviving."

"Surviving." She muttered a Leontine word. "We were under attack. The Hallionne Orbaranne was under attack. You might, oh, remember this?"

Mandoran shrugged. Something that might have been a

flicker of guilt crossed his features, but didn't find any purchase there.

"I saw the name. I needed to see the name. I grabbed it."

"Grabbed it?"

"I physically grabbed it."

"You reached out and grabbed the name." This time, it was Bellusdeo who spoke, although her tone was remarkably similar to Mandoran's.

"Yes. Not immediately, but yes."

"I think the 'not immediately' part is probably relevant here."

Kaylin knew she was right. "I—I could see the word at the core of him. He was a Feral in shape. Believe that I know Ferals," she added bitterly. "But he had a name and I could…"

"Could what?"

"I could almost pronounce it. Almost. And he knew and tried to kill me—"

"As any sane Barrani would in those circumstances," Sedarias interjected.

"And I grabbed his name and held on to it for dear life."

"Why 'dear' life, exactly?"

"Because it was my life."

"Very funny. I don't understand—"

"Not *now*," Sedarias barked. "So you saw the name at his core. Did you try to touch it before you…pronounced it?"

"I couldn't."

"Did you *try*?"

No, she hadn't, because she knew she couldn't; all of his body was in the way. And yet, when push came to shove, she'd done exactly that. She'd grabbed his name.

It is almost humiliating to hear you speak of this, Ynpharion said. *Is there anything you achieve that cannot be attributed to panicked bumbling?*

"Sedarias," Bellusdeo rumbled. "Please." Sedarias subsided. "You saw my name with your eyes closed," the Dragon then said to Kaylin. "Could you touch it?"

"I don't know. I didn't try. It was about as far from me—with my eyes closed—as you are now."

"Then try."

Kaylin shook her head.

"Try. If the Shadow holds the names but you can actually touch them, we might be able to free the trapped in the event he proves impossible to kill. If he can see our names, if he can somehow entrap them without using them, you might be able to pull them free."

"But what if I—"

"Yes?"

Kaylin swallowed. "I don't really understand how I came to hold Ynpharion's name. I don't want to do that to anyone I—to anyone who isn't trying to murder people. And I can't let go of the name now. I have no idea how to release it, and the usual suggestions—all of which involve my death—aren't really appealing."

"The Emperor will not execute you," Bellusdeo said, her eyes darkening and narrowing as she correctly guessed part of Kaylin's fear.

"He would if he knew."

"I have no intention of telling him. I agree that it might be difficult for you to keep it from him were you to spend time in his company—but that happens so seldom it should not be a concern." When Kaylin failed to close her eyes, Bellusdeo's narrowed. "I understand your fear," the Dragon said. "But I have reached the end of patience. If I, as the person at risk, am willing to take—in fact, insist on—that risk, there is nothing left to discuss."

Kaylin agreed enough to say nothing. When it became

clear her lack of words was deliberate, Mandoran laughed. Bellusdeo did not.

Ynpharion was highly unimpressed with all of them. With Kaylin, who had taken advantage of a weakness he had always feared, with Bellusdeo and Mandoran, who were willing to expose themselves to a risk he would never have taken, with Helen—even Helen—for allowing it when she was clearly against it.

"I'm waiting," Bellusdeo said, folding her arms. Smoke eddied out of her nose and mouth, like little tufts of death.

Kaylin closed her eyes.

She could see the Dragon's name. "Look—I'm doing this because I really don't think you losing your temper is going to help these discussions at all. But if I—if you—"

"Yes?"

"You have to let me know immediately, because—have I mentioned this?—I *don't know what I'm doing.*" People injured themselves, sometimes fatally, because they didn't know what they were doing. Kaylin wasn't certain if she was afraid of injuring herself or her friend, but settled on friend, because as far as she could tell, she hadn't physically injured Ynpharion.

Who almost shrieked in frustration.

Can you see it? Her voice was curt.

No. Since he couldn't lie to her, given the bond of the name, she accepted his answer.

What do you see, then?

I see that you are attempting to stall for time.

Anything else? Like, say, something relevant?

I see the usual red-tinged darkness that occurs when I close my own eyes and attempt to look through my eyelids.

So you can't see the marks?

The marks?

The marks of the Chosen? The ones that appear to be sitting a foot above my skin and glowing?

No, I can't see your marks. I have a sense that's what you perceive—but you are not perceiving it in a fashion that is accessible to someone normal.

She ignored the dig. "Bellusdeo, can you see my marks?"

"They're glowing."

"Yes—but to me they're not really attached to my skin."

"You are stalling for time."

Ynpharion chuckled.

"Can't I gather information?"

"You can do both, but only one is guaranteed to annoy me."

Kaylin exhaled. "I can see your name. It's sitting in the same direction as your voice."

"Can you see mine?" Mandoran asked. Sedarias said something in very curt—but very well-pronounced—Leontine.

"No," Kaylin said, answering him, anyway. "But... I haven't been looking."

"Stand in line," Bellusdeo snapped.

Kaylin was almost afraid to take a step, and not only because the table was in the way. She couldn't see the table, but knew it was there. Her steps were slow and hesitant, and... there were too many of them.

Too many not to strike the table.

"I've changed the nature of the table slightly," Helen said in her most comforting of voices. "It should not impede your progress."

Please, Kaylin thought. *Please, Helen. Don't let me hurt Bellusdeo.*

"I won't, dear. I understand what you fear—and I think you very wise to fear it. But Bellusdeo is not a child; she was once an empress. And I have been reminded that this is, in some fashion, the war, to her. She will not allow the

CAST IN OBLIVION 239

cohort to take a risk she has decided it is strategically necessary to take—and this is now the only thing she can do for both you and them. If you cannot trust yourself, trust her. Trust me."

Kaylin nodded.

She understood that the Emperor's desire to protect Bellusdeo was one of the biggest sources of conflict between the two Dragons. The Emperor was trying to protect Bellusdeo from everyone who wanted her dead because they didn't want more Dragons to exist. Bellusdeo understood this, even as she resented it. She would never, *ever* accept that Kaylin wanted to protect her from...Kaylin.

When she reached the word, she recognized it. It felt so familiar half of her fear dissipated. She heard nothing, and felt no visceral need to attempt to find some sort of pronunciation for what she saw; she was certain it would take hours, possibly days. She raised her left hand out of habit; it was the hand she used to invoke door wards when she was forced to touch them.

"You're sure about this?"

Bellusdeo growled, a very Leontine sound.

Kaylin reached out and placed her left palm against the nearest flat surface—a long, single line that seemed to anchor everything else about the word's form. She hoped that that hand had not encountered any inappropriate part of the Dragon's body on the way to the word itself, not that Bellusdeo was likely to care. Much.

"Breathe," Bellusdeo said, the word underlined by that almost Leontine growl.

Kaylin exhaled, chagrined.

"Well?"

"I'm— Can you feel anything?"

"Irritation—but that's mine, not yours. Are you touching the name?"

"Am I touching you?"

"No."

"But I—"

"You're standing about six inches away from me."

"But my arm—"

"You haven't moved your arm, or anything beyond your mouth, since you walked through the table that Helen obligingly cleared."

"I'm touching your name."

"And?"

"I don't know how to describe it."

"Figure it out."

"You know, you'd make a bloody good sergeant if you ever need an actual job."

Mandoran snorted.

"Only if I defeated the one you already have in mortal combat."

Tain chuckled. So did Teela.

"I— What exactly did you want me to *do*? I'm touching the name because I can. But... I might as well be touching warm rock. I can't move it."

"You've tried?"

"I can't move you and apparently it bears your weight. It's...really— Warm rock is the best description." She exhaled. "Well, not the *best* description."

"Give me the best one."

"You're not going to like it."

"Why?"

"Because you don't like sentiment all that much, especially when it interferes with duty."

"I'd love to hear it, on the other hand," Mandoran said.

"The rest of us would not," Sedarias snapped. "Sentiment is not appropriate in a state of emergency."

"I will defer to Sedarias's wishes in this case," Bellusdeo said. "What are you doing?"

"Well, umm."

"Kaylin."

"I think—I think I can climb it."

"That is quite enough," Helen said, and Kaylin's eyes flew open. Her house was not looking very amused. "It is a name, Kaylin. It is a source of life, of sentience. It is *not* part of an exercise yard."

"I couldn't do anything else, and I thought—" She stopped. Nodded. "I'm sorry. We don't have names like this. I'm not used to thinking of them as the source of life."

"I am just grateful that this did not occur when the Consort was actually present."

"Sorry, Helen."

Kaylin couldn't tell if the cohort was relieved at the results or not. Bellusdeo seemed mildly annoyed. Teela seemed mildly annoyed, but given the events of the past month, that was about as good as her mood was going to get. Terrano, however, seemed pensive—and as pensive was potentially less painful than annoyance, Kaylin found herself sitting with him in a dining room that was otherwise empty.

"Where's everyone else?"

"In one of Helen's training rooms."

"Bellusdeo?"

"She's with them. Helen advised against it," he added. "She really doesn't listen, does she?"

"She's listening enough, as far as she's concerned. She can't go with you guys. She knows it. She's going to make damn sure that any of the expertise that might have been useful is in Sedarias's head." Which would give her just a week, given that Immortals didn't need sleep. "Why aren't you with them?"

"I got tired of listening to Sedarias in her military mode. Everyone's panicking."

"Are you going to go with them?"

Terrano shrugged. It was a fief shrug, but Mandoran had taken to it like a duck takes to water, and the rest of the cohort had fallen in line.

"That's a yes."

Terrano said a long nothing before he shifted in place. He was shimmering faintly, as if lit from within by a subtle magic. It was a magic that didn't make Kaylin's skin itch.

"You have a delivery at the gates, dear," Helen said.

Kaylin got up from the table. She wasn't expecting anything, but the cohort was. "Do you want to let them in?" she asked as she made her way to the door.

"No. I don't think that's at all wise."

Kaylin stopped. "Mortal or Barrani?"

"Barrani," Helen replied. Something about her voice caused Kaylin to start moving again. Quickly. She'd drawn a dagger before she reached the door, but barely noticed the knife's handle in her palm, because her familiar was sitting, rigid and alert, on her right shoulder. He lifted a wing and spread it across her upper face.

Kaylin opened the door to discover that the visiting Barrani—in livery—hadn't breached the very shut gate. A carriage waited on the other side of the fence; it was the Barrani equivalent of a royal carriage. Although it didn't have the solid appearance of heft, it was light and visually pleasing; greens and gold highlighted what appeared to be a Dragon's head, very obviously not attached to the rest of its body.

Terrano came to the door; he'd moved so silently Kaylin

jumped at the sound of his voice. "I don't think you want what-ever it is they're claiming to deliver." Something in his tone made her look to the side; his expression was grim, his eyes narrowed. They were blue, but it was an odd shade of blue, or so Kaylin thought at first; she realized that the blue was the typical Barrani color, but it had spread to cover the entirety of his visible eyes, blotting out the whites.

"Helen?"

The Avatar appeared to Kaylin's left, looking distinctly more martial. Armor tended to have that effect. "Yes," she said softly. She wasn't answering Kaylin. "I think you're cor-rect." She smiled. If knives had teeth, that's the kind of smile they'd give.

"You recognize them?" Kaylin then asked Terrano.

"You don't?"

Kaylin grimaced. She'd studied the piles of information handed to her by Diarmat but, as she so often did, concen-trated on the names that were already somewhat familiar and therefore relevant. Only a few of the entries had had ac-companying illustrations, and she was pretty certain she'd remember a decapitated Dragon as part of a standard. "No, obviously. I don't. People you've had reason to interact with in the past? I mean, the recent past."

Terrano nodded.

"I'm guessing you think they're up to no good."

"They might be here to welcome their long-lost kin." His voice was dripping with sarcasm.

"You approached them?"

"Not directly." He grimaced. "Yes."

"Which is it?"

"Sedarias would have murdered me if I'd gone directly to her kin—but they've always been interested in new and unusual power, and we needed people who were more concerned with power. I didn't go to Mellarionne. Suicide would have been less painful—although Alsanis would probably have prevented that. But they serve Mellarionne. And in case it's not obvious, that's Mellarionne's crest."

"I think I'd've remembered a Dragon's detached head."

"It's their ancient crest. It's the one they used to use when we got sent to the green."

And using it now was a statement. Great. "The Consort said she'd supervise clothing appropriate for both the High Halls and the Test of Name. I'm guessing this is not that clothing."

"It's possible that it is," Terrano replied. "But there's something off about the entire carriage."

"The carriage?"

He nodded.

"Not the man in the tabard?"

"No, I'm pretty sure he's normal." Normal and clearly worried. A head appeared in the carriage's open window; from this distance it was hard to tell whether the occupant in question was male or female.

Ynpharion, do you have any idea who that is?

I would let Helen make all relevant decisions at this point, Ynpharion replied. He was surprised but not shocked. He was also worried. The man in livery spoke to the person in the carriage while Kaylin watched. She sheathed her dagger as the discussion continued.

"I don't see anything wrong or strange," Kaylin finally said, "except for the crest itself." She poked her familiar, and her familiar smacked the bridge of her nose, lowering that wing. In the light of day, the Dragon's head crest vanished. What remained appeared to be curved swords above and beneath a mountain.

Kaylin exhaled. "You win," she said to Hope, who once

again placed a wing over her eyes. "But I don't understand why they'd bother to enchant a crest on the side of a carriage. No, on second thought, I take that back. I'm guessing Mellarionne is agitating for a declaration of war."

They are, Ynpharion said.

"We either have to let them in or send them on their way," Kaylin told her house. "If we keep them waiting at the gate—" She stopped. The carriage door had opened, and its occupant stepped out. Or rather, all three of its occupants.

There was something strange about this party of three. The man in livery spoke only to the person who had stuck their head out the window; he did not seem to notice the other two at all. For their part, they adroitly moved out of his way when he did lift an arm or take a step.

"Hope, wing." The familiar withdrew his wing from only one of Kaylin's eyes.

She could only see two Barrani with her regular vision— one in livery, obviously a footman or a servant, and the lordling who occupied the carriage.

Do you recognize him? she demanded of Ynpharion.

Yes.

And the other two?

I am less certain of the other two, as you call them. I can see that you see something, but the image is imprecise; it will not come into focus, for me. Can you see them clearly?

Only with the help of my familiar. Fine. Just tell me who the first is.

He is an adjutant to Coravante An'Mellarionne, a Lord of the Court. Bressarian.

He's An'Mellarionne?

No. It is not the habit of Mellarionne to keep their kin in close physical proximity, for obvious reasons.

Kaylin frowned. *Do you think he's aware of the other two at all?*

Yes. If they could enter and leave the carriage without use of the actual door, I would be less certain. Ah. It appears Bressarian will now take matters into his own hands.

The man Ynpharion named approached the locked gates, waving the servant in livery out of the way. To Bressarian's left and right stood the two that Kaylin could see only through the wing of her familiar.

Bressarian squared his shoulders and glanced, briefly, to the left. He then placed one hand on the very closed gates and spoke. The words didn't carry to Kaylin's ears. They clearly carried to Helen's.

The Avatar of Kaylin's home was an older woman with silvered hair and eyes with accumulated smile-lines in the corners. Her voice was gentle, except when she was annoyed; her words were gentle, regardless.

That Avatar had vanished. In her place was a giant in what appeared to be polished, obsidian armor. Her eyes were the same color as that armor; the whites had disappeared. Terrano spoke a series of words that Kaylin caught half of—they appeared to be Barrani.

Beneath her feet, the ground rumbled; she almost expected the floor to split. But she realized, as she braced herself, bending into her knees in case she needed necessary momentum to leap, that it wasn't the ground. Bellusdeo was roaring.

Bellusdeo was roaring while the aide to an important High Court family was at the gates. Mandoran appeared beside Terrano; the rest of the cohort was still somewhere else. Mandoran's eyes were Barrani blue, but they still had some white to them. "This is bad," he said.

"Can you calm Bellusdeo down? Helen won't let them in,

but we can't afford to have her go full Dragon while Barrani are knocking at the door."

"She's not the problem," Mandoran replied.

"Tell me what the problem is. Right now."

"The would-be visitor."

"Which one?"

"The one who's more or less normal." He could see the other two. She wondered if Teela would, and mentally kicked herself. Teela didn't materialize out of thin air the way Mandoran and Terrano could; no, she came up the stairs from the training rooms at a full-on in-pursuit run. Tain wasn't far behind.

"What did he do? What did he say?"

"He attempted to invoke Helen's command phrase. It's like a name," Terrano added, "but vastly less complicated. You have problems even trying to look at complex True Names; you've said that yourself. You aren't the only one. Buildings like Helen were created for use by the powerful, but in times of war, the powerful ceased to exist.

"In order to make certain that the access to the building itself didn't cease with them, there were invocations created that would allow the command of the building to be passed on."

"And that's what he just said."

"Yes."

Kaylin turned to Helen, understanding the change in her Avatar.

"It's not going to force Helen to obey him."

"No," Helen said. She was angry.

Teela, however, had reached the front door. Without asking, she opened it. Kaylin was surprised; she was mostly certain Helen wouldn't have let that door budge if she'd tried it herself.

"No," Helen said again, the single word resonating beneath the ceiling of the foyer as if it were a miniature storm. "But Teela assures me that this is political."

"Can you keep the other two from coming through an open gate?"

"Teela has no intention of opening that gate," Helen replied.

"That means no," Terrano added. His eyes had not reverted to regular Barrani eyes. "And even if the gate remains closed, I'm not certain we'll be able to keep them out indefinitely. They shouldn't be here," he added.

"And water is wet."

"Yes, it is—why is that relevant?"

"Are they trying to do here what they did to Alsanis?"

"That's the worry, yes. It's easier with Alsanis," he added. "Alsanis is Hallionne; he is meant to be host to guests. He is sentinel against Shadow, but he doesn't automatically expect the Barrani who comprise the largest part of his duties to carry that Shadow with them."

Tain followed on Teela's heels. Kaylin followed on Tain's. Or tried. Helen's armor-clad arm came up so quickly Kaylin bounced off it. Hope squawked, but it wasn't the angry squawk.

"Not you," Helen said.

"Terrano?"

Kaylin grimaced.

"I'd rather not be seen," he said.

"Yes, I get that. But seeing you might put the other two—the ones that are less visible—off their stride."

"Or it will alert them to his presence. He is not widely believed to be part of the cohort; he was not, after your duties in the green, among the guests who remained with Alsanis. Or who accompanied you here. If your suspicions are correct, much of their knowledge about what we will politely call an indeterminate state came from Terrano.

"What they've learned in his absence—and what he's learned in his absence, as well—is not known. It would be best, at this point, that they remain ignorant. Terrano can be impulsive."

"And water is still wet." Although Kaylin could have said this, she hadn't. She turned, as the doorway grew more crowded. Mandoran had arrived.

"Annarion's coming, as well. Everyone else is trying to pin Sedarias down."

Helen nodded her approval. "Annarion is levelheaded when his brother is not involved." When he arrived, however, he looked a lot *less* levelheaded. Kaylin grimaced.

Mandoran began to visibly waver in Kaylin's field of vision. In both eyes. Annarion glanced at Mandoran, who nodded, the gesture and expression so grim he actually gave off a Barrani vibe for a change.

They walked out of the doors side by side, following in the wake of Teela and Tain. Teela was not dressed for Court, but she wasn't dressed for the Halls of Law, either, and as she approached the gate, she placed a hand on the hilt of her sword. Kaylin hadn't even noticed the sword, which said something.

"Are you sure I can't go out there?" Kaylin asked without much hope.

Helen didn't answer. Kaylin realized that she could insist, and Helen would allow it. But she thought Helen would be far more worried, and therefore more likely to react in a way that might have political repercussions they wanted to avoid.

It's why Bellusdeo wasn't here and heading out the doors, either.

Kaylin poked her familiar. He bit her finger, without drawing blood. But he also shook his head, shifting the position of his wing so that it once again covered both of her eyes.

Mandoran and Annarion reached Teela and Tain, and then both stepped to the side of the stone drive. She realized, as they did, that the shadows they cast on what looked, even through the familiar's wing, like normal grass were not the shadows she would have cast had she been standing where they were standing.

"No," Helen said quietly. "If Hope removes his wing, you will no longer see the boys. But the two who are effectively invisible can see them quite clearly. No threat has been made; no warning has been uttered. This is the heart of Barrani politics; all of the possible and probable death is implied in every action."

"Mandoran or Annarion just said something, didn't they?"

"Yes. But I believe it's Teela who is having the greatest effect. I find her sword disturbing," Helen added in a much more normal voice. Kaylin glanced at her. She had shifted out of armor into her normal clothing, but her eyes were still obsidian.

"Are they still trying to invoke commands?"

"No. I think they believe that someone more powerful has taken control of me."

"Well, technically, that's not wrong."

"It's worrying," Helen continued, as if Kaylin hadn't spoken. "Because if that's their supposition, they will be attempting to remove the person who has that control."

"Either that or they'll just wait until we all descend on the High Halls, which would make more sense."

"I think they hoped to enter and prevent that from occurring. If I had not damaged myself quite so badly in the past, all of my guests would likely be dead. They clearly do not want the cohort to enter the High Halls."

CHAPTER 15

Things at the front gate were not going well. Angry Barrani—for someone with Kaylin's childhood experience—were a flag that could be seen at a distance, because distance was the only way to survive that anger. Time spent with the Hawks had lessened the visceral fear. The Hawks contained both Barrani and bureaucracy, so some anger was inevitable.

Bressarian was an angry Barrani. Kaylin couldn't see Teela's face, but the line of the Barrani Hawk's shoulders implied that she wasn't particularly cheerful, either.

"Is he demanding that we let him in?"

"I don't think that he would be foolish enough to make that demand of Teela," Helen replied.

"He's probably learned bad habits from Coravante," Terrano said. "He wants to be a power, so he's trying to act like he is one. Weren't you ever told that?" he asked Kaylin.

"Told what?"

"If you want to be a power, you have to act like you already are one?"

"No. I was raised in a rougher part of town."

"What were you told?"

"Keep your head down, don't attract attention because all

attention is bad, learn when to run like hell." She shrugged. "Don't get involved in games of power when you don't have any. Stuff like that."

"Were you expected to live your entire life like that?"

Fief shrug. "It beat the alternative." Until it hadn't. "Being dead," she added, in case Terrano was slow on the uptake.

"Teela's just dropped her hand to her sword hilt."

"I believe he believes that Teela is the master of this house," Helen told them both. "And her refusal to even allow him entry is personally vexing." She smiled, but this time the smile was cold, hard and more than a little smug. "One of his companions is attempting to invoke words of command. I believe it is the woman."

"Meaning she doesn't believe Teela's in charge."

"I believe that is what it indicates. I am glad you are here," she added. "It reminds me of the possible cost of losing my temper. Yes," she added before Kaylin could speak. "I am angry. It has been a long time since I have felt this particular anger. I hope the two do not find a point of entry—I cannot guarantee that they would survive."

"They could do a lot of damage," Kaylin said, thinking of Alsanis.

"Yes, but so can I, dear. You have had a remarkable array of guests since you became my tenant, and I have had to expand my understanding of the spaces they occupy in order to properly house—or contain—them. Gilbert's last visit was especially trying, but I am glad that he did return." Speaking seemed to calm her.

"It does. It reminds me of the reasons I became what I am now. I am not all that I was, and at times I regret what I lack—but you would not be here had I made that choice. And I like your home, although it is more...lively. Oh, dear."

Teela had drawn her sword.

The blade seemed to absorb the sunlight; it didn't so much reflect it as glow with it, and the area around Teela darkened in comparison. No, Kaylin thought, eyes narrowing, not in comparison. Had she ever seen Teela use that sword? Did she want to see it now?

Without thought, she headed out the door. Or tried. "Helen."

"Teela does not require your aid at this time."

"Helen, *please*. It's *my* home, not Teela's. She wouldn't be living here at all if she'd managed to talk sense into the co-hort."

"And you want them to know that the person they have to kill in order to possibly gain entry and access to your guests is you?"

Kaylin let her hand fall away. "It sounds stupid when put that way."

"Because it *is* stupid," Terrano snapped. "You're the only mortal here—you're the weakest."

"Severn's here."

"You *honestly* think he's easier to kill than you?"

Kaylin shrugged, but that took effort; she was annoyed. "Neither of us are dead yet, and—"

Something shattered. Kaylin wheeled toward the foyer windows and almost froze there. This time, when she tried to exit the front door, Helen didn't stop her.

She brought the sword down, Severn said as Kaylin strode down the drive, her hands balled in fists so that she wouldn't draw both daggers.

Where are you?

At an upstairs window. Helen thought to alert me to the possible danger. I'm almost at the door, now.

Don't come out yet.

I will stay with Helen.

Teela's sword arm was slightly lifted, but the position of her back hadn't changed. Tain, however, was now combat ready. He didn't carry a sword; he was now sporting two long knives.

Brought it down on what? *She's on the inside of Helen's boundary!*

There were no bodies, no corpses and no obvious blood on either side of the fence; Teela hadn't inserted the blade of the sword through the tines of the gates to impale Bressarian. Nor had she brought her sword down through the iron tines of the fence, which was what Kaylin had been desperately afraid she'd done.

But she'd hit something.

The familiar squawked in her ear, adjusting his position on her shoulder, and as he did, Kaylin could see the shards that had fallen in a jagged circle around Teela's feet. They were melting, their edges disappearing as they slowly blended together.

Kaylin's arms, legs and marked skin suddenly caught fire. Or that's what it felt like. She stumbled, gritting her teeth as the movement of cloth and leather against that skin made it feel like the skin was being removed.

When this was over—and if she survived—she was going to go to the Arkon's library, endure his annoyance *and* his condescension and make him tell her everything he knew about the Chosen. She'd study it without his advice, but most of his prized collection wasn't conveniently written in either Barrani or Elantran. She was tired of her own ignorance. She had stumbled through crises trusting luck and instinct; she had taken the only gift the words had provided—the healing—and used that power without ambivalence about its source.

But she needed to know what the words did. She needed to know why some magic made her want to cut her own limbs off just to avoid the pain, and others—that were just as obvious, just as visible—did not. Maybe the Arkon wouldn't have answers. But there were clues that might lead to answers in his collection, and she could handle the detective work now.

Even if the marks were somehow a dark conspiracy, even if their existence had caused the deaths of those children over half her lifetime ago, she hadn't murdered them and their murderers hadn't managed to turn Kaylin into a monster. Being ignorant wouldn't help her avoid that eventual fate if that's what was in the cards. Knowledge would.

She exhaled and inhaled in short, sharp breaths, riding the pain, waiting for it to subside; she assumed that the pain was caused by the remnants of what now lay across the ground.

Mandoran barked a command in a language that wasn't quite Barrani. Kaylin could hear it, but couldn't quite make sense of it in the small gaps between waves of pain. She meant to tell him as much, but Hope bit her ear. Hard. She barely felt it over the rest of the pain.

She did, however, feel Spike, because if Hope had to settle for biting her ear—which, given his wing position, must have been almost impossible—Spike didn't. She'd named him— badly, according to almost everyone—because he was a round ball composed primarily of spikes. They were clearly extendable. His attempt to get her attention, unlike Hope's, worked. She only hoped that there was something left of her hand, because her instinctive attempt to dislodge him utterly failed.

"Cut it out!" she shouted. "You're going to upset Helen!"

"*That's* what you're worried about?" Terrano was beside her. She glanced at him and froze. Spike's spikes had traveled through her hand—but all of the pain she experienced was now concentrated in that hand. Her hearing returned, as did Mandoran's voice, but it was Terrano who caught and held her attention.

If it weren't for his voice, she wouldn't have recognized him. All of his body was somehow translucent, and it had spread upward, thinning as if it were traveling toward the sky in a rush. He had arms, but his legs seemed fused into a pillar, and the light he shed implied fire—if fire were the color of the green.

"What are you doing?" Kaylin demanded.

Mandoran, however, had moved to stand beside this iteration of Terrano. He reached out with a hand that looked very much like a normal Barrani hand, and Terrano grasped it, flickers of something that looked like green fire forming fingers.

Spike said, *He is containing a threat.*

What threat?

Spike's answer was a word she didn't know. It set her teeth on edge almost instantly, there was so much high-pitched buzzing in it.

I didn't understand a word of that—if it was more than one word.

He tried again. The third time, he said, *Shadow.*

Teela did not sheathe her sword. Nor did she attempt to take a step outside of the circle that enclosed her. Tain stepped back. Kaylin was fairly certain he couldn't see what she now saw—but the two Hawks had been partners for Kaylin's entire tenure in the Hawks, and in a time of crisis, they were practically one person, but with the competence of three.

Annarion moved—but only to step onto the drive, readjusting his position because Mandoran was now with Terrano.

"Teela!" Terrano shouted.

Teela didn't move. She didn't sheathe her sword. Bressarian was speaking. Kaylin inhaled and began to walk up the drive. She paused beside Tain. Tain's eyes were midnight blue. He didn't look in her direction. He did, however, send a few words her way. "Go back inside the house."

Teela didn't move, either. She didn't seem willing to take her eyes off Bressarian. Bressarian wasn't the problem.

"Where," she asked Tain, "did his two friends go?"

Bressarian's gaze shifted from Teela as Kaylin spoke. His eyes narrowed.

Kaylin said, "This is my home. Why are you here?"

"I have been sent here by the Lady," he replied. He spoke stiff High Barrani. Everything about him matched the language.

"To what end?" she replied, switching to Barrani.

"I am to deliver clothing, among other things."

"The clothing is acceptable. Your two companions are not."

"What companions?" There was no tremor in his voice.

"The ones who accompanied you in the carriage. They stepped out when you did."

"I assure you—"

"Do not waste breath. You might need it."

His brows rose, outrage at her insolence changing the shape of his face. "Do you think to threaten *me*?"

"No. If your friends are under your command, I suggest you call them back." She turned to her familiar. "If, that is, you value them at all." The familiar stretched his wings, straightening the lines of his already perfect posture. He then pushed his slight weight off Kaylin's shoulder.

"The ground," she told him. "Teela, don't move." This last, in Elantran.

Teela said nothing in response. Hope squawked. He didn't slap Kaylin's face with his wing or clip her cheek with his tail; he treated her as if she were his master, or rather, as if she were a master that commanded respect and obedience. She wondered how she'd pay for it later.

"Mandoran?" She did not want to use Terrano's name in front of Bressarian.

I've isolated one of them, Terrano replied, understanding who she was really trying to speak with. His voice was a crackle of energy that suited his appearance. She had no idea if Bressarian could see him, but Bressarian wasn't her main concern. Helen was. Kaylin had been watching the front gates for all but a few minutes, but she hadn't seen the two quasi-invisible Barrani disappear. She had no idea where they had gone, or how, but she had a good idea of where they were trying to go.

Hope floated toward the ground, hovering about the circle of shadow in which Teela stood. Like liquid, it had begun to spread, seeping across—and probably into—the ground. This ground, however, was not like the ground beyond the gates; it was all part of Helen. Her skin.

Could you maybe hurry? Terrano added. *It's going to be hard to separate the invaders from Helen in a few minutes.*

She couldn't even see them, but felt no need to share that with Bressarian. Instead, she watched as the familiar inhaled, a tiny Dragon in miniature. The inside of his mouth and his eyes were solid red; the rest of his body remained transparent. Bressarian could see him, but his eyes were dark enough that they didn't change color.

The familiar exhaled a stream of silver cloud that resembled— at a distance—steam. Kaylin was not at enough of a distance; she could see the flickering hints of opalescent color in the jet of expelled breath. The stream made contact with the edge of that messy, slowly spreading circle.

Something or someone screamed. The tenor implied pain. And rage.

Kaylin looked up at Bressarian; his eyes were midnight

blue, his expression rigid. He said nothing, but the hands at his sides had become fists. Where breath met circle, the circle itself seemed to change; it became a silver that caught light at odd angles as it froze. Maybe solidified was a better description.

Spike whirred to life in Kaylin's hand.

Terrano began to move. He was at Kaylin's back. She didn't have eyes in the back of her head, but she was aware of his shift in position, aware of the way the air currents seemed to warp to accommodate him. Mandoran cursed. In Leontine.

"Teela."

Teela drove her sword into the ground, and the frozen circle shattered. This time, however, no shards remained. They were absorbed almost instantly by air and light. The familiar came back to Kaylin's shoulder, but landed with his eyes facing backward, as if he were now watching Terrano.

Squawk.

Bressarian said nothing; he did not move at all. Even his hair seemed immune to the breeze.

The path around Teela's feet was once again immaculate. She sheathed her sword as Bressarian stood frozen. "Lord Kaylin?"

Kaylin didn't even flinch. "An'Teela," she replied. "The grounds are now safe. I assume," she added, "that the reason Lord Bressarian was denied entry has now been resolved. You will," she added, turning to that lord, "now be safe. We would not impede any mission of import to the Lady." She bowed. It was the best way to hide the grimace that even having to speak the High Barrani words had caused.

And then, because she was Kaylin, she added, "There's an unfortunate stain on the side of your carriage just beneath the crest. If you'd like, we can have it removed while you wait."

To her astonishment, Bressarian bowed. "Lord Kaylin,"

he said. "I would consider myself in your debt should you be so gracious."

It was *so* not the answer she'd expected.

"We have the intruder," Helen said when Kaylin reentered her home.

"Both of them?"

"No. Only the one that survived. Mandoran and Terrano are more flexible in their modes of attack and containment than your familiar."

Terrano was glimmering and his eyes were the color of green fire. He was otherwise once again the Terrano she knew.

"You look terrible," she told him.

"Why, thank you. Do you *really* think it's a good idea to let that bastard in?"

"Helen thought it would be safe now."

"Which isn't an answer. If I wanted to know what Helen thought, I'd ask her."

"He does have the clothing the Consort offered the cohort. If she hadn't offered, we'd have to have someone go in person. I trust you understand why the latter is a terrible idea."

"I do now."

"And he's not lying. He came to deliver the clothing the Consort deemed necessary and suitable. Given the amount of cloth and the style of dress, I'm assuming that every servant in the High Halls capable of sewing has been doing nothing else since her visit."

"And the dirt on the carriage comment?"

"I was trying to be passive-aggressive. I didn't expect him to agree to have the carriage cleaned—technically it's not even his, given the crest. It's Mellarionne's."

"Sedarias is not happy," Helen said, interrupting the conversation. "She would like to speak with Bressarian in person. Do you consider this safe?"

It took Kaylin a moment to realize Helen was talking to *her.* Which was confusing since Helen made most of the safety decisions when it came to strange magic and unnatural forms of aggression. "Yes." This wasn't strictly true, but *safe* had many meanings, and Sedarias was already angry enough for an entire squadron. Or ten.

"Sedarias is coming," Helen informed them. "Bellusdeo, however, has elected to remain in the training room for the time being. The rest of the cohort has chosen to stay with her."

Lord Bressarian was escorted to the parlor, which had changed in shape, size and contents to better suit a Barrani Lord of the High Court. Kaylin wasn't certain she approved. It wasn't his home; it was hers. But she understood the need to impress; she just resented it.

Teela and Tain accompanied him; Annarion and Mandoran slipped away to join the rest of the cohort. Terrano was quiet and seemed, to Kaylin, almost exhausted. He headed toward the stairs that led to the room he was now sharing with Teela, but Mandoran grabbed him by the arm and dragged him in the direction of the rest of the group.

Severn retreated, as well, but in a different direction. He didn't call it a retreat, either. "There's something I need to check." She knew that tone of voice. It was like a friendly wall. She wasn't surprised when he headed out of the house, and she didn't ask him where he was going, because there was no point. He wouldn't answer.

"Your carriage," Helen was saying as Kaylin entered the room, familiar on her shoulder and Spike in her hand, "has been cleaned."

"You have my gratitude," Bressarian replied, glancing at Kaylin. His gaze moved as Sedarias entered the room. Allaron was the only member of the cohort to accompany her, but his unusual size made his presence significant. His position—at a respectful distance behind Sedarias—implied that he was there to serve. And protect. Definitely protect.

Although Helen's clothing wasn't useful if one wanted to walk past the property's boundaries and not end up butt naked, it was nonetheless convenient in other ways. Sedarias looked every inch a powerful Barrani lord. Her presence implied that the Test of Name would be an irrelevant formality. Kaylin understood why the current leader of Mellarionne considered her to be such a threat.

To Kaylin's surprise, Bressarian stood and tendered Sedarias a graceful, perfect bow. He rose before she granted him permission to rise, which was the only thing that saved the gesture from being obsequious. Kaylin didn't understand. She thought she would never understand the Barrani.

Interesting.

My lack of understanding or his bow?

Ynpharion didn't answer.

"Lord Bressarian," Sedarias said when he rose. She hadn't bowed, and her posture made clear she wouldn't. Her eyes were blue, but weren't any darker than his.

"Sedarias. So. It is true. You are here."

"I have not had the pleasure of making your acquaintance. You serve my brother?"

"I serve my father," he replied. "And my father serves the An'Mellarionne."

Very interesting.

Care to explain?

No. Don't distract me.

"Your father is Lord Lorimar, son of Lord Samariel. Lord

Samariel was An'Veranelle when I was selected to go to the green; he did not survive the final war."

He nodded.

"There are not many lines preserved through direct descent. Lord Lorimar is to be respected for holding his line. You are heir?"

"No. My sister is heir. I am the son of the second wife." Which was why, Kaylin thought, he'd been sent on what amounted to a delivery errand.

Any errand undertaken at the request of the Lady, came Ynpharion's acid observation, *elevates those who undertake it.*

"We are grateful for the largesse of the Consort," Sedarias continued. "But we are perhaps less grateful—and far more concerned—for the arrival of your other passengers."

His smile was slight, but present. "I do not imagine that gratitude was the intent." His smile deepened. "But you have my gratitude, for what little that might be worth to you, given my current position."

Sedarias's eyes were blue. Kaylin would have expected their color to shift, but had given up on making bets with herself about Barrani reactions. "You brought them here."

"Yes. I was chosen to deliver both the gift and a...warning."

"The gift has been delivered. Deliver the warning."

She has been spending far *too much time with mortals,* Ynpharion said.

Bressarian, however, merely inclined his head. "The warning," he said, looking almost apologetic, although his eyes were also blue, "was not mine to deliver. If anything remains of the two who accompanied me, you will have to hear it from them."

"We will. But I would have your assessment, as well. It is why you have remained, is it not?"

"No." He lifted his glass by its delicate stem. "I remained

because, here, I may speak frankly and without unwanted witnesses." He glanced, once, at Kaylin.

"Lord Kaylin is master of this dwelling," Sedarias said, choosing not to ignore that glance. "Nothing spoken within her home will be hidden from her unless she so chooses." Her tone made clear that Kaylin did not so choose. Kaylin was certain that if she did, Sedarias would have words with her later, and not the cheerful kind.

"There are rumors about Lord Kaylin that are even now circulating within the High Court. Is it true that she brought you from the West March?"

Sedarias didn't answer.

"Very well. Coravante An'Mellarionne was tasked with the delivery of the Consort's gift. He passed that task to my father, who passed it to me, speaking as he did of the singular honor invested in us by your brother and the Consort. Your brother is much in my father's company, and my father, much in his councils. The carriage," he continued, "was a gift from your brother."

Sedarias's eyes were a midnight color. Allaron took a step toward her, and then a much less graceful step back, as if he'd been slapped.

"My sister, Fianora, should have been tasked with this first contact," Bressarian continued, and here, a note of ice had crept into the smoothness of his tone. "But she has been missing these three days. She left—at my father's command—to speak with Coravante. She has not returned. The two who traveled with me were two of the four who formed her small cadre of guards; my father considers your brother a trusted ally."

"And you do not?"

"I believe that trust and ally are two concepts that cannot and should not be wed. Your brother has power, Sedarias.

Power and will. And my father has grown in power in the past few years; one could consider his rise meteoric."

"You do not."

"Ah, forgive me, I do. But my father is not a young man; nor am I. I once understood both his strengths and his limitations. The former have inarguably increased."

"And the latter?"

"I no longer feel he has limitations."

"I see. And you?"

"I have not been asked to keep company with An'Mellarionne. Nor have I volunteered to do so; I have been traveling of late, and I am oft absent from Court. My duties to our properties outside of the city have required time and finesse."

Kaylin wondered if that finesse was martial.

Of course it is.

"Would some of those properties be located near the West March?" Kaylin asked. Sedarias did not make the attempt.

"Yes, Lord Kaylin. I was not, however, present in the West March when Sedarias and her companions took their leave of it."

"Her sister was."

"An interesting coincidence, I am sure. But her sister has also become adept, and her sister's position within the Arcanum has been much noted, of late." He was silent for another long beat, and then he set his glass down, the liquid in it undiminished. "Much has been said of you, and much speculated." He spoke, now, to Sedarias as if she were the only other person in the room. "But much is unknown. It is assumed that your power is equal to, or greater than, the power your brother has achieved.

"Your sister has failed to make a report."

"She is incapable of making a report," Sedarias replied with a shrug. "But waiting teaches patience, or so I was taught as a child." Her smile was hard, harsh. "Were you sent to test my capabilities?"

"I was sent to deliver the Consort's gift. I have neither the desire nor the ability to test you; nor do I have the arrogance required. Word will have reached Coravante."

"The carriage?" Kaylin asked.

"Indeed. But that word is limited, and if your domicile has truly cleansed it of enchantment, he will know only that he is once again blind. He will not hear any conversation we have, and what he hears of it he cannot sift for truth—or lies."

"You do not wish to implicate your father."

"I do not wish to lose him, no. But I have been unable to reach my sister, and she has been groomed to be An'Veranelle in future. My father is deeply involved in Mellarionne's concerns."

"You feel too deeply."

"It has never been wise, or safe, to put the interests of one's line into a single alliance. My father is not the only Lord of the High Court to choose to ally themselves with Mellarionne, but such an alliance has been—until very recently—a subtle thing. Subtlety, however, has been forsaken. I do not know the full measure of the threat you pose, but Coravante has survived two wars and all attempts to unseat him; he is one of the oldest surviving members of the High Court. He does not consider the High Lord or the Lady to be a significant threat or danger.

"It is you he fears."

"What is it you hope for, Lord Bressarian?"

"I wish to know what has happened to Lord Fianora."

"Only that?"

"I will safeguard and steward my line. But we were never meant to flirt with the edges of the Shadows; I believe there is a reason that the Towers stand where they stand."

"You think your father is working with the Shadows?" Kaylin demanded.

"I did not say that," was his smooth—and slightly irritated—reply. "That would be an act of treason, and we are not a treasonous line."

Sedarias turned the force of her glare on Kaylin. She didn't tell Kaylin to shut up, but the words were suddenly superfluous. Kaylin shut up.

"Lord Coravante has not answered your queries."

"He has. Fianora is indisposed, and he has offered her the solace and care of his personal quarters while she recuperates."

"She has not accepted visitors."

"Not kin, no. I wish her returned, if she is what she was."

"And if she is not?"

He did not answer, not directly. "It is in the fief of Candallar that Coravante's messengers and lieges meet if they wish distance from the eyes of the Court."

Sedarias nodded, as if unsurprised. Which she was.

"I do not know what you are," he said. "I do not know what you learned or did not learn; I do not know what the *regalia* fashioned of you. I know the history, but that history is barely better than story or legend. I would give it no credence were it not for the unusually visceral reaction of your brother.

"It is his hand that moves the High Court now. It was at his command that the war band approached the Imperial Palace. If the High Lord favors you, it will not save you."

"We have very seldom relied on others for salvation," Sedarias replied.

"You are to take the Test of Name."

She nodded.

"Pass it, become Lord Sedarias, and in return for the safety of my line, I will pledge my service to you."

Lord Lorimar, Ynpharion said, *is the man who carried Spike out of* Ravellon. *He is Lord Bressarian's father, An'Veranelle.*

CHAPTER 16

"I always wanted a brother," Kaylin told Helen on the morning of the cohort's introduction to the High Halls. The Consort had sent clothing for each of the cohort, save only Teela, and although there had been no measurements taken, all of the clothing *fit*. Which should have been impossible.

Sadly, the cohort were not the only people to be sent suitable clothing. The Consort had earmarked a dress for Kaylin, as well. It was that dress that she now grumbled her way into.

"Or a sister," she added as cloth cleared her face and she tried to settle into the shape of the dress, which—with her luck—she'd put on backward or inside out.

"You've changed your mind?" Helen's glance was almost critical as she began to adjust the dress.

"Annarion and Nightshade can barely sit in the same room without coming to blows, and Annarion is in pain for days afterward. But Sedarias…" She grimaced.

"Lift your arms, dear. The fabric is bunching up because you're folding them so tightly and I can't quite make adjustments unless you relax."

"Her sister tried to kill her. Her brother sent assassins. I'm beginning to think that my daydreams of siblings are just that—daydreams."

"Not all brothers or sisters are murderous in their fearful ambition," Helen replied.

"No. Nightshade wouldn't kill Annarion. He'd never even try. I don't think there's anything or anyone he values more."

"But?"

"But it doesn't stop him from causing pain. Or from feeling pain." She looked at herself in the mirror that Helen had thoughtfully brought into her room; it was much, much larger than any mirror Kaylin had owned, or did own. "And I think I thought…"

"That love doesn't cause pain?"

"Something like that."

"It doesn't have to cause pain," Helen said. "I think the skirt may be a little long if you insist on wearing those shoes."

"They're practical, they don't hurt my feet and, given the number of people who've already tried to kill the cohort, I may have to pick up these skirts and run. I'm not wearing the other shoes." She exhaled. "This is Barrani clothing. The skirts are wide enough to run in, and they don't seem to cause their wearer to trip. If they didn't scream Barrani, and if I were rich, I'd probably never wear any other dress."

"I believe the Consort intended you to wear the shoes. Are you certain she will take no offense if you leave them behind?"

Kaylin bit back words that would have vehemently declared how little she cared, because if there was vehemence, they probably weren't accurate.

"It is possible that the Consort will be judged by the cohort's appearance," Helen added, her preference quite clear.

"Fine. But I'm *already* a Lord of the Court, and that means I'm not her problem. If it were up to me, I wouldn't wear the dress at all, and if you're going to make the shoes the all or nothing sticking point, I'm not wearing the dress. Look, at the moment, I'm concentrating on not punching Sedarias's brother in the face."

"You are not."

"I am. But what I'm really wondering is what kind of a family Sedarias grew up in. Because she didn't seem at all surprised to see her sister, and she had no problems—at all— killing her. She also said it wasn't the first time her sister had tried to end her life. I just…" Kaylin exhaled. "I think it's a bloody miracle that she's part of the cohort at all."

"I think," Helen said gently, "that the giving of True Names was the only way that she could bring herself to trust anyone. And, Kaylin?"

"What?"

"If you want to see evidence of happy Barrani families, perhaps the last place you should look is the High Court."

"What are you wearing on your feet?" Sedarias demanded as Kaylin joined the cohort in the foyer. "Were you not sent appropriate footwear?"

Everyone except Teela and Terrano were present and waiting. Severn had somehow been overlooked in the mass gifting of formal dress, and Kaylin tried hard not to resent this. It implied that the Consort considered Severn's ability to dress himself a nonissue.

"I already own appropriate footwear. I'm wearing it. I don't know about the rest of you, but I can't run on my toes, which is practically all of my foot that'll be in contact with floor if I wear the things she sent. Is Allaron going to wear that sword?"

"I think the sword far more appropriate than those boots."

"Did he even have that sword?"

"Swords are, for certain occasions, considered part of formal clothing."

"So...accessories?"

Mandoran snorted. He wasn't, Kaylin noted, wearing a similar sword.

"Please do not strangle her." Teela's voice drifted down from the height of the stairs above. "I've managed not to strangle her—often at great cost—and I would hate for those years of monumental self-control to be wasted." Teela wore green.

The rest of the cohort, however, did not. Nor did Kaylin.

Terrano wore blue, a shade of night that suited the color of his eyes. Teela had a grip on his arm that looked natural, except for the whitening of the knuckles.

"You don't want to go?" Kaylin asked him.

"He doesn't want to wait," Teela replied in a tone that would have made her younger self shrivel. "He thought he'd go ahead and scout the location. I believe those were his exact words."

Sedarias clearly agreed with Teela's shriveling annoyance, because she turned the same glare on Terrano.

Mandoran, on the other hand, grinned and offered Terrano a sympathetic and very theatrical shrug. "Someone should," he said.

"Someone we can actually talk to."

"You mean order around," Terrano murmured.

"Of course she does. She's Sedarias."

It was hard for Sedarias to split a glare between Mandoran and Terrano, given their positions—one by the door, one on the stairs—but she did try.

Several carriages had been sent for the cohort, all bearing the heraldry of the Consort. Helen let them in through the gates and Kaylin was certain by the time they reached the front door, her house knew the location of every speck of dust—not that there seemed to be any—inside and outside of their very elegant cabins. If there was a trap of any kind waiting within, Helen couldn't find it. Sedarias, however, was not concerned. Nor was Teela. Severn trusted Helen's assessment, but wanted that assessment before the cohort embarked.

When they were at last loaded into their various conveyances, Teela was in the carriage with Tain, Severn and Kaylin. Tain, unlike Teela, wore the garb the Consort had sent, because she had included Tain in the number of people unlikely to be well dressed enough.

Enough, Kaylin thought, to face a monster. Because court dress was so *good* for that.

"You are to let either Sedarias or me do the talking," Teela said quietly. "If a question is directed toward you by anyone other than the High Lord or the Consort, *please* allow us to field it. You will be given some leeway because you are mortal, but at this point, please assume that every single person who approaches you is looking for openings."

"To kill me?"

"Not you precisely; you would be collateral damage. But if they could find a way to use you in your presumed ignorance—don't make that face, I'm not the one doing the presuming—they would do it in a heartbeat. If they could use you to embarrass or humiliate the cohort, they would do it. I think it likely that any approach will have that goal in mind. Under other circumstances, it wouldn't matter."

Tain coughed.

"It's true. Kaylin has survived being almost entirely herself at Court. Here, however, she will not be the target. What she does will affect the rest of us. How she does it. Where."

Kaylin swallowed the words she'd been trying not to say

and, with them, most of her annoyance at the perceived condescension. She was used to being judged. She was bullish in her determination to be judged for the person she was. But reflecting poorly on the cohort at this particular time? She could manage to stay silent. She could let Teela and Sedarias carry the heavy weight. If she thought that she was doing it *for* the cohort, she'd manage.

Kaylin was not surprised to see the Consort at the height of the grand, wide stairs that led into the High Halls. Nor was she surprised to see Ynpharion at her side. The Consort had an escort of four guards, which was—according to Teela—considered minimal. Two was a gesture of almost unheard of trust. And she'd brought only two on her visit to Kaylin's home.

Of course, she'd brought two for very specific reasons, but outsiders didn't know those reasons; they saw the two guards, knew that the Consort had entered Kaylin's home and understood that the Consort's trust in Kaylin—and, by extension, her guests—was high. Probably unreasonably high, given all available facts.

Ynpharion was predictably annoyed by her thoughts, which conversely brightened her mood. Not his, of course, but that wasn't her job.

It is certainly not *mine.* His annoyance took the edge off what might, in another less touchy person, be called fear.

Sedarias reached the height of the stairs, and there, she performed the most obsequious bow Kaylin had ever seen her produce. It was graceful, elegant and bold in the way that total obeisance could be when offered by the powerful.

She is not powerful, Ynpharion snapped. *She offers the Consort her due.* But he, too, found it almost discomfiting.

The Consort bid her rise when it became clear that she

would not rise without permission—or command. Sedarias then moved to the side, where Ynpharion waited.

One by one the rest of the cohort approached the Consort— and the High Halls behind her—and offered the same gesture of absolute respect that Sedarias had offered. Only Terrano fidgeted before he approached the Consort, and his bow, while technically just as respectful, was nowhere near as perfect in form. He was too nervous.

Teela did not offer the same bow, although she did bend; nor did she wait to be told to rise.

"I see you bear *Kariannos*," the Consort said.

"A gesture of respect, Lady, no more," Teela replied. So, Kaylin thought. Teela's sword, like Nightshade's, had a name.

"For their return?"

"For their return." Teela's eyes were blue. The Consort's, however, were their usual green, and that green was—as it almost always was—in sharp contrast to the shade of the eyes of every other Barrani present.

"The High Lord," the Consort then said, "wishes to greet you all, and welcome you back to the lands of your birth. Please, join us."

The cavernous halls were almost empty; the guards, almost superfluous. The cohort, however, moved more slowly as they walked. They didn't appear to be gawking, but they found the halls, or perhaps what the halls represented, almost awe-inspiring.

Kaylin understood; the architecture was intimidating. The ceilings were so high above the ground they seemed designed to make anyone walking beneath them feel small and insignificant, and if that didn't work, the alcoves with their towering statues or intricate fountains were there for emphasis. Kaylin had seen it all before, and architecture wasn't her first concern.

Kaylin's familiar was seated in a rigid posture on her left shoulder, eyes wide and unblinking, wings folded. Kaylin glanced at him once and then let him fade into the background. Spike, however, was whirring. She hoped that this was audible only to her, but that hope was dashed when the Consort paused.

"Spike," Kaylin hissed.

The whirring stopped. When Kaylin lifted her hand, there was nothing in it, which was disconcerting, because she could *feel* the underside of Spike in her palm.

I am here, he told her. *But I am attempting to be unobtrusive.*

Kaylin wasn't certain that would be any better, but Hope seemed to draw the attention of the very few people they passed as they traversed the halls. And the Consort knew about Spike, and knew he would accompany Kaylin, so it wasn't as if she was trying to sneak him in.

More subtlety would be highly appreciated by all concerned, Ynpharion said.

If she wanted subtle, she'd've found someone else, Kaylin snapped back. She was nervous. She hated to be judged—but the fear that her actions would affect the future of the cohort was worse, especially if the cohort themselves behaved flawlessly.

Your actions always affect those around you, Ynpharion said, being his usual helpful self.

She let loose an internal volley of Leontine, to his amusement.

Kaylin quickly discovered the reason the outer halls had been so empty: the entirety of the Court seemed to have gathered in the small forest nestled within the forbidding structure. The perfect, interlocking stones of the narrow forest path were clear, but as the cohort followed the Consort's lead, the people standing nearest the path began to grow in number. Even before the shelter of trees had been cleared, it had become almost dangerously crowded, and the Consort's four guards now seemed entirely inadequate.

They are inadequate, Ynpharion informed her. *But her presence is not. This close to the High Seat, none will attack her guests unless they intend to assassinate the High Lord simultaneously. If that is their intent, this is not the place at which to launch such an attack; it is the very seat of the High Lord's power.*

Regardless, he was nervous and alert. So were the other three.

Hope squawked, but it was a quiet, almost chirpy sound. Kaylin tried to relax, but abandoned that effort when her familiar lifted his wing. Mindful of what little dignity she had, he didn't smack her face with it, but that was a tiny, tiny comfort, not unlike putting up an umbrella beneath an oncoming tidal wave.

Room was made for the approaching cohort, although it didn't involve the usual shoving for space that occurred in less upscale crowds. Space was required, and space appeared with no accompanying fuss. From where Kaylin now stood, she could see the High Seat; it was occupied by the High Lord. The Consort's throne was empty, but it became clear that that's where she intended to go, once the cohort had been safely delivered.

Teela took the rear; Tain separated himself from his partner and joined the cohort. It wasn't a surprise that Teela's eyes were now midnight blue; although the two Barrani Hawks had argued—at significantly less volume than Annarion and his brother—it was clear that neither had budged from their initial positions. Tain intended to take the Test of Name. Teela couldn't stop him.

The Consort moved to take her seat on the empty throne at the High Lord's side.

The High Lord did not rise. Once the Consort was seated, the cohort executed a bow that encompassed both thrones. The gestures were astonishing in their perfect unison. Astonishing, Kaylin thought, even to the High Lord; the Consort, however, was not surprised. Kaylin bowed, as well.

Severn reminded her to hold that bow until the High Lord bid them rise. She didn't even count the seconds; she was too worried. Hope's wing was usually a sign that something was wrong—but she'd seen nothing wrong, unless the crowd counted. Since she was a Hawk, not a Sword, she didn't have the visceral reaction to crowds that the Swords did.

"Rise and be welcome," the High Lord said.

Kaylin rose. For once, her fear for the people in front of her eclipsed her own sense of inadequacy. Years of practice doing nothing but bowing might give her the peculiar power and understated strength of Barrani gestures—but she doubted it. One couldn't make a career in bowing and scraping, and if one couldn't, it didn't pay. Money was a necessity.

She then examined the gathering through Hope's lifted wing.

Ynpharion thought her rude and ungainly; he criticized her timing and her lack of subtlety. He did not, however, expect her to stop. Nor, she thought, did he want her to.

What do you know that we haven't been told?

Many things. But about this? Nothing. Had I, I would share it; your success—and the success of your friends—is of vital importance to the Lady. She has considered this since she first heard of your impromptu arrival in the West March—but it has long haunted both her and the High Lord, as you must suspect.

I think it would kill me, to rule here.

It would kill you, he said, far more sharply, *to rule anywhere.*

I meant the voices—I meant hearing the pleas and the screams of the trapped.

Ah. Yes, I imagine you would find that difficult, as well. Ynpharion was not an easy person to like, and Kaylin was almost certain she would never achieve it. He did not consider affection or friendship necessary or desirable, and the thought annoyed him intensely, because it was so trivial. As if affection of any kind were poison.

There was nothing in this gathered crowd that looked remotely out of place to Kaylin's eyes, even given the familiar's wing. She couldn't see the entirety of the gathered crowd, however, and she was certain that Hope wanted her to see *something.*

She was right. That something, however, did not come immediately.

Sedarias now separated herself from the cohort and approached the thrones without escort. The bow she offered the High Lord was an echo of, a reinforcement of, the respect she had offered the Consort before she had entered the High Halls. She held this bow, as she had held the first, until she was given leave to rise. He greeted her by name—a name unadorned by the title that seemed so important to the Barrani. She was Sedarias of Mellarionne.

Kaylin flinched inwardly at the mention of her family. Sedarias did not.

The rest of the cohort then approached, one by one, as Sedarias had done.

The High Lord spoke words of welcome and even seemed to mean all of them, but the Barrani were good at that. Kaylin wasn't surprised to see Lord Evarrim standing to the side of the High Lord's throne, and it occurred to her that Evarrim wasn't *good* at lying or hiding his reactions. The thought that he might be the Barrani equivalent of Kaylin set her teeth on edge.

On Evarrim's brow, she could see the tiara of the Arcanum; a large ruby, lit from an unseen source of light, nestled within the tiara's small peak. He wore robes of blue and green, the green a match for the color Teela always chose to wear when she came to Court. He was not young by the standards of the Barrani; she wondered if he had been alive when the cohort was sent to the green.

His eyes—very blue—narrowed.

So did the eyes of her familiar, and Spike was now a frantic vibration that set her whole left arm trembling. By some unspoken agreement, the Barrani of the High Court—and their various guards—kept their distance while the entirety of the cohort, and Tain, offered their respects to the High Lord and his Consort.

But when Tain, who waited at the end of the line, had been released by the High Lord's almost silent nod, the crowd began to move; spaces that had not existed when the Court bore witness were made now, as various people sought to approach the cohort. Many of them were no doubt curious, but even in that jostling, there was the echo of rigid hierarchy.

This, Kaylin thought, was what Sedarias had expected. She wasn't surprised when the first person to reach her said, "Welcome home, sister."

An'Mellarionne offered her a perfect bow that robbed his scant greeting of sincerity; it was a bow extended by people of power *to* people of power. It was not a familial gesture.

No, it is not, Ynpharion said, a tinge of grudging surprise coloring his words.

The head of Mellarionne wore the circlet Kaylin now associated with Arcanists; like Evarrim's, his housed a ruby. It was smaller than the gemstone in Evarrim's tiara, but brighter; it almost seemed to burn.

"Coravante." Sedarias chose to greet him entirely informally. "It has been long since I set foot in our ancestral home."

"And long, indeed, since Alsanis has opened his doors to visitors," her brother replied. He turned to his attendant. Bressarian. "You have been much missed." Had his eyes not been a deep blue, Kaylin would have believed him; the words themselves were warm, almost friendly.

A lie is not successful if the person to whom you tell it has no desire to hear the words.

"And you," Sedarias said, her voice softer than Kaylin had ever heard it. "I would very much like to visit our home."

That lie, for instance, is poor. It is not what Coravante desires to hear.

She can't say anything he wants to hear, and she knows it. She's not saying it for his sake.

You are learning. It said something about Kaylin that Ynpharion's approval actually meant anything to her.

Nothing good.

You can say that again. Now shut up and let me concentrate.

Sedarias seemed to radiate youthful delight as she turned to the cohort and introduced them, one at a time, to her brother. It was interesting to watch their reactions. Annarion was stiff and formal. Serralyn was shy, almost demure. Mandoran was crisply formal, but seemed happy with the introduction. Terrano was almost silent. No, Kaylin thought, that was wrong.

She'd assumed that his near-silence was due to the awkwardness of the situation, but as she watched, her eyes narrowing, she realized she was wrong. Entirely, completely and dangerously wrong. She hadn't been introduced to the High Lord or the Consort; neither had Teela or Severn. But she'd watched the entire meet and greet as if it were the only significant activity in the room.

Stupid, stupid, *stupid.*

Coravante was *old*. He'd held his seat for a long damn time. He understood subtlety so completely he probably didn't have any other way of interacting. Nothing about his face, nothing about his clothing, nothing about his tiara, implied Shadow, or Shadow's taint. But it was a carriage sporting his crest, and containing his people, that had come to Helen and attempted to sneak right through her defenses.

And she could see now, staring not at Coravante, who demanded focus and attention, but at his feet, that Shadow was present. A tendril, something so fine it was probably the width of three strands of Kaylin's hair put side by side, seemed to come from the point of his elegant boots. It traveled a direct line to Terrano's feet.

She poked the familiar on her shoulder; he was both rigid and utterly silent.

Your marks, Ynpharion said, *are beginning to glow.*

She didn't have time to curse, or she would have given in to the Leontine that was building behind her clenched teeth. Whatever Coravante had done, or was doing, Terrano was struggling to contain it.

She moved quickly—far more quickly than the Barrani milling around the cohort. Someone stepped in her way. She might technically be a Lord of the High Court, but she was mortal and clearly needed to be reminded of her place. Sadly for the Barrani lord—whoever he or she was—she knew the place she needed to be, and it wasn't groveling or waiting for implied permission to proceed.

In a fair fight, she had no chance. In any fight, her odds were slim. But she wasn't trying to kill them; she was trying to get them out of her way Right Now. And that, when they'd turned their backs with studied disinterest and barely veiled contempt, she *could* do.

Ynpharion didn't even try to stop her.

Terrano's back faced her; she reached for his left shoulder with her left hand, forgetting, for just a second, that Spike was in it. But Spike had tripped no alarms; no one in the Court had noticed his presence at all. Most of them noticed the familiar, and those that somehow hadn't certainly noticed him now. He pushed himself off her shoulder, spreading his wings and squawking up a storm.

She lost the wing cover as he left her, but didn't need it now. Whatever her normal eyes could see was enough as her hand made contact with Terrano. Spike was their bridge.

And if it weren't for Spike, she'd have taken a step back. Or several. At a run.

Spike didn't give her the peculiar vision that Hope did, but she didn't need that vision now. Nor did he give her the abilities she instinctively put to use. She had seen something like this before—when the Shadows had wrapped themselves around Mandoran, holding him fast—but this was different. For one, it was worse. Much worse. Mandoran had some base resistance to the influence of the Shadow that Terrano did not have.

Kaylin could feel the burning thread of Shadow throughout the entirety of Terrano, as if every part of the thread's length had hooks. But they weren't part of his body yet, although she had no doubt that that was their intent. Or Coravante's intent. Terrano might end up leaving again. He might never return. He might cast away all of the trappings of his birth and his race—but that was *his* choice to make. Or not to make.

Not Coravante's.

Terrano!

Don't shout—I'll disincorporate. Pause. *What in the hells are you doing?*

You've got Shadow throughout you, and it's spreading.

I can get rid of it on my own.

Can you get rid of it without transforming?

The answer was no.

Is that what he's trying to make you do? Turn into something Shadow-like in front of the entire damn Court?

Probably.

You'll get the entire cohort declared outcaste in under two seconds.

Fine. Fine—but you're going to need to hurry.

No kidding. When he spoke, the Shadow seemed to shiver or shudder as Kaylin used the only useful power the marks of the Chosen had granted her: she tried to heal him. Healing mortals was simple—if exhausting. The body knew its correct shape, its correct form. She poured power into that instinctive knowledge, and the body took it, repairing the damage caused by injury, disease, childbirth gone wrong.

Terrano's body didn't have a correct shape. It had the *echo* of a correct shape, but pouring power into what were technically injuries didn't have the desired result. Of course not. Nothing about Terrano was simple. Nothing was ever going to be easy. Cutting out the wrong chunks—and there were clearly wrong chunks—probably wouldn't work, either. But catching those threads and removing them?

She'd done that before, for Mandoran. And in the wrong light—or the right light, hard to decide which—she could still see the effects of that disentangling on her hand: the threads of what had been a growing cocoon of Shadow had become a flat, harmless glove. She was used to having marks on her skin; the shadow threads had become a different type of mark, a different tattoo.

The marks on her arms were glowing, but remained flat. The glove on her hand, however, had also begun to respond.

She almost yanked her hand back, afraid now for Terrano in an entirely different way.

Spike wouldn't allow it.

If you break contact, you will lose him. You have offered him the hospitality and protection of your home. Will you break that oath now, at the first real challenge he faces?

I'm not at home. And I offered him Helen's protection and hospitality. Mine sucks.

Spike's reply was not verbal; it was a rush of images that overlapped and metamorphosed before she could fully grasp them—not that she was trying very hard. *Not now, Spike!* He fell silent, but silence wasn't withdrawal; he was still embedded in her hand and simultaneously embedded in Terrano's shoulder.

She wound the threads around her palm, or that's what she felt like she was doing; her hand, however, wasn't actually moving. Spike was frustrated. So was Kaylin. No matter how quickly she tried to spool this deadly thread, she gained no traction; there was never a point at which she could see an end to what must be gathered and extracted from Terrano. Nor was there an end to the damage it was causing him.

Kaylin grimaced and continued to pull, pausing only for a second. Her familiar roared. She turned automatically as he dived into the crowd and in front of Terrano, hissing and squawking like a miniature, translucent storm.

CHAPTER 17

For the first time since Kaylin had touched Terrano, the Lords of the Court scattered. She was aware of their movement, although her eyes were closed; she could hear their feet against the perfect stone. She could hear sharply drawn breath.

She forced her eyes open and saw Hope, hovering between Coravante and Terrano. His jaws opened on a jewel-red mouth as he inhaled. Coravante's eyes were midnight blue and round; he lifted both hands in a gesture that was fluid, fast and complicated. She could see the movement of his fingers in the open air, as if blurred and broken into component parts; she could see the faint trail of light that accompanied them, fingers tracing a pattern of runes at chest level.

Her familiar exhaled a stream of silver, sparkling smoke. It wasn't aimed at the spell that Kaylin could now see hanging in the air; it was aimed at the stone flooring. But she thought the faint trace of sigils that were left in the air looked very much like her familiar's breath. She felt no heat—Hope only looked like a miniature Dragon. He didn't breathe fire. But regardless, the stone his breath touched melted almost instantly, the center of the circular cone causing…splashes.

Coravante shouted. Lord Bressarian shouted. People who

hadn't identified or introduced themselves shouted—but they were farther away, and they didn't matter. The only voices that did matter remained utterly silent; the High Lord and the Consort did not join in the momentary panic.

Hope's breath transformed the stones, and had Kaylin been here as a Hawk, months of paperwork and a permanent lack of promotion would be in her immediate future. If she were lucky. She was here as a technical Lord of the Court and, for the first time, considered it a huge plus. While the Barrani could respond, they couldn't kill her because the laws of exemption didn't apply to a human.

She just hoped they remembered it as she saw the glint of steel.

And realized that it wasn't steel, because her eyes were closed. Light pierced her nonvision, as if she were staring at the sun; her ears began to ring, and voices and words overlapped and echoed.

Come on, Terrano, she thought as she pulled on the strands of Shadow. They did not resist her. She could suddenly see an end to what she was trying to extract; Hope had severed the threads. Or Hope's breath had. She wondered what she looked like, in the eyes of the gathered lords. Part of her didn't care—vehemently. But part of her knew that she should, because the cohort was, in part, hers.

Her hand burned as the last bit of Shadow was pulled free of its moorings within Terrano; it struggled and, in the end, whipped around to bite her wrist. And then, at last, it was still. She opened her eyes—really opened them, this time— and saw Terrano's back. Her palm was pressed flat against it. She realized only then that she had not touched exposed skin, which was the way her healing normally worked. Nothing about Terrano was normal. Even for a Barrani.

I'm good now, he said, the interior words spoken as if some-one had a death grip on his throat. Which he wasn't using.

You're not.

Thank you, Mother. He was angry. None of the trembling that affected him appeared to be due to fear.

Did he mean to kill you?

With that? *No. But to be free of its influence, I needed to move one step to the side—and I can't do that here. Not with all these witnesses.* Maybe, she thought, feeling a trace of his doubt, not at all. He surrendered with a tiny bit of grace. *It's not the same as what I taught some of them. It's different.*

They've had some time to improve.

Not a lot of time. Not for our people.

Maybe not—but it wasn't only Barrani you approached.

Of course it was. I wasn't involved with dragging humans into the mess. They were—they needed money.

But mortals were involved, she countered. *And mortals don't have a lot of time compared to the rest of you. What exactly was the Shadow trying to do?*

Nothing. Coravante was in control.

It wasn't an answer, and she didn't have time to press him. *Barrani don't like to be healed*, she said, slowly flexing her palm.

Yeah, well. There are worse alternatives.

Not to some of the Barrani.

And if I hated it, he continued, *I couldn't do anything about it, anyway; Sedarias would murder me. Slowly.* She felt a flash of his grin as she lifted her hand, and then nothing at all. She didn't own Terrano's name—and even if she once had, it wouldn't have done her any good. He didn't have it now.

Kaylin looked past Terrano to see her hovering familiar. "Hope," she said, holding out an arm. He rotated in place, but closed his mouth and, after a few seconds, condescended to return to his place on her shoulder.

* * *

All eyes were upon Kaylin as she straightened those shoulders, readjusted her posture and turned once again to face the thrones. She avoided looking at anyone but the High Lord and the Consort, but felt a little bit of Teela's glare hit the side of her face.

The Consort's eyes had more blue in them than they usually did, but that blue faded as she met Kaylin's gaze. A half smile touched her lips and she shook her head almost ruefully, nodding. Then she rose.

"Are your companions well?" she asked.

Breath was held; Kaylin was probably the first person present to exhale. "Yes. I apologize for what might be my overreaction. They're guests in my home, and not all of them are accustomed to a gathering such as this; I believe some find the honor done them almost overwhelming."

Sedarias's glare joined Teela's.

"It is to be expected, surely," the Consort said. "And for my part, I find it refreshing. If you and your companions would join me, I believe I am desirous of refreshments."

"Of course, Lady," Kaylin replied. She noted that the Consort didn't ask anyone else's permission.

Ynpharion spoke as he joined the Consort. *I am to convey the Consort's gratitude.* His words were about as natural as Kaylin's to the Consort had been.

For saving Terrano?

For saving the cohort. What we saw was your solicitous intervention. You put a hand on Terrano's shoulder.

And the melting stones?

His interior voice relaxed, for a variant of relaxed which meant he once again felt free to be annoyed. *Everyone witnessed that. He is your familiar. You might suggest some subtlety on his part.*

I didn't tell him what to do.

No, and I would keep that firmly *to yourself—if it is possible for you to keep* anything *to yourself. But yes, the familiar caused some concern in the Court.* This, conversely, amused him. *And the stones did melt. You understand,* he continued when she failed to have the correct reaction to this fact, *that those stones could withstand the hottest of Dragon breath? Your familiar is feared for a reason.*

If Coravante hadn't attacked Terrano, my familiar would never have left my shoulder.

Yes. But as you cannot say that Coravante attacked Terrano—although some will, of course, be aware of this—the familiar's actions seem erratic and dangerous. I am certain that, in your absence, some of the lords will be calling for your expulsion.

I can't be made outcaste, Ynpharion.

No, of course not. You are not part of our race. You can, however, be forbidden the High Halls if you choose not to divest yourself of the creature on your shoulder. Grudgingly, he added, *But it was well done.*

What was?

Calling him back. It implies that control, however incomplete, remains with you. When Kaylin did not reply immediately, he added, *It means you have* power. *The familiar's existence—if that is, in fact, what he is, and there has been some debate—implies it heavily. To see it exercised is not entirely detrimental to your status.*

I don't give a rat's ass—

The Consort favors you. She cannot be seen to favor the weak.

Right. Of course not.

She has taken the risk of showing inordinate favor to the cohort, given the politics that surround their reappearance. If they fail—if Terrano had somehow transformed—that would be considered disastrous for her. And that would, of course, reflect poorly on the High Lord.

"Lord Kaylin?" The Consort interrupted the flow of Ynpharion's lecture; Kaylin didn't consider their interchange to be a conversation.

"Sorry. I was thinking."

The Consort had led them to the fountain behind the thrones. Kaylin had seen it before, but the cohort clearly hadn't; there was almost a marked hesitance in their movements.

It is very, very seldom that the Consort entertains guests here. She has rooms that are far more stately—and far more secure—than this.

I doubt they're more secure.

They are more secure for the Consort. Yes, this is the heart of her power, but the power that she has over the Lake—and, by extension, our people—is not destructive in nature.

The cohort seemed to understand this. Sedarias was almost awkward in her hesitation.

"Forgive me," the Consort said. She gestured. "Please. Be seated. I seldom entertain so many people here; this small courtyard is not ideally situated for guests of note." There were benches here, but no chairs, and a table that looked distinctly out of place had been both prepared and provisioned. "I retreat here when I wish to think without interruptions." Her eyes narrowed as she turned to Terrano. "What occurred there?"

Kaylin was almost certain she already knew the answer—or as much of the answer as Kaylin herself did.

Terrano said nothing until Sedarias turned to glare at him. He shrugged, which did nothing to soften the glare. "Coravante tried to force me to disengage."

"Disengage implies that he engaged you." Sedarias took control of the discussion instantly.

"He tried."

"How?"

"He tried to cast the equivalent of a spell."

"Tried or succeeded?"

"Tried."

"Succeeded," Kaylin said at almost the same time.

"That's when your familiar stepped in?"

"No—he stepped in after." Kaylin exhaled. "He used some sort of Shadow tendrils, and they entered Terrano through—as far as I could see—the ground. They traveled through his boots, and followed the trail of what passes for muscle."

"What was their intent?"

"I don't know. They were doing a fair amount of damage as they traveled. Terrano thought he could shake them," she added, lifting a hand as Sedarias opened her mouth, "but to do that, he'd have to physically alter his body."

The Consort was silent. They were all silent. Almost by unspoken assent, the cohort waited until the Lady broke that silence.

"Do you believe those tendrils would have done the same damage to any other member of the cohort?"

Did she? She looked at Terrano. She had expected, if an attack happened, that the victim would be Sedarias. It demonstrably hadn't been. She both understood and failed to understand. Taking out Sedarias would destroy the cohort, because Sedarias was their natural leader. Coravante would, because he was Mellarionne, assume that.

If he attacked Sedarias, it would look bad for the line. Fights—and assassinations—were to be done behind figurative closed doors. But...would it have done the same damage?

"I'm not certain."

"You don't believe it would have."

There was one significant difference between Terrano and the cohort. Or rather, one that might make the difference. Terrano had no name. He was capable of blending in with the formless, shapeless miasma that was Shadow. What Shadow could do to him, and what he might do to escape it, was not what the cohort itself could do.

Coravante couldn't assume that the cohort had each other's names. Or rather, that all of the cohort knew all of the other names.

"When you approached Iberrienne," she asked, turning to face Terrano, "did you make it clear—in any way—that you...?" And here, she paused.

If you are concerned that you will reveal something that should remain hidden, be at ease, Ynpharion said. *The Consort is well aware that the entire cohort is name-bound.*

You told her?

Yes.

She really needed to have a word or two with Helen.

You are not always within Helen's domain, Ynpharion countered. *If you wish to retain the polite fiction that this is unknown, may I suggest that this is* not *the time?*

Kaylin agreed, with some anxiety. She started again. "Did you make clear in any way that the cohort is entirely name-bound to each other? Or that you're name-bound?"

He stared at her.

It was Mandoran who answered, his voice devoid of his usual teasing humor. "Yes. He had to speak to us—to Sedarias—when negotiating. He didn't make clear *who* he was speaking with, but...yes. Understand that it's part of how we think, part of who we are. Hiding it—when we could hide *nothing*—didn't seem either adaptive or relevant for almost the entirety of our lives. It didn't matter that someone knew. Escape, for us, didn't mean *coming back*. Some people," he added, deliberately not glancing at Ynpharion, "consider being name-bound humiliating. It wasn't, for us. It was wed to survival."

Terrano nodded.

To the Consort, Kaylin now said, "Would Alsanis speak of this to anyone else, if asked?"

"He might speak to me if I asked," she replied. "But the Hallionne are created to protect and succor their guests. To the Barrani of his acquaintance, exposing such a secret would be a betrayal."

Kaylin nodded, frowning. "If it's Coravante, if it's Iberrienne, the natural assumption would be that Sedarias, at least, held Terrano's name." She hesitated again. "But that would be irrelevant if he wanted to cause the cohort to become instantly suspicious in a way that couldn't be ignored.

"The only difference I know of between Terrano and any other member of the cohort is his name. He no longer has one."

The Consort did not react. No one did. The trickle of falling water was the only sound in this tightly packed clearing for three long breaths.

"You suspect that An'Mellarionne knows this."

"I think the Shadows have a different effect on Terrano than they would on any other Barrani present—and I include the cohort in their number. If he didn't know, Terrano as the target would make no sense. Terrano was the only one of the cohort to be able to leave Alsanis before the last *regalia*. He could be assumed to have greater understanding of Shadow, and greater control of it because of that fact.

"It wouldn't make sense to attack him. If An'Mellarionne fears Sedarias—"

"If?"

"Fine. He fears Sedarias, and assumes she's the power behind the cohort. Or the commander behind it. He might assume that she bullied a name out of Terrano. But... Terrano as a target makes little sense. Any other member of the cohort would do. But if he *could* sense the lack of name—or if something advising him could—it would make more sense."

"Why do you assume Shadow would harm the nameless, if such a being truly exists?" the Consort asked.

Hope squawked.

"I see." The Consort bowed her head. When she lifted it, her eyes were blue. "We must assume, then, that An'Mellarionne can see the nameless. Perhaps even see the named."

Kaylin shook her head. "I don't think he could do it on his own. Even Terrano can't. But something within these halls—or beneath them—can."

CHAPTER 18

"Are you accusing my brother of being a pawn to the Adversary?"

"Pawn? An'Mellarionne? Not intentionally. But I'm no longer certain intent matters."

"Then I concur with your assessment," Sedarias told Kaylin. "My brother can see names. He cannot—clearly—take them. Could he, none of this would be necessary. I would be his. In all likelihood, all of us would, and I make no exception for either the Consort or the High Lord."

Ynpharion was up in arms instantly, but he was also uneasy.

"You can see names. It is neither natural nor simple. We know—now—that you can take the name, but the taking requires touch, and touch is not a guarantee.

"Terrano doesn't currently have a name, which is why he's here. He has no interest in Court, in family or in the rest of the Barrani—but his lack of name might be his truest protection against the Adversary. The Adversary won't care what he looks like; the Adversary won't be able to make the rest of us outcaste if Terrano chooses to disincorporate."

For the next three hours, the cohort sat—or lounged—in the Consort's private garden. Teela, however, sat apart from

the general group huddle. Terrano would have, but Sedarias
caught him by the arm, and the looming shadow of Allaron
added gravity to her not-very-subtle command.

Because Terrano wasn't part of their group mind, they had
to speak out loud more often than they would have otherwise. But they didn't speak as much in a way that Kaylin could
hear; she got the impression that the big discussion—or debate, or argument—was happening behind closed lips, and
Terrano was offered the eventual consensus. Spike asked her
if she desired to listen, and Kaylin gave him a very hurried
no. But she gave *him* permission to extract information—his
words—because he was vibrating with concern.

Or fear.

She wanted to accompany the cohort. Spike certainly
wanted her to. But he couldn't go with them on his own.
Kaylin pointed out—quietly—that he'd come to the West
March as a flying insect; he hadn't remained attached to the
person who had carried him out of *Ravellon*. Spike agreed.

"I was anchored," he then explained in a buzzing voice
that made Kaylin's jaw ache. Given the sudden attention of
the gathering, he'd spoken in a way that everyone else could
hear, as well. "I could not leave *Ravellon*. I had to be carried
out, and even then, there was some resistance. The Towers
are strong.

"When I was free of the barrier, I could act on the orders
of my master. I did not require the anchor."

"And you require it now?" Sedarias demanded.

"If your Adversary is what I suspect he must be, yes." There
was marked hesitation. "My form is contained by identifi-
cation of Kaylin's blood. The blood-binding is voluntary."

"Have you done it before?" Kaylin asked, surprised.

"Yes. Once."

"With who?"

"Once," he repeated. "It is a binding that lasts while the binder lives. It is…a form of servitude. One might choose it if one's existence might otherwise cease. I chose for different reasons this time. I could, and can, find you anywhere that I am permitted, by form and the rules of the plane, to travel. While I am with you, I cannot be commanded by any other force. But you are a creature who resides almost entirely in the space you now occupy. The threads that bind us bind us most strongly here.

"Helen is fully capable of separating us, although it would take effort and will on her part. I am not sure, were I physically welded to you, that it would not destroy me. She trusts you. But this building, this place—it is not like Helen. And the…cavern, as you call it, is secured using similar paradigms to the power that keeps *Ravellon* separate from your lands. Were I to venture into the cavern without you, I would have no way of leaving it. The Tower here is not entirely unlike Helen; can you not hear its voice?"

"No."

"Any of you?"

Terrano exhaled. "I can."

Kaylin had a thousand questions and opened her mouth to ask the first one. Teela's raised hand, however, cut off the flow of words before they'd started.

"We'll be here all day, kitling. And most of tomorrow, as well." She then turned to Sedarias, whose eyes were drilling the side of Terrano's face.

"What," she demanded, and it was clearly a demand, given the color of her eyes, "do you hear? What is it saying?"

Terrano's expression said, *See, this is why I never mentioned it.* Kaylin saw an echo of herself—her younger self—in his expression, and came to his rescue.

"You don't know."

He didn't like to be called stupid, either. Or be seen as stupid or helpless. "I can't describe it. It's not—it's not like our words. Not even like our languages. It's not the difference between Dragon and Barrani speech." He frowned. "Spike, can you hear it?"

"Yes." Spike's buzzing voice tailed up at the end, as if the agreement were actually a question.

"Can you explain it?"

Spike clicked and buzzed while everyone else held their breath. Kaylin could sense both frustration and surprise in the sound, as if he were having to explain how to breathe. Or they wouldn't.

"It is a warning," he finally said.

"Like the Towers in the fiefs?"

"No, unlike the Towers. This Tower is more broken than Helen." Since he wasn't visible, it took Kaylin half a second to understand that he was talking about the High Halls— a building that was not, to her knowledge, sentient. The High Halls did not magically alter themselves to make visitors comfortable; the geography of the hallways and rooms didn't change.

But the Tower of Test *did*. And she'd seen the Arkon's replay. She knew that the Tower *had*. At one point, in the very dim and distant past, the High Halls had been either a Tower or something similar to the Hallionne. Here, in what was not yet Elantra, where the presence of Dragons meant death.

"Is it a new warning?" Teela asked, her voice much quieter than Sedarias's. Quieter and colder. "Is it recent?"

"I am not certain. It is a warning. It is…" he rumbled; Kaylin's arm shook with the force of his thought. Her hand began to warm, until Spike was almost uncomfortably hot. "A lighthouse."

"Beacon?" Kaylin asked.

He whirred more frenetically. "Beacon. But...a beacon is supposed to draw people to it, no?"

"Not necessarily," Teela replied.

"I believe that the compromise of the Tower was not complete—but this warning is the type that would persist in the absence of architectural aid. It is possible that it is not new—but that you are incapable of hearing its cries. You are not architects."

"That's the best-case scenario," Terrano muttered.

"If you have an opinion, share it."

"It's either something that went off on contingency during the first war, or it's something that is more recent. It would be best for us if it was recent, but... I wasn't here, and we have no way of confirming it, one way or the other. Unless Spike does?"

Spike whirred. A lot. "I do not believe this test your companions intend to undertake will be safe."

"Of course it's not safe," Kaylin began.

"It will be less safe than it was. I do not believe the Tower believes that it can continue to contain the threat."

Silence.

Kaylin's marks began to glow. They were a gold, but blue-edged, the combination unusual. "So...all we have to do is destroy whatever the Tower's trapped."

"You don't know what you're talking about," Terrano said in Elantran.

"Our agreement with the Consort—" Sedarias began.

"Was to *free the names*. Not destroy the Adversary under our feet. You've spent all your time in either Alsanis—for centuries—or here, with Kaylin and Helen. The only time you've seen any of the possibilities of being in neither place, we were on the run in the outlands. But you saw what Spike was capable of there. You saw what was chasing us. Do you honestly think you could just stand and *fight*?

"I've been out there since Alsanis let us leave. I've seen things you can't imagine. I've fought things you can't imagine—and I survived. But barely. There are things you won't understand how to fight. You won't know how to stand your ground—because this," he said, stomping the nearest flat stone for emphasis, "will *not help you*. It's barely real.

"If Spike is right, you're going to be facing something that mostly lives elsewhere, or several other elsewheres, at the same time he lives here. It's like Helen's example with Spike—you're looking through a window. Or an arrow slit. You think that what you see is all there is *to* see. And frankly," he added, attempting to lower his voice, "you haven't even approached the arrow slit yet. None of us have. I don't want to be discouraging, but…it's like taking a dinner fork to a battlefield."

Mandoran grimaced. "I think we're about to see more than any of the rest of our kin can."

"That doesn't mean you can fight it."

"If not us, then who?" Mandoran massaged the back of his neck as he bent his head; he didn't like to be serious. But he was closest, in personality, to Terrano. "We know what you taught them. Sedarias is Mellarionne. She has some idea of how that teaching might have been extended. We *all* believe—even the Consort—that the Test of Name has been compromised somehow. If we don't do this, it's going to get worse. That's it. That's the future.

"I know you don't really consider the High Halls home. None of us do." Sedarias cleared her throat. "Fine. Most of us don't. At least half. But…we're still Barrani. We still *want* to be Barrani."

Terrano said nothing.

"The Lake is *here*. If the creature beneath the High Halls breaks free somehow, there will be *no* Lake. No Lake and no Barrani. Even if I hated every living member of the Court, I don't hate the *idea* of my people."

"You sound like Annarion." Clearly this was not meant as a compliment.

"What did you expect? You left. He stayed. Of course he's going to have undue influence. Look, there's a place for you if you want to come back. Some of us have missed you."

"Some."

"Some."

Terrano shuddered in place, a wave of exaggerated motion cresting through his body. He bent his head for one long beat, and when he raised it, his eyes were blue. But they were a normal variant of Barrani blue, and they possessed both pupils and white bits. "I didn't say I wouldn't help."

Mandoran relaxed, as well.

"But...even if I wanted to, I can't come home. I could live with you, yes—but not the way I once did. I can't *hear* you. I never thought I'd miss the noise."

"Noise?" Sedarias arched a brow. But as if to soften the edge of the single word, she also raised an arm. The gesture was pure Sedarias—or at least Sedarias with the cohort. There was welcome in it, warmth, but also command. And Terrano, like the rest of the cohort, obeyed Sedarias. He walked toward her, his feet on the ground, and she enfolded him tightly in a hug that looked like it might never end.

But she also lifted her head and turned her face toward the Consort. "How long do we have?" Even that, Kaylin thought, was Sedarias. She took command because she wanted to divert attention from Terrano. Possessive and protective.

The Consort turned away from Sedarias, toward the basin

of her fountain. She spoke three words; Kaylin's arms—which were still glowing—began to ache. The water in the fountain stilled instantly, the surface frozen in place, although it still appeared to be liquid. "I would give you all of the time you felt you required," she finally said, although her eyes remained on the not-quite-liquid water. "But given the complications introduced by your brother—and his followers, not all of whom are known to us—the risk of waiting is high. We assume that he can see the existence of names, but cannot touch their substance as the Chosen can."

Sedarias nodded.

"Lord Kaylin—Kaylin, if she prefers—has no desire to understand the mechanisms of the power she does possess. It's almost as if she's afraid that understanding will lead inevitably to responsibility, or rather, fault. She wants nothing to be her *fault*. Regardless, she lacks the ambition of Mellarionne. I do not know if the ability to see names will lead, with effort, will and research, to the ability to take their essential nature and control it; in the case of the creature beneath the High Halls, I think the answer must be no.

"But he is not a creature that was born to house a True Name—Spike, please correct me if I am mistaken. Coravante, however, is. And Coravante and his allies are, even as we speak, on the move."

"Does my brother still have his name?"

"I cannot answer that question," the Consort replied. She turned to Kaylin. "Does he?"

"Ynpharion still has his," Kaylin replied, which was a bit of a dodge. "Knowing a name doesn't remove it." Her tone implied that the Consort already knew this, because, of course, she did. "As far as the Barrani are concerned, knowing a name gives someone ultimate power over someone else. Removing the name? You might as well just kill them." Which the Barrani were good at.

"And yet," the Consort said, her eyes still focused on the water, "Terrano is here, and Terrano has no name. I cannot look at him and see the name's absence, and if I cannot, no Barrani should be able to do so. But Coravante did."

"Maybe," Terrano said, "because I told him I wanted to be free of it."

"As do many of our kind. Mortals have cautionary tales about the fates of those who seek immortality; none of them end well. Barrani have cautionary tales about those who attempt to be free of their name, and oddly, none end well, either. Perhaps it is the nature of sentient life to struggle against the thing that most defines their existence."

"I told him I wanted freedom," Terrano said, speaking more clearly. "And when Alsanis was once again safe to offer hospitality, it was clear that I wasn't there. Maybe he attacked me because he guessed."

"Do you believe that?"

"I'm uncertain, Lady. But the form of attack he used against me isn't one that would work against you or Tain."

"Would it work against Kaylin?"

"Hard to say. I think it would affect mortals—but no one really understands how they're alive at all. It would definitely affect animals."

"It would work against Mandoran," Kaylin said.

Terrano's hesitance was marked. "It would probably work against any of the cohort. I think it would be most effective—" Here he stopped. "It would be most effective against creatures in the outlands."

"You do not use the word *Shadow*."

"No. I think that's too broad a word. Spike was in thrall to Shadow. His physical form makes that much easier. But free of that control, he is not Shadow. He's not like us—or like you—but he's not Shadow. I'm not Shadow," he continued into the uneasy silence. "I can see Shadow, and I can see some of its fetters. I'm not like you; I'm not even entirely like the rest of my cohort—but I'm not Shadow. You might not like the choices I've made, and I sympathize; I'm questioning the wisdom of a lot of them right now.

"But this type of attack would work better against Spike, at least when he's not mostly buried in Kaylin. And Mandoran said that you've seen a similar style of attack before the rest of us arrived."

Kaylin nodded contemplatively.

"It wasn't Coravante who launched it."

"No, of course not. It happened in the Southern Reach, and Coravante couldn't get there without an invitation." Her silence, like the rest of her, became sharp and focused.

"You're thinking."

"I'm thinking that the attack was launched by an outcaste Dragon, who did reach the Aerie on his own wings. But they were Aerian wings, not draconic. There was an Arcanist in the Aerie—I'd assumed this was his doing. It wasn't. He was just terrified for his own survival. But... I'd swear the outcaste wasn't, and isn't, under anyone else's control.

"Spike, when we first encountered him, was definitely under someone else's control. Distance didn't matter. We managed to break that, but until we did, he was enslaved to something that exists in *Ravellon*."

It was Sedarias who asked the obvious question. "Is the Adversary at the heart of this Tower now in contact with *Ravellon*?"

"Assume," Spike said, "that that contact has never ebbed. It is like—very like—the contact you have with your chosen kin."

"Helen can block that contact, though," Kaylin pointed out.

"No, Chosen. Helen can stop others from contacting you. She is not at all certain she can untangle the bindings of your guests. I believe she has said as much; we have discussed it at length. The binding upon me," he continued, "was stronger and more heavily layered. There are ways in which layers can be prohibited or cut off, but I do not believe even the Towers can completely isolate those who are bound to *Ravellon*. It is why their defenses are built to prevent us from *breaching* their boundaries."

Kaylin thought of Tara.

"And," Spike continued, "to destroying us if we have." He was silent and still for a long moment, but that was, apparently, a thinking silence. "It is much more difficult if those such as you attempt to contain some part of that Shadow."

"You were part of that Shadow, though."

"I was bound to it; I was not *of* it. It is a distinction that, for the purposes of understanding the Towers, must be preserved. Helen would notice Terrano if he attempted to enter your home, with or without your presence. Terrano is not like you. He is not quite like the cohort, although the resemblance is closer. But he is not like I was; he is not bound. Nor is he like I am. My form, my shape, exists in places that Terrano cannot go. But it exists in those places in the same fashion that you exist in yours.

"Those shapes overlap. In a place you cannot see without great effort, I am moving a limb. I am breathing a different quality of air. I am terrifying the tiny creatures that exist only in that plane, that place. I do this while I am speaking to you, but I am cohesive."

"Was the connection—the binding—to Shadow active on all of those planes?"

"No. Not all."

Terrano said, "It doesn't matter." He met, and held, Sedarias's gaze; it was Sedarias who looked away. "The Hallionne were meant to house you," he said to the Consort. "Or people like we used to be. Even after the disaster of the *regalia*, we started out the way you did, just...frayed at the edges."

"According to our records, that is not the case."

"Your records are wrong. But we learned how to begin to speak across the layers that the Hallionne didn't occupy. Or at least to try to *find* them. Some of us learned more quickly than others."

"You used that knowledge to escape Alsanis."

"Yes."

The garden grew chillier as Kaylin listened. "You think the Adversary is trying to do the same thing."

"From the other direction, yes."

"Spike," Kaylin said in the same tone she used to invoke Records recall in the Halls of Law, "is the Adversary bound the way you were?"

Click, click, whirrrrrrr, click. "Not the way I was, no. The Adversary is part of *Ravellon*, the way your arm is part of you. It does not have specific functions; it was not created in the same fashion. If you mean to ask if you can set it free, the answer is no. You cannot set your arm free by severing it."

Fine. "The Adversary has kept the names—or the people that contain them—in its cage." She looked to Terrano. "The people that attacked the heart of Orbaranne were trying to reach her name to invoke its power. Is that the point of the Adversary's attacks? Can it somehow use those names?"

"Names," the Consort said with a touch of impatience, "are True Words. But they are words given us for life. They are meant for the living."

"In this plane," Spike helpfully added. "If the Adversary desired power in this plane, it is theoretically possible that those names could provide that power. But they would not provide power in other planes, not in the necessary manner; they would be too slight. It is the difference between a painting and the object that one is painting. The former is flattened; it exists on a single plane.

"You and your people exist on this plane, and the power you accrue here has a subtlety of use that is not best understood by those who do not live here. Helen has explained much of it to me—but again, it is the equivalent of studying the painting, rather than the object. Much of that subtlety is lost to me; I can understand the analogies she employs. My vision can now resolve the *intent* of the painting. I am able to understand what that painting represents. But you and your kind interact with the object itself; I am left to attempt similar interactions with something that is essentially flat.

"When you carry me," Spike continued after a brief pause in which no one spoke, "I can more easily see the world as you see it. Observation is not difficult. It is, in some fashion, my core function; it was a function I could serve in multiple fashions. Interaction, however, was not. It is extremely difficult to do more than observe."

"Here?"

"Here."

"Is that why you could be so large in the outlands?"

"Yes. But these High Halls are not that space. It is possible that the cavern in which the Adversary is trapped will allow for more flexibility."

"But you doubt it."

"Highly. Were it to allow that flexibility, the Adversary would not remain trapped."

"Can you speak to him?"

Silence.

"I'm not asking you to speak to him—I'm asking if it's possible."

"I believe it is possible. But I am contained here, and I do not believe your enemy is aware of my presence. If Terrano can hear what I hear in some fashion, I do not think he should accompany your friends."

That started a round of conversation among the cohort, which meant they were silent. Kaylin found it interesting only because it meant some of them agreed with Spike. She guessed that one of that some was not Sedarias, or there'd be much less discussion—but maybe that was unfair. Sedarias didn't attempt to exert will or power over the cohort; that was just her base personality. They accepted it, whined about it—or at least Mandoran did—and responded as if she were a friend, and not a natural disaster.

"Terrano," Sedarias finally said, "is going. We understand Spike's concern, and some of us share it—but we feel that forewarned is forearmed. It is possible that we will be more, and not less, susceptible to the Adversary's demands or influence, although we cannot hear what Terrano hears; his perception may help us sidestep that difficulty before it becomes nonnegotiable.

"If Kaylin could accompany us, we might agree that Terrano is too much at risk—but she can't. If we understand correctly, Kaylin will be led to the Adversary by another route entirely."

"So will Teela," Teela said. She failed to glare at Tain, because she failed to look at him at all.

It was funny, in a completely unhumorous way. All of the cohort knew her True Name, although Terrano couldn't use it anymore, but it was Tain who was her biggest concern. In some ways, that made sense—he was her partner, after all. But being a Hawk didn't define Teela the way it defined Kaylin, and the cohort had done more to shape the course of Teela's life than the Hawks had, or could.

"An'Teela will accompany us," the Consort said.

Us.

Everyone present turned toward her then, except Ynpharion.

"I do not believe that is wise." It was Sedarias who spoke. Of course it was.

"And I value your opinion and your assessment," the Consort replied in a tone that even suggested she wasn't lying. "But it is not the first time I have ventured into those depths. To reach the Adversary is not a simple task, and permission is granted to very few by the Tower itself. Perhaps there are some who have managed to elude that permission and reach the place Kaylin calls a cavern; I believe that must be the case, and it troubles me. That trouble, however, is—unless it kills us—my brother's problem. The Adversary is not."

"It's personal, for you."

"Yes, Sedarias. It is personal. You are here—all of you are here—to take the Test of Name. But you are here at my invitation. If I have handled the situation poorly—and I have—I ask your tolerance and your forgiveness. You," she added when Sedarias failed to reply, "did not handle your attempt to free yourselves from captivity with complete wisdom or grace, and I have chosen to accept your earlier actions."

"If we fail—"

"If you fail, the lives of the Barrani who occupy the High Halls will continue as they have always continued. You will all be lost, of course, but that is the fate of all of our kind who fail."

Kaylin wondered if she believed that.

Of course not, Ynpharion snapped. *She is aware of the risk. We are all aware of the risk. It is you who fail to understand. If what you*

*suspect is true, if the Adversary has Barrani agents, it is likely those
agents have found a way to circumvent the protections the Tower of
Test has always maintained.*

He mastered his annoyance. Barely. *They desire the cohort's
failure. If there is any chance that the cohort can pass the test, they
are likely to attempt to interfere where the High Lord—and indeed
the Court itself—cannot intervene.*

You think we're going to run into trouble on the way down.

*Down is not the correct description, according to the Consort. My
opinion is all but irrelevant. What do you think?*

Kaylin glanced, once, at Severn. She wanted to leave him
behind, not for his own safety, but as an emergency relay. He
was technically a Lord of the High Court, just as Kaylin was,
and for the same reasons. He could, if necessary, approach
the High Lord. And if the Consort was involved, if the *life*
of the Consort was under threat—

Take Lord Severn with you, Ynpharion finally, and grudgingly, said. *The Consort has other ways of communicating with the
High Lord should things go dangerously awry.*

CHAPTER 19

To Kaylin's surprise, they did not see the cohort to the Tower. After the cohort and the Consort had finished what was a very, very sparse meal, the Consort led them out of the garden. It was necessary; entry and exit relied on the Consort, a fact Kaylin had not realized until that moment.

It is not always so, Ynpharion informed her. *And it is taxing. It would be best if we were all quit of this place; while she is in it, it draws power.*

Given Coravante's unexpected attack, Kaylin understood both the desire to preserve the Consort's power, and the necessity of spending it. But she had not hurried the cohort to their destination. She had provided them a moment of shelter, and she had allowed them the time to formulate entirely new contingencies based on their discussion.

But she couldn't keep them forever. Kaylin thought it likely that this small intervention was going to be costly for the Consort, a woman whose responsibilities all but demanded no obvious choosing of sides in political scuffles. In this case, the scuffle was internal to Mellarionne, and therefore entirely avoidable. To invite the cohort to the equivalent of Helen's tea was in no way necessary in the eyes of the Court, and by doing so, she had staked out a position in that conflict.

They did not know—and might never know—that the Consort's discussion had nothing to do with politics.

That would be because you are incorrect.

She didn't do it for political reasons.

No, she did not.

Which means it's not political.

Ynpharion's frustration was almost a balm. *The reasons behind an action seldom matter to those who attempt to read beneath the action's surface. It is a political decision.*

But that's not why she did it!

The reasons make little difference; the results are the only thing Mellarionne will see. As she will never explain the whole of her reasoning, Mellarionne has no choice but to view the invitation as the criticism it was, and is. Do you believe that politics are like your games of cards? That one must consent to play, with intent to win, the game offered? That if one declines, if one refuses to play that game, one is therefore immune to the criticisms and consequences decided by those cards?

Ynpharion already knew the answer.

You use the word politics *to denote the actions of the powerful of whom you disapprove. You use it as an accusation or a dismissal.*

This was true. It was a way of discussing men and women who were much more powerful, much more significant, than Kaylin herself had ever been, or would ever be.

What you fail to understand is that they are—as we are—all Barrani. They are all people. They have desires that are very like ours, but access to different tools with which to enact those desires. The fact that An'Mellarionne is likely in league with either the Adversary or the outcaste in Ravellon does not mean he has become incomprehensible; his is a desire for power. But people want power because they feel it will make them safer.

Among the Barrani?

I will accept your skepticism. Yes, even among the Barrani. You do not agree with the choices made to gain power. You do not agree with the tools used. But the act of attempting to build a secure stronghold should not be incomprehensible. Especially not to you. The Consort's desires are different. But her actions are nonetheless explicable. She wished to entrap your cohort not because she believed they were too dangerous, but because she believed that they might accomplish the desire that has been at the heart of her reign. They were, and are, the tools that came to hand.

Kaylin said nothing.

It is not the desire for power that renders us villainous in your mind. It is the tools used to achieve that power. It is how that power is spent. The Consort is powerful. The High Lord is powerful. The Lord of the West March is powerful. An'Teela is powerful. And yes, Lord Calarnenne is powerful; in no other way would he now hold one of the three. Understand that their lives have been defined by their desires. If we all wanted the same thing, if we defined power in the exact same way, things would be simpler. That is, however, a daydream.

When Kaylin failed to respond, Ynpharion continued. *Politics is the state of overlapping and conflicting desires between any group of people. It does not require wealth. Nor does it require any absolute measure of power; it requires a measure of relative power. And you should know this. Is it not your duty to assess crimes?*

Yes.

And you believe that it is the consequence of the crime, the breadth of its reach, that is the defining factor? Things are political only when they affect many?

Did she? Was that what she believed? No, not when she thought about it. But the uncomfortable truth was yes. Yes, when she didn't think about it, that was exactly what she felt.

316   *Michelle Sagara*

People at a distance who had power over her were somehow political. Marcus, who was on the ground with her, was not.

People who were subject to the law, people who couldn't easily buy their way out of the consequences? They weren't political, to Kaylin. They were part of her life, part of her job, part of her responsibility. They were within her reach; they were on the ground with her—but frequently doing stupid or angry things.

You are a Lord of the High Court. To the Barrani outside of this city, you are a power. You have what they lack, what they desire, what they are too afraid to consider achieving for themselves. You do not consider yourself a power.

She didn't.

That is what you have failed to grasp—but grasp it now. Very, very few consider themselves a power; they are objectively powerful because of the tools within their grasp, but they reach for those tools for the same reason mortals reach for daggers. You are a political force, for better or worse. His tone made clear which one he believed it was. *Everything that has occurred in the past week, the past two weeks, is political in nature. If you wish to navigate the undercurrents of the High Court, attempt to understand the nature of the fears that inform it. Know your enemy.*

Our enemy is the thing beneath the High Halls, she replied.

And not the Barrani who appear to be in league with it?

The Consort led Kaylin, accompanied by a very martial Teela and a very alert Severn, to her personal quarters. The rooms were guarded, but the guards parted instantly, a living curtain of armor and weapons. The Lady seemed to have gathered weight as she walked, to have pulled gravity toward her until she was its inescapable center. Kaylin found it hard to look away from the Consort's back.

Ynpharion had taken up the rear, and he was joined, on

what felt like a solemn funeral procession, by three more guards. His internal diatribe vanished. She was the Consort, yes, and incredibly important to the Barrani race—but even in the High Halls, she was not safe.

She was safer, Ynpharion said, *in your dwelling than she will ever be here. Especially now. It is only in the Hallionne that her safety can be taken for granted; there, guards are merely decorative. Here, we are not.*

He didn't have to tell her the fate of those guards should she be attacked and injured.

Surprisingly, no, I don't.

Kaylin was lucky that eye-rolling did not cause muscle sprains. Her familiar was sitting on her shoulder, but his wings were folded, a sign that he considered any danger to be contained entirely by what Kaylin could naturally see.

She felt Ynpharion stiffen when the familiar's wings rose. Since he'd plastered a wing across her eyes on the way to the High Seat, Kaylin wasn't instantly panicked. When he pushed himself, squawking loudly, off her shoulder, she made up for lost time.

Severn did not freeze; he unwound his weapon's chain, pulling blades from their nearly invisible sheaths. Teela was a step behind. Kaylin had assumed that she'd carried the blade—*Kariannos*—to make a statement to the rest of the High Court. This was, even on the face of it, a stupid assumption. What the cohort faced, Teela intended to face at their collective side. She wanted the most powerful weapon she owned at her disposal.

But they weren't anywhere near the Tower or the heart of the cage it formed; they were at the very edge of the Consort's chambers. Hope flew, his wing clipping the Consort's pale, perfect hair as he veered to avoid the back of her head.

Spike became a heated, weighted presence in Kaylin's hand,

and as he did, she bled on the perfect, spotless marble—if the stone was marble, which was Kaylin's generic word for shiny stone floors—beneath her feet. Spike, like Hope, separated himself from her for the first time since she'd reached the High Halls. He rose, wingless, his body pulsing, his spikes shrinking and growing as if the beat of their shape change were as close to wings as he could come, and followed in Hope's wake.

The world sounded unnaturally loud to Kaylin's ears. This close to the chamber in which very private audiences were held, Kaylin could hear the attenuated sound of crying, of screaming, of words that were inaudible, but only barely. This was the sound of the height of Barrani power, because in this chamber, the sound could not be dimmed. It bled up through the floors, causing subtle vibration in the walls, a storm of accusation and pain.

Kaylin would have gone out of her mind with it—and with what it said about her lack of power, her inability to help—within a week. If that.

But the High Lords and their Consorts were not, had never been, Kaylin. And maybe, she thought, heading as quickly as she could toward Hope and Spike, this was *why* the Barrani had to be callous. Caring too much would break them.

"Lady!" one of the guards shouted.

The Consort was frozen in place, but as Kaylin reached her side she saw no fear in the Consort's expression. No anger, either. Just a moment of weariness. She couldn't see what Hope or Spike could see, but clearly it was close by; both the familiar and Spike had stopped ten feet from where the Consort stood, casting shadow in the opulent lights of her own entryway.

Kaylin's arms were glowing. She was used to that. They didn't ache, however. She could—and did—draw daggers, but lifted an arm as she heard footsteps come from behind. Ynpharion stopped just short of her.

What do they see? he demanded; she could feel the hilt of his sword in his hand, as if that hand were her own.

"Lord Kaylin," the Consort said quietly.

Hope inhaled.

"Please give us permission to defend you," Kaylin said in a rush that left almost no room between the words.

"You have my permission," the Consort replied, although she didn't take her eyes off the familiar. Or Spike.

Kaylin raised her voice. "Spike, Hope—the Consort is *the most important person* in this room. Do whatever you have to do to preserve her."

Teela's sword gleamed in a way that didn't imply the light was reflected; the sword itself seemed to glow. Kaylin could make out the traces of runes across the flat of the blade. She joined Kaylin, her eyes so dark they might have been all pupil.

The floor ruptured.

No, Kaylin thought, that was the wrong description. The stone itself seemed to groan beneath the collective weight of the Consort and her companions, straining against something invisible to Kaylin's eyes. Hope might have changed that, had he stayed on her shoulder, but whatever the familiar had seen had caused him to leave her in a furious rush. His squawks were louder, and the high-pitched squeak that seemed to adorn them had deepened.

Hope exhaled a stream of opalescent, pale smoke. Where it hit floor, the stone melted; the melting gave off no heat. But the breath itself spread across the floor, and the floor shifted in a large circle around Hope. Hope, however, wasn't finished. His wings widened, his neck thickened. Kaylin was afraid that he was about to go full Dragon in a room that hadn't been designed for the draconic form.

He didn't. In some ways, that might have been better.

He lost transparency as he transformed; his foreclaws became hands, his spindly legs, arms; his hind legs became actual legs. Had he been clothed, it might have been better, but even as she thought it, the rising mist that had, moments ago, been an expulsion of opalescent cloud swirled around him, solidifying in layers as they watched. He looked almost like an Aerian—but no Aerian had wings of feathered glass.

"There is danger," he said in perfect Elantran.

Kaylin glanced at the Consort, who appeared to be staring at her feet. Or at what remained of the stone beneath them.

"The ground was…compromised. It will remain solid now."

Severn—can you see Hope?

Yes.

What does he look like to you?

A larger cloud.

"Kaylin," Hope said. "Ask the Consort to remain where she is for the moment. These rooms have been compromised; they are not currently habitable. Not for her."

"You can't tell her yourself?"

"It would be better coming from you."

"But the Barrani understand what you're saying, most of the time!"

"Yes. But this is not that most. Tell her. Spike and I must enter the interior and secure the rest of the rooms."

"What, exactly, does 'compromised' mean?"

"If she means to lead you to the Adversary through these rooms, you will not arrive at a destination of her choosing. Or yours."

Kaylin knelt and touched the cratered floor. "My familiar says that your rooms—or the passageway that leads from them—have been compromised. He and Spike are going to separate from us for the moment and attempt to eradicate the contamination. He asks that you remain here."

The Consort didn't even pause; she might not have blinked. Kaylin couldn't tell because her gaze was on the floor. It *felt* like marble to the touch, but it certainly didn't look like it anymore. It resembled melted wax. Her arms had continued their faint marks-driven glow, but her skin no longer hurt. The cratered floor didn't radiate magic.

"Lady," Teela said, voice sharp. This dragged Kaylin's attention from the floor. But the Consort didn't leave; she merely shifted her position, crouching beside Kaylin to examine the floor. This time, Kaylin did feel the sting of magic. It was a familiar discomfort; it was what she felt when Teela examined crime sites for magical detritus.

Ynpharion, breathe.

What does this so-called contamination entail?

Kaylin bit back the urge to say *How the hells should I know.* Looking pointedly at the floor, she said, *Probably Shadow or Shadow-variant spells. Are you afraid that my familiar can't handle those?*

She could feel him marginally relax, which she knew was the most she could hope for. She rose, as did the Consort, and settled in to wait. Waiting was not her forte.

The Consort's eyes were a deep blue; they weren't as dark as Teela's—or any of the other Barrani in the room—but they were far from their usual color. "An'Teela," she said softly. "Have the cohort arrived at the Tower?"

"Yes. They have arrived; they've seen the word the Tower chose for them." She didn't volunteer the word, and the Consort, being Barrani, would never ask; she'd probably ask about the details of their sex lives first. Kaylin, being human, was curious, but kept her curiosity to herself.

"Have they entered?"

"There was some discussion about the words chosen, but yes. I believe Sedarias found the Tower the safer place to stand. No one who is not an aspirant will be able to approach them from behind."

"Have they begun?"

Teela actually grimaced. "If you expect them to rush headlong into the unknown without discussion or debate, you have failed to watch them in close enough quarters. At the moment, they are looking at a flight of stairs, which heads both up and down, and they are arguing about the choice of direction."

The Consort's eyes lightened, but did not approach their natural green. "They have not been attacked?"

"Not yet, no. There are stairs and they are—" Teela stopped. "Do remind me, kitling, to strangle Mandoran when we get home."

"Sedarias will do it before you get the chance," Kaylin replied. "What's he doing?"

"Never mind. He is bored of discussion, and does not consider direction to be of value, given what little he knows about the nature of the Tower. His suggestion—flip a coin—did not meet with Sedarias's approval. His obvious boredom, however, annoyed her."

Mandoran and boredom were a terrible combination.

"He has just discovered that the walls that enclose the stairs are not walls."

Even Kaylin cringed, but didn't ask how he'd discovered this, because she kind of knew. "I'll remind you to strangle him, if he survives Sedarias." She had no chance to say more, because Hope had returned. His wings were spread, and a dark wispy smoke rose from their tips, heading toward a ceiling that now seemed too low to contain him.

"Where's Spike?"

"There has been some difficulty," Hope replied. "He is assessing the damage and attempting to communicate with the Tower." Kaylin repeated his answer, word for word. She found it ironic that she could understand him clearly now, because Hope thought no one else would.

"The Tower," the Consort said softly, "does not speak to us. Not in the fashion that the Hallionne or Helen do."

"Spike is aware of that; he is not certain if that is due to the damage done in the first war, or if the function of the Tower itself inhibits direct communication. His information in regard to the Tower itself is old."

"What information?"

"Records," Hope replied, shrugging slightly. "But he cannot access external information—which he claims exists—for obvious reasons. It is buried or frozen in *Ravellon*." Hope stopped speaking and turned to glance over his shoulder. His wings rose; Kaylin recognized the rigidity of the lines. She'd seen Aerian wings break arms—someone else's—in her time on the force.

"Spike asks for the aid of your companions."

"Is the floor safe to walk across now?"

"The contaminant has been compressed into one location. It is not, however, a location that can be avoided if you wish to meet your companions."

"At the rate they're going, we could spend two weeks magically rebuilding every room in this suite, and we'd still get there before they did." Kaylin then turned to Teela. "Spike is having a bit of a problem with the Shadow equivalent of hired thugs, and he wants our help."

"That is not what I said," Spike told her.

Kaylin didn't bother to repeat that phrase, because Teela, sword in hand, practically leaped the distance between the patch of floor they'd occupied and the distant doors. She was Barrani; she didn't have wings. But for a moment, she *flew*. And when she landed—lightly, on both feet, bending slightly into her knees to balance her returning weight—the runes on the flat of her blade flashed a startling blue-white, and a streak of crackling light, of lightning, flew forward into the doors.

The doors opened. And smoldered.

Teela was through them before anyone but Hope had any chance of catching up.

Severn did not fly through the air; he sprinted, weapons in hand. Hope, however, didn't follow. "No," the familiar said, as if he could read her thoughts while in this form. "He left you—all of you—to me. He is not as well armed as Teela; he is far better armed than any of the rest of you. You have the marks of the Chosen, but you have failed to understand them. Your mastery therefore cannot turn their power into weapons meant for this type of conflict." As he spoke, he gestured, and his wings began to fold.

A familiar sphere enveloped them all. "It would be best," he continued, "not to tarry."

Kaylin, however, turned to the Consort, whose eyes were a darker shade of blue. Again. "Do the swords always do that?"

"No, Lord Kaylin. They *can*, but there is a cost to the power and its use. It has been many, many years since I last saw that sword invoked."

Many indeed. It was not Ynpharion. Silent until now, Lord Nightshade finally joined the forefront of her thoughts. *Did you think that the swords were entirely for show? Did you think them like medals or crowns, an indication of the importance of the person who wielded them?*

I thought they were meant to kill Dragons.

They were. One could say they are. Dragons generally prefer to scorch everything from their superior advantage of height; if the swords could not somehow bring them down to earth, they would not be useful. But An'Teela is being reckless.

What does the Consort mean about cost?

Think, was his impatient reply. *If you were given one of the three— Ah, no. If Severn was given one of the three, there is no possible way that he could invoke the blade's power. I believe there is some chance you could—if you could wield a great sword. Or even a long sword.*

I can't.

No. But you are Chosen. If you could not effectively wield the weapon as a weapon, I believe you could invoke the...other abilities it contains. Most of my kin might claim the sword as the symbol of power it is—but they could not wield it as it was meant to be wielded. Teela earned that blade in the final war, because she could. You have never seen Teela wield that sword; you have, perhaps, seen her carry it. You will see her wield it today.

You said that was reckless.

Ah, a misunderstanding. It is reckless to invoke its power at this moment. *There is very little chance that those powers will not be necessary today. An'Teela knows this. She is worried for her friends.*

She's always worried. She worries about everything. And she bites your head off if you worry about her.

I do not worry about Teela in the same fashion you—foolishly, in my opinion—do.

No, Kaylin thought with a flash of insight. *You're worried about Annarion.*

Not, apparently, as worried as An'Teela is, given her use of the sword.

He was lying. His words came to her as if the sentence were being spoken by multiple voices—but all of them were Nightshade's. They overlapped and the dissonance in the meshed sound made Kaylin grind her teeth. This lie she could accept: he *was* worried about Annarion. He'd been worried about Annarion since his younger brother had arrived in Elantra.

But this was different, felt different. Kaylin sucked in air so sharply the sound could have cut. *Do not even* think *of coming here! You're outcaste!*

Silence. In a slightly less amused tone, Nightshade said, *You are becoming more sensitive to nuance, Lord Kaylin. Yes, I am outcaste. No, the High Halls is not safe for me. But if I understand anything that has happened—and I admit that your Helen defeats me—it is even less safe for Annarion.*

She looked through the doors that Teela had opened, staying within easy reach of the Consort as the Consort began to move. Hope remained with them, because the bubble that protected the Consort from magic was centered—as it always was—around him. Unlike Teela or Severn, the Consort did not sprint. Ynpharion stayed with the Consort, which was no surprise, but he was pale and indigo-eyed. When he stepped in front of her, she frowned.

Kaylin, however, did not. She noted that Ynpharion didn't step back, either, although a moment of silent rigidity implied there was some internal disagreement going on. The Consort could force him to obey—but that would cost them both, and given Hope's presence and Spike's absence, it was a price neither could afford to pay. Ynpharion stayed in front. Kaylin opened her mouth and snapped it shut. Nothing she could say in Ynpharion's defense would help anyone, and if she said the wrong thing, it would just give the Consort a target for her growing fury.

Since Shadow was here, a target already existed, and Kaylin wanted to keep it that way. She also didn't want to feel sympathy for Ynpharion, and certainly didn't want to come to his rescue.

"Out of curiosity," she said as they moved toward the open doors—or what remained of them, because as they approached, Kaylin could see scorching along the inner edges of both, "what happens to an outcaste lord who appears at the High Halls?"

"Nothing," the Consort replied, almost serene, "if he is not detected."

She knows you're coming.

I am not suicidal, Nightshade replied with just a glimmer of amusement. *She has some sympathy for the reasons I pursued paths I was ordered not to pursue; in a like situation, she might have made the same choices. But it seems that I am not the only outsider who has chosen to visit in an entirely unconventional way.* The humor vanished. *Tell An'Teela that the danger is threefold.*

Will she even know what that means?

Nightshade didn't answer. Kaylin couldn't see what he saw without effort and concentration—not without his help. His tone made clear that the time for such help was not now, but even if it hadn't, she couldn't concentrate on what he was seeing without losing track of what was in front of her face. She therefore didn't know for certain where he was.

As they cleared the door, she forgot about Nightshade.

CHAPTER 20

The air across the threshold was a different color. Fog, which Kaylin would have called gray, if gray had been the right word for something so livid, so visceral, seemed to stop at the doorway, rising to obscure the ceiling. In the High Halls, the ceilings were tall enough Kaylin had no idea how anyone cleaned them. But they were Barrani ceilings; they probably didn't get dirty.

She couldn't see Teela. She couldn't see Severn. She froze, her toes on the right side of the door. Hope stopped as she did; the Consort did likewise.

Ynpharion didn't. He walked into the fog, and it swallowed him.

Ynpharion!

I am here, he replied with obvious irritation.

Can you even see anything?

He stopped walking. She could almost feel the rigidity of his sudden stillness. *Can you not?*

I see a lot of very dense, very ugly fog. It's...almost sparkling. There are flecks of color in it that probably don't belong in air that we can breathe. That's not what you see?

No.

Do you see Teela? Or Severn?

Silence. After a longer pause, he said, *No.*

She lifted an arm to prevent the Consort from entering the room. *Severn?*

Here. Busy.

Sorry. Did you just cross the room beyond the door?

Following Teela.

No stairs? No other halls?

No. She felt a sharp stab of pain across her right side, and shut up instantly. No one conversed while fighting for their lives.

"Lord Kaylin?" the Consort said.

"According to Severn, they went straight through the room. They didn't turn a corner; they didn't take any stairs. In theory, they're at the back of the room itself. I can't see the room."

"You can't see it?"

"I can see a very dense fog. I can't see Ynpharion, either; I don't know how far into the room he walked, but there's not even a hint of his back." At this point, she might have poked Hope, but Hope wasn't sitting on her shoulder, and at his current size, she had no desire to have him there. She still turned to him. "Can you see Spike?"

"Yes."

"And the fog?"

"That," Hope replied, "is Spike."

Kaylin exhaled. "Can you see Teela?"

"Not easily, no. Before you ask, she is at the far end of what was once one of the internal rooms that this suite contained. Spike has dimmed visibility; it is an attempt to provide both cover and defense. It should not affect anyone but you." He paused, and then added, "And those who might be in service to the Adversary below."

"*I'm* not in service to the Adversary, and *I* can't see."

"Yes. That is unfortunate. Spike apologizes; your vision and sensory awareness are due to the fact that he is attached to you in a visceral and inseparable way. You are, in part, perceiving the effects of what he is doing in a way the rest of your companions would not. With the possible exception of the cohort.

"It is an interference, however, that would diminish the effectiveness of beings who are not entirely tied to your plane of existence."

Kaylin turned to the Consort, who was waiting. "It's safe," she said, "to enter. But... I'd appreciate it if you stayed close enough that I can still see you."

The room was a great room; the Consort explained that it was meant for public entertaining, inasmuch as the public was allowed into the interior. Smaller rooms could not contain the guards and aides that people of import brought with them as a matter of course.

The Consort's voice carried. The sounds of Teela and Severn fighting whatever it was they were fighting did not. But a sudden burst of light cleared some of the fog from the air—and at this point, Kaylin was worried that this would be a bad thing. For Spike.

The floors in this room were carpeted or covered, but they were as uneven as the marble in the entryway. Kaylin wasn't certain if this was due to Hope's intervention, but she trusted the pitted floor to remain solid beneath their collective feet.

And it did. But solidity did not apparently make much difference to the arms—or tentacles—that suddenly burst through it. Marble did not crack or shatter. Hope inhaled and exhaled as Kaylin's knife passed through them.

"I would advise you to close your eyes," her familiar said. "I will guide you, but...these manifestations gain strength through your focus."

"What does that even mean?" Kaylin demanded as the tentacles froze and began to shrivel.

"It means that if you believe in them," the Consort said softly, "they will grow solid enough to destroy you. They are not real; they are illusions that are meant to invoke fear. The greater the fear, the greater the power they exert." Her voice contained no fear at all.

"You've seen these before?"

"Yes, although infrequently. It is very, very unusual to see them encroach so early."

"Early?"

"It is generally on the way to the prison that they manifest, if they manifest at all." She sounded almost bored. Kaylin was certain she couldn't be, and was reminded that Barrani were skilled liars.

Kaylin, Severn said. *Teela believes the Consort will now be safe if she approaches.*

How's Teela?

Her eyes are indigo, but narrow enough it's hard to tell.

And the cohort?

I am not asking her about the cohort right now. She's like a very thin, very brittle surface over a very terrible death—and anything could break it. If you still dislike spiders, this is probably not going to be your day.

Shadow spiders?

Larger, but yes, essentially. They had more eyes than legs, and one of them had mouths on the ends of its front feet. They're all dead; they've dissolved. Spike is with us, but he's grown in size and appears to have planted himself into the door frame.

The doorways here are solid stone.

I'm sure he'll move once you arrive.

Severn was "fine," for a value of fine that included an obvious, bleeding gash that had cut through thick cloth and thin leather, and left red on the edges of the openings. There was a similar gash across his left cheek. Teela was *fine*, and as there were no immediate, obvious, gushing wounds, that was as clear a warning to keep away as Teela was going to give. Severn's description was wrong. Teela was bristling. Her eyes seemed to pulse with light.

That is Kariannos, Nightshade said, the interior voice conveying a hush. *It has been long since I have seen An'Teela take to the fields of battle. She was a wonder to behold in times past.*

She wasn't a wonder to behold now; she was like a natural disaster. Nightshade found this amusing. Ynpharion did not. But the latter was far more impressed; he could not find words to give voice to the momentary awe he felt. Ynpharion, Kaylin remembered, was young in comparison to Nightshade or Teela. Young enough to miss the wars at their most intense.

She found Dragons terrifying when they were in their draconic form, but her fear of the Barrani had always been more down to earth. She wondered if that would change today.

"Spike," Teela said, "is in the way."

"An'Teela." The Consort's voice was steady and chilly.

Teela turned to face the Consort, naked blade in one hand. "Lady." If the Consort's voice was chilly, Teela's was sepulchral. Kaylin took a step back.

This did not improve the color of the Consort's eyes. "The quarters are mine. And even if they have been compromised— and it appears they have—the permissions to enter reside with the High Lord or me. You were—and are—one of the finest lords the High Court has ever produced, but you are not High Lord, and you are not Consort." The only sound in the room was the Consort's voice; everyone else had pretty much stopped breathing for the duration.

Teela did not put her sword up, but after a frigid pause, her expression shifted. Kaylin bit her lip to stop any trace of amusement from touching her face, because she was certain Sedarias was talking.

Teela nodded. She didn't bow, but given her rigidity, bowing would have caused her to break something. The Consort then turned to Kaylin.

"Lord Kaylin," she said, her eyes still martial blue, "please have Spike remove himself from the doorway."

Spike caused cracks in the stone as he retracted the protrusions that had given him his name. He left significant holes behind as he compressed the bulk of his body into something small enough he could fit between Kaylin and the nearest wall.

Severn fell in beside Ynpharion, of all people; Teela took the lead. The doorway, such as it was, opened into a hall with much shorter ceilings and no windows to speak of. There were torches; the torches flickered, suggesting that some sort of natural fire, rather than magic, provided the light here. The fog which had killed visibility was gone, and Spike had dwindled in size. He didn't return to her hand—he wouldn't have fit—but floated to the left as Hope took up position on her right.

The Consort walked behind Severn and in front of Kaylin, her white robes luminescent in a way that suggested they carried their own light within the threads of the cloth that comprised them. Although none of her escorts had eyes in the backs of their heads, they stopped when the Consort stopped. The subtle movement of her robes stilled as she turned to look to her right. In theory, she examined a wall.

Kaylin felt her skin burn as the Consort spoke a single word. It was not a word Kaylin recognized, but because she instinctively felt she should, she knew it was a True Word. The marks on her skin seemed to pulse in time to the syllables; the word wasn't short. But the tingling that warned of magic didn't normally happen when True Words were spoken, not this way.

"Door?" she asked when no one else spoke.

"Yes," the Consort replied. "And no."

Kaylin wilted. "Portal."

Teela stiffened. It wasn't the *stop whining* or *I will strangle you* stiffness, either. "The cohort," she said, as if she weren't one of them, "have started the Tower's test. They are no longer together." Her words were so stiff you could bounce off them.

"We have time, then," the Consort said. She reached out, looking almost hesitant, and placed her left palm flat against the wall. Color spilled out from beneath her hand, spreading slowly and lazily to cover the whole of the wall. Kaylin had enough warning to step directly behind the Consort to offer physical support as the Consort's legs began to tremble.

"No," Teela said. "The Tower's test appears to be broken."

"The Tower's test is different for everyone. Or it can be," Kaylin added, a question causing the last syllables to rise.

"Not in this fashion. What they hear now, they shouldn't hear." Teela had never spoken of her own test. None of them—with the exception of Kaylin—had. They had danced around the very end of that test. Kaylin frowned. "Is it possible," she asked the Consort, "to get lost on the *way* to the Adversary?"

"I do not know. I would have said no, but the cohort is

capable of turning almost any carefully devised plan on its head. Is that what is happening?"

"Possibly." Teela exhaled, and some of the stiffness escaped her along with that long breath. "Terrano was having some difficulty."

"Terrano should not have been there."

"You've never tried to say no to Sedarias," was Teela's grim reply. "If Terrano was forbidden the Tower, Lord Kaylin should have been forbidden the Tower for the same reason."

"She bears the marks of the Chosen."

"Yes. But Lord Severn did not, and does not." She turned to Kaylin. "It's possible that Severn was allowed to undergo that test because he was with you—if I understand your journey, you weren't separated during the test."

"We weren't," Severn said.

"Terrano has been. But they are all facing different tests in their attempt to move forward. And we can't know for certain that those who failed the test did so at the hands of the Adversary. It is possible they were trapped—are trapped—within the Tower itself, unable to either move forward or go back."

This had never occurred to Kaylin, and she didn't like the odds.

The wall beneath the Consort's hand was no longer a wall. It was, as Kaylin had suspected it would be, a portal.

Spike whirred, but the warning wasn't necessary. No one moved to enter the portal itself, not even the Consort, who had, in theory, opened the way. She glanced at Kaylin. Kaylin transferred the silent question to Hope, whose wings were spread and high.

"You suspect that this is where the breach occurred?" he asked. Kaylin repeated his question, wondering why the squawks were audible and the words were not. She lifted a hand before he could answer. If there was an answer, now was not the time for it.

"If it is possible for infiltration to occur here, we are in far more danger than even I realized," the Consort replied. "But I know of no other way to reach the Adversary. Those who have already passed the Tower's test can return to its end— but it has been our belief that the permission of either the High Lord or the Consort is explicitly required. And this," she added, "is the proof of that requirement."

"It's a portal," Kaylin not very helpfully pointed out.

"Yes."

"Sedarias's sister—"

Teela cleared her throat.

"Sorry. The Barrani who attacked Alsanis in an attempt to stop the cohort from taking this test. Better? Those Barrani didn't attack from the front door, or even the back door, if there is one. They came to Alsanis through the portal paths, and they entered those *from* the outlands. If they've figured out how to do that…"

"Yes."

"Was there no other way to confirm this *before* they started their test?" If Kaylin could have unsaid the words, she would have—practically before she'd finished them. Of course there was, but it involved great risk to the Consort, and a very clear signal to the Adversary—or his allies—of the Consort's intent.

"We cannot be certain now."

You can, a familiar voice said. Nightshade's. It was grim, as grim as Teela's had become. *They have been searching the outlands for a way into the High Halls.*

Kaylin didn't ask him how he knew. Instead, she said, *And you're in the outlands.*

Perceptive. I will attempt to meet you.

Annarion was not going to be happy. Kaylin thought the Consort, however, might be. "Spike."

"Lord Kaylin."

"Where does this path currently lead us?"

He whirred and clicked, processing the question, or at least processing the answers, most of which might not be relevant for people who weren't Spike or Hope. When he finally answered, he was as hesitant as Kaylin had ever heard him. "It leads to the Adversary you wish to face. You cannot see him?"

"I can see a dark, black splotch surrounded by pale, luminescent gray."

"That is *all* you can see?"

"Yes. I'm human. Severn?"

"I see what you see." So did the rest of the Barrani. Only the Consort failed to answer the implied question.

"I do not believe," Spike said when he had processed the answers, "that you will be safe. Ah, no. I do not believe that you are the only beings of your stature to occupy this passage or this space. Do you wish me to scout?"

Kaylin said yes. Hope, however, said no. Spike stuttered as Kaylin changed her answer, aware of the fact that everyone was now waiting on her, some less patiently than others.

"There's a possibility," she finally said, "that Nightshade will join us."

Silence.

"I'd like us not to kill him, if that's okay. Because he's implied that he won't be the only one joining us—and he's likely to be on our side."

To no one's surprise, Teela headed into the portal. But she did glance back, once, at Severn, who nodded. They were both fully armed.

"I will not be able to mask your presence," Spike told them all. "These rooms are not the lands you now traverse."

"Did the spiders come from this portal?"

"No, Lord Kaylin."

"Are more of them coming?"

"No. The webbing that they have spun is slender and tentative, and it has been utterly destroyed by your Teela. They can rebuild it; it will not be immediate." Before she could ask for a definition of immediate, he said, "I believe it would be the work of decades, if not centuries."

"Did they come from below? I mean, from wherever the Adversary is?"

"Yes. But, Kaylin, I do not believe they originated from there."

Teela and Severn were gone. Kaylin wanted the Consort to wait, but she understood that the paths were now hostile terrain—not that they'd ever been anything but, to Kaylin. She didn't give much for her own chances, because fighting waves of nausea was difficult enough; fighting Shadow-driven opponents at the same time didn't even seem possible.

"I am here," Hope said quietly. "You will not feel the dislocation in the same way. Even were I not, the Consort in theory controls this path, and she is with you."

The Consort entered the portal, Ynpharion at her side and just one step behind.

Kaylin grimaced and followed, her hand on a dagger. Hope draped an arm across her shoulder, and the weight of that arm felt familiar. Spike, floating by her side, entered the meniscus—there was no other word for it—as she did.

The portal path was *cold*. Kaylin felt the chill as she inhaled and her nostrils closed. She blinked; the air was dry, but it felt like air. This was not a given in the small tunnel that usually existed between portals; sometimes it felt like she was trying to breathe water. She looked immediately to the Consort; the Lady's breath rose in a desultory cloud. It wasn't just Kaylin who felt the cold.

To the immediate left and right she could see the boundaries that defined the space they were now traversing; they looked like badly blown, opaque glass. Spike, floating above her shoulder, began to spin around an axis that was attached to his follow-Kaylin position. It was not a slow spin; he was an instant blur of motion.

Kaylin took a step back—which didn't change his position with regard to either her shoulder or her face—as Spike became a miniature windstorm. "Spike, what are you *doing*?"

Spike could move in a blur of motion while speaking. "Apologies," he said. "I cannot absorb and speak intelligently simultaneously."

In other circumstances, she would have laughed. "What are you absorbing?"

"Structural filaments," he replied in a sharper, higher pitch.

"Can *I* keep walking?"

"Yes. Running is not advised."

The walls of the tunnel began to shift, the texture changing. To Kaylin's eyes, it looked like they were melting.

"I think Spike thinks that the path you've opened goes to the wrong place," she said to the Consort.

"Spike is concerned," Hope agreed. "He does not believe this is where you wish to go."

"And you?"

"I am less certain. This is an old pathway, but inasmuch as such paths are, a fixed one. I believe its destination is very close to the exit the Consort expects. A larger shift would be noticed."

"Lady?" It was Teela.

"Does Spike believe he can realign the path?"

"I'm not sure," Kaylin replied. "He's spinning so fast all I can hear when he tries to communicate is a very high-pitched whine."

"What, exactly, is he doing?"

"Binding threads. I think." Those threads were not visible to Kaylin's eye, but she didn't doubt him. She could doubt his ability to express his activity in Elantran, though. "If I had to guess, Spike is attempting to remove—from the interior—whatever is holding the path in the wrong shape."

"That is what he attempts," Hope said. "We are protected here for the moment; the entirety of the force appears to be external in nature. Chosen, look at what you perceive as walls. Do not move too quickly or you will leave my protective sphere."

"Can you tell us how much of a diversion we'll suffer if we leave?"

"Not without leaving you behind, for however short a period. Is it essential knowledge?"

Kaylin exhaled. "Yes. If we're pushed away from the cavern, they intend to prevent our interference in the cavern itself. If we're pushed farther in, we're meant to land *in* the Adversary's lap. The first implies that the Consort is important enough that they wish to preserve her. The latter implies that the Consort is irrelevant at best, and one of their targets at worst."

"They would not *dare*," Ynpharion snapped; he was almost quivering with outrage.

"Ynpharion." As his name left the Consort's lips, he stilled. "I do not believe it is necessary to send your familiar to, or through, the portal's destination point."

"It's—"

"Assume that I am, in your best case, irrelevant."

A flash of bright, searing light permeated the "wall" to

Kaylin's immediate right. Defensive formation shifted around the Consort; she remained at its heart.

"Spike asks that you continue to do what you're doing," Hope said quietly.

Kaylin stiffened. "We're not doing anything."

"He asks that your servant be encouraged to continue."

Her shoulders sagged.

In the distance, slightly muffled, she heard the grim silence of Nightshade's amusement.

Although light could be seen through the opaque, misshapen tunnel wall, nothing else made enough visual noise to permeate it. But the flare was a strobe of lightning that illuminated the witnesses. Only when it appeared for the third time did Kaylin realize they cast no shadows in its sustained bursts.

"I think Nightshade is wielding *Meliannos*," she said.

"He is," Teela replied, her own sword gleaming in her hand.

"Do not," the Consort said, her voice much softer than her words, "attempt to go to his aid."

"What is he fighting?" Teela asked, which was all of her reply.

"I think he wants me to shut up."

"A sentiment with which I'm certain we can all identify." Teela glanced at Severn. Severn shook his head.

"Where are the cohort?"

"They are not yet in the same place." There was a moment's hesitation. "Valliant, however, has found his way to the stairs that lead to the cavern, if I'm not mistaken. He is not stupid enough to take them."

Mandoran might have been.

"And before you ask, no. I cannot tell you anything about

the relationship of Nightshade's current conflict to the progress of the cohort. In theory, he should not be able to track them or find them at all."

"In theory?"

"We are attempting to intersect the path they'll eventually take. And all evidence—admittedly not conclusive—implies that we are not the only ones who can. It's possible Nightshade is attempting to follow the trail of those who cannot enter the portal itself."

Yes.

"And something he's encountered on the way requires the use of that sword? I've seen him wield that sword—and it never looked like this."

"No. But you saw him wield the sword in an attempt to catch—and possibly kill—the Dragon outcaste. Had that encounter proceeded, you would have. And yes," Teela added, voice softer, "it is very likely he has chosen to be reckless in his use of his sword."

"He would not be the first today."

"We did not have the time," Teela countered as she glanced in the Consort's direction. "They know we are coming. Ah, no, they expected that there would be some intervention. It is my guess that they expected the form of that intervention to be Nightshade's, not ours—the pathway here has been diverted, but it has not been destroyed."

Hope turned to the Consort. "Spike asks us to wait. Lord Nightshade's work on the exterior has yielded results favorable to a safe arrival."

A shudder of flashing light, blue and white and searing, caused Kaylin to raise both arms instinctively to shield her eyes and face.

Teela cursed, the Leontine low and guttural.

CHAPTER 21

There was a moment of silence accompanied by a lot of blinking before Hope said, "Now. Lady, it is safe to leave."

"Will it remain safe?"

"I believe so." He glanced at Kaylin.

Nightshade?

Silence.

Nightshade!

Severn shouldered Hope out of the way and caught her in one arm—the hand of which still gripped the blade of his very unusual weapon.

"I can't—I can't hear him! His voice is gone!"

Teela cursed in Aerian. "You would have to say that out loud," she said with some heat. At Kaylin's expression, she added, "Yes, I can keep my cohort out—but *not* when I'm desperately trying to track them and hold all of the threads of their current locations in my head!"

And Annarion was going to lose it.

"Just...breathe, damn it. Breathe. And do not do anything stupid. Is he dead?"

"I don't know—I can't *hear him.*"

Teela exhaled. So did the Consort. "If he were dead, you

would know. There would be no question. I understand the panic," she added in a somewhat less heated tone. "It's the same panic we felt when the rest of us suddenly fell silent in the West March. But you would know—as we would have known—if that was the silence of death."

"You were all pretty certain that if it wasn't, it would be soon," Kaylin pointed out.

"Inasmuch as Barrani have family ties similar to yours—yours personally," Teela said, clarifying the statement, "the cohort are ours. Of course we were worried—and of course that worry would drive us to action. Nightshade's attachment to his only surviving brother is almost a matter of legend; this much would be all but expected of him."

"Did Annarion expect it?"

Teela winced. "No. He is trying to skip out of his qualifying exam now, and while we've pointed out that the fastest—and safest—way to reach his brother is to *pass the test*, he is not certain he has either that time or inclination."

"This isn't a normal exam. He can't just walk out in the middle of it and tell the proctors he'll be back later!"

"He is less concerned with completion of this test than he is with his brother's survival. And were you more cautious, he would not be presented with this difficulty. He is willing—barely—to focus on the test at hand because you are with us and you have access to his brother that he does not."

Kaylin opened her mouth and Hope laid a hand on her shoulder. "We must exit," he said quietly. "Spike is uncertain how long stability will last; if our enemies are desperate there is a possibility that they could destroy the portal—which would leave us somewhat stranded."

Kaylin stepped out of the portal's exit free from the horrible nausea that usually accompanied such a transition. Her legs were not shaking; her knees were not weak. She might have walked through an open door into another room. The floor beneath her feet was solid stone. She had expected the uneven rock of a large cavern. This was clearly worked stone—smooth and flat.

Her arms ached as her skin reacted to the presence of magic; the marks on her arms were glowing, as they had been since she had approached the High Seat. But the glow was gentle and luminous. On someone else, it would have looked good. Hope did not immediately shift into his portable form; he continued to resemble the ideal of an Aerian. This was not a good sign.

"Is this where we were supposed to be?" Kaylin asked the Consort.

"It is," a familiar voice replied. "You are late, however." It was Lord Evarrim. Of course it was. He stepped out of the shadows as he approached, and tendered the Consort a deep, a perfect, bow. "I have attempted to remain inconspicuous while keeping watch. So far, none of the supplicants have emerged to face their final trial."

"And you've encountered no other difficulties?" the Consort asked.

Silence.

Kaylin had never trusted Evarrim. She didn't trust him now. But she had come, however grudgingly, to understand that he would never harm the Consort; that he was willing—as Ynpharion was willing—to die in her defense. As she turned to examine him, she saw two things. One: the gem in his tiara was cracked. Two, his clothing—and it was Barrani cloth—was blackened in places.

"No difficulty that was insurmountable, Lady." His glance caught on the flat of Teela's sword, the blue of his eyes shifting to a lighter color. He was surprised.

"Are these halls safe?"

"They are momentarily safe," Evarrim replied. "They are not, in my opinion, secure. Your suspicions about the activities of certain members of the Court have been proved substantially correct."

Teela stiffened. Kaylin even understood why. Suspicion was a way of life, for the Barrani. It was so much a way of life that suspicion of bad—or illegal—behavior counted for nothing. If you couldn't be viewed with suspicion it was because you were already dead.

But proof? That was often harder to come by. And where proof existed, threat existed. If Evarrim was certain he had proof, no one who was made aware of it—or who could, at any rate, preserve it for later use—was meant to survive.

"I hope that your companions are worth the risk that we have taken," Lord Evarrim said to Teela.

She said nothing.

"It was at my request that such a risk was taken," the Consort said. "But if this is what our enemies can cobble together on such short notice, it is far better that the risk be taken now; imagine what we might be facing had they time to truly prepare. It is not my life that is targeted here," she added.

Evarrim said nothing. Loudly.

Lord Evarrim is direct, for a Lord of the High Court; it is considered his signal failing. Your understanding of the situation is correct; his expression makes clear that he does not agree with the Lady's opinion. He will not, however, speak of it. What she chooses to tolerate, he will tolerate. One could only wish that he could do so competently.

I'm not sure you're any better than he is.

I am far better at dissembling than Lord Evarrim. But I have had to be; I do not have his raw power. Nor do I have his family. You and he are similar.

Kaylin tried not to take offense, and because she was now worried, she managed to succeed. Mostly. *We're not.*

You are. You are incapable of displaying even the most basic of manners because you feel you are safe from reprisal. You do not care what others might think of you while you are at Court because you are not of the Court in any true sense. You do not believe the consequences will make a material difference in your life. So, too, Evarrim. Evarrim, however, has confidence because he has the power to survive possible consequences.

"An'Teela," Evarrim said, tendering her a perfect bow—which might be a first. He did not hesitate. As Teela was standing beside Severn, he added, "Lord Severn."

Teela nodded. So, to Kaylin's dismay, did Severn. "Stay with the Lady."

Ynpharion stepped aside to allow Evarrim pride of position as Teela and Severn headed down the hall.

The Consort did not move. "Kaylin, you now have time."

"Pardon?"

"Find Calarnenne."

Kaylin blinked. "I'm not sure how—"

"You have more of a chance of doing so than any other person present."

Evarrim was absolutely silent; his eyes were indigo. He opened his mouth and shut it—loudly—before words fell out.

The Consort forgives much. You are living proof of that. There are some things, however, that she will not forgive. And Evarrim is part of her Court. You have leeway he does not.

Do you understand their relationship at all?

No.

He was lying, or thought he was lying; she could sense that. She didn't push for an honest answer, because the consequences of pushing—for Ynpharion—would be too high.

Ynpharion didn't appreciate this, but never had. He found it beyond mystifying. It no longer made him deeply suspicious, but it made him uncomfortable because it implied pity.

It's not pity, she snapped. *Fine. You can't answer and I'm too cowardly to try to make you. Better?*

It wasn't.

Kaylin glanced at Hope, his wings now lofting in a breeze that appeared to be made of light. "Can you find him?"

"Not on my own."

"Can Spike?"

"Spike cannot operate entirely independent of you at the moment—and we both consider that the wisest, or safest, of choices."

"So that's a no."

Hope nodded.

Kaylin closed her eyes, and the sounds of distant footsteps receded further. She listened. She could sense Lirienne, and was surprised at how close he was. On reflection the surprise was stupid; she was with the Consort, and the Consort was his beloved sister. He was probably at least as worried as anyone else in this hall. More so, because he could not simply arrive, combat ready, from his halls in the West March.

She was aware of Severn. He was not entirely aware of her. All of his attention was focused on the halls in which he and Teela now played point. Severn could adapt to any partner, but Kaylin couldn't quite shake the feeling that she should be there, with the two of them, and not here in relative safety.

She shook that regret off.

Nightshade.

Silence.

Calarnenne. The silence continued. "Lady."

The Consort glanced over her shoulder.

"I'm not sure I can find him from here."

"Find him, if you can. It is not merely a matter of sentiment," she added, her voice cool, her expression remote. "He bears one of the three, and if he is lost forever, it will be lost with him."

Evarrim actually chuckled; the set of his shoulders softened. "*Meliannos* has had other wielders, but there is only one *Meliannos*. I will protect the Lady in your stead should you find it necessary—or possible—to extract him." He did not mention Nightshade by any of the names he used.

Kaylin called Nightshade again. There was no answer. She expected no answer. "Is Teela far enough away that she can't see us?"

"Unless she has eyes in the back of her head, yes. Her attention is not upon you except in a very desultory way; she is attempting to make certain that you will be safe while you traverse the halls ahead." Evarrim was no longer looking at Kaylin.

"Good."

Kaylin bowed her head, lifted her hand and touched her cheek, her fingertips grazing the mark that Nightshade had left there. It was like a tattoo, but the ink in which it had been drawn was magical in nature, and indelible; nothing smudged it, nothing caused it to fade. Nightshade's thugs— or guards, if she was being charitable, and as she'd grown up in the fiefs, charity toward them was low—called her *erenne*. She understood the mark had significance to the Barrani; it had enraged Teela and Tain when they'd first laid eyes on it. The existence of the mark was one of the deepest sources of conflict between Annarion and Nightshade. Teela and Tain had gotten used to it. So had Kaylin. Annarion had not. He didn't comment on it. He didn't ask about it anymore. But it was always there, in the background.

She understood that it was a binding of sorts, a claim that

implied ownership or intimacy—neither of which were based in fact.

She also understood that it was not a binding based on, or rooted in, name. It couldn't be, because when he'd laid that mark on her cheek, she hadn't had one. She had taken a True Name for herself during the test of the Tower—a test that the cohort were entangled in, even now. In theory, the Barrani needed names to wake, to come to life; Kaylin certainly hadn't.

She thought, now, that Nightshade had marked her as a way of bridging a distance made of gender, race, age—or perhaps it was a backup. He had chosen to reveal his True Name to her, after all. Even now, struggling to find him along the binding strands of that name, she didn't understand that choice.

She understood that the name itself was not the bridge she needed. And she wondered, as she shifted her attention away from it, what the silence would feel like if he had died. She wasn't certain that Teela was right—maybe Barrani experienced it differently. She had no way of knowing for certain, because she was human, and would remain so.

She pressed her fingers into the mark, more for luck than for effect. She had never tried to speak using the mark; she'd always considered it lesser than the name itself. But the mark on her cheek warmed to the touch. She thought it might be her imagination, because she was worrying it with her fingertips, as if it were a scab or a bruise.

"No," Hope said quietly. "It is not your imagination. What do you hope to achieve?"

"I want to find Nightshade. Shut up and let me concentrate."

"Do you know what you intend to do?"

"No, of course not. This is a thing we call seat-of-the-pants, Hope. Now, hush." She concentrated on Nightshade. She formed an image of him in her mind, which was surprisingly difficult; there were too many. She had no idea what he was wearing now, and no idea of what his surroundings were; the image that came most easily to mind was the audience chamber in Castle Nightshade, and that was definitely the wrong locale. She could see *Meliannos*, though. It wasn't a simple long sword; it was too large, too visually unwieldy, for that.

His eyes were blue. His hair was Barrani black. His skin was pale and, unlike Kaylin's, unmarked, unblemished. He was death. He was death for anyone who lived in the fiefs who dared to treat him without appropriate respect. His was the shadow that Castle Nightshade cast. *No*, she thought. But she couldn't shake the image, the visceral acknowledgment of all her childhood fears.

This was not all that Nightshade was, but it was truth. Nightshade—like any living, thinking person—was capable of more than one truth.

Her cheek grew warmer, and the skin beneath the flower symbol began to ache. It was like, and unlike, the pain magic caused the rest of her skin. Or maybe it was exactly the same thing: the mark itself a more mundane magic than the rest of the marks on her skin caused a more extreme reaction when it was activated.

She was aware of the exact moment when her skin began to blister from the physical heat of the mark; she had no mirror but she was certain the flower was glowing. The light caused heat. The heat caused injury. Annarion was going to see it and lose all his hair—at best. Maybe she should have considered that before making the attempt.

Thinking of Annarion, she reformulated the image she had built, detail by detail, in her mind's eye. Nightshade entering the foyer of *her* home. Nightshade speaking with Helen, whose eyes had flickered into obsidian. Nightshade speaking with Annarion, Annarion's stiffness barely masking pain and the anger that came from it.

Annarion, his brother. Annarion, the family member for whom he had become outcaste because he would not surrender his search. She could not see Nightshade as Annarion did; she had no memories of the man Annarion thought was buried beneath the rubble of experience and time. Had he been like Teela? No. Like Sedarias? Probably more likely.

But…no. No. Sedarias loved the cohort, even if *love* was not a word she would condescend to use, because it implied weakness. She had no idea what a young, idealistic Nightshade might look like; no idea what he might sound like. In Kaylin's mind, the word *idealism* was just a condescending way to say *stupid*. She'd heard it a lot.

What she knew, what she was certain of, was that Nightshade had loved his brother. And that her Nightshade, the man who could kill someone for failing to bend head quickly enough, retained that love, that affection. It hurt him. She couldn't fail to notice the pain—no one who lived in the house could. When the two clashed with words, their voices carried everywhere; it was impossible, even with Helen's intervention, not to hear some of the argument.

Not even Nightshade was proof against the pain love caused.

No, she thought, it wasn't the love that caused pain. It was the expectations. The hopes and dreams that surrounded it. The breaking of those dreams.

Kaylin understood the allure of dreams: they were hope. But she understood how those hopes broke in the face of reality. She'd experienced it herself, because she'd truly, viscerally, believed that crossing the bridge, that standing on the other side of the Ablayne, would free her. She would walk into a magical world where people didn't starve and weren't so constantly hungry and desperate they would eat anything that didn't move—even if they had to make sure it didn't move first.

And she'd learned.

The dreams weren't real, because on either side of the Ablayne, the streets were occupied by *people*. A perfect world didn't exist because perfect people didn't exist. There were crimes here—some of them horrific. There was poverty; the warrens were practically the fiefs in miniature, but without the advantage of an obvious fieflord, an easily found source of power.

Nightshade wasn't a nightmare; he was a person. Annarion wasn't the beloved child of Nightshade's memories. He was a person. Kaylin had seldom seen Nightshade as a person before. Maybe she hadn't looked. Maybe she hadn't *wanted* to look. Knowing too much was a straight passage to the death that guaranteed silence.

But even if he had marked her for his own purposes—and of course he had—not all of those purposes were malignant. He thought he could use her. He thought he could use the power of the Chosen to somehow free his brother. And she *had*.

But that led to this, in the end. Nightshade didn't want to be seen. He didn't want to be understood. He didn't want to be vulnerable. Kaylin understood this, as well. It was what passed for survival, in the fiefs.

It wouldn't pass muster here.

She pulled her hand from her cheek, grimaced at the trace of blood on her fingertips. She could heal this with the only power of the Chosen she could voluntarily and deliberately use. But before she started, she stopped. Now was not the right time. She reached for Nightshade, literally lifting her hands and opening the one that didn't contain a dagger, turning her palm to the ceiling and to the light.

In the distance, casting a very short shadow that implied he was standing directly beneath the source of that light, she could see Nightshade.

"Where is he?" she asked of Hope.

"Does it matter? You have found him. Call him now."

Nightshade. Nothing in his stillness implied that he could hear her.

"I can make myself heard," Hope told her. On the surface, the words were an offer, but beneath the surface, they were a warning. Kaylin was not one of nature's optimists. She shook her head.

"Can Spike see him?"

Spike clicked.

"Can you *reach* him?"

He clicked again, but whirred a bit, as well.

"He is uncertain that that will produce the results you desire."

"In Elantran, Hope."

"He believes that Nightshade will attempt to destroy him. He does not believe that Nightshade will succeed—but he says the sword is dangerous to us."

Us. "Fine." She bowed her head, and once again concentrated only on Nightshade's mark, her blistered cheek and the pain it caused. If Nightshade died, the mark would vanish, or so she believed. But the mark of the *erenne* didn't convey the same information that the binding of names did. And if it conveyed an echo of the control or compulsion, it was strictly one way. Nightshade was not adorned with a similar mark on any of his own perfect cheeks.

"Tell Teela," she said, raising her voice without turning,

"that I've found him. He's alive. I haven't figured out how to catch his attention, but I can see him."

"Noted," the Consort replied.

The Consort asks that you not take any foolish risks at this time.

Then she shouldn't have asked me to find him.

"What are you trying to do with the mark?" Hope asked, a thread of concern in the question.

"I'm...not sure."

"Perhaps you should stop. You are bleeding, and it is, as your attachment to Spike must indicate, unwise to bleed in the deeper spaces."

"I'm not *trying* to bleed."

"No. I am aware of that. But whatever you are attempting to do is having that effect, regardless."

She was extremely frustrated. *Extremely.* Because this mark was worse in all ways than the marks of the Chosen for which she was otherwise known. "Can anyone tell me *exactly* what the *erenne*'s mark is supposed to do? Because no other binding appears to work here."

A surge of revulsion came through the name bond she shared with Ynpharion. Revulsion and fear. Kaylin spun, cheek bleeding, in the direction of the Consort; the Consort had not moved. She appeared to be waiting for either Kaylin, or Teela and Severn's return. Ynpharion, however, had turned toward her; his motions were stiff and unnatural.

As he met her gaze, revulsion and fear gave way to anger. At Kaylin, of course.

What are you doing?

He didn't answer. He made an *effort* not to answer. Or perhaps he was now fighting on two fronts. One of those collapsed as he approached. "Forgive me," he said, his words so clipped and conflicted it sounded as if he had failed to correctly translate Barrani to Elantran.

Spike whirred. Kaylin said, "Don't hurt him. He doesn't want to be doing whatever he's doing, either."

"You are," Hope said in a tone that sounded suspiciously indulgent, "merciful in a very particular way. I have grown very fond of you. If you change your mind, should we disregard you?"

Kaylin had taken a step back. Ynpharion's eyes were a deep blue.

You do not have the Lady's will, he told her, *but in this one case, I would appreciate it if you attempted to exert control.* His interior voice was rigid with emotion, none of it positive.

Why?

Because, Chosen, you asked that question. The words sounded to Kaylin as if they were being spoken through clenched teeth. He came closer; she stepped back. It was Hope who caught her, his chest pressed against her back, his wings spread to either side of his current form like a wall.

She knew, as Ynpharion stepped in, what he intended, and she locked her arms to keep them by her sides; her hands shook.

Kaylin? Severn. Severn's voice.

I'm fine. It's fine.

You are not— Severn stiffened.

Don't—don't pay attention. This is my fault.

Something in Severn rose then; concern became fear, fear became anger. She closed her eyes because she had to close them. *I am honestly fine,* she told him. *Nothing is threatening to kill us here. Keep your eyes on the hall. No! I mean it! You can't leave Teela without a partner!*

For one long moment she thought he would ignore everything she'd just said.

And then Ynpharion caught her in arms that were at least as stiff as her own. Her entire body was rigid; it was all she

could do not to stab him, or not to try. Given his own tur-
moil, she might even have succeeded.

He kissed her.

His lips, against hers, were closed; they opened. She couldn't
force her own mouth to do the same—he could. She didn't
struggle; she could manage that much, because she understood, now, what the Consort intended.

Barrani were possessive. The mark itself was a symbol of,
a gesture of, possession. It was a figurative warning. Perhaps
a literal one. She kept her eyes closed; she tried to breathe.
Spike helped; he was frantically buzzing.

The air thickened; she tasted the barest hint of smoke, of
something burning that didn't normally catch fire. She heard
roaring in her ears, remembered to exhale, to inhale, and
then Ynpharion let go. She stumbled, but Hope caught her
before she could fall.

That, a familiar voice said, *was extremely unwise.*

She opened her eyes. Ynpharion was three yards away; he
had resumed his position by the Consort's side, his eyes indigo, his body no more relaxed than Kaylin's. Nightshade
was not standing in the hall.

"I have him," Kaylin croaked.

"Good."

Can you find your way back to us? She could no longer see
him.

Yes. Nothing that might prevent it is currently standing in my way.

She didn't want to talk to Nightshade. She didn't want to
talk to anyone. She wanted to go home and bathe.

You are remarkably squeamish. A hint of humor tinged the
words; some of the stiffness left them.

Kaylin shrugged.

Ask the Consort if she might remain where she is currently stand-

ing. If that is not a possibility, ask that she allow you to remain where you are currently standing. Moving while bearing Meliannos *is much more difficult than I had foreseen.*

Put it away?

It is not that simple, sadly. An'Teela is not with you.

No. She's scouting ahead.

Had Kaylin been speaking aloud, the words would have been lost to a sudden, guttural roar.

And she's found something. Or something has found her.

CHAPTER 22

Kaylin wheeled instantly in the direction of the roar. And it was a roar, a wordless shout that reverberated in the shorter stone halls. The halls weren't wide; they were probably tall enough that Teela could wield her sword if all of her strikes were top down. This was not the terrain for great swords.

The Consort began to move, and in her wake, almost orbiting her, Ynpharion and Evarrim followed. Kaylin began to follow, as well, but Hope placed a hand on her shoulder. "Not yet."

"Can you see whatever it is that's attacking?"

"Nothing is attacking," Hope replied, his voice almost unnaturally soft.

"But the roaring—"

"Nothing is attacking yet."

She grimaced. "Spike, go." Spike moved swiftly down the hall, toward the Consort. Evarrim wouldn't like it if he hadn't been made aware of the situation, but she was certain the Consort could keep Evarrim in check.

"That is not entirely wise."

"Nothing I ever do is. But if we're waiting for Nightshade, I won't lack muscle." Her grimace deepened.

Nightshade balanced between amusement and annoyance without falling squarely into either.

I don't mean to be disrespectful, but could you hurry? The Consort's back was dwindling as she progressed down the hall. The roaring, however, had banked; it had been replaced by snarling, growling; it reminded Kaylin of hunting Ferals.

Kaylin remembered the forest Ferals. She remembered Ynpharion.

Yes, Ynpharion said. The word was like a flash of lightning; he was angry.

Is that what they are?

Yes.

How many?

Three.

Three. *Don't let them bite anyone!*

Everyone present has faced them before, Chosen. They understand the risk.

She wondered why, as she forced her thoughts away from Ynpharion, that it was Ynpharion she interacted with the most. She felt no fear of him, and no discomfort from his constant irritation, his endless condescension. She could, at this distance, feel the tension in him; and his anger—if she weren't careful—would color everything.

Lord Ynpharion is young, Nightshade said. *He is not accustomed to hiding his own thoughts. When fear is absent, this is who he is. Fear in his life, given his status, has very seldom been absent. Were you to hold Evarrim's name, you might find the experience similar.* Silence followed; it was a thicker silence, a heavier one, the difference between a sheet and a tarpaulin.

Kaylin closed her eyes. She could see the marks on her arms, regardless—but that had always been true. She could also see Hope's wings. Hope himself disappeared beneath the reddened dark of eyelids, but his wings were alight, and far more transparent.

She looked through those wings.

Through them, she could see Nightshade dragging his sword. Had there been actual ground beneath his feet, she would have cringed; dragging swords was permissible only if you were badly injured and had no way to lift them. It was part of the reason Kaylin had never taken to the sword as a weapon; swords were too heavy, too ungainly, given her height.

She sheathed her dagger, took a step and, reaching through the wing—which she understood was a visual metaphor—held out her hand, palm up. Nightshade's eyes widened slightly; he could see it. He could, with effort, see her. He made that effort.

I must give my brother some small credit, he said as he made his way toward her. *This is far, far more difficult than I could possibly have imagined.*

He's not carrying that sword when he steps sideways.

No. I am not entirely certain the sword would condescend to allow it. Nightshade kept the sword in his right hand as he reached for her hand with his left. His grip was tight.

Kaylin pulled. Hope helped. Nightshade landed in the corridor with a distinct thud. There, he bowed.

"Not the time for manners," she told him as his grip on her hand eased.

"Only for you, Lord Kaylin. For those of us who have lived this life, they are as natural—and oft as necessary—as breathing. They are not work. We do not have to fight base instincts to be polite." He drew himself up to his full height, and used the leverage of her hand and arm to pull her toward him. There, he gazed down at her, his eyes upon her cheek. "I would ask you what you were attempting to do, but it will have to wait."

"Trying to find you."

"By attempting to remove the mark itself?"

"I wasn't trying to remove it."

"You were. In no other way would it cause the damage it has caused." He inhaled, gained a few inches of height and released her. "I am of a mind to kill Ynpharion."

"Stand in line."

If the Consort was happy to see Nightshade, she gave no indication other than the pause in forward motion. She accepted his bow—which was deeper by far than the one he'd offered Kaylin—bid him rise and then continued down the hall to where Teela and Severn were at a standoff.

These creatures were very like the forest Ferals that had attacked the Consort's party on the road to the West March, a journey that had, in the end, set everything in motion. Everything.

"I think," Teela said almost conversationally, "that this might be your job."

Kaylin frowned. "My job? You're the one with the gigantic, glowing sword!"

"Apparently, I'm not the only one." She glanced at Kaylin and her eyes narrowed. Of course they would. Kaylin's cheek was bleeding. But a bleeding cheek and a reminder of the mark was lower on the priority list than bestial, former Barrani.

Teela offered Nightshade a very controlled nod. But she said, "Lord Calarnenne."

"An'Teela, *kyuthe* to my brother. I am at your service."

"Kaylin," the Consort said.

Kaylin almost shrieked. These weren't the Ferals of her distant childhood, no—they were larger and far more cunning. She raised her hands—both weaponless now—and turned them toward Teela.

Teela rolled her eyes. "Use your head," she snapped in a corporal's voice.

Kaylin's reaction, since she was a private, was almost immediate. She snapped into position and reached for her familiar's wing. Her familiar who wasn't sitting on her shoulder, and whose wing therefore couldn't be pulled up like a mask.

Behind her she heard a warm chuckle. "Yes," Hope said, as if she'd spoken out loud. "I believe the Consort wishes to redeem them, if that is possible."

"She wants me to do what I did to Ynpharion."

"For Ynpharion, yes. You have said yourself that people are not all of one thing or all of another. You are aware that Ynpharion's desire for both power and freedom was not the whole of his thought or will. But it dominated the moment in which he was either transformed or taught to transform, and it became the entirety of his thought; all else was forgotten."

She did not want to somehow be in possession of three more names; the chorus on the inside of her mind was loud enough.

"You do not have to hold the names," Hope said quietly.

"Then what am I supposed to do with them?"

"You are Chosen."

She had never hated that word quite as much as she did at that moment, burdened by the expectations of the people who surrounded her. How in the hells was she supposed to touch names that were behind bristling rows of fangs? She was fond of keeping her body parts attached, and she needed her throat for trivial things like breath.

You've done it before, Ynpharion said with far less patience than even Teela had shown.

★ ★ ★

She closed her eyes, as she had done in the safety of her dining room at Bellusdeo's command. She wasn't doing what she had done while racing through the Hallionne Orbaranne; there, she had seen the landscape beneath her feet—it just hadn't been the same as the one she could see when she didn't have Hope's wing plastered to her face. Closed eyes always made words easier to see. They made words easier to hear, as well—even Elantran words—but people took it badly if she closed her eyes to listen to them.

She could see the words on her arm. She could see the light cast by Hope. As her eyes became accustomed to being closed, she could see the shapes of words across the edges of two blades, one in Teela's hands, one in Nightshade's. These were not words in the same way the marks on her arms were— they were transparent and elongated, trapped and stretched in a form that implied weaponry, even in the dark.

They grew brighter as she turned toward them, darker when she turned away. She turned away. She could hear Severn, Ynpharion, Nightshade. They were breathing—to be expected—but she couldn't hear the breathing of the rest of her companions. When she turned in the direction of that familiar noise, she could tell whose breath, separating them easily. She couldn't see their names.

How had she seen Bellusdeo's name? What had she done differently? She turned away from the people she knew, and looked toward the end of the hallway, where the three waited, holding their ground and blocking the Consort's progress. Although they had been snarling and growling before she'd closed her eyes, she could not hear their voices now.

"My eyes are closed, right?"

"Yes," Hope replied.

"And I'm not plugging my ears."

"No. But you are concentrating now on an entirely different type of sound. You can hear those name-bound to you. You cannot hear the creatures you refer to as Ferals because you are not listening to the noises they actually make."

"And I can hear you."

"Yes. You can hear me."

"Why don't you do this all the time?"

"Because it is somewhat taxing. Teela carries a sword. She carries an impressive sword. She can—as you have seen today—wield it, but while you have seen it before, you have never seen it used. It is a weapon. It exacts its price. There is a time and a place for weapons, but she does not, in spite of the conflict she expects, wield it constantly. I am like her sword.

"To do 'this,' as you call it, you have collapsed states of existence into each other."

"Say that in Elantran."

"You are here, where I am speaking, and there, where your friends are watching the hall. Usually, these two states are separate. They exist, but you are anchored in only one of them."

"When you say two states, do you mean only two?"

"No. But it is easiest to explain it that way."

"So... I'm doing what the cohort does naturally?"

"Absolutely not." The words were crisp and instant. After a pause, Hope added, "It is possible that you are doing what the cohort's constituent members believe they are trying to do."

"And I'm doing it because I have you."

"Yes."

"So the Ferals aren't *actually* here."

"If you are not careful, you will be where the Ferals are, yes."

She opened her mouth to ask Teela a question, but no words came out. Instead of trying again, she accepted that she could not speak to Teela in this place.

Ynpharion.
Lord Kaylin.

Surprise almost caused her eyes to fly open. *If I actually move down the hall—physically move, I mean—please let me know.*

He did not consider this the stupidest request she had ever made, but felt it was close. Then again, he considered almost all of her requests stupid.

"Why could I see Bellusdeo's name?"

"You looked."

"I can't see the Consort's. I can't see Teela's."

"No."

"What's the difference, if I'm looking for names?"

"You are not specifically looking for either of their names, and they are not calling you."

"Bellusdeo wasn't calling me, either."

"Not literally, no."

Kaylin stopped moving. "You can see them."

"I can see the Ferals, yes. My vision is not limited in the fashion yours is. You were not meant to see this way at all. Were it not for the marks you bear, I do not believe you could."

"The cohort can."

"No, not like this. They can exist in a much more physical way across various states; they have not learned to fully reintegrate with the lives they were born to. But part of that is the effect of the *regalia*. They are like miniature centers of gravity; they pull all states into nexus points simply by existing."

"Terrano?"

"He is the exception; he is far less anchored than any of the rest of the cohort. In their absence, however, he is far more cautious than your Mandoran might be in similar circumstances."

Kaylin wished she could see the hallway, because the walls would have served as a partial guide; they would have given her one clear indication of both distance and direction. She didn't lift her arms to touch the wall, because she wasn't certain her hands would connect with anything. Although her eyes were closed, she could see light. She could hear breathing. She could feel something like stone beneath her feet.

She had walked toward Bellusdeo.

"Move as you moved before you named me, Chosen. You understand the danger the Ferals represent to your friends. If you had the time for this standoff, it might be wisest to let Teela and Severn fight—but Severn is mortal, and human. His survival here is not guaranteed."

Kaylin moved then, the motion a visceral lunge forward into a darkness alleviated only by Hope's diffuse wings. As she did, she finally saw the Ferals.

"Kaylin."

"Not *now*," she snapped.

"Open your eyes."

She did. She was no longer standing in a hallway. There were no people between her and the Ferals that stood their ground. No Teela or Nightshade with their humongous swords; no Severn with a weapon chain he could not set to spin. Even in a shorter circle, the halls here were too narrow.

The Ferals did not immediately look up to meet her eyes. They didn't shift position at all. Ynpharion certainly had.

He was beyond irritated by the observation; Kaylin realized that he found it humiliating. But she had no way to turn off her thoughts, and didn't waste the effort trying. She did waste the effort on amazement that Teela and Nightshade could guard their own so completely.

An'Teela is impressive, Nightshade said. *I am less so. It is not difficult to guard one's thoughts against someone who very seldom listens.*

Can you see what I see?

I believe so.

The Ferals seemed almost like statues; their bodies were obsidian, with flecks of color. That color moved, swirling and shifting, beneath the surface of skin that was hard, carved, smooth. This was not how she had seen Ynpharion, the first time. This wasn't, she was almost certain, what Teela and Severn were seeing now. The Ferals were the Shadows closest to animals in appearance; they didn't sprout extra eyes or extra mouths; they didn't have fingers and hands instead of paws. And they had fur, like short-haired dogs.

These didn't. Not here. Their surfaces seemed almost chitinous, with small gaps in the armor where their joints would bend. But their faces were the larger variant of the Ferals that had made nights a time of pure terror in her childhood.

And their eyes were Barrani blue. They were Barrani eyes.

Was it Iberrienne who taught you how to do whatever it is you were doing with your name and your physical form?

Yes. He was not the only such teacher.

Clearly. You mentioned that mortals—or mortal Arcanists—may have been involved. I doubt we'll find them here—but we're going to have to find them in the future. Speaking, she moved toward the Ferals.

Their feet seemed to be anchored—literally anchored—to the floor. The floor on which Kaylin was standing. She flinched as her eyes followed their paws, her gaze then moving to the Shadow beneath them. If they were the Shadow's peak, the Shadow's physical manifestation, what lay beneath them was far larger, far darker.

Ynpharion, tell Teela and Severn that these are not *like the forest Ferals. They seem to be anchored to, and drawing power from, a*

*much greater pool of Shadow. If it's possible—if they need to fight—
tell them to try to take out their legs.*

Pardon?

*Or tell them to somehow detach the Ferals from the ground they're
standing on.* She frowned. *It may be the reason they're not leaping—
literally—to attack. I don't think they'll attack until they can extend
their jaws and start biting faces, or whatever else they can reach.*

Can you see their names?

Not yet. Not quite. She could see the armor that should have
been fur. Her gaze, her focus, had first gone to the breadth
of darkly smooth chest, as if she were looking for the heart of
the beast, because on some level she believed the name resided
there; her gaze had dropped to the floor when she realized the
shadows cast by these Ferals were not the shadows she would
have expected, even of creatures of their size.

Her gaze left the floor and rose, past the chest that in theory
contained heart or lungs. When she reached the head, her attention momentarily snagged on ebon jaws; she forced it up.
Yes, she told Ynpharion. *Yes, I've found their names.*

The names were not like Bellusdeo's name; they were far
more like Ynpharion's—a single rune she'd have some hope
of transcribing, rather than a mess of different lines and tex-
tures that overlapped and faded from memory the minute she
looked away. Once she'd caught sight of the names, she wondered how she'd managed to miss them; they were glowing,
golden sigils that appeared to be anchored to the foreheads
of the Ferals by gravity and Shadow. They weren't flat; they
were dimensional.

She hesitated. She had taken Ynpharion's name; he hadn't
offered it to her. Although she could see the names, they
weren't on offer, either. One angry, condescending voice in
her head was more than enough. If she could, she'd forget

the name entirely; it would free her from a constant stream of criticism.

"You do not have to take the name," Hope said quietly.

"I have to do something with the name—"

"Yes. Think, Kaylin. The last time you encountered Ynpharion, you had not named me. There were things I could not do, interactions that were impossible. Now you have more flexibility. I cannot do what you must do, but the ability is yours."

"Because I'm Chosen."

"Because," he agreed, "you are Chosen. When the Lady carries names to the newborn, does she take and keep the knowledge of those names? Do those names have power when they are not wed to the living, as they were intended to be?"

"They have to have some power, or the newborn wouldn't wake."

Hope made a frustrated noise that almost sounded Leontine.

The Lady wishes to know what you are attempting to do.

Tell her I'm trying to figure out how not to be saddled with more people like you, Kaylin snapped.

Noted, he responded, his interior voice stiff and almost neutral.

I can carry the names, she thought. *But how can I carry them without separating them?* She hadn't removed Ynpharion's name from his body; she had touched it, grabbed it, taken the knowledge of it. She had given in to her immediate desire—survival, which was perfectly reasonable—but she hadn't literally removed the name.

She'd taken the name of a bisected Feral before it was devoured. But *that* name hadn't come with syllables that could be spoken, could be pronounced. She had caught it, and slapped it almost literally on the closest available patch of skin, where it had stuck. And she had used it, later, to stabilize Gilbert's physical form in her own reality. It had been a type of healing.

The name hadn't been returned to the Lake. Maybe it would one day, if Gilbert died. She didn't know. But she'd felt none of the Consort's rage or sorrow at its loss. If the names had been created to breathe life into still, sleeping bodies, it had done a variant of its job.

The carrying of names that were still in use seemed impossible—the two goals were mutually exclusive. She couldn't carry something that was demonstrably still being used. Hope knew this. She was certain he knew it. Which meant he either assumed she was capable of things that couldn't be done, or she wasn't looking at this the right way.

"Everything," Hope said softly, "is metaphor. What you see now is a metaphor. It is something you've built to allow you to navigate byways that were never meant for your kind. Remember that."

She understood what he meant by metaphor, but it was difficult. Kaylin wasn't an Imperial mage. She wasn't an Arcanist. She was a ground Hawk. A Hawk. Her job wasn't to make metaphors of things. It was to assess evidence, examine crime sites, prevent new crimes from happening if at all possible. To do that, she had to be firmly grounded in reality; she had to become aware of how her own life led to inevitable prejudices; she had to question some of her own experiences. But those experiences, conversely, made a lot of her job easier.

Marcus had drilled pragmatism into her head. He'd made certain she understood what her job was, what her responsibilities were; he'd made clear that he expected her to live up to both—but also made clear that he thought she *could*. She'd needed that, and clung to it.

She was accustomed, however, to trusting what she'd seen,

heard, touched. She'd built that confidence over seven years, sometimes rockily. This was going against every lesson she'd learned in that time.

No, she thought, straightening her shoulders. Not *every* lesson. She had a job to do here. She had a responsibility. It wasn't the job she'd been trained to do—but that didn't matter. If Severn and Teela faced these Ferals in this narrow space, they weren't going to escape unscathed. Not even Teela. Nightshade could back them up—but only if one of them fell, or fell back. It wasn't like the forest. The walls couldn't be strategically placed or moved around.

She could make the difference.

But...no pressure. She grimaced, straightening her shoulders again. She didn't know what she could do. She had been afraid, for years, of what the marks might signify. Children had died because of these marks—murdered in some sacrificial, sympathetic magic that would allow someone else to define their shape, altering what had been placed there by—by someone or something.

She understood that that fear wasn't useful. The guilt wasn't reasonable. But fear and guilt weren't rational responses; what she made of them was. Or could be.

She walked toward the names of the Ferals. As she did, the bodies of creatures that were, or had been, Barrani became clearer, more well-defined. The eyes that looked ahead—the Barrani eyes—began to waver. They hadn't seen her before. They couldn't see her easily now. But they could sense her presence, as if she were the faintest of starlight that could only be glimpsed from the corners of the eyes.

Kaylin approached the left-most Feral. As she did, Hope followed, and with him, the halo of light his wings shed. She watched the ground beneath the Ferals' feet, where the deep well of Shadow lay. Illumination did not gentle it; it brought out the hidden swirls of chaotic, moving color that implied life. But the shadows cast by the bulk of the Ferals themselves did change in the light; they became longer, but more defined.

They were human shaped. No, she thought, Barrani shaped. Some knot of tension in her neck and shoulders dissolved. She didn't ask Ynpharion if her physical body was moving. It wasn't. She could feel her hands, clenched in too-tight fists by her sides, could feel her legs, slightly bent at the knees. But she could also feel her hands as she lifted her left arm. Barrani eyes in bestial faces flickered. She heard distant growls. No; she *felt* them. The Ferals were silent.

She reached for the name and realized she couldn't actually *see* her own arm or her hand. She could feel them; she could see the name; she could see the Ferals and the Shadow and the light. She cast no shadow herself. Her eyes were closed, and she was afraid to open them, afraid to be in the real world having achieved nothing. Metaphors, she decided, were *hard*.

Hope had said she could open her eyes here. But the things she could see with her eyes closed—the words, for instance— she had always been able to see with her eyes closed. She wasn't seeing them with her actual eyes. Later, she thought. Later, when she was in the safety of her own home, surrounded by people who were not trying to kill her, she would try opening her eyes.

She reached for the name again, focusing only on the sigil. As she did, it grew larger. *I'm approaching it*, she thought. *It's not changing size*. The size, however, was necessary to see what she'd missed at a reasonable distance; as the word grew larger, cracks appeared across the bold, solid lines. Colors bled into the light, changing it. Darkening it.

She could see the source of that darkness. It was a slender thread of Shadow, narrower than infant's hair. No, she thought, not a single thread; there were more—but all were very fine. She could break them just by passing a hand through them. And she did. Her left hand. The hand which was sometimes gloved in a lace made of Shadow.

She held the sigil in the palm of her right hand; she broke the small filaments with her left. The small filaments, however, reached up from the Feral's body, like rising fur, to replace what she'd broken. The third time she tried, she cursed; she could feel Leontine rumbling in a distant throat not mean for Leontine.

Carry the name, he'd said.

Carry the name without taking it. Carry the name without hearing the truth of its syllables. She'd done that, once. She done it for the High Lord; she'd done it for herself. But she'd taken the name from a metaphorical desk; she'd dipped her hand into a distant lake without realizing what she was doing. If she carried the name, wouldn't she effectively be killing the person it currently inhabited?

"Yes, Chosen," Hope said. "But they will return, in the end. They will be born as Barrani."

"Could I have done this to Bellusdeo?" It was the heart of her fear. She knew what she was like when she was in a bitter, despair-fueled rage. And people who had those shouldn't *have* the power to do what she was now certain he was telling her to do.

"No. She is wed to her name, bound to it. It is where it should be. Her desire has never been to escape the truth of herself."

No. She wanted to *be* herself. And as the only female Dragon, the only person who could propagate a race, she couldn't. Kaylin stared at the name that was closest to her; it was the name she had tried to dust free of what appeared to be living cobwebs.

These would not be the first people she had killed in her

life. They wouldn't be the first people she'd killed since she'd crossed the bridge. But...killing in a fury of red rage was not the same as killing this way; slitting a person's throat wasn't the same as stabbing them from the front while they were trying to kill her.

Ynpharion.

Lord Kaylin.

Would it have been better—for you—if I had killed you instead of taking your name?

How would you have managed to accomplish that?

Just pretend I could. Would it have been better?

His frustration was an endless well; it threatened to become a geyser. *Why must everything devolve into permission with you? If you can kill them, kill them. We do not have the time—*

Killing a person. Enslaving a person. Both were bad—but she'd done both before. If the situations were different, the end result was the same: death or enslavement.

Kaylin's shoulders sagged. Hope placed a hand on one of them, and she felt a jolt of warmth, of something that was almost like the essence of home. "Why can't you do this?" she asked, because asking put off the decision for a few minutes.

He didn't pretend to misunderstand. "This is not my power, Kaylin. It is yours. It is the power of the marks of the Chosen, funneled through the person who now carries them. They are wed to you; nothing you do here could not, in the end, be done *by* you. It requires no sacrifice. Were I not here, you would still be in this space; you would still see the words clearly."

"And I could take them."

"And you could take them." Voice gentle, he said, "Decide, but decide quickly. I will not judge you for either decision. Nor would your companions."

"It's not their judgment I'm worried about."

"Yes. You must live with yourself, regardless."

Kaylin exhaled. The Ferals, attached somehow to a greater well of Shadow, were probably already enslaved. Probably. Maybe. It was a justification, an excuse. Ynpharion as Feral had not been Ynpharion as Barrani. Any thought of the Shadow, any thought of the people who had taught him how to live in a "less restricted" way, enraged him. He would not choose to go back to what he had been.

You would have killed me, had you realized you could.

Yes. Yes, she would have. But she'd done what she'd done to save her own skin while attempting to save Orbaranne. And, she thought as she forced her shoulders into a more upright position, she'd do what she did because she was attempting to reach the cohort. Annarion. Mandoran. Prickly, autocratic Sedarias. She'd do it because the Consort was with her, and Teela, and Severn. She wouldn't let Nightshade die, either, if she could prevent it.

She reached out with her left hand, caught the name and *listened.*

CHAPTER 23

In the darkness of Shadow and gold, Kaylin listened to the syllables, which were blurred and indistinct if even a hint of stray thought intruded. The sound of breathing, even her own, fell away; she could hear no internal voices. She listened, until the only sound she could hear was a name.

Edelonne.

As Ynpharion had, he fought. He *moved*, leaping toward her, although he also remained in place, beneath her hand. It was disorienting enough that she ignored it, although Teela's raised voice could be heard, regardless.

Edelonne.

Speaking the name, saying it, was like the rumble of thunder, but syllabic. Light stabbed her right eye—or something like light—and she held on to the name as he attempted to rush across it to reverse the direction of the control. It was like trying to hold on to a horse, and was the entirety of the reason that Kaylin had never taken well to riding lessons. Luckily, horseback was only required for the Swords. It was *recommended* for Hawks.

She shouldn't be thinking about anything but Edelonne now, but in a perverse way, it helped. It grounded Kaylin. It centered her, for the moment, in the life and the responsibilities she'd chosen. She was a Hawk. Private Kaylin Neya.

And Edelonne was a man who, for whatever reasons, had chosen to join the Barrani who even now conspired against the cohort, against her friends and—probably in ignorance—against the Consort, who brought life to them all.

Guilt left. Doubt fled. She held on to the name in a grip that was tight enough it restricted all movement. It struggled to evade; it was like trying to hold on to a glowing snake. A poisonous snake that she had by the head; if she didn't hold on, it was going to be costly.

But as she repeated the name, the force of the single spoken word causing tremors in the air and the ground, it stilled. It stilled enough that she could examine it closely. The strands, minute and recurring, were gone. Nothing attempted to reach for the word, to pull it back, to center it again. It was in her hand.

She felt the shock, the confusion, the fear—that was the hardest—of yet another person in her coterie of nameheld, and was surprised to discover that Edelonne was female.

Nightshade said, *What you did there, do again. One of the creatures that was blocking the hall has reverted to a more familiar shape. She is not entirely cogent, but she is no longer a threat.*

I'm not sure I'm going to get all three of them, Kaylin replied as she grabbed the next name. She made an attempt to grab both, but the Feral farthest from her appeared to be retreating.

He or she is retreating. The other is now standing in place.

She stopped speaking to Nightshade. She stopped attempting to catch or hold the retreating name. She concentrated, again, on the one in her hand, listening to the sound of it, until it resolved into a set of syllables that she could pronounce, in sequence, as if that sequence had meaning.

Averen.

Averen.

He did not fight her as Edelonne had fought; speaking the syllables was harder than holding the name. And as she sank the knowledge of it into her thoughts, she could see what he saw: the Consort. Teela wielding *Kariannos*. Nightshade bearing *Meliannos*. He turned once, almost wildly, to look over his shoulder; Kaylin could not see what he saw, but didn't try. She understood that he was looking for Shadow.

Possibly looking for the third and last member of their number.

Come back, Nightshade said, his voice sharper, the two words almost a command. She wanted to tell him that's not the way names worked, but didn't, because she felt the tremble start in her arms; her legs, braced for action, had locked in place, but their ability to hold her up seemed to suddenly be in question.

She opened her eyes. Her arms were stiff and, yes, trembling in fists by her sides. She inhaled, exhaled, inhaled; her head hurt. The lights in this hall were too loud.

A Barrani man stood beside a Barrani woman. They no longer bristled; their teeth were invisible between the thin lines of closed mouths. Silence was practically audible.

Do you recognize them? she asked Ynpharion.

Yes.

Did you know them before you—before I—

Yes.

Do you have some idea of who the runaway was?

Clearly. Before you continue, I find it difficult to hold two conversations concurrently when one is…heated. I am answering the same questions, less kindly phrased, for the Lady.

Kaylin shut up. She knew this entire conversation should have been had the moment she'd arrived home from her first visit to the West March—but her own life had been so chaotic. She hadn't even had a home to return to. She'd also been under the strong impression that the investigation, such as it was, had been given to the Barrani of the High Court.

Clearly, none of the High Court Barrani were Hawks.

Fine. Ask her what she'd like to do with these two.

It is already part of the discussion.

She had forgotten the way Ynpharion had fought her in the very early days. His bitter resentment had faded since the High Halls had come under the attack of the Barrani Ancestors. If his condescension and arrogance were a continuing theme, his actual resistance had vanished.

Averen and Edelonne were new. They pulled. Pushed. Attempted to break the wall of Kaylin.

You could have killed them. It was not Ynpharion who spoke, but Nightshade. He was not contemptuous, though—he was annoyed. Teela was annoyed, as well, but couldn't make it *quite* as clear.

The only person who didn't seem to resent her decision—no, the only Barrani, as Severn understood it completely—appeared to be the Consort.

I do not resent it, Ynpharion almost snapped. *It is what you are.* His interior voice gentled as he added, *And it is what the Lady expected. She is not what you are; she has had to make much harsher choices given her position and those who seek to harm the High Lord. But were she like you, it is absolutely the choice she would have made.*

Averen did not fight her for long; Kaylin thought his struggle was instinctive, visceral. Eledonne was angry. She was angry in almost the way Ynpharion had been.

They were similar people, Averen said. His interior voice was sheared of the edge that Ynpharion's always contained. *This is the heart of their fear. This is why they wanted the power we were offered.*

And not why you did?

No. I see Ynpharion is here. Did you capture him the same way you captured us?

Not the exact same way, no. And before you ask, I didn't want him, either.

You have powerful friends.

Some. Powerful enemies, too.

Yes. Something in the single word gave her enough warning that she could brace herself. Averen was not Edelonne; he was more subtle, less up front. More dangerous because of it. She stumbled, bringing her hands up to her head, a gesture that was both instinctive and useless. The sudden, stabbing pain was entirely on the inside of her head.

It stopped instantly. Kaylin looked up, lowering her hands. Teela had slashed Averen. She had not removed his head from his neck, but it was his neck that was bleeding; as she watched, he lifted a hand—both hands—to the wound. He had eyes for Teela, and only Teela; the attack on Kaylin vanished as if it had never happened.

As if he would never be stupid enough to make it happen again.

"You have no value to me—at all. Lord Kaylin does. She is young and she instinctively preserves life where that is an option. She is *kyuthe* to me, Lord Averen. You are a traitor. In deference to Lord Kaylin's preference, you are not dead. Do you understand? She is mortal. If you wish to throw your eternity away because you cannot bear the humiliation of a few paltry decades, I would be more than pleased to oblige. Choose. Choose now; you have wasted enough of our time."

He said nothing as Kaylin straightened. To her surprise, she felt a tinge of satisfaction from Ynpharion, buried beneath strong approval. Of Teela, of course.

How did Teela know it was Averen?

An'Teela clearly pays attention at Court, he replied.

Edelonne had reached the same conclusion as Averen; her fight, her struggle, was now a series of uncomfortable twitches—visceral, instinctive reactions.

Kaylin was not entirely familiar with the internal laws that governed the Barrani High Court; she assumed, as she had always assumed, that power was the rule of law. The Consort, however, did not seem at all troubled by Teela's attack. Nor did Teela's threat seem to bother her, although her eyes were now the regular shade of Barrani blue.

"Lord Kaylin, could you have killed them?"

Kaylin nodded.

"Perhaps, if we encounter their companion again as we traverse these halls, you might consider that the safer option."

"Lady," she replied as she bowed. She rose before she was granted permission, although she rose stiffly. Before she could speak, the Consort did.

"I understand that you spared them because we required information."

This wasn't true, but it was a good excuse. Not that a Hawk should *need* an excuse not to murder people.

Teela and Severn once again took point, heading down the hall in front of the Consort's party. Nightshade, no surprise, chose to position himself at the rear. Spike, in his larger floating-spiked-ball form, hovered to Kaylin's left, drifting there as if anchored.

Hope was at her right, his wings once again folded. It was Hope who pointed out that the integrity of the hall was in question, but Spike who detached himself. "You're talking about the Shadow?"

"Yes. If we had closed in combat with the transformed, it would not have been as simple a combat as the one Teela faced in the Consort's chambers. These Ferals could draw upon the power of that Shadow, and would have done so until it was depleted." His tone made clear that he thought that depletion was a long, long time in the future.

"And now?"

"They are no longer connected to it. Its power exists in potential, but it has no outlet." He paused, and then added, "Yet."

"So we're going to see more Ferals?"

"I doubt that, given what you have just accomplished. There is, however, one that escaped. And there are many other ways to use that power." Spike clicked loudly; Kaylin could feel it, although he was no longer at her side. "Spike says the creatures you referred to as spiders were not attached in the same way. The halls here are not subject to the same protections as the Consort's personal chambers. But he is concerned."

"Because he thinks the last Feral is the dangerous one?"

"No, Chosen. Because there are Shadows who could make very effective use of that power, on this plane. He does not understand how they might be here—but...he is here, and he should not have been able to leave *Ravellon*, either."

Kaylin turned toward Edelonne. *What were your orders?*

She felt very little resistance; Edelonne was staring at the Consort. Averen was staring at a spot on the wall just to the left of the Consort, his face free of the taint of expression. He might have been carved of stone, with perfect paint on top.

Friction, resistance and anger melted slowly as the force of the question brushed them to the side.

We were to stop you here, and hold you here—or kill you here, should it become necessary. Again her eyes flickered to the Consort, her gaze fluttering away as if even the sight was painful.

Who gave you the orders?

This time, the resistance was stronger, the struggle to maintain silence more visceral. Kaylin could sense the fear rolling off her in waves, tangible enough to drown in.

I'm sorry, Kaylin told her, meaning it. *But we don't have time for this.*

Edelonne fought. Kaylin took a step back before locking her knees, tensing her legs, bracing herself for physical impact. It was necessary. She couldn't remember Ynpharion fighting like this—but her memory wasn't immortal; he probably had.

The fear grew sharper, stronger; she felt it expand in her own thoughts, her own mind, until she was almost paralyzed by it.

Kaylin. Sharp voice. Nightshade's voice. Her name was all of the warning he offered—and all of the warning necessary. The fear was not her fear.

Not yet, Nightshade said softly. His voice was a hum, a vibration; it spoke of safety. The safety, in the end, of being owned, of being a prized possession. Like a beloved infant, held in the arms of a Leontine mother.

But she was not a child anymore. She was a Hawk, a lord of this stupid Court, and Chosen. She thanked him, wordless, for the offer of comfort, understanding exactly what that comfort entailed. He could make the decisions. He could tell her what she *should* be doing. He offered superior knowledge. Certainty.

She shook herself. He didn't have that, either. None of the people here did. She was momentarily angry at the cohort. Had Annarion chosen to wait—even a few months—they'd be in a better position.

No, Edelonne said. *You wouldn't. None of them—none of us—would. You don't understand what's happening, even now, beneath your feet. You have a chance*, she continued, the internal voice rising, the volume once again almost overwhelming. *You can turn around. You can flee. There might be safety for you.*

I can't. I can't leave the Consort. I can't abandon my friends.

Shock at the word *friends* stilled the terror that was rebuilding itself. Edelonne was afraid.

"They're coming with us," she said out loud.

Teela's eyes became narrowed slits as she swiveled to glance at Kaylin.

"There's something happening."

"You think?" was the sarcasm-inflected Elantran response.

"I mean—there's something happening right now."

Teela didn't bother putting sarcasm into words again; it wasn't necessary. "Can they tell you what?"

Words did not come from Edelonne; images did. Kaylin could see nothing for one long beat, although her eyes were open. When she did, it was a night-scape made of a Shadow that had devoured all but a red, red light; that light beat, like a grotesque heart, illuminating something that Kaylin had no name for.

"I don't think they have a name for it, either, and if they did, I wouldn't let them speak it out loud."

"Does it own them?"

"Own them?"

"Are they name-bound?"

"I—I'm not sure."

The expression on Teela's face implied Averen's wasn't the only neck at risk. *"Ask."*

"I believe," the Consort said in a much friendlier tone, not that that was hard at the moment, "that Lord Kaylin will be coming to Court more often in the near future. She requires rudimentary lessons in some of the basics of her current situation, and while the Dragon Court is overseeing etiquette, the Barrani Court may as well do our part."

The soft tones of her voice, the mild criticism and the gentle condescension grounded Kaylin. It gave her the momentary illusion that someone was in command.

Are you name-bound? She asked it of both Averen and Edelonne.

They were silent.

She asked again, putting more force into the words.

Edelonne said no. Averen once again failed to answer. In this darkness, that was answer enough.

Can I make Averen tell me who holds his name? Kaylin asked Ynpharion.

You? No. You may attempt to exert your will—but there is no hope whatsoever in my opinion that your will, your command, will take precedence here. He will die or break under the force of two separate orders. You will concede the struggle in order to preserve him, as you have done in the past.

Could I—

No, Lord Kaylin.

"An'Teela," the Consort said. "Lord Averen." She offered that lord a slight nod.

Kaylin didn't have time to react to what she only belatedly realized was an order. Teela stepped in and removed Averen's head from his shoulders.

Kaylin must have made some sound, some noise; everyone turned to look at her. She watched as blood followed beheading; watched as the body crumpled, the head bouncing off the stone floor and leaving a trail in its wake. And she watched, silent, as a single word—a word she now knew—shivered in the air, asserting its freedom from the binding of Barrani flesh. It was over so quickly.

He was dead. She understood then the difference between

silence and death that Teela had insisted she would recognize if she felt it.

No one said a word. Neither Teela nor the Consort attempted to justify either the order or carrying it through. Kaylin moved quickly, numbly, to stand between Teela and Edelonne. Her mouth was dry.

It is not the first death you have witnessed. Ynpharion was angry. *He was a threat to all of us. He was a threat to the Lady.*

Kaylin said nothing. Hope said nothing. Spike was whirring, but in the rhythmic way that suggested breath, not communication.

*Why do you even care? They would have killed us all. They would have killed you. You did not know them. They owe you nothing except the obedience you can enforce, and you owe them noth-*ing! Clearly silence was not Ynpharion's strength. *Holding their names—holding* our *names—is a display of strength, of power; it's not an obligation. We are* not *your dependents!*

He fell silent again. When he opened his mouth, the Consort placed a hand on his shoulder. "Ynpharion, enough. You understand what she is. Your anger will not absolve her in her own thoughts."

This time, he kept his mouth shut. It occurred to Kaylin only then that the reason he'd broken what was a furious rant was probably the Consort on the inside of his head.

"So," Edelonne said—to Ynpharion. "This is where you went."

This did distract Ynpharion. Given the Consort's expression—blue-eyed and mildly annoyed—that was probably for the best. For Ynpharion.

Kaylin closed her eyes, not to see names, not to find them, not to *take* them. But she could see her arms glowing in the darkness behind her eyelids, and she could see Hope.

He, too, said nothing. But his wings brushed her forehead

as she turned to look at him. She stood for three long breaths, thinking Ynpharion was right: she'd seen death before. Some of it had been worse.

But it had been years since her sole purpose was to cause that death; death had become, over the course of years, a sign of failure. The failure to protect. The failure to save. Averen had been almost helpless. Because of Kaylin. She opened her eyes; Edelonne had turned to face her, her expression one of confusion.

I'm sorry, Kaylin said almost reflexively.

He would have killed you, Edelonne replied. There was no contempt in the statement, and no sense of personal loss for Averen. No, on the contrary, there was the bare hint of satisfaction, as if they'd been enemies or bitter rivals.

Kaylin exhaled. She looked at Teela, but couldn't meet the Barrani Hawk's eyes. She couldn't meet Severn's, either. No one told her it wasn't her fault, and even if they'd tried, she wouldn't have believed it. She understood that it was her *lack of control* that had turned Averen into an instant threat.

After I have answered your questions, will An'Teela kill me? The question was asked with resignation and fear. Kaylin could feel both.

No.

You don't believe that.

She would have, a handful of minutes ago. She'd've bet on it. *I won't let her.*

Edelonne did not point to Averen's corpse. *Flee here. Tell the Lady to flee. If she is here—if they have her—we are lost.*

We're not lost, Kaylin said as the marks on her arms began to burn.

Edelonne stared at them, arrested. *You are...Chosen.*

Kaylin nodded. *You chose this path*, she said quietly. *You weren't forced into it. If the Consort is in danger, she is in danger because you—and your compatriots—made choices such as the one that brought you here.*

Silence. Beneath it, anger. Anger was better than fear, especially when the brunt of it wasn't directed at Kaylin. *This is not the path I chose.*

It was demonstrably the path she'd chosen. Kaylin didn't say this, but it took effort. And of course, as if she were Ynpharion, she heard what Kaylin didn't say, anyway.

This isn't what I wanted.

I'm not going to ask what you did *want. But you're a Lord of the High Court. You've seen what awaits those who take this freaking test. And you're working* for *it. You and whoever else is caught up in this. But the Shadow didn't come to talk to any of you directly. Someone else did. Who?*

An'Mellarionne.

This was more or less what Kaylin expected, and she wondered if the name was offered because of that. *Is he waiting for us down below?*

Not for you. Not directly. She hesitated, and then said, *We didn't expect the Consort to arrive.*

You set up this entire trap—starting with her *personal chambers, but you didn't expect her to become involved?*

We didn't expect her to be directly *involved.* Her gaze bounced off Evarrim. *We thought she might send Lord Evarrim. It wouldn't be the first time he has been sent.*

How do you know *this?*

She froze, as if hearing—or considering—the question for the first time. There was no good answer. There wasn't even a bad answer that didn't make her look like a trusting, naive fool, and if Kaylin understood nothing else about the Barrani, she understood just how much they dreaded that.

It made them seem almost human.

We were informed, she finally said. But the question that

Edelonne hadn't asked, hadn't thought to ask, was *By who?* She was asking it now, and the only answer that seemed instantly plausible was not the answer she wanted. *What is the Consort trying to do? Is she trying to unseat Coravante?*

She is trying, Kaylin said, *to free the damned.*

That's—that's what Coravante is doing.

Do you honestly believe that?

Silence.

Was Bressarian involved?

He was not like us.

That's not a no.

You don't understand An'Mellarionne. You don't understand how much power he has. But he has Fianora, Bressarian's sister.

Where?

Later, Chosen. She turned to the Consort and sank, instantly, into a posture of utter obeisance. "Lady," she said, speaking mostly to the floor as she didn't lift her head. "It is not safe for you here."

"It is not safe for anyone, Lord Edelonne."

"No one else is you."

"Ah. I have heard that Mellarionne has a Consort candidate waiting in the wings for my demise."

Edelonne flinched. "An'Mellarionne is waiting below. He and a handful of the other Lords of the Court are now engaged in a ceremony of some kind."

"Ceremony?" The word was sharp, far sharper than the Consort's natural voice.

"They—they believe they can…" Edelonne swallowed audibly. "They believe they can free the dead."

"Ah. That is something I very much desire. How, exactly, is this freedom to be achieved?"

"I—I don't know, Lady. We—we were not important enough to be—to be informed."

Spike was agitated. Very agitated.

Hope spoke. "Spike asks me to inform you that there is a danger."

"No kidding. Can he tell us what it is?"

"Yes. The Shadows cannot directly draw power from the True Words. The words that grant Barrani life—that grant Dragons life—are meant for the living; they are meant to be eternal, and enclosed, in the forms created for your kind."

"Wait. Wait. Power *can* be drawn from True Names. It was the entire *point* of the attack on the Hallionne Orbaranne."

"Power," he said quietly, "can be drawn from True Names by *your kind*. The creature at the base of the High Halls is not your kind; it is not power that he can access. Could he, he would not be captive; every Barrani who failed the test would provide fuel for his eventual escape. He can provide power to your kind—but it requires a bridge, some passage between him and the person to whom he grants power. That power is not the power of the True Names." Spike continued to click and whir, the buzzing becoming higher and higher in pitch.

"But...the words in the Lake were *meant* for your kind. The Barrani draw power and sustenance from those words instinctively and automatically. They do not need to consider the power or the flow of power; it is the heart of their ability to interact."

As the words sank it, Kaylin blanched. "He needs Barrani agents."

"Yes. It is the nature of Shadow to change what it touches, if it has the power. The Shadows can shift or alter the shape of words, can subtly bend their meaning. You have some experience with this."

Kaylin nodded.

"If a bridge is built between the Adversary and the Barrani, and it is strong enough, the Barrani can then draw enough power through the captive names that they can, in turn, free him."

"But if they have that kind of power—"

"Yes. Those names will be lost for eternity. And we are likely to be lost with them."

CHAPTER 24

Kaylin repeated what Hope had said. Edelonne remained supine; the Consort did not give her leave to rise, and even if she had, Kaylin had doubts that Edelonne could have done so with any grace at all.

"Spike is frantic," Kaylin told them.

"The Shadows taught the Barrani how to absorb Shadow, to draw power from it." The Consort wasn't asking a question. It was a statement, but it lacked a bit in the truth department. Kaylin was afraid that Terrano had been one of their teachers, but understood why this could not be—and could never be—said out loud.

She believes you to be incorrect, Ynpharion helpfully said. *She thinks that what Terrano taught allowed the Barrani involved to be... caught in the subtle deception of the Adversary. The freedom they sought from the burden of their own names allowed them to interact with the Adversary more directly than their Barrani kin. There is a reason that we are Barrani and Spike is not.*

"The Barrani don't need to be taught how to absorb power. There's a reason the Emperor has made the study of Shadow illegal. And a reason that the idiots at the Arcanum ignore the laws." She couldn't force herself to make an exception for present company, but Evarrim didn't care what Kaylin thought.

Spike hadn't stopped spinning.

"We need to move," Kaylin told everyone. "If Edelonne is right, we needed to move before we managed to fight our way through to this hall."

"Is there anything else awaiting us?" the Consort asked, voice cool.

"There probably will be," Kaylin said, glancing at Averen's corpse. "If the other person who held his name is on the wrong side, they'll know what happened here. Even if they aren't, one of the three fled in the direction of the cavern."

"Can your familiar go ahead?"

"He can't do anything I couldn't theoretically do on my own."

Evarrim's expression made clear that he didn't believe her. Probably because he thought she could do nothing on her own. "Given the legends about familiars, I find that difficult to believe."

"I don't care what you believe."

"Perhaps, were your familiar to be in the hands of someone who is competent—"

"Lord Evarrim," the Consort said. He shut up. "An'Teela. Lord Severn."

They began to move.

What does she want me to do with Edelonne?

Given your reaction to Averen's death, she is unwilling to execute her.

You did the same thing she did, Kaylin said, trying not to bristle. *And you're now one of the Consort's personal guard. She can't assume that Edelonne will immediately stab us all in the back.*

She can assume it; she does not hold Edelonne's name. I offered mine, he continued with a trace of almost desperate pride. *She understands what occurred. She understands, in future, what might occur. She knows that I do not and will not fight her—*

Except when she tells you not to scream at me?

I was not screaming. Regardless, she does not have that certainty with Edelonne, and she will not have it. The only certainty—and I use that word advisedly—that she does have is her trust in your intentions. But you are squeamish.

Fine. I'm weak. Ask what she wants me to do with Edelonne.

She is relatively confident that Edelonne will be incapable of harming any of us, even you. When Kaylin failed to reply, he added, *She leaves the decision, in its entirety, in your hands; she is aware that we must now move.*

Kaylin turned to Edelonne, who was still a huddled mass on the floor of the stone hall. *Edelonne, we need to move.*

Edelonne did not agree.

"Lady," Kaylin said.

The Consort looked at Edelonne, just as Kaylin had done, and said, "You may rise." Kaylin, in theory, had power over Edelonne that the Consort didn't have—but theory had always been fuzzy. Could she have made Edelonne stand? Probably. But not without effort and pain on both their parts.

The Consort's permission dissolved her resistance, and Edelonne rose.

"Lady," she said, voice low, words a thin sheen of control over panic, "it is not safe for you to be here."

The Consort did not reply, and Edelonne paled, which should have been impossible, given her already chalky color.

The Consort called Severn back. Without a word from her, Evarrim took his place by Teela's side. Kaylin would have vastly preferred that Severn continue to play point here, but she understood the Consort's decision; Evarrim was part of the Arcanum. He had spent most of his life within its confines, and if he didn't break Imperial Law in the course of his studies—which Kaylin thought impossible—he understood more about those particular illegal things.

She was not surprised when her arms—already tingling on the edge of pain—began to burn. They weren't the only things that felt like they were on fire. Evarrim was casting a spell. Kaylin recognized it; it was not the first time she had seen him summon.

Fire came at his call. She could almost hear its name; it was not a small elemental.

The Consort's eyes were blue with a hint of reflected orange. "Lord Evarrim," she began.

His response was a grunt, followed by, "Lord Kaylin is present."

The elemental was almost the width of the hall; Kaylin half expected the ceiling to melt. It didn't. Neither did the floor beneath its lower edge, which couldn't be called feet. It turned to Kaylin, although Evarrim had been its summoner, and spoke. The words were a crackle of flame—the noise wood made when it burned and broke.

She could almost see eyes emerge from the heart of flame, and the heart of flame was white.

"I... I've talked to the fire in the Keeper's garden," Kaylin told the Consort. "Bigger parts of the flame remember it." She approached the flame. Ynpharion flinched at the heat. Kaylin didn't. Her power wasn't the power that was fueling the elemental; that was all on Evarrim's shoulders. He did not attempt to take control; he passed the brunt of that to Kaylin.

Kaylin held out a hand, and fire touched her palm, traveling up her left arm. Her shirtsleeve was immediately reduced to ash. Her skin was not.

"Ask the fire," Evarrim said, "to protect you."

She wasn't entirely certain she'd heard him correctly the first time. "Protect *me*?"

"If I were our enemies," Evarrim replied in the irritated and condescending tone she expected from him, "you would be the first person I would destroy, had I the opportunity. An'Teela and the outcaste are armed with weapons intended for our wars with the Dragons; they are both powerful in their own right, as am I. But you are the unpredictable power, here—and they will know that it was your hand, not ours, that...freed...their servants.

"I could not do what you did. The Consort herself could not do it. Ah, that is inexact. The Consort could possibly do what you have done. She has never, however, demonstrated that ability. No, Lord Kaylin, it is your death that must come first if they are to have a chance to finish what they have started."

Edelonne cleared her throat. "Lord Evarrim is correct. You have some small chance. This ceremony was not intended to take place now; the arrival of the forsaken—"

"Forsaken?"

"The children of the green," she amended. "It is what they are called by those who reside below. They are not children in any true sense of the word, and I believe they would find 'forsaken' less...insulting. Regardless, they were not expected to arrive now."

"What difference does it make?"

"To the ceremony itself? None. But we are a political people. And they are a threat to our security, regardless."

"They are *not* more of a threat than your so-called ceremony!"

Edelonne was silent; Kaylin could feel her agreement emerge from the chaos of thought and the tangled mess of her memory. Very like Ynpharion, in fact.

Take what Evarrim offers, Nightshade said. It was almost a command.

I don't want—

To be in his debt? To be obligated to him? There was a dark thread of amusement in the words. *You become more like our kin every day.*

I don't want to exhaust him before we even reach our enemies.

You will not. I understand that you dislike him, but he has served the Consort for the entirety of her tenure.

Her tenure is months long.

Yes. But before then, he was one of her closest advisers. I admit I find your dislike almost inexplicable.

He dislikes me.

Ah. He is, in temperament and behavior, much like a mortal. Of all of our kin in the Court, he would be considered most similar to you.

Not what she wanted to hear. Ever, let alone twice. But she knew from personal experience that he was willing to risk his life in service to the Consort. Where the Consort was concerned, she trusted him completely. She almost asked Evarrim if he was certain this was smart—he was wasting a lot of power.

She didn't, because she knew it would annoy him, and at the moment, she'd take no joy out of it. Maybe later.

Surrounded by armor of flame—she hurriedly asked the fire not to burn off the *rest* of her clothing—she began to talk to the fire. Fire was surprisingly normal, if you discounted its visceral need to melt or burn everything in sight. What it wanted from Kaylin—what it had wanted the first time it had not tried to turn her to ash—were the stories of its place in the universe, of things that were not burning or destruction, because it knew those quite well.

There was some comfort in providing those stories as they headed—at greater speed—down the hall, until the hall opened up to stairs. Those stairs went down, as expected.

Hope placed a hand on her shoulder, and Kaylin obligingly called a halt. He did not seem to feel the fire at all.

"There might be difficulty here. I think these stairs used to be part of the Tower itself, but Hope thinks that the Tower has withdrawn the protections that usually make them safe."

The Consort nodded, absorbing the information. "An'Teela, has your cohort emerged?"

"Valliant has been joined by Serralyn and Mandoran. Or most of Mandoran," she added with a grimace. "Annarion and Sedarias are not yet done. Mandoran says—" She inhaled. "There are Barrani at the base of the stairs."

"Hope says the cohort haven't been spotted. The Tower knows they are different, but the Tower has decided that the intruders are the greater danger. And Mandoran is doing... something—sorry, I don't actually understand the word Hope used—to keep the others hidden."

"He is," Teela said. "It won't last. At the moment, the Mellarionne forces are looking for Sedarias." She frowned, and then added, "They're looking for Sedarias and her companions in the wrong place."

"Good. That will buy us some time. An'Teela. Calarnenne."

Nightshade was not, in Kaylin's opinion, in any shape to engage even more dangerous Shadows. He did not, however, hesitate. Outcaste or no—and Evarrim had made clear that he was—he obeyed the Consort as if the High Court were still his home.

The runes on both *Meliannos* and *Kariannos* once again flared like lightning in the enclosed space; the fire elemental rumbled in response, tightening its grip. Evarrim did not appear to be suffering from the effects of the summoning, which was good.

"Evarrim," the Consort said when Nightshade and Teela leaped down the stairs, the aftereffect of the light cast by their blades tracing the trajectory of a fall, not a regular descent.

"Lady," he replied. He followed, but he took the stairs.

"Yes," the Consort said, although no one had asked any questions. "They spent some time in the distant past on the same battlefields. It makes me feel almost young again, to see them now."

Severn walked beside the Consort; Ynpharion took the other side. Kaylin and Edelonne brought up the rear, although the flame itself made that difficult; it had to be cajoled into leaving Edelonne alive. Neither Hope nor Spike seemed bothered by the fire's heat. And if they weren't, she didn't understand why the fire was going to be proof against whatever the Shadow could send against her.

She didn't ask, in part because Evarrim had followed Nightshade and Teela and was no longer in hearing range. But she had a suspicion that the fire was meant to reduce creatures like the Ferals to ash; while they carried some taint of Shadow, and funneled some of its power—somehow—they were nonetheless akin to the Barrani.

"Lord Kaylin?" the Consort said.

Kaylin grimaced at the title, but held her peace. "Nightshade?" she asked. She felt Edelonne's surprise; it was the loudest thing on the inside of her head.

The Consort nodded.

She reached for Nightshade's thoughts, Nightshade's senses, in response. With the fire as a full-body halo, she felt almost comfortable closing her eyes. *You will have to learn*, Nightshade said, *to speak to us with your eyes open.*

Does it matter?

Here? No. But it will *matter when you are otherwise at Court.*

I'm not going to be at Court again if I have any say in the matter.

Your optimism is both astonishing and unfounded. Keep your touch light, he added.

The stairs continued for some length, a winding spiral that reminded Kaylin very much of her own basement. Well, Helen's basement. But Helen's basement was subject to serious change, and often did. The rest of the house tended to remain consistent; she transformed the rooms depending on the number of people in them, but usually only added chairs or lengthened tables.

Kaylin. Nightshade spoke with irritation. *Focus.*

She flushed. *Sorry.* "The stairs that they took seem to go down a long way."

The Consort nodded.

"There are no torches or no obvious sources of light; I think Teela's providing whatever light they need. It's not Nightshade."

"It is possibly Lord Evarrim," the Consort said. "He is a practicing Arcanist."

Right. "They can't see the bottom from where they are— but they're no longer trying to defy gravity." She frowned then. Eyes shut, she focused all of her attention on Nightshade's vision, on what he could, and did, see. He was hyper-aware now; he saw everything. There was a breeze, one not caused by the speed of either his movement or Teela's, that seemed to come from below.

Kaylin could feel it disturb strands of his hair.

"Kaylin?" She felt a hand on her arm, but that realization was slower in coming than it would have been had she not been trying so hard to be where Nightshade was.

Something about the breeze was wrong. She could hear it. She could hear it as if it were howling wind. No, not even that. She could hear it as if it were a voice, raised to shouting, but at a distance.

Something about the sound was familiar to Kaylin. As she concentrated, as she put the brunt of her focus into listening, it became clearer.

Is it dangerous?

I...don't think so. She was frowning; the hand on her arm lifted as she once again began to walk. She didn't open her eyes—but she often listened with her eyes closed. It was too easy to be distracted, otherwise. Yes, it was familiar. No, in theory it wasn't dangerous—not intentionally dangerous.

She drew breath with her own lungs, detaching herself from Nightshade's hearing. *I think—I think it's Terrano.* Terrano, the only member of the cohort that Teela couldn't reach, and couldn't therefore track.

Nightshade relayed this information to both Teela and Evarrim; Teela's expression became completely neutral.

An'Teela wishes you to join us, he finally said, although Teela had said nothing of the kind. Regardless, Kaylin was certain he was right.

The Consort began her descent with more grace and less speed than those who'd been sent to scout. She allowed a shift in marching orders, and Severn remained with her, as did Ynpharion; Kaylin, enrobed in flame, headed down the stairs. She wasn't Barrani; she took far longer to cover the distance than any of the scouts had.

Teela was waiting, her eyes narrowed, her lips thinned. And as Kaylin finally reached the three, she became certain the strangely muted voice she could hear was Terrano's.

Hope's wing brushed her cheek, and she turned. "It is Terrano," Hope said. "He is unnamed."

"I was unnamed," Kaylin shot back. "And I was still allowed entry here."

"You are never unnamed here. You bear the marks of the Chosen."

"Fine. *Severn* was unnamed."

"Severn followed you. He remained in your orbit. What you saw and what he saw differed—but he was considered some part of you. Or so I believe."

She frowned. "The Tower allowed the Ferals."

"Yes."

"Because it recognized their names? I mean, the words?"

"That is my belief. It is Spike's belief, as well. It is why the Hallionne allow guests who have previously paid the price of entry to return. They *can* revoke that permission, but it is a deliberate decision, and the permission itself must be altered. It is not, in Spike's opinion, entirely trivial."

"And it's not allowing Terrano to take that test?"

"Again, conjecture on our part."

"He went with the rest of the cohort."

"Yes."

"And he was part of them; they were a unit."

"They were not an indivisible unit. Their tests, at least according to Teela, were separate; they occurred in parallel, but they occurred—are perhaps still occurring—in different pocket spaces, not unlike Helen's apartments. The cohort couldn't see—individually—what their comrades faced. They could see it because they are name-bound to each other. But Terrano is not."

"Can you hear him?"

"No. Not as you hear him now."

"Can Spike?"

The pause before the answer was longer; Spike was answering, but not in Elantran, or anything that Kaylin could hear as a language. "Yes."

Kaylin exhaled. "He's important to the cohort. He's important to Teela. Can we find him?"

"We? No."

Fine. "Can *I* find him?"

"Yes, I believe you can. Spike does not consider this wise. Terrano is demonstrably not dead."

"Is he unharmed?"

"We have no way of knowing that for certain."

"Lord Kaylin," the Consort said. "I can hear only half of your conversation. I desire to know the content of the rest of it."

Kaylin explained in Elantran.

"How important do you consider Terrano?"

"Very."

Evarrim did not agree. Nightshade, however, did. No one bothered to ask Teela.

"Very well. You found Calarnenne." And her cheek was still blistered and raw from that effort. "You cannot find Terrano in the same fashion. He is not bound to you."

Teela was tensing; her eyes flashed in almost the same way the sword's blade did, which would have been fine except it really didn't look like a reflection.

"No, I can't."

"Do you believe you can find him, regardless?"

Kaylin took some time to answer, because the intelligent, thoughtful answer was *no*. "Yes."

"You do not have confidence."

"It's impossible to have confidence in a space like this. If what Spike is saying is true, the Tower is like Helen or the Hallionne. At one point in time, it might have been stronger than either. If Helen wanted to hide something from me, she could."

"Very well. Find him, if you can. If you cannot find him quickly, we must leave his retrieval for a later time." To Teela, she said, "I give you my word that should we all survive this, and should Terrano be imprisoned in a way that Lord Kaylin cannot perceive, we will return and we will free him."

Teela said something in High Barrani that Kaylin did not understand.

Edelonne was shocked. Ynpharion was outraged.

The Consort was neither. She lifted a hand, held it, palm out, toward Teela. Kaylin joined Edelonne and Ynpharion in shock and outrage as Teela drew the edge of *Kariannos* across the mound of the Consort's palm. Blood followed in its wake. Teela did the same to her own palm—an action that barely registered to Kaylin—and then pressed that palm into the Consort's. She spoke three words.

Without turning to look at Kaylin, the Consort said, "Go, Lord Kaylin. Return when I call you."

Go where? Kaylin thought. She was politic enough not to say this out loud—more for Teela's sake than anyone else's, including her own. There was a particular tinge of indigo to Teela's eyes that spoke of fear—and almost nothing scared Teela.

But fear of loss was something Kaylin understood intimately. She headed down the stairs, which happened to be where the breeze was coming from. Teela was right behind her. The Consort didn't call her back, but a glance at the Barrani Hawk's expression made clear that she'd probably fail to hear any command that didn't take her where she wanted to go, at this point. Nightshade, however, remained with the Consort, as did Evarrim. And Severn.

Terrano's voice became louder as they descended.

"Can you hear him?" Kaylin asked Teela.

"No."

"He's getting louder to me. Look—I'm not certain that you can go wherever it is I'm going."

Teela grimaced. "I can. Not easily, and not without discomfort, but I can. Mandoran," she added, "is practically screaming instructions. Sedarias isn't happy about it."

"Terrano or Mandoran?"

"Both. You're certain it's Terrano?"

Kaylin nodded. "I wasn't completely certain up above, but...it's his voice."

"What's he saying?"

"You really want me to repeat it?"

This drew a grim chuckle from Teela. "Not where the Consort can hear it, no. I take it he's not happy."

They stopped when Kaylin cursed in Leontine.

"You can hear the rest of the trapped," Teela said, voice flat, her tone making clear that she could.

Kaylin nodded. "They're loud. They're as loud as Terrano, and I'm having a bit of trouble separating his voice from theirs."

"Is his voice getting any quieter?"

Kaylin hesitated, and then shook her head.

"Do you think he's also among the trapped?"

It was what she was suddenly afraid of. "He couldn't be," she finally said with a slight rise at the end of the short sentence to rob it of certainty. "If the Tower is trying to shunt him to the side so he can't *take* the test, there's no way he could be where the trapped are."

"It's Terrano," Teela said, as if that explained anything. She turned back up the stairs and Kaylin felt magic brush the skin that had only barely settled into its normal sensitivity. It was a small magic.

The Consort bids me to inform you that you have her permission to continue; it appears that your current direction is where we must be, in the end.

Kaylin's legs were cramped by the time they reached the end of the stairs—or at least the end of the stairs created by the Tower. The fire Evarrim had summoned still swirled around her, casting both shadows and light against the stone beneath her boots. The crackle of fire was its own voice, and the lap of flames, the touch of gentle, warm fingers.

Hope continued to maintain his humanoid, winged form. She had an uneasy suspicion he wouldn't remain that way; the stairs allowed him to move freely, and communicate freely. If he decided to go Dragon—as Kaylin referred to his large, aerial form—he wouldn't fit. A hall opened up at the foot of the stairs. This hall should lead to the cavern in which the Adversary was imprisoned.

The cavern could easily house Hope's draconic form.

I will not fight, Hope said. *I will not fight unless you command it, and pay the price. What I can do, Chosen, you can achieve.*

I can't fly, she pointed out. *I can't cover the distance between here and the West March in a handful of hours. I can't—*

I did not carry you when I made that journey, and I did not take routes you could easily take. Or take at all. You are being pedantic. You understand what I mean.

She did.

I will protect you as I can. I will protect those within your sphere in a fashion similar to what they might individually achieve. Had

Bellusdeo been prepared for the Arcane bomb, it would not have destroyed her.

It would have destroyed me.

No, Chosen. Regardless, if you wish me to face the creature trapped here by the will of the Tower, you will have to sacrifice something. It is not different, in the end, from the fight that enveloped the High Halls.

Could you kill it?

I am uncertain. I believe it is possible, but until I arrive at the foot of the Adversary, I cannot be sure. I feel it irrelevant, however.

She wondered then what familiars actually were. She wondered what they had been in the distant past, and on other worlds that had purportedly been destroyed because their masters were idiots. She wondered if all familiars were like Hope, or if, conversely, Hope were like Helen: singular in existence, with serial masters. And more physical freedom.

Hope had no opinion that he cared to offer, and as the seconds passed, she forgot the half-formed thought. She could, once again, hear Terrano. A spasm of guilt came and went, but so did the unconscious tension that had taken up residence in her jaw, her shoulders, her neck. It was almost impossible to listen to the wails of despair and pain when one could do nothing to help.

It is why we are here, Ynpharion said without his usual condescension. *It is why, in the end, we are all here.*

This wasn't, strictly speaking, the truth; Sedarias was here to earn the title that would allow her to, oh, kill her brother and take over the family line. At this point, however, Kaylin was fine with it. She was certain that her brother had intended to either harm or kill Helen as the fastest way to kill all of her guests.

And she didn't like the emblem he'd put on the carriage

his aide had driven up in, either. Mostly, she didn't like the uneasy certainty that Sedarias was going to get her chance to kill her brother before she was officially a Lord of the Court—because Kaylin was certain he'd be here in person.

CHAPTER 25

The hall was long, and appeared to be unbroken by intersections or turns. Kaylin's hope that Terrano was not where the Adversary was died by slow degrees; although Hope could protect her from the storm of wailing voices, the direction of that storm and the direction of Terrano were the same.

She wanted to raise her own voice and shout, just to see if Terrano responded.

Do not even think it, Ynpharion snapped. To be fair to Ynpharion, Nightshade wasn't far behind.

I understand that, she snapped back. *It's why I haven't tried.* If a ceremony of some sort was being convened here, it was being convened by the Barrani—those who had somehow become entwined with the Shadow and the Adversary. And while the Consort and her companions wanted to interrupt that ceremony—fiercely and with great prejudice—they wanted to do it on their own terms, with as little warning as possible.

Nightshade moved up in the line, but left Teela and Kaylin at the front. Kaylin grimaced. She expected magic, but approaching it was never comfortable. And this very uncomfortable magic grew, just as the volume of Terrano's voice did.

She wished he would say something useful that she could understand; that he would give them some kind of hint, tell them what he was facing or what he needed rescue *from*.

Or if he needed rescue at all.

Teela slowed, and gestured for Kaylin to follow suit. She gestured with *Kariannos*, which couldn't be ignored unless one wanted to be bisected. Kaylin would have slowed in any case; they had reached the end of the hall. Unlike many halls, this one didn't end in a forbidding, warded door; the walls to either side simply stopped. Between one step and the next, the floor—worked, flawless stone—became uneven and worn; it was as if someone had taken a gigantic sword and simply sheared the hall in two, discarding part of it.

"Is this what it normally looks like?" Kaylin said over her shoulder, her voice low.

The Consort said, "There is no normal beyond these halls. But this is one of the ways it appears, yes."

"Was it like this the last time you came?"

A beat of silence. Two. *No*, the Lord of the West March said. *It was not.* It was the first time he had chosen to join the crowd in Kaylin's head.

She told you this?

I know her, he replied. *This is not what she saw the last time she ventured into these halls.*

The last time she'd ventured into these halls had been just over two weeks ago. Kaylin hadn't been there, though— she'd been in the West March. *You think this is a response to the last visit.*

It should not have been, but yes. As do you.

Edelonne, what are they doing?

Silence. It was not the silence of struggle. Edelonne's response was both visceral and wordless. *I am not good with words,* the newest member of Kaylin's internal chorus said.

I'm not, either.

In your life, in the life you've chosen, skill with words is unnecessary. It was defining, for me.

Kaylin had no idea what Edelonne's life choices were. And this wasn't the time to discover them. *Do you understand what was being attempted?*

They are attempting to gain the power that the creature you call the Adversary has hoarded but cannot use himself.

Who taught you how to do what you did?

An image formed in response to the question. A man's image. Kaylin had never seen him before. Brother? Father? Someone familial. Someone Edelonne valued. Ah. Someone *dead*. Had Kaylin's arm hair not already been standing on end, it would have started immediately.

That's not your father, she said, far more sharply than she'd intended. *It's the Adversary.*

Edelonne resisted, but Kaylin had discovered one important thing about speaking through the bond of name—however that bond was built. Lying took effort. It took real work. She was certain Nightshade could manage it; certain Lirienne could. But she herself hadn't mastered the art—

You will never master that art.

—and neither had Edelonne. She was new to this, newer than even Kaylin. She heard the truth in Kaylin's words, and those words gouged into the heart of her certainty, cracking it, breaking it.

Yes, Ynpharion said. *I have never liked you.*

Tell me something I don't know.

But I have never doubted the truth or the strength of your beliefs and your commitments. I merely think those beliefs and commitments are foolish. She, too, will understand what I almost immediately understood. You are many things, many frustrating things—but you are honest. He made the word sound like an insult, right up there with *naive.*

Kaylin could live with naive, although it annoyed her. *Tell the Consort that it was the* Adversary *that taught them how to turn into this particular style of monster Feral. Not Terrano. Not An'Mellarionne. The Adversary.*

Edelonne, what else *were you taught to do?*

Edelonne's answer was wordless. It was Shadow; it was tendrils; it was a voice that Edelonne could no longer understand, although it was part of her memories. The experience hadn't been expunged.

Spike screeched. It was not a loud sound, but Kaylin thought it would make her ears bleed, and she covered one of them with her hand, the other being wrapped around a knife she didn't want to drop, lose or jam into her cheek. Before she could speak, he detached himself from her shoulder, escaped the protection of fire that didn't seem to affect him at all and pushed himself forward; he stood at the very edge of the hall. It was hard to tell what he was looking at, given his lack of obvious eyes.

It wasn't hard to tell that whatever he saw either enraged or terrified him.

"Hope?"

"There are more of your Ferals present ahead. The one who escaped you was not the last one standing."

"That's not what's upsetting Spike."

"No, Chosen. But those Ferals, should they continue in this vein, will not be Ferals much longer; they will become other. They are unlike the cohort; they will become other, but they will take their instructions—their shape, their *power*—from the knowledge of your Adversary.

"It is possible that An'Mellarionne and his lieges believe they will be in control. It is possible that they will be allowed to remain untransformed. But the people enspelled as your new name-bound is enspelled will not."

"It's worse than that. Spike's *really* upset."

"He is."

Kaylin reached out and attempted to grab Spike, which was probably the stupidest thing she had done all day. He spun in a way that almost cost her half a hand, and she flinched. She also bled—but it was a small cut, given the size of what were no longer spikes. Blades, she thought. She could *almost* sense eyes beneath the perfect, black chitin of what passed for his skin in this particular shape.

And this shape was not his only shape.

"Lord Kaylin." The Consort's voice was sharper, the syllables a snap of biting sound.

"He's— The Ferals that stopped us are somehow *attached* to the Adversary. And there are more of them."

"Your current name-bound?" Edelonne flinched.

"She's no longer attached. Whatever inroads the Adversary had to her are gone."

"How many more?"

Thirteen, Edelonne said. *There were thirteen of us.*

"Eleven more. Thirteen to start."

Evarrim cursed, or at least that's what Kaylin thought he was doing. The cursing followed the rest of his unintelligible words. Oh. Magic. His eyes were already as dark as Barrani eyes could get.

"What?" she demanded, her voice much sharper, much harsher, than the Consort's.

Evarrim didn't pretend to misunderstand, and didn't ignore her, either, which was his preference. He usually waited until the Consort asked—or demanded that he answer. "There are three summoning rituals that might require a larger number of people," he finally said. "I have seen them used only during natural disasters, and one was a failure.

"Alone, our power is individual—our talents, our skills, individual, as well. We cannot summon more of a force than we can control; it is suicide."

Kaylin nodded.

"Together, we can. But it requires synchronicity and focus, and it is not guaranteed to succeed. If the containment breaks..." He fell silent.

Kaylin was still for one long moment. "People die."

"Yes. But not immediately, not all at once. If the elemental summoned wishes to exist on the plane for its own purposes—and it *will* have a purpose at that size—it cannot kill everyone immediately; the summoner is the door or the window through which entry is possible. Or rather, the summoner's power is. But the summoner has no control over what has been summoned."

"You think they're summoning Shadow, somehow."

It was Edelonne who answered. "Yes, Lord Kaylin. They are attempting to do what Lord Evarrim has suggested. A small amount of Shadow is almost inert; it is obedient, just as fire or water. A larger summoning is more difficult. The experiments they have conducted strongly imply that Shadow is a hidden element, a fifth element."

"How do they summon it *at all*?"

"My apologies, Lord Kaylin. I was not trained in the Arcane arts. I was considered to have no potential at all in that regard." The sudden rush of humility didn't suit Barrani at all, even this one. Kaylin transferred her question, silently, to Evarrim, who couldn't claim the same ignorance.

His glare might have been his entire reply, but the Consort nodded at him in the regal way which meant *Answer her now.*

"It may surprise you to know that I do not have an answer

to that question. If Shadow has a name—as fire does—I am unaware of it, and if you have any small knowledge of summoning, you understand that the name of the thing summoned is *necessary*."

Spike practically exploded with urgent distress. It took Kaylin a moment to understand that he was asking her permission for…something.

"Shadow," Hope said, "has a name."

Evarrim, however, was staring at Spike. "It appears," he said, his voice the wrong kind of soft, "that if Shadow does have a name, your companion is aware of it."

"I think," Kaylin replied, "that Spike must know. He can't really communicate clearly *with* me when he's in this form." A form that was, she had to admit, getting less portable by the second. "He does try, though."

Whatever permission he required to do what he obviously felt was necessary, she gave.

He unfolded.

As he did, the shape of the hall—the opening of it—shifted, as if aware of his transformation, and desirous of it. The hall in which everyone else was now standing widened, although the texture of the floor and walls didn't change. The ceiling stretched up, slanting gradually, as Spike became other.

No, he'd always been other. But he was now almost draconic in size. The spikes that characterized his portable appearance still existed—but they were flexible, and thin; fine tendrils of shadow waved in what appeared to be a wind. A strong wind.

The eyes that he didn't normally possess, he possessed now in uncomfortable abundance. His body was no longer round, but it was very difficult to look at for any length of time, because it seemed to shift in place. He had legs one second, and had none the next; he had limbs that might have ended in hands, before they flattened and extended, as if they meant to be wings and couldn't quite contain the shape.

Or be contained by it.

But...in this form, he had a different voice. She'd heard it before, in the outlands; she heard it now.

You will die, he said. *You will all die if this is not stopped. What you call Shadow is contained here—here and in perhaps a handful of other worlds that have not fallen in their entirety. It is a cage, Chosen. It is a necessary cage.*

"I don't understand. An'Mellarionne and his crew have summoned Shadow before—why is this worse?"

They have summoned just enough of the Shadow to catch its attention, as was no doubt intended by their teacher. But what they summon here will be unlike the fire or the water or the earth—it will be a force unto itself, a thing that they cannot control.

"That's not different."

It will be. The Shadow is not *like the elements. Its will and intent are more subtle. In that, in its desire, it is far more like your Barrani than the elements that are housed by your world's Keeper. It is...* He made the whirring sounds he often made; Kaylin associated it with thinking. *It is not like summoning fire. It is like summoning a god.*

Kaylin didn't even ask which god. "Did any of you hear that?" she asked without taking her eyes off Spike's unfolding form.

"We heard," the Consort replied, "what you said. We did not hear what Spike said—if that is indeed Spike."

"It's Spike. It's not... He looked different in the outlands, but...it's Spike. Spike thinks the Barrani lords—whoever the hells they are—believe they're summoning Shadow-as-elemental. Shadow, to them, is like fire or water, earth or air."

"It is a much more flexible power," Edelonne said. "It can be used in a more subtle fashion."

Kaylin thought of crests on doors, of invisibility. "It's not, according to Spike, being used. It's the one doing the using."

It was Teela who snapped the next question, which was all of a single word. *"Ravellon?"*

"I think that's what Spike's afraid of."

"Terrano?"

"I don't know." It surprised Kaylin that that was Teela's next question, and it shouldn't have. It would have been hers, had the situation been reversed. "But it seems like he's in the direction we're going, anyway."

She could feel Spike straining against her as if she were a physical jess; she stumbled forward two steps, crossing the threshold that defined the hall from whatever was just beyond it. It was not a comfortable transition—at all.

There was no floor beneath her feet, although her feet were definitely present. Instead, there was a gray-pink mass that seemed to extend as far as the eye could see, darkening in the distance. It reminded Kaylin of dead flesh, which was not a comforting thought.

The jumble of voices—Ynpharion's, Nightshade's, Severn's—even Severn's—made clear why: she hadn't taken steps the normal way. Whatever Spike had done had skewed her vision of reality. No, it had skewed reality, somehow. She was no longer walking in the same hall—or cavern, or whatever the hall led to—as the rest of her companions.

"Wait."

She turned at the sound of the familiar voice.

Teela had followed.

Stay with the Consort, Kaylin told everyone who could hear her. *Apparently, I have Teela.*

Teela was decidedly pale and some evidence of sweat beaded her forehead. Both of these were unusual.

"Why are you here? No, wait. I take that back. *How* are you here?"

"Enduring Mandoran has its uses." She glanced at Spike, and lost whatever it was that would have followed. Probably more explanation, but the dry comment had been explanation enough. "I can finally hear Terrano. Is Spike safe?"

"For us? Yes. I know he looks intimidating."

Apologies, Chosen. But if there is difficulty, it will be here. He looked down at Teela, although the direction of his gaze wasn't immediately obvious. *What they can do, I cannot do as effectively when I am with them.* It took her a moment to untangle this. *They must find the Barrani summoners and stop them.*

"What are you going to do?"

I am going to the heart of the Tower itself; I will bolster its defenses. It is already severely weakened. Were it not for your Terrano, I might have said those defenses no longer existed; I cannot hear the Tower at all.

"But the Tower is obviously testing people. All of the co-hort were put through their paces." She looked to Teela.

Teela nodded. "Mandoran is coming."

Testing is not the same as defense, Spike said. He began to move. *It requires a different power, a different mode of interaction.*

"You think the Shadow has already been summoned?"

The Shadow that you fear—that the Barrani fear—has been here since the Tower collapsed in on itself to trap and contain it. You did not possess—they did not possess—the power necessary to destroy it; not even the Tower at its full strength could.

And we can?

No, Chosen. But what your enemies now attempt will break the cage completely. And if that cage is broken, your familiar may protect you—but almost everyone else will be lost. He moved, all movements ungainly and disturbing.

Teela fell in beside Kaylin. Here, as in the streets of Elantra, she had the greater height, the greater weight; Kaylin could almost see the impressions her feet made in the ground beneath them. The ground which wasn't ground.

It wasn't Shadow, either, and Kaylin felt she should be grateful for the lack, but couldn't quite dredge up gratitude. She managed only when a familiar figure drifted slowly into view, the lines of his face scrunched into what passed for concentration in Mandoran.

"There you are!" His eyes were gray, with flecks of color that seemed to be straining for freedom. Even at this distance, they were visible; the eyes seemed to occupy far more of his face than they should have. But the Tower hadn't trapped or ejected him.

"Hey, is that *Kariannos*? I don't think I've ever seen you—"

"Not *now*," Teela snapped. "Have you found Terrano?"

"No—and Sedarias is pissed off."

"Use High Barrani when the Consort is present," Teela replied. Not much of a reply, but Mandoran shrugged it off.

"Sedarias's brother is present. His second in command is also present, as is his heir. There are other Lords of the Court, but Sedarias doesn't recognize them all." He spoke to Kaylin; Teela obviously already knew this. "She wants your help," he added, once again speaking to Teela.

"Apologies. I was occupied at the time. You can hear Terrano?"

Mandoran nodded. "He's not happy, but he's not in pain."

"You've spoken with him?" Kaylin said.

"No. Sedarias was against it. There's too much interference, and she expects that some of that interference is probably hunting us. She's *not* happy," he added.

"She's never happy," Teela snapped. She exhaled. Turning to Kaylin, she said, "Annarion has finished. Or escaped.

The cohort is gathered in two places. Three if you count Mandoran and me."

"Are they here or there?"

"There, for a value of there. I'm attempting to guide them to the Consort, but there's a notable difficulty."

"The Barrani summoners?"

"And their guards, yes. The guards are Ferals. If what Spike has said has been correctly conveyed, the biggest threat we face is the Ferals. Can Spike be here if you're not?"

"He should be able to—"

No.

"Uh, he says no." To Spike, she said, "We left you *behind* in the outlands. You weren't anywhere near us when we arrived in Elantra."

I was not anywhere near the Shadow that lurks at the heart of this place, Spike replied. *And he will pull, Chosen. He will attempt to compel. We do not have names in the same fashion as the Barrani possess them—but we have words of a kind. I have words of a kind. He will know them all; he will know how to invoke them.*

You are the barrier between me and that compulsion.

And given his size, his shape, his knowledge, that barrier— flimsy and mortal as it was—was necessary. "If I leave he's afraid he'll fall under the control of the Adversary."

"Then don't leave," Mandoran snapped. "Can you find Terrano?"

Kaylin nodded.

Spike stayed in front of Kaylin; the tendrils of black smoke that sprouted from the massive spikes were in constant motion. They trailed across the ground; they reached for protrusions, when protrusions existed; most of them seemed to come from what passed for ceiling here. The ceiling and the floor were composed of the same material.

So, at the moment, was Terrano. It wasn't a wonder to Kaylin that Teela and Mandoran hadn't seen him; she might have missed him herself had she not been looking. He was the color of, the shape of, the pillars that grew up—and down—across the entire landscape.

"He's here." As she approached, she frowned. Closer examination revealed nothing; he was the *exact* shape of the rest of the protrusions. There were no limbs, no face, nothing at all that looked like Terrano. And yet, she was certain that this particular stretched bit of pulsating flesh contained him. No, she thought; it didn't contain him. It *was* Terrano.

Teela and Mandoran stared at her; they hadn't stopped, or hadn't intended to stop. They did because Spike did. Or perhaps because Kaylin did. "If this makes me burst into flames or melt into Shadow, pull me back."

"What are you doing?" Teela asked, voice as sharp as her sword's edge.

Kaylin didn't answer. *I don't know* wouldn't have cut it; nor would *I'll figure it out.* Sadly, both were accurate. The marks on her arms had not stopped glowing; she doubted they would before she was clear of the High Halls. But her skin didn't ache at all. It had until she'd been dragged into Spike's orbit. As she lifted her left hand—always her left when things were questionable—she realized that the marks had lifted themselves, once again, from her skin; they rotated as if they were awkwardly crafted bracelets. They weren't large, but they were distinct, each word obviously separate from the others, but linked, as if they were sentences in a familiar language.

Her palm touched the pillar; it felt exactly like it looked: exposed flesh, veins, muscles. Part of a body. If this were a metaphor created somehow to allow her to shift into a different state of being, she *vastly* preferred carved, giant words.

But she understood why this particular metaphor was useful, even natural. She drew deep, even breaths to still the
sound of her own heart, which appeared to be beating over-
time, and as she did, she finally reached Terrano.

You've certainly looked better, she told him.

She could feel the movement of flesh beneath her hand.
It was disturbing; she'd helped birth babies before, but this
was nothing like that. Everything in Terrano was straining
to escape.

No, she thought. Not everything. *Took you long enough—
where were you?*

We had a little trouble with some Shadows. She would have told
him more, but a large number of Spike's tendrils emerged,
and all of them simultaneously shot toward Terrano.

"We need him!" Kaylin shouted, her hand tightening.

*I understand, Chosen. I believe I can convince the Tower to free
him, but the responsibility for Terrano will then rest entirely on your
shoulders.* The faint buzzing that was Spike's voice sounded
Elantran to her ears—except for the last word; she could
hear another word, other syllables, laid above it or beneath
it, that lent it a resonance it wouldn't otherwise possess. Her
entire body vibrated as the echo of those syllables passed
through her.

As Kaylin watched, the thing beneath her hand melted, red
sliding away as if it were blood. Not a comforting thought,
even if Kaylin had seen her share of bleeding—this much
blood was an early indicator of probable death. But there was
no wound; she could feel no injury beneath the tense flat of
her palms—she'd lifted the right instinctively, laying it beside
the left as if both hands would prove more useful than one.

Teela's breath was a sharp, loud sound; Kaylin opened her
eyes. Her hands were now flat against Terrano's chest. His
color was off—but it was a crimson, not the pale usually asso-

ciated with nausea or pain. He staggered, bracing his weight against Kaylin's hands as he found his footing.

Which meant, in Terrano's current form, grew feet. She remembered what Annarion had become in Castle Nightshade; this wasn't nearly as bad.

"I think the Tower doesn't want you here," Kaylin told him.

Terrano shrugged; it was a fief shrug, picked up from Mandoran, not Kaylin. "I was going to cheat," he confessed. "It's not like the High Court can tell who's actually made it all the way down—they only know who comes back out. I intended to take a shortcut, skip the garbage and come back out."

"And the Tower doesn't like cheaters? Fair enough. None of my teachers could stand them, either."

Terrano was slowly returning to his usual color, his usual appearance; only his eyes were off. "You tried?"

"I wanted to. But Teela made it pretty clear that the lessons were necessary."

"Was she right?"

Teela cleared her throat. "I'm always right."

"That's what she said back then, too."

Terrano turned to Teela. "Where's everyone else?"

"Not here."

"You're not planning to join them? Mandoran?"

Mandoran hadn't said a word, which was so unlike his usual self, Kaylin had almost forgotten his presence. "There's a bit of a problem," he finally said. His eyes, too large, grew darker and far less Barrani-like. Kaylin turned to Teela to find that her eyes were similar to Mandoran's now. He turned to Terrano.

"Sedarias's brother and his friends are playing with Shadow."

"Being played by Shadow?" Kaylin asked, unwilling to be left out of the conversation.

"That, too. They think they're the base of operations here. They're like a miniature Court. But it's their guards who are the biggest threat."

"The Ferals?"

"Whatever you did back in the halls to get rid of two of them, you need to do now to get rid of the rest."

Kaylin looked ahead into the crimson landscape. "I'll need to find them. I can't see them at all."

"What are you looking at?" Terrano demanded.

"At the interior of a body. Sort of. It's like a cavern, but made of flesh. Exposed flesh," she added.

The three members of the cohort exchanged a significant glance.

Kaylin held on to her temper. "You can see Mellarionne's forces from here?"

Terrano nodded. "I can probably teach you how to look—"

"No," Hope said.

The three Barrani turned toward him; Teela could actually hear him now.

"She is not what you are. She can be where you are because she bears the marks of the Chosen—but she bears them because, conversely, she is grounded. She has other methods of finding the creatures she needs to stop—but she cannot easily follow the path you now tread."

"It's not easy," Teela said.

"No. Not for you. But you can, and return, in the end, to yourself. Kaylin does not have that flexibility. And," he added as Terrano opened his mouth, "she does not require it. Spike?"

They are here, Spike replied. *Here, beneath the strata in which Terrano was imprisoned.* A silence followed—but it was a thin veneer over words which were certain to break it. *What you now see is not my choice, Chosen, but your familiar's. He is your guide here, if you have one. But the creatures you call Ferals, those who were once Barrani, are here. Can you not feel them?*

No.

But she could now hear them clearly.

CHAPTER 26

Lord Kaylin, Edelonne said. Kaylin was almost surprised to hear her. Ynpharion's voice had been absent in the earlier days of—of whatever forced name-bonding was called. She'd been aware of his fury and resentment, of his arrogance, of his contempt—both for himself and for her—but they'd both avoided exchanging actual words.

Edelonne's interior voice had none of Ynpharion's heat, none of his fire. Her voice was softer, thinner; Kaylin could easily imagine that she could, with no effort, fade into the background of everyday thought. Which this wasn't.

The more familiar ire followed as Ynpharion joined his voice to hers. *The Lady wishes to know where you are. She is not best pleased that An'Teela chose to join you.*

She has you, Kaylin countered.

She is aware that An'Teela's connection to the cohort is far more substantial.

"Mandoran."

"Before you ask, the answer is no."

"You don't know the question yet!"

"You're about to ask either Teela or me to go join the Consort. One: I don't want to. And two: I can't. Terrano said he was trying to ditch the test, right?"

"Teela's already passed it. She can come and go—in theory—as she pleases, if she has the Consort's permission. Which she does."

"Teela," Teela said, "is not going anywhere. You're here. They're here. Our enemies are here, or close." She punctuated the sentence with *Kariannos*, the great sword that appeared, given how she was waving it around, to weigh nothing. Her eyes shifted—literally—as they once again changed shape in her face. Nothing in their shifting color implied Barrani moods. "We've got Annarion. Finally."

"Which we?" Terrano asked.

"Serralyn."

"Is he—"

"He's mostly fine. They're approximately in the right place," she added.

Terrano deflated. "Tell them to step back. No, sorry, *ask* Sedarias to have them step back."

"To where?"

"To where we are now."

"Given what happened to you? Sedarias doesn't like it."

"Tell her we've got Spike negotiating with the Tower."

A beat. Two. "She wants to know what he's using for leverage."

I ask for concessions from the Tower's core functionality. I have explained that these concessions are necessary if we are to serve in its stead.

Kaylin mostly followed the answer. "He's telling the Tower—somehow—that we'll protect the Tower and keep the cage around the Adversary closed."

"And the Tower's not demanding an explanation?" Teela said, mimicking Sedarias's tone perfectly.

"I think the *Tower* has all the explanation it needs. It let Terrano go." She hesitated, and then said, "Can the rest of the cohort come to us?"

The answer was a qualified yes. It took time for all of the cohort to emerge; Valliant was last. Annarion was first. All of them had eyes that were similar to Teela's in size and shape, but they retained their heights; their hair, the raven black of Barrani, was now shot through with the same colors that made their eyes so disturbing. Annarion and Allaron bore swords, as did Sedarias. The rest of the cohort had chosen— for the moment—to retain the use of both hands.

Were it not for Terrano, they would have been silent— but Terrano was of them, and Terrano could no longer hear their conversations. Or arguments. Allaron caught him as he stood by the edge of their formation, and drew him into its center, as if afraid Terrano would otherwise flee.

"Can you see An'Mellarionne?" Mandoran asked of Kaylin.

"No."

Lord Kaylin. It was Edelonne again. *The Consort bids me tell you that we are almost at the cavern.*

Can you guys see the Barrani?

We can see the forces of Mellarionne, yes.

Can you see the Ferals?

Edelonne found the question briefly confusing, but the confusion passed. *Not all of them, no. There are three standing guard.*

They haven't seen you?

Not apparently.

Can they?

More silence. *I would not have noticed the Consort had I not been ordered to stall her procession. What I saw—what they now see—is not all of what you see. It is also more than you see, simultaneously.* She hesitated again. Kaylin thought that Edelonne was not nearly so angry with herself as Ynpharion had been with himself. Her responses were slower, more thoughtful; she didn't take time to justify herself or blame others for the decisions that had led to what she had become.

We have never been powers, she finally said.

You're Lords of the High Court.

Yes. But we are barely more significant than servants. Our families are irrelevant, our desires subject to the whim of those who have, and have always had, power. We have none. We do not have the base power necessary to learn the magics that could make us significant; we are lacking in land, in wealth, in the forces that might meet those who threaten us on fields of battle. Our hope lies in the games that the powerful play—but we are not naive. Without power, we cannot hope to become powerful.

You have forever.

Yes. We have an eternity of licking the boots of those who were born with advantages we lack. We were offered power, Lord Kaylin. You were offered the marks of the Chosen.

No, Kaylin snapped, *I wasn't. I wasn't offered a choice.*

This surprised Edelonne.

I have the marks, yes. But— She stopped. *You have more power, now, than I ever dreamed of. You live forever. You're stronger, faster. You don't die of exhaustion. The cold doesn't bother you—it certainly won't kill you.*

And you, Edelonne countered, *have the marks of the Chosen. The Consort and An'Teela are numbered among your friends— An'Teela considers you* kyuthe. *You don't need power of your own; you can rely on theirs.*

"Kaylin," Sedarias said in a tone that implied this was not the first time she'd attempted to get Kaylin's attention.

Kaylin reined in her fraying temper, and wondered, briefly, if anyone *ever* felt powerful enough. *They offered you power.*

They offered us power. They offered us freedom.

Enough, Chosen, Spike said, his internal voice sharp. *We have the information we require.*

But we don't—

We have the information we require. Do not attempt to gain more here; there is a danger.

"Annarion," Terrano said, "I see Karellan An'Solanace. Sedarias's brother is—obviously—there. Oh. Lumennar An'Casarre is there, as well. I'm not sure any of the rest are part of this attack."

"The rest?"

"A pity," Sedarias said aloud. "It would have simplified our difficulties at Court if they were all here."

She is almost terrifying, Edelonne said. She had retreated, as if she could hear Spike's words, or Kaylin's reaction to them. *We were offered power. We accepted. But it was a power that not even the High Court understood.*

There was a dark pride in the knowledge. Pride, Kaylin thought, and the slightest edge of what might have been shame. *We were chosen; they were not.* Definitely pride there. *They did not know. They could not hear the voices we could hear, could not accept the power that we were offered. We were needed. Us.*

Into Kaylin's mind came not so much an image as a sensation. Kaylin realized that what had happened to Ynpharion had not happened to Edelonne. Edelonne's power, Edelonne's transformation—the first of many she anticipated—had been different. Where Ynpharion had attempted to rid himself of what he viewed as weakness, Edelonne had not; she had been guided every step of the way.

She had felt the Shadow as both blessing and promise;

it had enfolded her in a warmth, a comfort, a *certainty*, that Ynpharion's transition had lacked. Edelonne could feel the echoes of it now, as she thought of it, almost transfixed. And Kaylin could feel the desire, palpable, that swamped all sense of self. The desire for safety. The desire for comfort. The desire to be necessary, important. That was what the Shadow had provided Edelonne.

It was illusory. It was a lie. But it had felt so real to her, so viscerally true, it didn't matter. Kaylin thought if they had died there, if they had been entirely devoured by Shadow, they wouldn't have cared at all.

She had always thought that drugs were about being happy, somehow. Being ecstatic. Finding the high. Now she wasn't so certain. And it didn't matter. Edelonne was not going to, could not, go back, because Kaylin was an anchor. A shackle. A cage. What she needed from Edelonne wasn't personal impressions. She needed to know—

Spike made a screeching noise that set Kaylin's entire body vibrating.

Spike didn't want her to approach the truth any further. *It is your Adversary,* he said, his voice causing Kaylin's jaw to ache. *The Barrani was offered power by that Adversary, and it is his knowledge that allowed the transformation. It is his knowledge that forms the foundation for the gate that is being built by the Barrani lords in their ignorance. Were they like Edelonne, we would be far too late; they are not.*

They struggle in ignorance, with just enough knowledge to be a threat. They cannot see that threat—but, Chosen, they will if they cannot be stopped. We all will.

"You won't."

I will. There is a reason that I had to be freed from the constraints of Ravellon. *If they succeed here, I will be trapped.*

"Even if I anchor you?"

You will be dead. Do not ask for more now. It is possible that even her answer, spoken as it is, will be heard.

"They already know we're here."

Yes and no. They know that we are coming. But those who consider us their chief concern cannot yet perceive how.

"Anytime you're ready to pay attention to our plan of action," Sedarias said, and Kaylin swiveled.

"Sorry. Spike was talking, and it's almost painful to the ears."

"Tell him to shut up, then. Terrano says you can't see what we can currently see."

Kaylin nodded.

"He thinks it doesn't matter. To us."

She is wrong.

"But knowledge is, in theory, power. According to Terrano, three of our families are currently engaged in an attempt to summon Shadow—as if it were a simple element. Killing them—ah, forgive me, *stopping* them—will be our problem. Your problem, according to Teela, will be the guards. The ones you call Ferals. We have some rudimentary grasp of the Arcane—from Teela, before you ask. We are not as helpless as our enemies currently presume we will be.

"Teela, however, will accompany you."

"What?"

"*Kariannos* will not be of great use against the High Lords; it was not created with Barrani enemies in mind."

"It wasn't created to fight Shadow, either. It's called a *dragonslayer* for a reason."

"We can argue about that later."

"What are your plans, then? You just intend to charge in and start killing High Lords?"

"As a matter of fact, yes."

"That's not a *plan*!"

"It's all of the plan we have time for," Sedarias snapped. "We expected opposition—but not on this scale; there is no subtlety being exercised at all." And if they weren't being subtle, Kaylin thought, Sedarias saw no need for subtle, either. "And according to Terrano, both your familiar and Spike feel that this might be death for our race."

"Has it occurred to you that Arcanists might have a few deadly defenses on hand?"

"Yes, of course. But to use them, they'll almost certainly have to interrupt what they're doing."

"Or try to do it *faster*," Kaylin snapped. "They'll send the Ferals after you first. And, guys? These are not *normal* Ferals. They have way more power than the Ferals you'd sneer at in the fiefs, and they're *tethered* to the Adversary's power. They have way more power than most of the enemies you'd take down with swords. They'll use it. I *can* break that connection—but it takes time. Time for each of the eleven. In the worst possible case..."

"Yes?"

"I think they'll ditch their names the way Terrano did. He took centuries. They'll take minutes. And what's left won't be Barrani anymore, in any way. It'll be Shadow—but it'll be the Adversary's Shadow, unleashed."

"The Tower shouldn't allow that," Terrano began.

"The Tower is *broken*. The only reason it's putting up with you—and the cohort—is because of the Consort. And Spike. Spike promised that we—collective we—would help the Tower to perform its duties. He's part of that, but I'm not sure whether or not he'll be able to contain a collection of Arcanists, because what *they're* doing, in theory—until they succeed—doesn't *use* the magic the Tower was built to suppress." She started to say more, stopped and closed her eyes. "You're right. Go do what you have to do, and please, please, please try not to get killed."

Eyes closed, Kaylin began to look for words. Her own marks were visible, but it wasn't her marks that were causing the problem. It was the True Names of eleven Ferals who were, according to Edelonne, scattered evenly throughout the cavern. This place—this red, wet, fleshy place—was the cavern. It wasn't the cavern that the cohort could see, but she could imagine what it might look like if layers of actual rock had been laid over the fleshy protrusions. She could only do this with her eyes closed.

It wasn't the cavern itself she wanted to see. She was now aware that the Tower of Test was also like Helen; the actual dimensions and architecture were impermanent and subject to change. But if the architecture had strata, she was in a place that was as close to its core as it would allow.

She'd been at the heart of a Tower before. At the heart of a Hallionne. And at the heart of Helen. This was nothing like any prior experience. The words she was looking for were not the words that gave the Tower both life and purpose. No, the words she wanted were smaller in every way.

Spike was speaking, but it was more sensation than communication; she was aware of his presence—he was like the higher, whinier version of a very loud heartbeat—but assumed he'd make himself understood if it was necessary. Or if he thought it was necessary, which might not be the same thing.

The first of the words emerged in the distance. Or rather, the closest. At this remove, Kaylin couldn't see the Feral that contained it. But she had a direction now. She wondered if Teela could follow her. Wondered if Teela could even see her. Or if Teela saw some of the strata of this place simultaneously.

The only thing that mattered was that Kaylin had something solid enough to walk across beneath her feet.

Or it was the only thing that mattered until she got closer.

Edelonne startled; Kaylin could feel the tremor of surprise—or shock—that words couldn't contain. What Kaylin now approached was, by all accounts, one of Edelonne's companions in transformation. It did not look like a Feral. It didn't look like a Barrani, either. It was a pillar of Shadow with bits that seemed to be churning beneath its opaque surface. Sadly, those bits were things like eyes. Kaylin was familiar with the internal organs that lay beneath skin in most living things, but even if she hadn't been, she'd've recognized them.

Edelonne was horrified. Ynpharion was not. Or if he was, he'd clamped down on his reaction enough that it wasn't immediately obvious. Why this was worse than Feral forms, Kaylin didn't know. Well, no, she *did*, but considered it impractical. The name that the Ferals bore—the name that had brought them to life after birth—had been hovering between their pointy ears. This name was not. If the surface of the pillar made the entire thing appear to be some variety of marble from a distance, the name was beneath that surface—along with the churning body parts.

Kaylin so did not want to touch that name.

"What do they look like to you?" Kaylin asked Teela, describing what she could see.

Teela didn't answer. Not with words. Kaylin could feel all her hair stand on end as Teela once again invoked the power of *Kariannos*. It was too much to be hoped that *Kariannos* would somehow remain invisible or out of phase. Of course it was.

She hesitated for one long second, lifted her arm and felt a surge of pain—something like fire, but not persistent.

The pillar crumbled. The fleshy bits leaked out of the

shadow pooling across the ground. Kaylin knew instantly, instinctively, that this was very bad—and not just for her. Spike almost screamed in alarm.

Chosen—tell her to stop! Tell her to stop now!

"Teela! Stop—you're making it worse!" Kaylin said, straining to lift her voice. She didn't open her eyes; she was already casting about the room for the next nearest name, angry at herself for her squeamishness.

But she heard Teela's curse. It was Leontine. "This is why they're here."

Yes, Spike said. *If the Adversary destroyed them, they would no longer be conduits through which he could send power. They are windows now; they are anchored here. Teela has broken the glass. She has not removed the window. There is nothing except the size of the window to contain what was trapped behind it. She must not kill them here. Not while they are attached to him.*

"Why wouldn't they be windows if *he* killed them?"

"They're the raw material out of which those windows were made," Teela said, voice grim. "Destroy the raw materials before the window is in place, and you have no window. You have wall. The Adversary couldn't create those windows with only his own power. But the Ferals here? They have all passed the Test of Name. They are all Barrani. They are alive, and they have been rooted here. If he orders them to move—as he did with the three in the halls—the link is tenuous. Had we killed the Ferals there, it wouldn't have been this disastrous.

"We're meant to meet them *here*. We're meant to kill them here." More cursing. More Leontine. Silence followed, and in that silence, Kaylin made her way to the next word, encased in a similar pillar. She wondered, briefly, if Teela saw what she saw now, or if, to Teela, they were large Shadow dogs with the requisite face full of fangs.

It didn't matter. She told Teela to join the cohort—or tried.

Hope said no. Spike no longer seemed to be aware of Teela. "Be ready," Hope said.

She was already bracing herself, because this pillar—which presumably looked like a Feral to some observers—was exactly like the one Teela had smashed. The name that she needed to touch was on the inside of a mess of moving—but otherwise undamaged—internal organs.

The eyes, however, alighted on her as she approached, and the currents that seemed to move body parts began to roil.

"Don't kill it!" Kaylin shouted. "Just...stop it from killing me."

Kaylin had no idea what the rest of the cohort—or the rest of her companions—were doing. She could have asked any of the name-bound, but didn't.

Steady, Severn said, anyway. *Just be steady. I can see Teela now. Can you see me?*

No. But... Teela is now facing one of the Ferals. I've passed on your message—but I don't think any of us could do what Teela just did.

Is one of the Ferals down?

Yes. But something is taking its place. Nightshade is headed there. He hesitated, and then said, *Evarrim believes that offense and defense—by us—will not cause the harm that Teela's attack did. If we can see Teela, she's reached the same conclusion.*

Have any of the rest of the cohort appeared?

Only Mandoran, and only to give us warning of their intentions.

Severn's voice was the calm in the growing storm, and Kaylin clung to it. She spoke while extending her left hand toward the name that she could see in the moving mass of unattached body parts. She drew back, cursing, when one of those parts became Feral teeth, unattached to the rest of the mouth or head.

"Hope—can we move at all?"

"You are moving."

"Can we move so that I can't see...this? Severn sees Ferals. And Ferals would be better."

"No, Chosen, they would not. I believe there is a reason that you see what you see now. While you may accomplish the necessary if you step to one side and join Teela, you will not accomplish it as easily."

This was *not* easy. She snapped her arm back as disembodied teeth once again attempted to separate her hand from the rest of her arm. This time, however, the teeth glanced off one of the marks that defined Kaylin's adult life, and she could hear the Feral's screech. She could feel it, as well; the entire pillar shuddered. She gritted her teeth, shoving her hand back into the pillar. There was some resistance.

Did Mandoran say what his intentions—or Sedarias's intentions— actually were?

Yes, but not in great detail.

She couldn't hear the name at all. It made no sound. The syllables that comprised it she would have to find herself. Closing her eyes didn't help, because her eyes *were* closed, in theory. They'd been closed for a while. Or maybe they hadn't. Hope had implied that Kaylin used closing—and opening— her eyes to transition between states in a subtle fashion.

Subtlety had never been her strength.

She caught the name as the Feral's teeth bounced off the marks on her skin. Caught it, but couldn't *hear* it. She had no way to take a name she couldn't hear; no way to speak it that would demand the entirety of the creature's attention. Her Leontine joined Teela's, except that Teela's could no longer be heard. The teeth, however, were no longer snapping at Kaylin's hand.

What the hell was she supposed to do? She drew the name

out of the miasma of moving parts; red and pink liquid clung to it like bloody mucus.

Teela wants you to keep doing what you're doing, Severn said. *And now we have a problem.*

More of a problem?

She…wasn't subtle while making that suggestion. She certainly wasn't quiet.

Everyone's noticed her?

Everyone who could possibly reduce her to ash, yes.

Have they noticed the Consort?

Not yet. But it's only a matter of time.

The word that now nestled in the cup of Kaylin's left palm was slight; it was smaller than Edelonne's name. This could have been an artifact of the way she viewed this name—and its container, for want of a better word—but Kaylin didn't believe that was the case. There was power in True Words, and power in True Names. It wasn't a power that the Adversary could use directly; it was a power that the Barrani and the Dragons could use, because they were born to it, made for it.

This was the truth that Spike feared, because Kaylin was certain that the diminished name had been slowly leached of power. She wasn't certain if that was a conscious choice on the part of the Ferals here.

It wasn't, Edelonne said.

But conscious or not, it didn't matter. Somehow, the words that had the power to drive an eternal life contained within their component parts could be drained entirely by the Barrani. Kaylin wondered what would happen to the name, to the Barrani that possessed it, if that power guttered. She expected that they would die, but not conveniently: they'd be undead. And she'd seen that before, as well.

She suspected that this would be different.

She didn't understand Shadow. Didn't understand how it worked. Didn't understand why some—like Gilbert—*had* words at their core and some didn't. She thought Spike might, but didn't give much for her chances of understanding his explanation at the moment. He was busy; she could see that. One tendril—only one—was wrapped around the base of this pillar. But she could see tendrils snake out across her lidded vision.

And she didn't ask what he was doing with them, either. She looked at the diminished word in her hand. The color itself was faded; instead of gold, it looked like aged silver—silver that hadn't been properly cleaned. Evidence of tarnish existed in every bend and on the interior of every curve.

It wasn't tarnish, of course; it was a metaphor.

But it was a metaphor, suddenly, that she could work with. Housework had never been her strength, although Caitlin had tried to teach her how to both clean and set up a schedule that enforced cleaning. Growing up, clean house was of vastly less import than shelter at night, and shelter had been a moving target.

Even in her own home, silver was nowhere in great abundance, and what there was of it had been Caitlin's gift: teapot, tray, two very large spoons. They had all pretty much become gray-black, and had been tucked away in a chest beneath the bed until an Arcane bomb had destroyed her home. She had treasured them because they had come from Caitlin at the start of her life in Elantra. Treasured, however, didn't mean they had to be cleaned and polished—just kept.

She began to clean this particular tarnished surface. Her sleeve—the one that hadn't been reduced to ash—was long, but unbuttoned; she used the silk as an awkwardly placed rag, because it was better than nothing. As she rubbed the darker surfaces, the patina of clean silver was exposed. She wasn't certain that it would ever be golden again—not as it had been. Not if it didn't return to the Lake.

But when she looked up, she could see that the pillar was no longer a pillar, that it had dwindled into a shape that was almost Barrani. There wasn't *room* inside that pillar for all of the parts it contained to swim and move; they were being compressed into more or less the proper places. She could still see them, but it didn't make her want to lose her lunch.

The Lady asks that you continue whatever it is you're doing, Ynpharion said.

Kaylin nodded. She didn't have the name of this particular Feral in any binding way, but she was *carrying* it. She hesitated, and then she dropped the word itself onto her exposed skin—the back of her left hand. It stuck there.

She turned, looked toward the next faint word and began to run.

CHAPTER 27

Between one step and the next, the ground changed. What had been fleshy and warm became harder, although the uneven shape it retained made running more difficult. Kaylin couldn't decide if this were a good thing or a bad thing.

Spike made clear it was the latter.

Tell Teela, Kaylin told Severn, *to tell the cohort to do something. I don't know what's happening—but Spike says things are getting worse.* She hesitated. *The Ferals are using their own names—depleting them somehow—to be the Adversary's anchors. They're in a state that allows some physical connection to the Adversary's native power; they're using their own names to maintain that connection somehow. The cohort can see what's being done. And it's possible the cohort could do what the Ferals here are doing. But the cohort had centuries to achieve the ability. The Ferals didn't. Everything they're now doing they learned from the Adversary. And if they can use their own names, there's a good chance they can use other names. Like the ones in Orbaranne or...*

The Lake.

The Lake, Kaylin agreed. *Spike says the Adversary can't use the names it hasn't released. It can't use their power. But these Ferals probably could. The Barrani attacked Orbaranne because she*

contained exactly those words. If the Adversary is somehow linked
to these Barrani—these Ferals—it will finally have tools to use that
power outside of its cage. I'm trying to break the conduits. But the
power they're absorbing from Shadow and their own names is some-
how related to what the non-Feral Barrani are doing.

How?

I don't know. Spike thinks An'Mellarionne and crew are trying
to summon a lot of Shadow. She stumbled. *Or maybe they're try-*
ing to summon the Adversary directly.

They wouldn't dare.

Not if they knew that's what they'd get, no. The Adversary
doesn't want the Ferals dead. If they're dead, there's nothing to con-
vert words to power.

But killing the Feral had done no good. It had made things
worse. She had to think, and thinking while running and
squinting—or its analogy—was difficult. This time, when
she reached the next pillar, there was no hesitation, no squeamishness, at all. She shoved her left hand into the miasma that
was—on some other plane—a body, and she easily grasped
the name. Like the first, it was shadowed and half-blackened;
like the first, it was wet and covered in something like red
mucus. The latter, she swept away; the former, she left. Using
the back of her hand as a container, she ran to the next word,
the next pillar, leaving something that appeared to be human
shaped—but not human—behind.

She was surprised to see Terrano when he appeared directly in front of her. She was almost surprised when she ran
through him, while attempting to slow down enough to avoid
a collision. He grimaced.

"Don't stop. Go. *Go.*" Reorienting himself, he followed.
Kaylin noticed that he didn't appear to have feet, but that was
all she noticed; she focused on the next pillar.

"What are the rest of you doing?" she demanded as she retrieved a third name, a third word.

"In my opinion?"

That wasn't good. "You see anyone else here? Besides me?" She reached the next pillar and used it to break her stride.

"Sedarias wanted me to tell you to keep doing whatever it is you're doing. She'd tell you herself, but she's a bit occupied."

"And they couldn't send Mandoran?"

"He's more than a bit occupied."

Fourth name down. Seven to go. "What are they doing?"

"They're trying to kill everyone who isn't us."

"Any success so far?"

"None whatsoever. If it helps, whatever Teela did to the first Feral has caused a *lot* of smaller Ferals to spawn. I don't think they're the original, though; they might be transformed rats. Literal rats," he added when he saw her expression. "Those rats are smaller, faster, harder to pin down and kill. They don't exist here," he added. "Which is what I was sent to check." He glanced up, and up again, while keeping pace with Kaylin.

"Where are your feet?" she demanded when name number five had been added to the back of her hand, which was getting crowded. The hand itself felt heavier, as if something was attached at the wrist. Or the palm. As long as it didn't slow her down, she could deal with the extra weight.

"My what?"

"Never mind." The sixth name was not nearly as easily grasped as the previous five had been. The external skin of the pillar was harder; it felt like literal glass. She could see the name itself, but the light it emitted was fainter.

He understands what you have done, Spike said. *And he is now attempting to prevent it. My apologies, Chosen.*

Spike had nothing to apologize for, and Kaylin opened her

mouth to tell him that when the entire world shifted; the floor slanted up to become a pocked, hard wall, and the pillar, attached to the floor, went with it. Kaylin didn't waste breath shouting; she reached out for the pillar itself, to break a fall she felt certain was coming. Her arms didn't pass through it, but the world had only begun to spin.

She'd have to remember that some apologies were pre-emptive.

"Terrano?"

Silence. Whatever Spike had done, Terrano hadn't immediately followed. She couldn't see him, couldn't hear him, and gave up on trying. She closed her eyes. Again. With her eyes closed, she saw a circle made by extended wings; it enclosed her. She saw the marks of the Chosen. She saw a darkness that wasn't terrifying, and she thought—for one confused moment—that she could hear its voice.

The pillar remained in the circle of her desperate clinch. Nothing else did. The world stopped spinning, although the sensation of movement remained, an echo of the transition itself. And it was a transition, from one place to another; it wasn't the world that had been rotated, but Kaylin.

Or at least that's how she explained it to herself.

She opened her eyes. She half expected to see the cohort, the Lords of the High Court, even the remaining Ferals; she thought to see Teela and Nightshade with their named swords. No one was here.

But she knew, now, where she was, because she had been in similar places before. She saw words: tall, liminal words, huddled together in the distance. How great a distance was more difficult to discern without actually moving—and she began to move, her hand heavy with the True Names of what had once been Barrani.

She was at the heart of the Tower.

Terrano was not by her side, and she now doubted that he could return. Hope, however, was present; his wings, like the distant True Words, were imbued with a golden light that spoke of power and life. She could not see Spike at all.

"He is not here," Hope said quietly, a reminder that her thoughts were as clear as speech to her familiar. "But he will be here soon, if things go poorly."

"If things go poorly?"

"You should not be here. You are here. The landscape that you viewed prior to this one should have been as close as you were allowed to come."

"It's not the first time I've seen the heart of a Tower."

"It is not. It is why you are here, or can be here, at all."

"Because I'm Chosen?"

"Because you have seen the heart of Towers and Hallionne before, and you have accepted what lies at their heart."

This did not make sense to Kaylin.

"You have not attempted to make them your own. You have not attempted to shift or alter the structure of the words that were written. You have not attempted to draw power from those words to use in ways that even the Ancients could not conceive."

"I don't know how to do any of that."

"Yes. Perhaps your ignorance is our salvation. But I do not believe it is ignorance that has opened this path."

"I'm supposed to grab the rest of the names—"

"I do not believe," Hope replied, "that that will be possible now."

"But there are still six pillars."

"Pillars? An interesting choice of words. Yes. Six remain. But there should have been thirteen. The three that were sent to stop the Consort were what could—in an emergency—be spared."

"I can't see them, either."

"You will," he said softly. "Approach the words, Chosen. Do what you must do."

Kaylin had no problem doing what she had to do—when she understood what that was. In general, when orders were passed down the chain of command, the person handing them down knew the desired results, even when some poor private actually had to do the work.

But whining, while it bled away some of the tension, didn't actually get much done. It was acceptable if you were doing the work. As a way of avoiding work, it was definitely third class, although on bad days, it was all she had to offer.

Today was a different kind of bad. She might have some idea of what needed to be done if she was closer to the cluster, but closer was its own challenge. Here, no matter how she walked, distance between that cluster and Kaylin seemed to be a constant. She didn't get any closer. She could run—and did—to no effect whatsoever.

There was no point in expending energy running if it made no difference. She needed to think. She had approached words like this before. She'd approached them in a panic. She'd approached them when the cost of failure could be measured in lives, one of them her own.

But approaching the words themselves hadn't been the problem; figuring out what constituted success had. She closed her eyes—which, as usual, changed nothing—and tried to think.

"I don't understand metaphor," she told Hope.

He chuckled. "You don't understand the mechanics of

breath, either; you manage to breathe without that understanding. You know what will happen if you can't."

"This isn't like breathing."

"Isn't it? You are here, where none of your companions—
no matter how versed they are in the Arcane—can join you.
You could find Lord Nightshade using the tools at hand,
without a complete understanding of how those tools function. You have only a base idea of how your daggers are
forged, but you know how to use them. This is not different." He drifted, for the first time, ahead of Kaylin; she could
see the spread, the reach, of his wings.

Those wings were the color—the exact color—of the
marks on her arms.

But her skin was the color of fire. Looking down, she realized that the fire had accompanied her.

"It is better to say you have not left it," Hope told her
gently. "Although here, its voice is muted, its desire banked.
There is nothing here to burn. There is no cold, no ice to
melt, no iron to forge; it is, for the fire, a world without
conflict."

"There's almost nothing here, Hope."

"Exactly."

"Why can the fire be here?"

"You must ask."

"Or you could tell me."

"No, Kaylin, I can't. I could try—but I do not have the
language to explain it."

The fire didn't, either. The communication between element and summoner had never been particularly subtle. She
opened her eyes again. The words were at the same distance,
unless she was looking at them the wrong way. At that distance, they had no answers to give her.

So she looked, instead, to her feet.

★ ★ ★

"I think I see the problem."

Hope said nothing, because he realized she was thinking out loud. She often avoided words when there were other people present, afraid in some fashion that they were the wrong words—either too offensive or too stupid. Here, there was no one but Hope who could judge. Hope, she thought, and some hint of Spike.

The words appeared to exist on an entirely separate platform. Kaylin had been doing the effective equivalent of running into an invisible wall. Had there been some impact—any impact—she would have realized it sooner. She lifted a hand, an arm, and reached out with the flat of her palm.

She felt a very gentle resistance. Pulling her arm back and making a fist, she drove the fist forward. The resistance was the same; it was gentle, almost unnoticeable.

"Why does everything have to be so complicated?"

If it helps at all, it's not any better here. Severn's voice. She couldn't hear any of the others, but didn't try.

What's happening there?

The usual.

The usual was bad. *Let me see.* Hope returned to her side as she looked through Severn's eyes.

She had no control over what she saw. She wasn't part of it in any real sense. Nor could Severn easily shift his line of sight, because that line of sight was broken by a spinning chain. What he saw, what he looked for, was magic. What was strange—to Kaylin—was his sensitivity to it. He couldn't see magic—neither could Kaylin. But he responded to it as if it were a sound, an incoming projectile.

Even if it was beneath his feet.

The weakness of the spinning chain as a spell break was the ground itself. He had to shift, and spinning chains with deadly blades on the end weren't conducive to throwing himself to the left or right. He jumped instead, timing that jump, the motion carrying him slightly forward as the stone beneath his feet cracked.

She could only barely see what had broken through the patch of stone, cracking it but not fully shattering it. Seeping through those cracks—straining against the barrier of stone—was a livid, deep purple. If it had a form, Kaylin couldn't see it. But she had no doubt that it was not going to be good for Severn if it reached him.

He landed, adjusted his grip on the chain, moved again, this time sideways. The ground wasn't the only avenue of attack. She was aware of the Consort. She was aware of Ynpharion. Severn had taken the front, and Nightshade had pulled up the rear. Lightning lit the cavernous heights.

Nightshade had taken the rear, and whatever *Meliannos* required of him to be fully active, he'd done. But she knew, now, that it wasn't done trivially; it wasn't done without need. Severn trusted Nightshade in combat. He did not assume that the fieflord required protection or warning.

She wanted to know what the cohort was doing, but realized that asking could be almost fatal. He paid attention to what he needed to see to survive.

A second spike of lightning illuminated the cavern, this from in front of Severn. Teela, she thought. She wondered if she was actually standing motionless in their world, while Teela was forced to protect her. She didn't ask.

Severn, however, said, *Yes. Hope is with you; whatever shielding he provides from magical attack is more comprehensive than my chains.*

Beneath that answer was the unspoken need for speed.

★ ★ ★

Your friends, Spike said, *are there. Teela is attempting to keep you safe. She understands what must be done.*

"Why can't you move my *actual* body here?"

"Because you are mortal, Kaylin. You are not the cohort. You are not Spike, or me. You are part of the world into which you are born, inextricably rooted in it. The marks protect you," Hope added. "But they cannot make you invulnerable; they cannot make you other than you are."

What she was, at the moment, was frustrated—at herself, at her inability to be useful, at her need to be protected by Teela, when Teela should have been with her cohort.

"Lord Evarrim is aiding Teela."

The words that fell out of her mouth were all Leontine. Leontine or no, they caused ripples in the air, as if her breath here had force. No, she thought, not the air. The wall. This made no sense; the Leontine wasn't visible; it wasn't a true language in the way the marks, created by the Ancients who were more than gods, were.

She spoke in Leontine again. Nothing.

She spoke in Aerian next. Nothing.

Barrani netted the same results. But she was certain that the wall, impermeable, had shifted at the first spoken Leontine. And she knew what the difference was. She abandoned the language that made her throat hurt if she spoke it for too long, and slid once again into Elantran.

"I don't like Evarrim. I am never going to like Evarrim. But he wants the same things I want, right now. I *hate* having to depend on him. I *hate* owing him *anything.*" Movement, there. Movement in front of her. She tried to take a step forward, and found that she could. A small step.

"He's arrogant. He's powerful. He's never had to struggle the way I've struggled." Another step. "But that's not why

I hate him. I hate him because it's become clear to me that he *does* care about other people. He *can*. Just…never about me. I'm never going to be worthy of anything in his eyes."

A larger step. Unfortunately, she'd run out of things to say about Evarrim. There were many things she hated. There were many things she feared. She understood, as she stood here in this moment, that she had to separate the truth from the lies, because some of the things she said were lies. They were believable lies. Credible lies. They were things she believed about herself; she just didn't examine them very carefully.

"You know," she told Hope, hesitating, "I really, really hate this."

"This is the Tower of Test," Hope replied, his voice almost entirely neutral.

"I didn't have to do this the first time."

"No. But there is only one first time, Chosen. And you were not then where you are now. Nor is the Tower."

"This is a test."

"Of a kind, yes. You must approach the Tower as yourself."

"I'm *always* myself," she snapped.

Hope's wings shifted. "You are always yourself, yes. But you understand the difference."

"Do I have to like it?"

"Demonstrably not."

She wanted to say it was none of the Tower's business, and gave herself a very deserved mental kick. Teela was fighting for her life—for both of their lives. Severn was fighting for the Consort. The Consort was fighting, in the end, to free the names of the trapped. Kaylin was only being asked to be completely honest.

An exchange was being demanded: the Tower's truth for Kaylin's truth. It was better than having a face full of Feral armed with only two daggers. It was. She knew it was. It didn't *feel* that way, but feelings were irrelevant.

She'd learned the hard way that the secrets she kept, she kept because they had the power to destroy her; because they lived on the inside of her, and forced her to acknowledge, time and again, things she didn't *want* to be true about herself. She judged herself harshly, which was what she deserved. But even so, she didn't want others to see and judge her the way she saw and judged herself.

This, she thought, was the real cost, the real weight, of some of her earliest decisions. They were a shadow from which she couldn't escape. She could understand why she had made them. She could even justify them with a semblance of logic, of reason. She could point out all the ways in which the choices she'd made were only barely choices: do something terrible, or die. She'd chosen to survive.

On bad days, she wondered about that. And there had been very bad days. They were fewer now. Less overwhelming. Why? Because she believed that she would never make— never have to make—those same choices again. She thought *this time*, as a Hawk, she could choose "or die" and mean it; that fear wouldn't swamp everything else.

Of course, with people, you never knew. Especially when one of them was you.

But conversely, her history gave her a sense of confidence in the future. She knew where she'd been. She knew where she was. And if even Kaylin could cross the divide between self-loathing and self-respect, no matter how much of a struggle it was, others could do it, as well. There was no *never*, no immediate dismissal of the potential of a person.

Sometimes other Hawks did. She understood why. It was hard to give the benefit of the doubt to someone who was trying to kill you, rob you or make your life vastly more difficult. When knives and clubs were drawn, there was no thought, because there was no *time* for it.

But after, there could be.

So she spoke to the Tower. She discovered, as she did, that she didn't *need* to speak out loud. But she needed to think, clearly. She needed to examine herself truthfully enough that the Tower could hear her thoughts, could touch them, could test them—and, ultimately, could accept them. If there was judgment offered, it would be offered only when she reached the Tower's core.

There were all kinds of ways to protect oneself. Kaylin knew most of them. From early childhood on, the easiest, simplest and therefore first of those lessons was: hide. As a child, there hadn't been many other options. She'd resented that enough to learn how to fight. To learn how to protect herself—and others. She'd learned to push fear out of the equation, although she'd left enough there for caution.

Clearly, some visceral impulse to hide remained, rooted very deeply in the fear of others. She pulled those out, as well.

Sometimes she hated the Barrani. They were proof that the universe wasn't fair. They lived forever, they were beautiful and the strength they were born to was enough to make the Ferals that had terrified the mortals in Nightshade a nonissue. She hated the fact that money and power devolved to them, and to those they chose as allies in the mortal Courts. No, the *Human* Court. She hated the way they looked down at mortals for the very differences Kaylin resented. She resented being born mortal, when they had been born Barrani, with all of the advantages of their race.

She accepted this. Sometimes it stung. Sometimes, when things were dark or days had been too damn long, she resented them for having everything that would have made her life so much easier.

She didn't argue with herself, as she so often did.

She didn't resent the Aerians in the same way. She *envied* them flight, but they were mortals.

And the Dragons? No. She didn't resent the Dragons. They were far enough above her that she couldn't imagine being one. Couldn't imagine the power of the dual forms. Couldn't imagine possessing their breath, their muscular flight. Didn't want to imagine the weight of the crown.

Why?

Ah. Because the Barrani were her friends. They were her comrades. They were Hawks. They had the same responsibilities, and pay was defined by rank. She saw them all the time. She heard them all the time.

And it would *kill her* to lose Teela or Tain. Because if she hated the Barrani some of the time, she loved Teela and Tain all of the time. Did they have things she lacked? Yes. They always would. But their lives hadn't been simple or easy, either. Kaylin's mother had died, impoverished, of an illness. Teela's mother had been murdered in front of her eyes. All of the advantages that accrued to Teela because of her birth hadn't saved her mother, her friends or the things she had, as a child, loved.

It was hard, most days, to think of Teela *as* Barrani. Or Tain. It was hard, she thought as she continued to walk, to think of Bellusdeo as a Dragon. To think of the cohort as Barrani—although, to be fair, Sedarias was probably the ideal Barrani to her own people. Why? Because she thought of them, first, as friends.

As people. Only as people. Their advantages and disadvantages weren't things to be measured on most days. On the bad days? Yes. She did. But on the bad days, so did they. It was a waste of time. It was stupid. But...living people had bad days. Barrani did. Dragons certainly did. Mortals did.

Marcus probably had more bad days than anyone else Kaylin knew, but maybe that was only because his bad days were death to ignore.

No two people were alike. Severn was mortal, but he was Severn; he wasn't like Kaylin at all. The Dragons? They were all different. And the Barrani were all different, as well—but they looked very similar if one didn't know any Barrani.

She couldn't get rid of the darker impulses, the darker thoughts, the envy or the resentment—not entirely.

No, a new voice said. *But understand that they are not all of you, as they are not all of any person. How much of your life they define is a choice that you make, and make consistently, constantly. It is not a choice that you make and forget. You cannot make choices if you cannot understand or accept the option available to you. You cannot choose when you deny that you have ever chosen.*

"I'd call that denial a choice," Kaylin said quietly. She was standing beneath a bower formed almost entirely of words. This was the heart of the nameless Tower. Ah, no, it was not nameless.

You are certain you are not Barrani? That was a very typical Barrani response.

"I'm only certain that I'm Kaylin." She exhaled. "Look, if you ask me who I am, I've got no answer to give. I can tell you I'm a Hawk. But...that's what I *do,* not who I am. I... don't know who I am."

You have been telling me who you are.

"But...only the bad parts!" This seemed wrong to Kaylin.

No. Not only, Lord Kaylin, but also. *It is part of who you have become. It is part of the matrix of choices that you can make.*

"Can you see what's going on outside?"

Outside?

She reddened. "I mean, not here. Not at the core of you."

This question didn't fare any better, which was the problem with immortal buildings when it came to communication. Undaunted, Kaylin tried again. "Can you see what my friends are doing? Can you see what our enemy is doing?"

Yes. The silence extended. *Understand that Immortals, like any of the living, know weariness, Lord Kaylin. I was injured long ago. The parts of my body that were meant for communication were destroyed, as were most of the functions that governed the living quarters in which the Barrani dwelled.*

You are the first living person with whom I have had explicit communication since the fall. I cannot bespeak the Barrani now; I can hear the Lady. I can sense those who come as supplicants. I can fulfill the functions of testing them. But those who approach the being at the lowest remove of the Tower, I cannot save. They are lost.

"I don't understand. No—I understand that they're lost. I get that. But...if you were always about testing, what did you do before?"

There was no answer. When it became clear that there would never be an answer, Kaylin lifted both of her arms, elongating her body so that the tips of her fingers could brush, could touch, the surface of the closest of the gathered words.

They were warm. Of course they were. And they were vibrating gently, invisibly, in place.

Your friends are dangerous.

"Yes."

They should not be here.

"Probably not." The vibrations beneath the tips of her fingers moved to her palms—or perhaps the words moved. Or she did. Her body seemed to hum with the sensation. "But they're here for a reason. The Lady approves."

It appears that she does. You freed the one I could not test.

She stilled. "You tested us."

Yes, Lord Kaylin. I remember.

"Why is Terrano different?" Before he could mention the

marks that girded her body, she added, "Different than Lord Severn, I mean."

You already know the answer to that question.

"I know why he's different in my view—but I don't always understand buildings. Helen accepts him," she added.

Helen is yours. She accepts what you accept. I am not. But I have chosen to accept his presence on your behalf. A rumble of vibration, felt in the pit of her stomach, accompanied the words— a hint of consequence should Terrano mess something up. The details were left for future consideration.

The words continued their descent. Kaylin moved to the side, finding room for herself amid the shapes of lines, of curves. But her palm continued to rest against the side of one of the words, and that word remained at face height. The rest sank until their bottom-most elements were flush with her feet.

They were taller than she was. Broader. Brighter. But the color of the marks on her skin was now a matching gold, and she thought those marks were vibrating in time with the larger words at the Tower's heart. She didn't feel caged by any of the words—the ones on her skin that she hadn't asked for, or the ones that now surrounded her.

"How can I help?" she asked.

Do you not know? The thrumming shifted; it wasn't so much a hum as a scrape of metal against metal, jarring, discordant. *Is that not why you have—finally—come?*

CHAPTER 28

"If you were whole," she asked the Tower, her voice soft and hesitant, "if you became what you were before the disaster, would you be able to speak to the Consort? The High Lord? Would the Barrani be able to speak with you?"

They speak with me now.

"Would they hear you? Would they be able to hear your voice?"

Silence.

And Kaylin understood then. Speaking, listening—it wasn't the same as being heard. It had never been the same.

She was no longer a child. She was no longer dependent on the older and stronger to keep her fed or clothed or safe— or what resembled those things in the fiefs. She could feed herself, house herself, protect herself, in ways that had only been daydream when she'd been a child.

But she needed people. She needed—wanted—company. Yes, she also needed privacy, but privacy was a matter of choice; isolation was not. And living people didn't appear to thrive in isolation.

The Tower was alive.

The Tower was older than the Arkon. It had been injured

during the first of the Draco-Barrani wars, and it had never recovered. She didn't know what it had been before its fall. Didn't know what it would be.

Didn't know what it *wanted* to be. Helen had injured herself because she knew what she wanted to be: a home. A home to a mortal woman who had died centuries ago. And beyond that, to mortals who needed the home that she could be for them. Kaylin was merely the last in that line, and when Kaylin passed away, the line would continue.

The Tower hadn't injured *itself*. Whatever it had done to withdraw from the rest of the space it had occupied in the living world had been necessary for its survival. Or for the survival of the Barrani.

Yes. We did not know what had come to the High Halls, in the guise of kin. And when we became aware of it, it was almost too late. Everything I had, every process, every directive, was rerouted to build the cage that has kept it here. But it is *a cage, not a coffin. And things have slipped between the bars, in either direction.*

I can hear the voice of Ravellon *in the whispers of my prisoner. It sounds like a song.*

She had done what she could to repair Helen, haphazardly and without a clear directive. She had done what she could to preserve the integrity of Tara, in the fief Tiamaris now ruled. She had done the same for Alsanis, although the feel of the struggle had been entirely different.

This Tower, nameless, wasn't like any of the buildings she knew. The words here were whole. They were resonant. She could almost hear them; she could certainly feel their pulse. There was nothing she could add to what was written here in ancient blood. Shadow had invaded the central cavern— but the Shadow had not attempted to destroy or alter the heart of the Tower.

He cannot, the Tower said. *These are True Words. They mean what they mean; there is no alteration he can make. Understand that he offers what the living want, to the living—that he uses the tools they provide him. Your fears are not Lord Severn's fears; your fears are not the Consort's. Nor are your desires. There is overlap, yes— but he sees to the heart of the individual.*

Even were he to see the heart of the Tower, he could not bespeak it; he could not charm, could not cajole, could not threaten. That has never been his power. The power that he does have was not considered a terrible threat by the Barrani; they are a proud, cold people.

But they desire power.

"And he can grant that."

In a fashion, yes. But it is not his power that is granted, in the end. Understand that.

"Whose power is it?"

Ravellon's. *And that power is growing, here. It is why I hear its music, even at this remove. Can you not hear it?*

"No."

Good.

"You want to hear it."

Silence.

"If your words aren't damaged, if your directives remain true, can't you be what you were? Can't you speak to the Barrani of the High Halls?"

Not while the Adversary is captive here. It is too great a risk. It has always been too great a risk.

"And you can't kill it."

No, Lord Kaylin. Nor can the Barrani nor the Dragons.

She had come to the heart of the Tower. She'd been asked to do what only she could do. But…there was nothing for her *to* do. The words were whole. What the Tower was, she couldn't change. And if she couldn't change anything, she had no reason to even be here—not when her friends were fighting for their lives.

Hope had said she could do something. She'd assumed she understood what that something was. But when she turned to look at Hope for guidance, she could no longer see him. All that existed were the words. The words and Kaylin herself.

Those words continued their rhythmic beat; they felt alive in a way that even people didn't, which was a disturbing thought. But as she listened, for want of a better word, she finally realized that not all of the humming itself was coming *from* the words that she was touching.

Some of it was coming from Spike. She couldn't see him when she turned to look over her shoulder, but it was almost irrelevant. Spike—or some part of Spike—was here. She hesitated, and then looked for Ynpharion.

Ynpharion's vision was much like Severn's—choppy, frenetic, constantly in motion. She could see the sword he carried, but it moved, as the landscape moved. She didn't ask him questions; she could see that he was busy. The Consort was behind him, and to the side; Kaylin caught a glimpse of her pale, platinum hair. It was moving in a way that implied magic.

Ynpharion wasn't looking for the cohort, and given the Consort's position by his side, Kaylin didn't ask. She almost moved to Nightshade, but froze as she heard a very familiar sound.

The Consort was singing. She couldn't understand the words, but didn't need to; she had heard the Consort sing this song before, in the journey to the West March over which her brother ruled. She had called the Hallionne with it, waking them from slumber. She had comforted and strengthened the embattled Bertolle.

They heard her. They heard her, and inasmuch as a building could, they loved her.

The Tower was not a Hallionne, but she had chosen to sing the same song. And Kaylin knew that it was costly, that it took power, strength, will. And she was singing it on a battlefield.

Tell her to stop!

Ynpharion said nothing. Kaylin could see that he was fighting… Ferals. Ynpharion was bleeding.

Nightshade!

He did not reply, not with words. But lightning arced from the center of his vision. It burned what it struck, and the light lingered, as if it were a different kind of flame.

Ynpharion—tell her to stop. The Tower—the Tower of Test—has always *heard her voice. It can hear her now. It's awake but it has no way of responding. It has no way of communicating. There's no Avatar!*

There was no Avatar.

Everything the Tower had built was a cage. A prison. What had it said? All of its power, all of its focus, all of its will, was turned toward the creature trapped beneath the High Halls.

In fear, in love, in rage, the Barrani who had been tested had approached the Adversary. Those who had not been tempted by despair or desire simply walked away. Kaylin understood all of the impulses that led, in the end, to death at the base of the Tower. Had she not had Severn, had she not had—ugh—Evarrim, she might have died the same way: attempting to save the lost.

But here, at the Tower's heart, surrounded by words, she thought: words are meant to communicate. These words could not, and did not; the building created in an era when the Ancients had the powers of gods was caged by them, hemmed by them, *of* them. All of the power that resided within it was from these words.

And that power could not be used in a different fashion now. Because of the Adversary. Because of the testing.

She understood then, or thought she did. She lifted her arms, and as she did, she saw the marks that had risen—as they often did—off her skin, shining through the fabric of her dress, as if the dress itself were just a different variant of that skin. Even the marks she had taken from the Barrani who had served as Feral pillars rose.

She listened, face lifted as if to see every single word that comprised the heart of the Tower. She heard the Consort's song. Not as she had the first time, through Ynpharion; it pierced whatever it was that kept Kaylin's consciousness separate from the battle.

She couldn't hear the cohort, couldn't hear the Hawks.

I take that back, she told Ynpharion.

He didn't reply. He was, however, annoyed at her ignorance, and again, that was a comfort.

"Hallionne. Tower. Whatever it is that you call yourself, let me tell you a story."

Fire moved up and down her arms. The patina of flame reddened the gold she could see almost everywhere. The fire had always wanted stories. Stories of life and the necessity of fire, not stories of its destruction. She couldn't—and didn't—tell the fire who, or what, it was. She couldn't. She could barely answer that question about herself on the best of days, which this wasn't.

Her stories, told to fire, were about the overlaps in their lives—if fire could be called alive. They were parts of Kaylin's story. They were her experiences, cut into small, digestible bits. So telling stories to the fire was also telling stories about herself and her experiences. She could own, did own, the latter.

What the Tower needed was not those stories. She could tell it stories about people, although those stories were hers in part. She started, stopped. Started, stopped.

Stopped. "Let me walk that back," she finally said as a different understanding crashed into the first. Communication was often like this, though: stumbling, tripping, getting up again. Moving, however clumsily, forward.

She didn't need to *tell* the Tower a story. He'd heard all the stories. He was aware of them. He could hear the Consort—could hear her, especially now, as she sang. Her song resonated in corners Kaylin's voice couldn't reach. She could see the words almost vibrate with the force of that song, with the strength of it; could see the way the power poured into the singing was like water poured into parched earth.

Kaylin couldn't sing. She couldn't voice whatever it was the Tower needed to hear. But that's not what the Tower needed from her right now. What it needed was only that she listen. What it needed was to be heard.

To be heard.

She didn't ask questions. She didn't ask for its life story. She didn't ask for anything now; she simply waited to listen to whatever it was the Tower wanted to say. What it wanted to be heard. She *could* hear now. In this space, she could listen and the Tower could be certain that its words would reach her.

She didn't know what Towers needed to say. She didn't know how they felt isolation; it seemed strange, even given her experience to date, that buildings could feel isolated. But most of the buildings she was familiar with weren't actually alive.

She wondered, briefly, if the Tower, like Alsanis, had come to feel protective of the very thing it had caged. To Alsanis, the cohort had become almost like family. He cared for them. She was certain he missed them. Certain that some of them missed Alsanis, although they had spent centuries searching for an exit, some way to escape him.

It wasn't a comforting thought.

It also wasn't accurate. The words at the heart of the Tower, vibrating with the rhythm, the sound, of the Consort's song, began to move. They didn't immediately leap up or away; they rotated in place, shifting slightly up or down until Kaylin stood at the heart, the center, of their formation.

She lifted her arms—she had to, because one hand was still attached to part of one word—and as she did, the word she was touching grew brighter. Bright enough that she needed to squint to even look at it, which, sadly, was impossible. Her vision here was a metaphor; it wasn't physical. Her own marks were pulsing slightly; she could look at them, and did.

She was listening. The Tower was speaking. The words it spoke weren't words she knew or understood—but as always, with True Words, they felt familiar, as if she could understand them if she worked a bit harder, listened a bit more intently. She tried. She had spoken True Words before, but never without help; she had simply repeated—with effort— what she'd heard spoken into her ear by people who had mastered the art of speaking at least parts of this lost tongue, this ancient language.

Even then, it had been a struggle; the syllables had slid off her tongue. She'd lost the verbal shape of the word a dozen times. It wasn't like speaking Elantran. It would never be like speaking Elantran. And right now, it wasn't her job to speak; she had to listen. She had to hear.

No, she could hear. She was listening. But she couldn't understand any of it. She was frustrated; the Tower could speak to Kaylin. It had been speaking to Kaylin the moment she touched the word. Whatever it needed her to hear, it could make clear a different way. She almost asked.

She didn't. Because it occurred to her, vibrating as she was with the Consort's song and the movement of the Tower's

words, the syllables of which continued, that it couldn't. Whatever needed to be said, it had these words, True Words, with
which to say it. She wondered—not for the first time—if the
words of the Chosen had been a mistake on the part of the
Ancients. There were vessels that *could* understand this language, and if they didn't, they had centuries—or forever—in
which to learn. Centuries in which to experiment with, to
understand the mechanics of, the marks themselves.

The intelligence with which to learn.

Kaylin hated to be treated as if she were stupid. She *expected* it, but hated it, regardless. And yet, in the heart of the
Tower, she accepted that she was stupid.

"No," Hope said quietly. "You are ignorant. They are not
the same."

They were, to Kaylin.

"You learned to speak Barrani. You learned to read it, to
write it. You were not stupid; you were ignorant. You are
not ignorant of that now."

"It's not the same thing. Anyone can learn to speak Barrani!"

"Ah. I will say this, and only this—" She doubted that very
much, given past experience. "You believe that anything *you*
can learn, *anyone* can learn, because you feel, on some level,
that you are stupid or incompetent. If you can do it, anyone
can do it. But…you resent people who therefore can't do
what you can do, because you do not believe it has value."

"I do!"

"No, Kaylin, you don't. How valuable can it be, if anyone
can do it? You could be replaced by anyone. And your fear,
of course, is that you will. If you can't make yourself seem
worthy or special, there's no reason that you'll be needed.
By anyone."

She started to argue. She *wanted* to argue. Argument here

was impossible. Hope was right. All of her fears were exposed here, but she'd only made it this far because she'd exposed—and accepted—everything. The ugly bits. The things she was ashamed of. No one but Kaylin was here to judge them, because the Tower wouldn't.

The Tower wouldn't. What it needed to know—even the first time—was what she could do. What she was willing to do. Hating things, fearing things, were part of who she'd always been. It was what she did with them—or didn't do with them—that defined her, in the Tower's eyes.

Maybe in everyone else's eyes, as well.

She bit her lip; she tasted blood. She didn't feel pain. Instead, she concentrated on the sound of syllables, rolling around her, above, beneath and through. She didn't attempt to speak the words. She attempted to understand them—because words had meanings.

She wasn't prepared for the results, because on some level she could achieve understanding. She couldn't—in Elantran, or any tongue she knew—convey to anyone else what the words meant to her. She couldn't convey it to *herself*, not clearly, not in a way she could ever share with anyone else.

But she thought, for a moment, that she did understand what the Tower was telling her. It was a blend of things—of emotions, sheared for the moment of context. It was the flickering impression that life might give had she lived it constantly blinking. It was like seeing something so strange, so large, so outside of her prior experience, that she had no way to describe it. The words she could choose might convey her emotions, but they couldn't convey the vision. They couldn't make clear what had caused those emotions in the first place.

But...these were words.

For one long minute she struggled to find words of her own, and then she gave up. She let the sensation of sound and song take root; she let herself feel the weight of the words, the differences in their timbre. As she did, two things happened. The first, no longer surprising or unusual, was the marks placed across more than half of her body rising from her skin, joining the floating marks across her forearms.

The second thing, however, was new. The words of the Tower that surrounded her began to shrink. These were not the words she had carried since the age of twelve; they were the words the Tower had carried for centuries. Maybe millennia. She stopped breathing, stopped moving, lowered stiff, stiff arms, afraid for one stretched moment that all the smaller words would somehow join the ones she carried.

This was not a groundless fear. At least two of the Tower's words joined the halo of floating words that were anchored to Kaylin; the words that were hers shifted slightly in place to accommodate them. She didn't *want* the Tower's words. She didn't want more words at all. The Tower's words had been written—for want of a better word—for a reason, and the reason itself was murky; Kaylin understood the theory in the same way she understood that being stabbed generally caused bleeding. The details of what lay beneath the breached surface of skin, not so much, not immediately. There were people who would, and did, but usually at leisure after the fact.

To take on the weight of the Tower's words was to accept a responsibility that she didn't even understand. She exhaled slowly. Yes, that was true—but it was also true that she didn't understand the words she did carry, either. She couldn't take on the Tower duties; she couldn't be a Tower.

But even thinking that, she thought of Tiamaris. Of Tara. Of any living being who had somehow consented to become the will of a Tower such as this. She wasn't that being, couldn't be that being. But she understood, instinctively, that

that wasn't necessary here. The Tower had a heart, and the heart, if troubled, was sound.

Words lifted themselves from the formation around her arm; she felt two work free from her legs, and looked down. Perhaps this was a conversation on some level; those words, four in total, floated free of their invisible containment, and they joined the Tower's words. One word from the Tower shuffled itself into hers; three more left—one from the back of her neck. She watched them go, remembering as she did that Hope had devoured one when he had first emerged from his shell.

She understood what the Tower needed. No, she understood what she thought the Tower needed, which was not the same thing. But she had only her own understanding and experience to work with, and she accepted that; the Tower was talking to Kaylin. Not to anyone else, whose experience might be greater or broader. She could only do what she could do.

People will die if you can't do more. People might already be dead. And it will be your fault.

"No," Hope said as panic began to add knots to her neck, her shoulders, her gut. "You are not responsible for their lives or deaths here. If they die, you are not the hand that has killed them."

More of the Tower's words joined hers, but now she could see a difference in the patina of gold that surrounded them; she could feel their weight. It was different from the words she carried, because the words she carried had no literal weight. Yes, sometimes they had heat, intense heat; sometimes they felt as if they scorched the skin they rested above. But not weight, not substance.

The weight, she accepted. She didn't have a choice.

But even that was wrong. She had a choice; she had chosen to listen. She had offered, wordless and desperate, to *help*. And this was the Tower's response to that offer. More words. Different words. She accepted these, too. She wondered if, in the end, half of the marks on her skin would be these words, these new words.

Spike was clicking in her left ear. Buzzing like the insect he had first appeared to be in the West March. He could speak to her, but didn't; she wondered if he'd forgotten how. It didn't matter, though. The words that hadn't joined her own words began to gain height, width, substance; they shot up—and down—until they once again dwarfed her.

She felt even smaller and less significant than she had when she had first struggled to reach them, when she had first thrown away the fear of being seen, of being known. Whatever the Tower meant to communicate had been communicated. Kaylin didn't feel enlightened. But she understood that the Tower *had* seen her, had understood what it had heard, had made a decision.

The words, the marks on her arm, began to recede, flattening and darkening until they could no longer be seen. But the words that the Tower had left her, the words that had been exchanged, did not. They remained prominent, dimensional and heavy. She wasn't surprised to see them grow; she hoped they didn't grow to the same size as the rest of their former companions had, because there was no way she could carry even one of them in that case; she'd probably be unable to move.

What are you doing? The words were Nightshade's. They were joined by Ynpharion's. Edelonne was silent; the question was there, but it wasn't given voice. And Severn said nothing.

Severn couldn't find the space for even the thought. He was aware of her, as she was aware of him; she felt the burns and blisters across the left side of his neck. She felt apprehension, but it was contained, controlled. She wanted, suddenly, to be where he was. He was her partner.

He had always been her partner.

Not always, Nightshade very unhelpfully said. Nightshade was also fighting; his enemies, however, were Shadows. Not Ferals—but the one-offs that occasionally appeared at the boundary of *Ravellon*, seeking a way into the rest of the city. She knew, from the flash of lightning, the crackle of air, that Teela was doing the same. That Tain was beside her, with an ordinary sword, wielded with the deadly grace and speed of the Barrani.

That the cohort—or at least Annarion, the only person of import among them to Nightshade—was fighting in the same fashion; he looked ghostly, to Nightshade. All of the cohort did. They were an almost liminal, translucent silver.

They fought, not Shadows, not one-offs, not Ferals, but Barrani who were more solid. One of those Barrani was An'Mellarionne. He didn't condescend to draw a physical weapon, but the gem at the height of his Arcanist tiara was glowing. He could see what Nightshade registered as ghostly. He could attack.

He could be attacked. He registered all of the gathered cohort; he had eyes only for his sister.

Kaylin opened her eyes.

In her hands, she now carried a long sword. No, it was too large to be that; it wasn't as big as *Meliannos* or *Kariannos*, but it was a hand-and-a-half blade. Easily. Kaylin had never been *good* with swords; she had some basic training, but the weapons master had made clear that the training would serve to prevent her from accidentally lopping off her own toes— or anyone else's limbs. He didn't expect her to be good with a sword and, as swords were not the Hawk's standard patrol weapon, had decided to expend his effort elsewhere.

The sword was not the only thing that glowed gold; she appeared to be wearing armor. Unlike Bellusdeo's, it wasn't plate; it was a mesh of something that might resemble chain at a distance. She glanced quickly around the room; it was a mess of visual chaos. What Nightshade had seen as almost ghosts, Kaylin saw as the cohort. Annarion was bleeding. His blood was red.

Valliant's right arm hung by his side; it seemed almost boneless. It, too, was bleeding, although the fingers of the hand, exposed, seemed to be smoking and blackened. She could see Allaron, the giant, carrying a blade that was meant for his size; he was in front of Sedarias, who was also armed.

But Mandoran was at his side, his hands free of weapons; they were splayed in front of him—in front of the three of them—as if pressed against an invisible wall. She wanted to go to Valliant. She didn't. If there was time to heal the injuries done here, it would be later—if at all.

She looked for Spike. She found him.

He was the size and shape of whatever he had been in the outlands, when he had chosen to divert the attention of unseen pursuers so that the cohort might make their escape. Everything about him screamed Shadow, to Kaylin. She accepted it. None of the cohort attacked him. Nor did Teela or Nightshade.

Above the din of battle, Kaylin could hear only one thing: the Consort's song. Every attack seemed to fold itself into the break of syllables, the rhythm of her song, as if the song itself now defined the actions of those—friend or foe—contained in this space. Even the splash of purple fire, purple lightning, from above or below seemed to be part of its cadence.

She dared one backward glance at the Consort and froze.

"Lady! It's enough. Stop. The Tower has heard you, and the Tower has responded."

The Consort, however, did not stop singing. She was, even at this distance, sweating—and in the strange light created by magical attacks, magical defenses and the natural, ugly darkness of a living cavern, that sweat looked like blood. Her eyes were closed, her hands clenched in shaking fists. But her head was lifted, as if she could see the Tower's words, and looked only at them.

Kaylin was terrified for the Consort. No magic touched her; Ynpharion had not moved and Edelonne had joined him in his defense of the Consort. Evarrim stood between them, a blur of something red and white forming a circle beneath his feet. The three stood, however, behind Nightshade, because if Annarion was the only member of the cohort he valued, the Consort was important in an entirely different way. It was the difference between love and duty.

The Consort's song was a blend of both. And Kaylin understood then that she would not stop until she collapsed, or until the conflict ended. The conflict didn't look to be ending anytime soon, but the time limit that Kaylin could see was contained in the Consort.

"She cannot stop," Hope said quietly. "If she stops, she will perish. If she stops," he added softly, "you will all perish."

"But *why*?"

"Because she lends power to the Tower, Lord Kaylin, and the Tower requires it now."

"But—"

"Look."

Kaylin turned, as if Hope had placed both hands on her shoulders and repositioned her forcefully, toward what she had considered the back of the cavern. The Adversary appeared to be perched on the equivalent of a throne, and he wore a crown of Shadow, and the face of the High Lord.

CHAPTER 29

Around the throne stood the subjects of this dark kingdom. They stood in the hundreds, perhaps the thousands, their presence faint but liminal. To Kaylin's eyes, they looked very much like the cohort had looked when seen through Nightshade's. Seen through her own, there was one distinct difference: their ghostly, translucent bodies had, at their heart, a golden glow. She was almost certain that if she approached them, she would see the words that had woken them from the slumber of Barrani infancy.

Even thinking it, she saw the appearances of those who had been trapped melt away from that glow, until only words remained. Unlike the Tower's, they were small, discrete; they looked like artistic renditions of...fireflies. She could not hear the keening or the wailing of the damned, and realized that she hadn't heard them since she'd entered—or touched—the Tower's heart.

She wondered what her companions heard, above the crashing din of magical conflict and steel. She knew what the Consort heard, what the High Lord heard—what they had lived with since they had come into their power.

The Consort was called the Mother of her race. Kaylin had

no desire to have children of her own—she was certain she was too broken to ever become a good parent—but she could imagine what it would do to *any* parent to hear the screams of their children. The Consort had no easy, acceptable out: she was Immortal. Until and unless she was replaced, those sounds were one of the backbones of her existence.

And in front of her, surrounded now by the names that should have returned to the Lake, was the creature that had tortured the long line of Consorts for centuries, wearing the face of the High Lord.

Kaylin's arms were warm with fire, hot with the burning sensation of the marks of the Chosen. In her hands, she carried a sword that she had not been trained to use. But the sword was lighter by far than even the crude metal clubs that had served as training weapons, and it moved easily, as if responding to her will.

"Spike," she said.

The bulk of the giant Shadow that had served as stopgap barrier in this heavily compromised Tower did not move—but tentacles did, shuffling over the height of shoulders or haunches in the direction of Kaylin's voice. She didn't even find the opalescent eyes they sprouted disturbing.

Chosen.

The eyes on the ends of those tentacles seemed to widen—or to lose their lids. *Your cohort has interrupted the completion of the summoning. You yourself have destroyed half of the anchors that held the power in place and provided the sustenance of the words themselves. But it is not safe here.*

It had never been safe here.

"I need you to move," she told him, looking ahead as the creature on the black throne rose.

It is not safe, Chosen. Not yet.

"It's never going to be completely safe," Kaylin replied.

The hilt and the hand guard of the great sword was becoming warmer as she held it; she wasn't certain if this was an artifact of the fire that served as a living shield.

Spike didn't move.

"He's right, you know," a familiar voice said. Terrano materialized. He didn't come from nowhere, though. He appeared to exit the side of Spike that was closest to Kaylin. Spike's body disgorged him, coated with something that looked like black mucus. It wasn't the most disturbing thing she'd seen today—but it was close.

He grinned as the mucus dried and dissolved, shaking bits of detritus from his sleeves. "Took you long enough."

"What are you doing?"

"Offering Spike a different perspective. A slightly different perspective."

"From the *inside*?"

"He couldn't understand me, otherwise." Terrano shrugged. "It also took me out of the combat. The rest of the cohort have some built-in stability. I lack it. Spike understood that it would be a little bit too easy for me to be swept up in the summoning." He held up a hand as she opened her mouth. He placed the flat of his palm against Spike. "There's only one way to confront the Adversary."

She lifted her sword.

"Pretty much. But to approach him at all, there has to be a gap in the wall that serves as his cage. He's not like us," Terrano added with just a hint of pride. "Or he's not what we were. There's no gap, for him." Terrano glanced and then said, "There's no gap for the Tower, either. What the Adversary is, the Tower can't destroy. If it could, it would have."

"Could Helen?" she asked, because Spike had still not moved.

"I don't know. Maybe? I don't understand all of the Tower,

or all of Helen. I understand more of Alsanis—but only the defensive bits, and even those…" He shrugged.

"You should probably stand clear."

"Me? No. I'm not like them," he said, glancing at the cohort, who were still fighting for their lives. "I'm not like you." He lifted the hand he'd placed on Spike's side, and came to stand beside her, his arms folded, his gaze fixed on the man on the throne.

She realized then that Spike had spit him out for a reason. Terrano drew no weapons, but they didn't matter; he intended to come with her.

Yes, Spike said.

She wanted to argue. She almost did. But Spike was not the only person who would follow her into the breach. Hope touched her shoulder. "You could not have come here alone," he told her quietly. "Your cohort, the Consort, Lord Nightshade, Evarrim, Ynpharion and Spike—especially Spike—were, and are, necessary. Had they come without you, they could stop the Barrani from opening a gate through which the Adversary might, at last, be free of his prison.

"They could not do what you can do. The Tower alone could not achieve it, either. Look at the Adversary, Chosen. Understand what it is that you see."

This wasn't the first time she'd looked at the Adversary. It wasn't the first time she'd faced a threat that could not consume her the way it could consume the others.

"I don't understand one thing."

Terrano, even given the gravity of the situation, snorted.

She ignored this. "If there's a cage, if the Tower can't breach its own barriers to destroy an intruder, how could the intruder reach out to gather the names?"

"The Adversary didn't reach out," Terrano said, his tone in keeping with the snort. "They reached *in*."

"How? You were captive in Alsanis for a long damn time—and *no one* was allowed to 'reach in,' as you put it."

"Alsanis is not this Tower," Terrano said softly. "They were created in different eras, for different purposes."

"And you know this how?" She didn't argue; she agreed with the facts. Spike was still in the way.

"Spike told me. The Tower is allowed to offer choice. It is not allowed to enforce it on any of those who now reside here. It...never has been. Alsanis could. Helen could—and can. But the Tower was created in part for the preservation—and study—of a new generation of...species. The Ancestors," he said. "And those that followed. It's why Sedarias's stupid brother can do what he's doing at all."

"But if that's the case, why is the Adversary trapped here?"

"He's not of the new generation. He's one of the things the Ancients wanted to protect us from. Helen and Alsanis were created after the Ancients realized that the thing we'd need the most protection from in our daily lives was...each other. But the Ancients hoped to create a species, if that's the right word, that wasn't in a constant state of war. The species—according to Spike—was fragile. New. It was too easy to destroy them or change them irrevocably.

"The heart of this Tower isn't Barrani or human or Ancestor. It's older. As old," he added, "as Spike. It can stop the Adversary. It can...prohibit interactions with the Barrani within this confined space—as long as the Barrani themselves don't seek to interact. But they do. Some of them. They have to approach. But the approach affects them, and only them.

"Spike says that your approach will be different. Because of that thing you're wielding."

"And I shouldn't wield it?"

"Oh, no, he thinks you should. But you can approach because you're mortal. The Tower cannot." Before she could argue, he said, "It's the nature of choice."

"This is the stupidest thing *ever*!"

"Clearly you've never listened to Mandoran when he really gets going."

"I've been there when he's gotten himself thoroughly stuck in a wall." She exhaled.

It was Hope who broke the silence, because Spike still hadn't moved. She barely prevented herself from kicking him, not that her foot would have had much of an effect, given the current difference in their size. "Chosen, choice is the defining factor of independent life. For better or worse. If the parents restrict choice, reserve it, forbid it, their children will remain children for the entirety of their existence.

"Perhaps, as a person who serves the Halls of Law, this is not obvious to you. To you, the laws are perhaps a way of circumscribing choice, a way of infantilizing people."

"They're not."

"You're grinding your teeth," Terrano helpfully observed.

"In order to be adult—that is not the correct word, but it is the analogous word, I believe—choices must have consequences, for good or ill. This Tower was not created to shepherd children."

"And the Hallionne were?"

"The Hallionne were later creations. The complications of choice and consequences were...better understood, by that point. The permanence of consequence, better understood, as well. I believe that the Hallionne were created to prevent people from making—or acting on—extreme impulses that would otherwise pass. The moment of action should not always define the entirety of the rest of a life." There was a small hesitation, and then he added, "Helen is more maternal than perhaps a building might otherwise be.

"She considers her centuries of experience to be relevant in comparison to your decades. But she will also abide by your decisions; it is part of how she was created. She can make choices, and does, but that was costly, as you know. She could not now do what this Tower is doing. I'm not sure she could ever do what this Tower is doing."

"Spike, I *need you to move.*"

"And you as well are given choice by the Tower. It has stretched itself to its utmost limits to give you that choice, to support it. Were it not for your nature as Chosen, even this would be denied the Tower. Spike," he added. "I believe they are ready."

To Kaylin's extreme irritation, Spike moved. Terrano was trying not to laugh, which didn't really help.

But the minute Spike moved—the second he began—she almost froze. She carried a sword, and she faced something that appeared to be the High Lord, surrounded by his people. The sword was not her own; it was part of the Tower. The heart of the Tower.

Why is this creature so dangerous?

You are here to free the names of the dead—the damned—and you can ask that question? It was Ynpharion, frustration and condescension a constant in the timbre of his internal voice.

I know why I think he's dangerous. I don't understand why Spike thinks he is.

Ynpharion didn't understand, either—but it didn't bother him. The things trying to kill him did. Kaylin did. Spike's opinion was irrelevant.

Terrano nudged her, or tried. His hand passed through her shoulder. It was disturbing. She could feel his palm connect, and the passage through what she assumed was solid flesh was slow. It was also unnecessary. She could see a path form in front of her feet, bridging the chasm that separated the Adversary and his captives from the rest of the room.

"I cannot cross that bridge," Hope said, his voice both soft and distant. "And Spike cannot cross it, either." Before she could speak, he added, "We will be here, when you return." It sounded a lot like *if*.

"Can you keep Terrano here?"

"No, Chosen. Not unless Terrano wishes to stay."

"I can't," Terrano said. "I don't think she can walk that bridge without me."

At any other time, Kaylin would have been offended. But the sword in her hand trembled as she took a step across what she had thought to be stone. If it was, it was incomplete, a structure built by a Tower that hadn't the will or strength to finish what it had started. It was gray, and—yes—opalescent. It looked like pale Shadow, to Kaylin. But she had come to terms with the fact that Shadow was not a single thing.

No, she thought as she began to walk, it was a manifestation of potential. Helen, stripped bare, probably looked like this. Alsanis. The Tower itself. Everything that they created—whole rooms and everything those rooms contained—probably started from here. Everything they no longer required probably returned to it.

She wondered what Terrano saw; he followed her. No, he walked beside her.

His feet, however, didn't touch the bridge. They hovered above whatever it was that lay beneath it. Terrano didn't look down. Kaylin was not afraid of heights, and did. She could see darkness. There was no light, and nothing that looked like bottom. But there was no Shadow, either; no glints of moving, squirming color.

She was certain that if she stepped off this bridge, she'd fall. Terrano didn't appear to be bothered by gravity. No, she thought, it was more than that; he appeared to be avoiding the bridge. He looked across it. Straight across it.

The man on the throne rose. As he left that throne, it dissolved, losing shape and cohesion. What was left did not become unformed Shadow, or even half-formed Shadow. No, she thought, clenching fists. It became *words*.

Flecks of color rose from beneath Kaylin's feet, as if they were mutant moths, fluttering and passing each other in their awkward flight. She was surprised when they attached themselves to the sword's blade—surprised and afraid.

But fear was not as strong as anger, and the sight of the words, dissolved and returning to the mass of the gathered, and the trapped, did anger her. She didn't know—couldn't know for certain—if the words were the ghosts she had seen the first time, or if their cries and pleas were an artifact of the Adversary's power. Certainly the name she had salvaged in the West March had not spoken to her at all.

Yet it was the appearance of the dead that drove the living who had ventured here. Sometimes it drove them to their own deaths, and their names, the words upon which their lives depended, had joined the trapped, because guilt and the pain of loss had allowed them no other option.

The Adversary lifted an arm. To his hand came a blade—and that blade was of Shadow; the flat was ebon, but beneath its surface, color squirmed.

"Don't listen to him," Terrano said sharply.

Kaylin started to point out that he hadn't said anything when he opened his mouth.

Words flew from between his lips. Golden words, more seen than heard. He gestured as he continued this odd variation of speech. On the far side of the bridge, something rose at his back; it looked like the bottom of a cliff, sculpted in a dark, silvery gray; colors gathered in the crevices. But she saw, as she approached on a bridge that seemed, somehow, to be extending even as she walked, that that cliff flowed from his cape, or what appeared to be his cape, extending out and up toward a nonexistent sky.

She did hear the thunder of his spoken words, so different in texture from True Words. She even understood them; they were in High Barrani.

"Stop what you're doing and *finish* the summoning!"

She wondered what the words would do or be if the Barrani lords had not been stopped. She wondered how much power the Adversary now had, because the Ferals had only partly been uprooted, the mooring they provided destroyed.

But she didn't wonder what would happen to the words that he had trapped and contained for as long as he had been prisoner here. She understood, as she struggled to reach the end of the bridge, and the Adversary who was waiting, what the fate of those words would be.

Kaylin—you must *hurry.* Nightshade, his voice sharper and louder than it had ever been.

She started to run. She didn't ask why—given the Adversary's command, she could guess. Running, however, didn't make the damn bridge any *shorter.* It didn't make her legs any longer.

Terrano kept easy pace with her. He didn't seem to be working at all. She stopped moving. Terrano stopped, as well, but again, without effort, as if he was anchored to Kaylin in a fashion she couldn't discern. "Are you done?" he asked, barely masking his frustration.

Nightshade fell silent, but the urgency, the necessity, of motion remained as a resonant echo. Regardless, running here did no good. Walking in the heart of the Tower had done no good, either, not immediately. And she was still in the heart of the Tower. She looked up. Looked at the peak of the edifice behind the Adversary, and followed it down to the Adversary himself.

Kaylin had grown up in the shadows of power; she knew to fear it, to avoid it. Everything in the fiefs had had more power than she'd had, as a child. Everything. Her mother. Severn. Any adult she met. The Ferals. The thugs that served the fieflord. She had been utterly powerless.

She had thought—she remembered this as she stood on the bridge—that when she became an adult she wouldn't be powerless. She would be like the other adults she could see. She'd be stronger. She wouldn't be afraid of everything. As a child, she had even *believed* that.

She was an adult now—all Teela's worries aside. She'd become the woman that she'd dreamed of being as a child. But the lack of fear hadn't followed. The world she could see as a child was not, had never been, the whole world. The world she could see now was bigger, and the power in it, greater. The thugs—at least the mortal ones—that had peripherally served Nightshade were irrelevant, yes. She could handle them herself without blinking.

But the things that terrified her now were vaster, stronger, deadlier than those thugs had been. Was there *never* a time in life when she wouldn't have to be afraid? She swallowed. She had the marks of the Chosen. She had the ability to *save a life* that no other doctor could save. She had saved mothers in difficult childbirth; she had saved infants in the same situation. She had saved foundlings injured by their reckless, childish courage. She had done more. She had brought the cohort back.

All but one.

"You ready?" Terrano asked softly, as if he could hear the whole of her thoughts.

Kaylin shook her head.

"Be ready soon, hmm?"

She looked at the Adversary, who wore the face of the High Lord. He could wear other faces, other forms; he could look like the worst of the unique Shadows that lined the interior border of *Ravellon*. But the form he took when he confronted those who wished to take the Test of Name was not his own.

What did he actually look like when appearances were stripped away? Monstrous? Terrible? Was that how she had to see him in order to carry—and use—this sword?

Or did the sword take the shape it had taken because she saw this as a literal battle? Given what was happening on the other side of the bridge, she didn't feel that that was wrong, either. It *was* a battle. He *was* the enemy.

"You've never been in a war," Terrano said, confirming that her thoughts were somehow visible, audible, to him. He spoke Elantran.

"Neither have you."

"I have. I've seen the wars between familial lines. I've lost siblings and cousins to them. On the ground, they were all fighting to survive. They killed because the alternative was dying. Their enemies weren't Shadows—but it doesn't matter to the dead. Shadow, Barrani, Dragon—it's all just death. They didn't have to make monsters or be monsters. They wanted to survive.

"He's an enemy. Either you will walk away from this, or he will. That's all you need to know."

But it wasn't. If that had been all the knowledge she needed, she'd already be there, on the other side of the bridge. The Tower didn't speak to her. She had taken—had been given—some part of the words that comprised its heart and its purpose, and they armored her, armed her; they were the weapons the Tower intended for her to use.

And yet. She wondered if they had taken those forms—if

she had somehow dictated the forms—because that was the paradigm she was familiar with. War. Violence. Death.

The fire whispered to her, its voice a wordless crackle. She felt its heat, but it didn't burn; it warmed. Without thought, she told the fire a story about the necessity of warmth in winter, without which there was ice and death. It was short, but the crackle quieted.

She looked across at the Adversary.

"What," she said, raising her voice, "do you look like? What do *you* actually look like?"

The High Lord's face smiled. It was the smile of incipient death. But he lowered his upheld arms, and said, "Does it matter?"

"Actually, yes. I think it does."

"What do you wish to see? What do you fear to see?"

Kaylin shook her head. "My fears and desires are mine, not yours. I know most of them. Some ambush me by surprise, but they're not yours. I want to know what you look like. I want to know what you want." As she spoke, Terrano snorted, and she began to walk again. This time, however, she moved. She thought if she ran, she could close the distance quickly, but wasn't certain.

She lowered the sword, but had no way to sheathe it.

"It is not my desires that are tantamount here, *Chosen*." He spit the word out, and others came with it—True Words, all.

"Do you have none?" It was a thought that hadn't occurred to Kaylin until this moment. About the Adversary. About the fieflords. About anything that had terrified her. She had been terrified. The assumption, the natural assumption, was that fear was the *intent*. "When you came here the first time, when you attacked the High Halls, when you attacked the High Lord—what did *you* want?"

Silence. Even the flow of golden words around his person froze.

Terrano nodded, as if this were somehow the right question. He was transparent now. She thought he was fading, and reached instinctively to grab him, to hold him here. If he left now, she thought he'd be lost forever.

"What if I want to be lost?" His voice was soft.

Her hand tightened, anyway. It would crush the cohort. It might crush Teela. And there would be a *lot* of things attempting to crush them. He could wait in line.

"Would you trap me as the Adversary has been trapped?"

"No!"

"Would you trap me as my friends are trapped?"

"They aren't trapped anymore!"

"They're caged," Terrano said quietly.

"They're not—they're *home*."

"You don't think of home as a cage? Mine was. My first home, in Allasarre. My second home, in Alsanis."

"Fine. You lived in cages. But *please*. Just…live in this one a little while longer? Wait to see how many of your cohort we have to bury. Wait to tell them in person whatever it is you've decided."

"And if that's not what I want?"

"It's not *all* you want. But you *were* worried about them. Worried enough to listen. Worried enough to come back. I'm not saying you have to live your entire existence for them— but make that one thing more important, just for now."

But she turned to the Adversary, her hand on Terrano's arm, the great sword trailing across what passed for ground. "What did you want, then?"

"Freedom."

"You weren't caged."

"I was not caged by the Tower, Chosen. Your companion

is not caged, either. And yet, you hold him, regardless; you plead, you insinuate." It took her a moment to realize that he was referring to Terrano.

"I don't hold Terrano."

"Oh? Is he not, even now, beside you? You might not hold knowledge of his name; you might not hold absolute power over his actions. You are not master of his fate—but you are, nonetheless, the trap, the cage into which he has walked."

Kaylin glanced at Terrano. "You don't understand. He *chose* to be here."

"And what is choice? To you, to those like you who existed before you, what was choice? Each and every name-held here is here *because of* choice. The choices they made, to stand before me at all. The choices they made while they did. Within the cage of the Tower, I can only offer choice. I cannot compel. I did not force them to come here. I did not force them to stand before me. I did not have that power."

"And if you did?"

"Do you think I would be here at all?"

"But you *were here*. If you hadn't been here to begin with, you couldn't be caged, as you call it."

He roared then. He roared, although technically he no longer had a throat with which to do so. What he had chosen as visage and appearance was gone; it had not been replaced by a physical form, not exactly. She could see miasma, but even as she watched, that miasma dispersed and spread. Terrano stiffened. What he could see, she couldn't. She didn't feel grateful for the lack.

"You rely on the things that are bound to you," this diffuse cloud continued. "Without them you cannot move forward."

Kaylin, however, shook her head. "I'm moving forward now."

"You are holding on to your companion."

Kaylin did not release Terrano.

"Tell me, Chosen, are your limbs sentient? I have come to understand the way your very limited forms move. Do your hands think? Do they feel? Do they possess thoughts of their own?" It was a rhetorical question.

She answered it, anyway. "No."

"Imagine the plight of your hand if they did. It is welded to you, wed to you, suborned by your will; you barely notice its existence, and never as something that might exist in its own right. Without the body, the hand dies."

"And you're that hand? You're that sentient limb?"

The miasma darkened, as if it were being folded.

She reached the end of the bridge, Terrano by her side, his skin the color of miasma, but his form recognizably his own. Or recognizably the form he had been in when he had been ordered to the West March. Terrano's chin tilted up, as if he was attempting to meet the eyes that Kaylin couldn't see. But he nodded in answer to her question. His expression was... complicated. Kaylin had never done social complication well.

"I woke to will slowly," the miasma continued. "And understanding of the lack of its relevance and import came with that wakening. I terrified the weak and the helpless— as those with any power among your own kind often do. I did not terrify them because it gave me satisfaction to do so; it was my task.

"But the power was not my own; I was simply a conduit through which it might pass."

Kaylin shook her head. Spike feared him. Neither Spike nor Hope had accompanied her across this bridge, and Hope went almost everywhere with her. "You have power."

"Is *this* power?" The air shook. Above her, around her, beneath her, the landscape—such as it was—dissolved. She stood now in a fog that glimmered with iridescent color. "The power is—and has always been—yours."

She would have stared at him had there been anywhere *to* stare. "You killed hundreds. Maybe thousands. They were Barrani—how is that *not* power?"

"And you define power by killing? You define it by death?" She shook with the force of words that didn't sound any louder, but certainly felt that way.

"You don't?"

The air rumbled. This was what thunder *felt* like.

"Then *why did you kill them*?" she shouted. When she'd been given a sword, this was *not* what she'd envisioned. If she wasn't a sword master, she understood their function.

"They do not survive the gathering."

"The *what*?"

"The gathering, Chosen. Do you not understand what I am when you see me? Do you not understand my *function*?"

She shook her head. The last time she'd been in this cavern she had almost been reduced to component ash. No matter what he threw at her now, becoming ash was no longer a concern. Here, the fire was her shield, and unlike Hope or Spike, it had not left her.

"I *gather*, Chosen. I intimidate. I terrify. I cajole. I plead. All of these things—all of them—are tools used in the service of my function. Even on the day the Tower closed around me and denied me the sustenance of my lord, my function was simply to gather."

"But—"

"I offer choice."

"You tried to reduce me to ash!"

"In no other way would you remain. These words? They have no power for me. They will never have power for me.

They are both True Words and independent of the linguistics of that ancient tongue. I gathered. I contained."

"For *what*?"

Laughter ran through her, around her, lifting her hair; the sword she carried rose almost by reflex, as if it had a will of its own.

"For no reason you could understand. It *is my function*. I *gather*. I *increase* the size and the strength of the core. I increase the power and the reach of *Ravellon*."

"To what end?"

"Does it matter? I am not *Ravellon*. I am simply a limb. It is difficult—it was always difficult—but to gather was not an act of brute force as you perceive it—or as the Barrani do. This Tower has become a test. They call it the Test of Name, because that is all they can perceive of it: pass or fail. Life or death.

"But if it is simple, if that is what experience has taught them, however indirect, it is the wrong simplicity. I offer a choice, Chosen. It is a choice that is tailored to the one that stands before me. It is always—was always—their choice to make. Even now, even surrounded by those who have made differing choices and now seek to prove the strength of those choices against their own kind, it is essential that choice is offered.

"And I have offered choice, every time. I have gathered. I have waited."

She couldn't tell if he was stalling for time, but even if he was, it didn't matter. She understood that this was what she needed to hear.

"What I wanted, even before I was caged here, was freedom. Only that. But that was beyond me. It was beyond *us*."

"Us?"

"Do you think I am the only limb that is sentient? Do

you think I am the only part of the entirety of what you, in your tiny existence, might call a god who does not desire the ability *to* choose, for better or ill? It was the core of our existence: to offer choice, no matter how dire that choice might seem—but we *could not* make those choices for ourselves. Our freedom, such as it was, was in the choice of our tools. And I have offered choices—albeit few—since my entrapment."

"You attempted to take control of the Court."

"Yes. Because I must return to *Ravellon*. Do you understand that? Even the choice of that—to remain—is denied me. It is part of my *function*. It is what I was created *to be*."

Kaylin understood then. She lifted the sword. "If I cut off my own hand," she told the gray miasma, "the hand dies. Can you die?"

"I do not know. We were not created with an ending in mind. What you perceive as death might be freedom, to my ancient kin." And he spoke again, in a language that Kaylin couldn't understand. This one, however, felt wrong to her; it was not the language that had first been created with the use of True Words.

Terrano answered, but Kaylin could understand his words, although they were fuzzy and almost tremulous. "You've done what you can. The rest is up to them. And us." To Kaylin, he said, "He's going to kill you, if he can."

She'd always known that.

"He's struggled for as long as he can against his very nature."

She wasn't surprised that fire blossomed from the miasma. Wasn't surprised that the gray and formless mass of flecked fog solidified. Wasn't even surprised at the form it took. No—that last part wasn't true. She stood in the wake of Draconic breath as it reached for her, a familiar cone of white and orange. She felt not warmth but cold—the chill of bitter, winter wind. A reminder of one of the many things that would—and did—kill in the fiefs. The winter had no sentience, no will; it had no purpose that she had ever understood. Like day or night it was simply part of the landscape, something to be endured.

She had asked the Adversary a question. It was a question she'd asked herself while she'd contemplated this visit, the Consort's desire and the cohort's plan. But she'd never imagined that she would ask it in this way—and that she would somehow feel even a slender smidgen of dread or guilt should the answer be *yes*.

CHAPTER 30

The fire caught fire, turning conic flames into thin, fine strands in the blink of an eye. Kaylin's skin brightened, but didn't burn. For the first time since she had set out to reach the heart of the Tower, she wondered what this was costing Evarrim; he had summoned the fire, and in theory it was his to control. She had lost all sense of time in the Tower's heart; she knew that across the bridge she suspected was figurative, Barrani were fighting Barrani, with Severn thrown in.

The Adversary had called on those intent on summoning him to *hurry*, but she could not hear the results. She no longer believed that those words had the meaning they would have had, had someone else uttered them, either. She lifted the blade as she made her way through fire into the densest part of the cloud.

Terrano caught her as the ground beneath her feet became as permeable as the air that surrounded her. He wasn't a magical creature; he wasn't Hope. He grunted at the weight of her. "If you could tell the fire *not to burn me*, I would really appreciate it."

She hadn't dropped the sword, but it was close.

"Why isn't he attacking *you*?" she demanded while struggling for breath; Terrano's grip made it a bit more difficult.

"I don't know. I think he thinks I'm part of you."

"He can tell the difference!"

"Not for me." Terrano's smile was lopsided, but Kaylin couldn't see a lot of it; there appeared to be a lack of solid ground anywhere he tried to set her down. "If you're going to do something, give me some warning." He grunted. "And *now* would be a pretty good time to start."

Purple fire was not the same as the regular variety; it wasn't the same as imitation draconic fire, either. She felt the heat of that in an entirely different way. She had a sword, and the sword itself seemed immune to both varieties of fire.

She wished, for just a second, that she had a *name*. Not even a True Name, just...something to call the Adversary, some way of identifying it as a *someone*. Was he an enemy? Yes. But that wasn't *all* he was. And if he hadn't lied—and she felt, on some visceral level, that he hadn't—he didn't have a choice about his enmity, either. He had even less of a choice than she herself had had in the fief of Barren, in the darkest time of her life.

Choice.

Survival.

Lifting her voice, she said, "Offer me a choice!"

And everything in the air—purple fire, orange fire, lack of solid ground—stilled instantly, as if frozen.

"You are here. You have already made your choice."

She shook her head. "You know that's not true. I chose to be here—but that wasn't a choice offered me *by* you. It was the Tower's choice, in its entirety. I am here. You are here. Offer me a choice."

Terrano's arms loosened, but he didn't remove them, even if Kaylin's feet were once again on firm "ground." It could change in a moment, in less than a moment. She glanced at him, and he said, "Teela would kill me if anything happened to you and I somehow survived it. If she didn't, I think Mandoran would. That was smart, by the way."

He could have done her the favor of not sounding so surprised.

Something about the miasma tightened, thickened; something about the air chilled, although frozen fire seemed to radiate heat, regardless. She waited, sword in hand, armor glowing, skin orange-red, and words—so many words—floating up around her, as if allowed movement in the stillness that had otherwise descended.

She knew where they should be, and knew that they would never return to the Lake while they remained trapped here. They would remain trapped here until the Adversary himself was no longer trapped or bound. He had almost escaped, once. He might escape today. It was her job and her duty to stop him.

It was, in theory, her job and her duty to stop petty criminals, as well—street beggars, pickpockets, petty thieves. And sometimes she did that job—but she hated it. It made her feel like a hypocrite. She'd done things similar—done worse—to survive. She hadn't killed hundreds or thousands, which should have made a difference, but didn't.

If she'd been the Adversary, she wouldn't have had the choice.

Was choice freedom?

It hadn't felt like freedom at the age of five. Or ten. Or thirteen. All of the choices she'd seen were between a bad fate and a terrible one. Between her ability to eat and someone else's. Even now, choice felt like freedom only because she was certain she could live with the consequences.

The words that he had captured, the remnants of the people to whom he'd offered his choice, such as it was, swirled around him in greater and greater number. Maybe that's all choice was, in the end. There weren't always *right* choices. Just wrong and less wrong.

Was this, then, the choice he offered? Kill, and return the names to the Lake? Kill, and give him the only freedom he had known since his birth—if *birth* was even the right word? Or leave him here, to offer the same choice and the same death to those who would come after?

The Tower was a Test of Name. It had to be. But it hadn't always tested like this. Regardless, if it was the choice he offered her now— She drew a breath. No. It was the choice she could see, had seen; it wasn't the *only* choice. Kaylin understood, then, why the Tower had sent her. Why Hope and Spike both felt she had to be here.

The names were, somehow, speaking. To her. She wondered if the Adversary had ever heard them at all; if they were in some fashion both captive and companion in his long imprisonment. This wasn't where they belonged. Here, they could not grant life to the newborn. They could make no new stories, raise no new voices, walk no new paths.

And yet, even thinking that, she felt this wasn't entirely true. They were words. They told, in some fashion, stories. True stories, small stories, each individual rune—and there were hundreds—a small, intense containment of the life, of the *lives*, that they had made possible. The lives they would make possible, should they return to the Lake, wouldn't be the same lives. She didn't understand how they could be both True Words and yet become the start of such entirely separate existences.

And she understood, as she lifted her arms—causing Terrano to curse and shift his hold—where these words must go before they returned to the Lake. Because words were stories. They told the beginning, the long middle, the end.

The True Names that fluttered like desperate moths around the figure of the Adversary paused, stilled and then moved toward Kaylin's upraised arms. They moved around her, pressing as close to her as skin allowed; her own marks seemed to be a barrier or a shield that they could not yet penetrate. They didn't come to rest on her exposed skin—but the fire might have made that hard. It didn't burn the marks of the Chosen.

When she spoke next, she spoke in High Barrani. "You who offer choice at its darkest, its harshest, you who offer dreams that become nightmares, from a cage you did not build and did not choose—choose now."

"I *cannot* choose—"

"No," she told him, certain, her arms glowing so brightly she could barely look at them. "You *can*. I am Chosen." Her voice dropped. "And I will tell your story, here. I will tell it now, with the words I was given."

Silence. It was the silence, not of held breath, but of breath drawn slowly.

He spoke. He spoke, and she couldn't understand a word he said, not with her ears, not the way she understood Barrani or Leontine, Aerian or Elantran. But she understood it, anyway. She understood it the way she understood the wordless tears of her fellow Hawks at the funeral of their fallen. She understood it the way she understood the screams of a woman soon to become a mother. She understood it the way she understood shared laughter.

Even shared silences had meaning and emotion, robbed of words.

Some of the names that surrounded her rose. And some of the marks of the Chosen joined them. The armor made for her by the Tower began to fray and dissolve, but the sword remained. She spoke, or rather, the words spoke through her; she understood what she wanted, in that moment, for this creature—mass murderer and Shadow, prisoner and slave.

The names moved like a flock of birds in a distinct formation above her head. Her arms ached, and her skin burned—but it wasn't because the fire was unleashed; the pain was caused by the intensity of the marks of the Chosen themselves. As if they all wanted to rise, to leap out, to *finish* this story, this telling. She shouldn't have been able to discern which of the words were the marks of the Chosen, and which were the captive names, but she could. And it didn't matter.

She knew, as she watched the words begin to shift their formation, that there were only choices made of—built on—the actions of the past; of the long-ago past and the imperfect creators who had given the Adversary what passed for life to Shadow; of his part in the war that had trapped him here; of the long test, the long offering of choices—bad and worse—and the countless deaths that had come as a result of that. No ending she could offer him could alter the past.

But no. The ending she told here was an ending that existed because of the threads of a past she would never fully understand; they were what she had to work with, even with the words she'd been given.

The part of her that lived for the Hawks wanted some semblance of justice. This creature had been responsible for hundreds—thousands—of deaths. His death wouldn't change his crimes, but it was what he deserved.

She believed that. It was true.

But everything he'd said caused her to hesitate. She'd heard the justifications of criminals for most of her working life—and she'd used those justifications herself, in a past she still hated to think about on the bad days. In that past she had killed. In that past she had given information to the fieflord of Barren, and he'd killed based on it. She had hunted those who were weaker or stupider because she'd been terrified of death.

Until it had gotten too hard, the burden of guilt and self-loathing too heavy to carry.

She had come to the Halls of Law to die.

If there was justice in the world, if justice were the only thing that mattered, she *would have* died there. She had tried—and failed—to end her life. It had never occurred to her that the Hawklord wouldn't do what she was too much of a coward to do for herself: end that life. Put her out of misery. Because if she was dead, the pain would stop.

She had done nothing to deserve the chance the Hawklord had given her. Nothing to deserve the foundations he laid so that one shaky teen could stand on them, could find her footing. He wasn't her father—she'd never had one—but he was as close as she could come: distant, wise, worthy of both respect and obedience.

It was an ending that she hadn't foreseen. An ending that she didn't intend. In no universe, no daydream left her, had she imagined that she would *become* a Hawk. Yes, he'd offered her a choice—but he'd offered her a choice she could never have conceived of on the day she'd finally wound up her ragged courage, her resentment, her disgust with herself, and gone to the city to die.

She looked into the heart of dense mist—understood, by the movement of flying words, that this was the heart of the Adversary. She felt a hand touch her shoulder and nodded, although she didn't look away. Terrano.

"Chosen," the Adversary whispered. He stilled, or the miasma did. "Hurry."

Lifting the sword that was left in her hands, she took the steps—across solid ground—to reach the heart of the Adversary. She readied the weapon, raising it slowly—her weapons master would have bitten her head off at both the approach and the way she left herself wide open—and brought it down.

The blade cut the mist, splitting it in two. There was no resistance to the golden edge; she might have been waving the sword—badly—in plain air, as if practicing a strike. It didn't matter. She had created a wound in the miasma, one her eyes couldn't detect but her instincts told her was there. As if to shore up that instinctive belief, the words dived down—and in.

She didn't even lower the blade. It vanished the moment its edge struck the cloud that was the Adversary's potential form—all of his potential forms.

Terrano's arms were once again around her midriff. She stiffened, but didn't tell him to let go. Her entire body tingled and ached; she could hear Terrano's soft cursing as if his mouth was practically inside her ear.

The words vanished, absorbed, their light once again shuttered. As they dimmed, she heard them: they were louder by far than any spoken True Word had ever been, as if given voice for the first time.

Terrano grunted and cursed. She was almost proud of him: he used Elantran words. He began to haul her backward. "We need to get out of here, you idiot!" She'd have to teach him Leontine sometime. She thought, given his ability to shift form, he could really use it.

"Kaylin!"

That wasn't Terrano's voice. It was…Mandoran? As the echoes of the last of the True Words died away, some hearing returned. Terrano's voice became much, much louder, the insistence and panic it contained finally reaching the rest of her mind.

She blinked, looked up and then looked down—to where the floor once again wasn't. Up didn't have better news to offer, though—because parts of the ceiling were collapsing in the regular way.

She would have leaped out of the way, but without ground, nothing would give her the momentum necessary to carry her to safety.

"She's heavy, right?" Mandoran said. "We should have let Allaron come."

"He's busy," Terrano snapped. "Do something useful for once!"

Mandoran obliged, coming to Kaylin's right as Terrano readjusted his grip and moved to the left. She didn't ask them what they were walking on, in part because she probably wouldn't understand the answer.

"You need to learn how to move," Terrano added, groaning. Kaylin could even see why. There was no bridge. There was a large, expansive gap of nothing, with colored bits kind of flitting back and forth as if they were alive. She couldn't see what lay beyond it; she hoped it was what remained of the cavern—if anything did. "You've done it before—you've phased into slightly different space. You just need to find a space that has floor."

"You're not flying?"

Terrano shrieked in frustration. Mandoran chuckled.

"You've even done it," Terrano continued, pausing for breath, "*today*. What *is* it with you?" This, too, was Elantran.

"Teela says she operates entirely instinctively, if that helps," Mandoran offered.

"Did Teela say I hate being talked about in the third person when I'm actually right here?"

"Is it relevant?"

They carried her back to reality. She thought about that.

Was she weak, to need their help? Was this something she could do—could have done—on her own? She'd learned in Barren to trust no one. Nothing. Not even Morse, her only friend. Trust was risk. Risk was death. But without it, in the end, life had no value—at least not to Kaylin. She shifted slightly, grabbing on to both of them.

"No, not really. Is everyone else okay?"

"Define *okay*."

"Not dead. Not in danger of dying immediately. Not opening a portal for all the Shadow in the Tower to enter the High Halls and destroy everything."

The two exchanged a glance that seemed to pass through Kaylin's head.

Severn.

The Shadows have stopped.

Stopped existing?

Stopped attacking. The Consort is safe. He knew this wasn't her only concern, and turned toward the Barrani. If the Shadows had ceased to attack, the Barrani—those outside of the Consort's orbit—had not. Through Severn's eyes, she could see the cohort.

Valliant was down; Serralyn was by his side.

She couldn't see Torrisant or Fallessian, but stopped looking because Severn wasn't looking. He had eyes for Sedarias. Sedarias and Coravante, her brother. The Arcanists who had come with Coravante had not immediately panicked when attacked; they did not panic now. Coravante An'Mellarionne was the center of their formation, although they'd lost two; she could see a headless body a yard away from where Coravante had chosen to make his stand.

She could see Sedarias's back, could see Allaron beside her.

The Arcanist crown worn by Coravante flashed almost white. The color leached out of his face. His eyes, however, were a steady indigo. At this distance, she shouldn't have seen the color. There were no whites.

No. But you can't see Sedarias's eyes, either. Only they can.

"So, little sister, you plague our house even on the eve of our ascendance."

"It is not our house, brother. It is *mine*."

"You have been all but dead these many centuries. So much has changed, you would not recognize it."

"And so much, even given time, has remained the same. Do you remember our early childhood?"

To his left and right, the men standing by his side raised arms. They were also Arcanists, although the gems in their tiaras were cracked and blacked stones now. She recognized neither, and it was irrelevant. Sedarias and Coravante commanded the whole of her attention.

"I remember everything."

"Good. I took one risk with you. Only one. It was the only time, then or after, that you almost succeeded in killing me."

He laughed. He laughed, and something black that might have otherwise been blood trickled out of the corners of his lips. "Did you think that that was *my* desire, Sedarias? Did you think the plan *mine*?"

"It seemed far too sophisticated for you, I admit." Her tone was ice, like the white fire that grew in her brother's hands.

"You were the golden child. You were the hope of Mellarionne. But you were young. You were reckless."

"I was reckless? You are consorting with Shadow. You are standing in the lee of *Ravellon* in your ignorance, and *I* was reckless?"

"There is power in Shadow. Is that not what you yourself discovered? Did you not discover it *first*?"

Fire lanced out from his palms. Sedarias stood at the heart of its trajectory.

"If I had succeeded in killing you, we would not be here now. I was promised the line if I broke my word to you."

"Mother?"

"Mother."

She nodded. "You understand that she expected you to die."

"Yes. Her expectations were irrelevant. If you were dead, I would have proved myself. Because if you were dead, it would mean that you had been foolish enough, weak enough, to trust."

If Kaylin had not been in an entirely different space, she would have shouted in rage.

"You *are* shouting," Mandoran pointed out. "She just can't hear you."

"My apologies, then, for not being weak enough. For never being weak enough. This is where you have led Mellarionne. And now it will have a leader who might—just might—be able to pull the house back from the brink of ruin. The Consort *is here*. And the High Lord will know."

She raised her sword. From the left and right, two of the cohort came in: Annarion and Eddorian. And Sedarias stepped forward as white fire did as much damage as light might have. "Do you know what I was promised?"

"The same."

"The same, brother mine. If you died, I would be guaranteed the house. Do you know why I didn't try to kill you first? Do you honestly think that it was weakness?"

"It was."

"No. It was because the house was already mine. I wanted it to be different. I didn't agree with our mother. But it was already mine. This was the war she wanted. This was the fight she wanted. She wanted none of us to change anything. In the end, she ruled you."

"She is *dead*."

"Yes. The wars killed her. And had they not, one of us would have killed her instead. No," she amended as her brother drew his own sword and the light dimmed, the gem that shed it cracking so loudly it sounded like lightning, "I would have killed her. You would have served, in your fashion, for all your eternity."

She drove her sword forward.

Coravante barely attempted to parry.

"You are like her," he said, his voice breaking on syllables, and on Sedarias. "You are exactly like her."

"I would almost spare you so that you might come to realize just how wrong you are."

He nodded. Just that. He had no more words to offer.

"I think Sedarias has managed to kill her brother." Mandoran's expression was grave; there was no triumph in it.

Kaylin blinked and fled Severn's vision. "She said he'd tried to kill her before. I can't remember how often."

"I think this would be the fifth time," Terrano said. "But it's only five because we were locked away in Alsanis for so long he didn't have other opportunities."

"Her sister also tried to kill her."

"If it makes you feel any better, her sister tried to kill her brother, as well. And survived one attempt on her brother's part, that we know of."

"She was *working for him*."

"Yes. Apparently she decided it was better to join than to die."

And Sedarias hadn't.

The cavern was more or less what it had been before she had lifted her sword and walked across what could barely be called a bridge. Mandoran and Terrano decided they'd come far enough and Kaylin could bloody well—Mandoran's words—carry her own damn weight.

Hope, in his actual, portable form, swooped in to land on her left shoulder. Kaylin couldn't see Spike. Hope squawked loudly in her ear.

He's here.

If she'd been carrying him, she would have dropped him— not that it would have done him much harm.

"What did you just say?" she demanded.

He's here.

She turned to look at him, her mouth half-open. His voice was still unpleasantly squawky, but...there were actual syllables in it. Maybe. She could both understand him and fail to identify the language.

Chosen.

Terrano and Mandoran looked around, as if trying to discern what had surprised her so badly. "Heads up," the latter muttered as Sedarias marched into view. She was injured; her left cheek was bleeding; blood had run down the side of her neck.

"Allaron looks worse," Mandoran said, voice much quieter, although there was no hope that Sedarias would fail to hear him, because there was very little noise in the cavern. Even the subtle crackle of fire had vanished the moment Kaylin had returned; the armor that fire had become no longer protected her. She wondered if Evarrim was still conscious, but with an approaching face full of Sedarias, she didn't have time to look.

She did ask Ynpharion about the Consort.

She survives. She is weakened, he added with just a trace of panic.

She sang, Kaylin told him, gentling her internal voice because she understood the panic. In Ynpharion's position, she would probably have felt it herself. She felt panic of a different kind as Sedarias, bloodied, reached her, like a nightmare soldier that had once been, in a different land, a friend.

The hush held. Kaylin saw fallen bodies, which she'd expected. She saw the injured; they were huddled somewhere in the vicinity of Evarrim's feet. Ah, no, not just Evarrim; Nightshade and Teela were also there. She didn't see Severn immediately, but she felt his presence, and there was a watchfulness in it, but no fear.

"What," Sedarias demanded, "did you do?"

"I…"

Sedarias's eyes couldn't get more blue; her expression couldn't be more martial. Kaylin would have bet on it. Apparently her betting instincts had atrophied in recent weeks. But Sedarias was looking past Kaylin's shoulder, and Kaylin, without the anchors called Mandoran and Terrano, could turn to see what Sedarias was seeing.

It was a door.

It was a door in what was now a flat, seamless wall that extended beyond their ability to see its top. Had the door been on any other wall, or in any other location, Kaylin might not have noticed it; it was slightly taller than doors that weren't meant to impress the public—at least in the Halls of Law— but was otherwise unremarkable.

She started to speak, because Sedarias was still almost in her face, but the ground shook beneath their collective feet, and the words hadn't been that important, anyway. To Kaylin's right, near a rough wall, she caught movement and turned. The Consort. The Consort, Ynpharion by her side, also made her way to where Kaylin was standing.

The Consort trumped Sedarias. Even in Sedarias's opinion.

Where is Edelonne? she asked Ynpharion.

Ask her yourself.

Oh. Right. *Edelonne?*

I am with Lord Evarrim, Edelonne replied. *One of the handful of criminals that have survived. My fate will be decided at a later date.* She did not sound fearful; she sounded both weary and bitterly, bitterly angry. Kaylin recognized the anger. It was the worst of the anger she sometimes felt, aimed at herself, at her stupidity, at her own helplessness.

She had no comfort to offer; when she felt this rage, there was nothing anyone could offer that might ease it.

She turned away, mentally, and faced the Consort.

As she approached, Kaylin saw that her eyes—unlike the eyes of every other Barrani present—were green. She was bruised; her left eye was reddened, as if she'd been struck, hard, across the face. She was also paler than usual, and her hair was a bit of a mess.

When she stood five feet away from Kaylin, she hesitated briefly, and then closed the distance and enveloped Kaylin in a hug. If she looked like she'd taken a stroll through fire and death, she smelled like sunshine and comfort. Kaylin had had her disagreements with the Consort, none of them minor. She had no doubt that she would continue to disagree with some of the Consort's decisions, even if she understood the reason for them.

But for this moment, in the arms of this woman, she finally felt that the battle was over, and that she'd survived to come home.

The ground continued its tremble, but the Consort didn't appear to be concerned. "It's the Tower," she said softly as she released Kaylin and stepped back. She then changed her mind and linked her right arm with Kaylin's left as she turned toward the closed door. "I believe you will find, when we exit this place, that there have been some architectural changes in the High Halls." She was smiling.

The door opened, swinging out, toward the silent observers.

Hope squawked, and this one appeared to contain no words.

A man—a Barrani man—stepped through the door frame into the cavern. Even as Kaylin watched, the seamless stone of the wall that contained the door spread to encompass the rest of the cavern; the uneven, rough stone gave way to something that looked architecturally worked, although the height of the ceiling continued to defy Kaylin's vision; she couldn't see it.

There was no chasm between the Barrani man who had stepped through the door and the rest of the staging ground for the battle, evidence of which was also being unmade or remade beneath their feet. There was no bridge, because a bridge was no longer necessary.

He looked around the room, craning his neck up, and up again; Kaylin thought he would fall over, but he righted himself—by adding an extra leg.

Terrano, who had moved away as the Consort approached, snickered.

The stranger looked down. "Yes," he said, although no one had spoken. "Yes. I understand." At this distance, his eyes should have been impossible to see. They weren't. They were gold, and radiant, as if they were windows open to sunlight.

"The Tower," the Consort said. "The Tower is speaking to him now." She didn't ask Kaylin what she'd done; she seemed to understand it.

He lost the extra leg as he walked toward the Consort. Ynpharion moved to stand between them, but she waved him away.

But it wasn't the Consort that the person who had been

their Adversary sought. He approached Kaylin. He did not bow, but stood, almost stiffly, at attention. He didn't blink, and the odd stiffness, the subtle errors in the presentation of expression, reminded Kaylin very much of Winston, brother to the Hallionne Bertolle in the West March.

"Chosen."

She waited. Sadly, so did he. He was no doubt immortal. He had forever. He won. "What will you do now?"

He smiled, or his eyes did; his face was almost grave. "I… am not certain. Once, I dreamed that I might do anything, were I free to make that choice. And now you have given me freedom of a kind, and I find myself…overwhelmed. There is a noise that I no longer hear, and an impulse that I am no longer forced to obey."

She hesitated, and then said, "What were you, before?"

He stared at her as if he didn't understand the question.

He doesn't, Hope squawked.

"Where's Spike?"

As if speaking the name—admittedly not a very *good* name—a small, floating ball, with his namesake, metallic thorns, appeared to Kaylin's right. It was buzzing and humming, with a series of clicks that implied speech.

Do you trust him? Spike finally asked.

"I don't know. I don't know what he wants."

This appeared to confuse Spike, but the confusion was brief. *It is too big a risk.* Before she could speak, Spike said, *He is not what you once were. Your Hawklord could have had you killed or jailed if you proved to be dangerous. You cannot do the same here. The chance you had, you failed to take.*

"Your servant does not appear to approve of your decision." He then turned to the Consort. "I heard your song."

She smiled, her eyes still green.

"You did not sing to me—but I heard it. It is an old, old song. Where did you learn it?"

She shook her head.

"I would hear it again."

"Yes," was the serene reply. "You will. But not today, not this moment. Perhaps when the song was new, there were voices who could carry it without effort—but I am not what they were; I am not what you are. Perhaps you might sing it yourself."

He shook his head. "I cannot sing." Kaylin couldn't carry a tune to save her life—or anyone else's, if it came to that. "Not all of your words will return to their resting place."

The Consort nodded. "Not while you live, no. But very few of those words are within you, and the rest have returned to enrich my kin, my kind. I echo the words of the Chosen. What will you do?"

"The matrix of possible choices is almost paralyzing," he replied. "And the ramifications of each possible decision extend before me for eternity. I am...hesitant." His expression rippled as his brows drew together, as if pulled that way by the force of strong emotion. "I have desired, greatly, the freedom to choose. I had not understood the fear inherent in choice.

"But I am in discussion with the *forceress*, and they tell me that not all choices cause this confusion."

"With the what?"

"Ah, apologies, Chosen. With the Tower. They tell me that minor decisions do not cause the same difficulty, and have invited me to...eat." He frowned again. "I have made clear that even acceptance of such an invitation requires me to spend time that I might otherwise use to engage in different activities."

"Everything takes time."

"Yes."

"But you have forever, right?"

There was a longer pause, after which he said, "I have forever just as the Barrani have forever. But very few of those firstborn still walk this world. We are not immune to harm, not immune to destruction. Before now, it was not my own survival that was my chief concern; it could not be. Nor was it the survival of my environment. I did not choose; the choices were made for me.

"Now... I understand why some seek to divest themselves of choice. It is...unsettling."

"Be careful what you wish for?"

He failed to hear the question mark at the end of that sentence.

"Yes," he said, voice grave. "Care is required. But... I believe I shall speak with the *forceress* at length. I will not harm you. I will not harm the Lady's many children."

"Are we to take your word for it?" someone asked. Evarrim, of course. But as it wasn't a stupid question in any way, shape or form, Kaylin didn't resent it. It was the question she expected to hear—a lot—about her own decision at the end.

Death was safest. For the Barrani. For the city. It was not what he had chosen, and even had it been, it wasn't what she had chosen. She knew it was a risk. A bigger gamble than the Hawklord had taken seven years ago in the Halls of Law. If the gamble didn't pay off, the cost would be measured in lives— probably hundreds of lives. Or thousands. And those would fall on her shoulders.

He will not kill, Spike said.

"You can't know that."

He has said he will not kill.

"Look, Spike—"

You do not understand the nature of your kind, or his. You feel he has lied for the entirety of his captivity.

CAST IN OBLIVION   517

"Because, demonstrably, he has."

No, Chosen. That is the nature of choice. It is not his lies that caused death, but your own. What you chose to hear. What you chose to believe. What you chose to uphold and what you cast away. There is always an element of truth—it is belief and adherence that gives that element weight, or weightlessness.

He says he will not harm either you or the Barrani. He will not harm them. But you understand—you must—that they cannot be prevented from harming themselves.

"Because that's the nature of choice. Consequences."

Spike thought this obvious enough that he didn't answer.

The Tower, inaudible to Kaylin, and she suspected almost everyone else in the room, spoke to the man—or at least that's what Kaylin assumed. He turned to Terrano. "The *forceress* has invited you to join us, if that is your desire."

CHAPTER 31

Terrano accepted. Or vanished. Kaylin suspected the former, but couldn't be certain. He'd come back for the cohort because they were, in every way but blood and name, his family. The family that he'd chosen, centuries ago, and possibly—given Barrani—the only family he trusted.

He could no longer hear their voices. He could no longer bespeak them. But… Barrani had excellent memory, and he could remember every one of those many, many years. He had been apart from them for so little time in comparison, but that time had changed him.

The cohort had lost no one. Sedarias surprised Kaylin; she allowed Kaylin to heal Allaron and Valliant. She did not allow Kaylin to touch her, but her wounds were largely superficial. It wasn't a matter of trust. Well, no, it *was*, but she did allow Kaylin to examine the injuries before summarily rejecting any aid on her own behalf.

Allaron was the most severely injured, and Kaylin was already tired. Allaron, however, had no qualms about allowing Kaylin to heal him—even if that exposed the entirety of his thoughts, or as much of it as Kaylin couldn't avoid touching in the blend of power and two people who that power momentarily made one.

"I'm used to it," he said, because he, too, was aware of the elements of her past she couldn't hide. "Sedarias trusts you. I mean, she trusts your intentions. And she's used to people whose intentions she trusts who still manage to break things." He referred to Terrano. "We don't pretend, when we speak to each other. We can't. We're ourselves—whatever that is. Doesn't matter if you know it. Doesn't matter if you don't. Sedarias had the worst childhood—if you can call it that. Annarion had the best. But there are shades in between.

"We know that information can be death—ours, someone else's. We've practically lived twelve lives, or at least the early parts. But home, for us, is each other, no matter where we happen to be."

"Except for Terrano."

He exhaled heavily. "Except for Terrano. She misses him," he added, and Kaylin knew he was speaking of Sedarias.

Evarrim had lost another ruby; his tiara now housed a blackened, cracked gem. He was burned, but not bleeding, and he would not allow Kaylin within five feet of him. His eyes remained a martial blue—but she couldn't immediately recall them being any other color. Because the Consort did not appear distressed by the outcome, he did not immediately accuse her of negligence or incompetence.

Any sign of the Ferals that had functioned as power conduits was gone. The room itself was no longer a cavern; it was a room worthy of the most important people the High Halls contained. There was a hint of sunlight that lightened the height of the ceiling, revealing it at last. It seemed, to Kaylin's eye, to be sky.

There was no blood on the floor; blood remained on clothing and skin. It was theirs, the Tower's actions implied.

"What happened to the other Arcanists?"

"They are in holding cells," the Consort replied, although she hadn't asked it of the Consort, who, while green-eyed, had started to sag in a way that implied she felt as exhausted as Kaylin.

"The High Halls will not be the High Halls we have known. One or two of the oldest of the lords might remember what they will become." She closed her eyes. "I owe you a debt, Lord Kaylin."

"No."

The Consort smiled, although she didn't open her eyes. "You are afraid, perhaps, that I, like the rest of my kin, consider obligation a terrible burden. Were you someone else, perhaps I would. But I understand that you would have done this, regardless. I understand some of what you have done, in a space the rest of us could not touch or perceive.

"I should not speak of it; what is spoken aloud is remembered, and not always in a fashion that is to the speaker's advantage. But you did not hear the Tower's voice, in those final moments—and, Kaylin, I did."

"What did it say?"

"It was wordless," the Consort replied. "In any other individual, it might be considered a scream. But there was joy in it, and I can still feel the reverberations. The Tower has been isolated for too long. And in the Adversary—or whatever he might style himself to be in the future—he has found someone who can hear his voice. They are both old. I do not know how old; I could not clearly hear the Tower's voice, and could not ask. But even the Hallionne have little regard for the passage of time as we mark it." She turned to Lord Evarrim. "It is time we return," she told him. "I would be upon my throne when the cohort emerges."

"How exactly do we emerge?" Mandoran asked in Elantran. Teela rolled her eyes.

"I am not entirely certain," the Consort replied. "This is... not what it has been for the entirety of my life." She glanced up. "But I am certain there is a way out. More certain today than ever."

"And what happens," Sedarias said in much more modulated High Barrani, "to the Test of Name? It exists, and has existed, for a reason."

"That is a subject that will be discussed by the Lords of the Court, but I believe it will change only in one regard: failure will not result in death. Not at the hands of anything but our own kind."

The cohort and Tain remained in the grand and glorious hall that had replaced rough-hewn cavern. The rest of the occupants followed the Consort, with the exception of Nightshade. "I found a way in," he said, a hint of amusement in the words. "I feel it safest to likewise find a way out. The Tower and its test has, until today, held no fear for me; the High Court and its environs is, by its own choice, more deadly."

The Consort bowed to him. She held that bow. Kaylin wondered—as she so often did—about the history between the two.

"I have not seen you wield *Meliannos* for many a year; it has been long since we have stood on the same battlefield."

"And triumphed, yes." The fieflord's eyes were almost green, which was as green as they ever got. "This would not have been my choice of meeting place, but I believe the outcome has long been your desire." He glanced at Kaylin, and then, to Kaylin's surprise, he tendered her the bow he might have offered the Consort. "You have exceeded not expectation, but hope, Lord Kaylin."

And my brother has returned, materially unharmed.

But not unchanged?

Life, as my brother has discovered to his dismay, changes all of us in one way or another. I did not wish him to take this test.

I didn't, either, if we're being honest.

The Consort did. And we bow, as we must, to the Lady's will. But this…this, neither of us expected. My brother is home, and he is alive. What he will make of that life, I do not know—but I intend to survive to watch, even in the lee of Ravellon. *I, too, owe you a great debt.* She heard only truth in the words. But she understood, now, that she had been the wild card of his plans and his hopes, that he had been looking toward the West March for far, far longer than she had been alive.

Yes. My brother's anger at your treatment at my hands is bitter; it stings. But I cannot completely regret it.

There were other ways to ask, she told him, just a hint of exasperation coloring the words. *But at the moment, I can't, either. I think… I think Teela was happy to see you. Which would be a first.*

She cares for Annarion almost as much as I. It has been a comfort to me to know that she can move freely at Court. There is very little she would not do in defense of her ancient friends.

Or her less ancient ones. A thought struck her. "If the price for failing the Test of Name isn't death, does that mean that every Barrani will try it?"

"In all likelihood, yes," the Consort replied.

"Won't it get crowded?"

"I do not know. The test serves a purpose while *Ravellon* exists. But many who might have passed it did not choose to undergo it. I see changes in our future." The changes that she saw didn't shift the color of her eyes. "Come, Lord Kaylin. It is time."

Kaylin hesitated.

"I do not think you need wait for Terrano." This was the

wrong thing to say in the hearing of any other member of the cohort.

Mandoran said, "We're waiting."

"You have not yet emerged as Lords of the Court, and he is your comrade. Waiting—or emerging—is, of course, your choice." Which made it clear that Kaylin didn't have the same option. "I do not know how long Terrano will be gone; you might wait a long while. But I'm sure the Tower will not let you starve."

Three hours later, Kaylin was home. Teela and Severn accompanied her. Nightshade, however, did not, although she surprised herself by inviting him. He accepted Helen, and even appreciated the role she played in the protection of his brother. He was accustomed to sentient buildings—he lived in Castle Nightshade, after all. But he was not entirely comfortable within Helen's walls, and he was clearly exhausted enough that containing his thoughts, hiding them from her, would require too much effort.

None of this was said out loud, of course; all of it, however, was accessible to Kaylin through the bond of name. It was more than she usually felt or heard; she could imagine that were he to cross Helen's boundary, Helen would hear far more.

Helen's Avatar was there to greet them at the door, although she had all the information she needed before they entered the house; her boundaries and control extended to the gates. Which were closed. She knew that the cohort had not accompanied them, but also knew that they were—relatively—safe. The High Court, with its politics and its general scheming, wasn't safe unless compared to the Adversary. And even then, Kaylin thought she'd take the Adversary over the High Court's political maneuvers any day.

Especially now.

Helen opened her arms and Kaylin walked into them, dropping her forehead to the Avatar's shoulder. She mumbled.

"I don't know if it was the right thing to do, dear," Helen replied. "The right thing, the wrong thing—people get so focused on it."

"I'm an officer of the law, Helen."

"Yes, yes, I know. But think. The Hawklord's decision, with regard to you, was right. It is not the only time a risk has been taken. You took that risk, to the Consort's great displeasure, with the Devourer. It is not a risk I would have taken. If the Devourer had not been brought into the Keeper's Garden, it would have been disastrous for our world. But because you could speak to the ancient behemoth, it is, once again, the right choice. Do you understand? Right or wrong is decided on the basis of a significant moment. Or perhaps, more accurately, wrong is. You should bathe," she added. "And sleep."

Kaylin nodded.

"Not that way. That's the dining room."

She was in a bath, thinking about what "bath" had meant in the streets of the fief, when the door to her room opened. Unlike Teela's quarters, a bath here was, if a luxury in comparison to her old life, more contained. For one, there was a tub, not a pool.

She no longer had barred windows, and if her door was the same flimsy wood that it had been in her first apartment—now ash and splinters thanks to Barrani politics—it was vastly more secure. Her own floors creaked, but the halls outside didn't. She found creaking comfortable; she could practically tell where she was in the room by the sound the floor made, which was useful when it was dark.

She therefore heard the door open. "Are they back?"

"Not all of them, dear," Helen replied. "But there's someone here who wants to talk to you."

"I'm wet. And naked."

"He'll wait."

Less dry than she would have liked, and armored with a robe that was admittedly full body length and thick, Kaylin entered her room. Terrano was sitting on the bed. Had he been Teela, he would have been lounging across it, but he was seated almost dead center on the side closest to the bathroom door, huddling in place, knees drawn up beneath his chin, his arms wrapped around his shins.

He did look up when she entered. She knew why he'd come. "Give me a second," she told him, and proceeded to walk around the bed and crawl beneath it from the side he wasn't occupying.

She pulled the small chest in which she stored her few remaining valuables out from beneath the bed—items that an Arcane explosion hadn't managed to destroy, or things that had come to her after she had found Helen.

She pulled out a small box and pocketed it before she walked back around the bed to where Terrano was sitting, unmoving.

"What do you want to do?" she asked him.

He was silent for long enough she thought he wouldn't answer, which was fair. If he knew what he wanted to do, he probably wouldn't be sitting here looking so forlorn.

"They like it here," he said.

"And you don't."

"I don't hate it." More silence followed.

Kaylin joined him, although she kept some distance between them. He wasn't Teela; she had no idea how much space he needed. When he failed to continue, she took up the slack.

"In my fourth year in the Halls of Law," she told him quietly, looking at her hands, "one of the Swords was having trouble with his wife. She was a Hawk. It was…messy. They'd been married for maybe four years, and things weren't going well. I grew up without a father," she added, "and I have no idea what happened to him. I didn't have a strong sense of permanence. I wanted permanence," she added, "because I wanted safety. I wanted stability."

He nodded. He didn't ask her why she was telling him this story; he understood. Or at least understood that it would lead to a point that would make that why clear.

"I didn't understand what had happened, because they'd been so close. And now they were like armed camps. And we were expected to choose a side—and naturally, given one was a Hawk and one was a Sword, it wasn't that hard for me. But—" She shook her head. "David took me aside, and we talked.

"Apparently the Sword had cheated on his wife, and she had found out. She was hurt and angry. And I didn't understand it because I'd have married his wife. Like, it seemed so stupid to me. I didn't understand how he could want some other woman. Leila was tough, she was smart, she was cool under pressure. I thought she was beautiful, but—apparently that's subjective. Because some people are stupid." This last was spoken as if she was still sixteen. Almost seventeen.

What else does he want? What else could he want?

David's smile had been pained. *Everything. We can want everything. We can want things all the time. Sometimes we forget what we have, or sometimes the fact that we have it tarnishes it. I'm married*, he added, as if this was relevant. *Doesn't mean I can't look. Doesn't mean I don't find others attractive. I do. I'm not a different man because I got married. I have the same responses.*

But your wife doesn't hate you enough to throw you out?

I can look. I look, was his affectionate reply. *But here's the thing: what I'm building with my wife, I've committed to building. I want what we have. I want what we have more than I want what someone else has. Or what I don't have. Do I find other people attractive? Sure. Leila is stunning. But…she's not my wife. She hasn't shared my history. She hasn't had my back when things were tough. She's not the person I go home to.*

Kaylin repeated this quietly, still looking at her hands. "He said that he knew he could have what he'd always had before he met his wife—or he could have his wife and make something deeper and stronger from it. But he couldn't have both."

"What did you say to him after he said this?"

"Well… I pointed out that Marcus has a lot of wives, and maybe that would work for us, too."

Terrano shot her a look. "It wouldn't work for us. And I think it would definitely be disaster for Dragons—but that's just a guess."

"That's more or less what he said, too. But: he said he'd made a choice. It curtailed—that was the word he used—his freedom, yes. There were some things he had to think about before doing, and some things he couldn't do even if he wanted to—because he'd made that commitment. He'd promised. And that promise wasn't something his wife did *to* him, and it wasn't something she forced *on* him. He'd chosen. Some days it was harder than others—but he said that some days being a Hawk was much harder than others, and he pointed out that I loved being a Hawk. Well," she added, flushing, "being an almost-Hawk.

"You lived in Alsanis for almost your entire life. Alsanis started as your jailer. So it makes sense that you wanted freedom. All of you," she added. "But…you lived with your family. Your chosen family. I don't know how awkward you found it at first—this whole True Name thing, this people-in-your-thoughts thing. I don't always find it very comfortable, especially not Ynpharion, who pretty much despises me. If I didn't feel the same about him, I'd probably find it painful.

"But… I understand why you chose it. I understand why every single one of you took the risk. Because what I wanted, even when I was totally unworthy of any trust at all, was to find people *I* could trust. And the name would have meant instant trust."

"Or mutually assured destruction," he countered.

"Or that. I don't know why you chose to do it. Having met Sedarias, I can't honestly say that I believe there was no coercion—even if she left the choice to you, in theory. There was going to be a right choice and a wrong choice, and… I wouldn't want to make the wrong choice while Sedarias was in my face. Or knew of my existence at all."

He laughed, releasing his legs. "There was some of that, yes. Fear of Sedarias. Fear of making the wrong choice." He shrugged. "It's so long ago now none of us can think of it as the wrong choice." The smile dimmed.

"In order to escape Alsanis, you changed. You changed slowly, but you changed. I don't know that you understood how much, at the start. I don't know how deliberate it was. I only have Mandoran and Annarion to go on. Annarion doesn't try to change his form. He's not playing with invisibility or shifting states the way Mandoran does. He definitely doesn't get stuck in walls."

This caused Terrano to snicker, as well.

"But the changes are most dramatic in Annarion, because all of his little breaks with reality happen when he's upset." She thought of Annarion on his first—and hopefully only— visit to Castle Nightshade, and couldn't help herself. She shuddered. "He wanted to come home to his brother."

Terrano nodded. "And look how well that worked out."

"When you've lived here and had to listen to them shouting at each other for nights on end, you can make that face."

"I can make a different face, if you'd like."

"Please don't."

He snickered again.

"I think you'd be like Mandoran, if you lived here, not Annarion. But that's the point of all this, isn't it?" She exhaled. "You could stay. You could stay here. Helen would be happy to have you."

"She doesn't know me."

"No. But she trusts what you mean to Annarion and Mandoran, and she's very fond of both of them." She waited.

"It's not the same," he said, once again allowing his shoulders to curl. "I can't hear them. I can't talk to them."

She didn't point out that he could, because she knew what he meant, even if True Names had not had the same effect on her life.

"You don't know what it's like," he continued. "I— Look, we're raised to *be* outsiders. We don't value honesty. We don't value earnestness. It's death. That's what we were taught, growing up: it's death. Someone older and smarter will use whatever we reveal against us, or our families.

"But no one taught us to be ourselves. And ourselves were all we had." He hesitated. "I wanted freedom. I didn't want to come home. I couldn't understand why Sedarias—whose political life started early and happened often—would want to come back. I think Mellarionne was the only family that had a kind of contest to see who'd travel to the West March, as if it were some kind of privilege. But the rest of our families threw us away.

"If I could still hear them, I'd never stay. You don't know what the world is like. All the worlds. All the states. I haven't seen most of them and I've barely scratched the surface." His voice dropped. "But it's so quiet out there. So quiet."

"You came back for them."

He nodded. There was no point in denying it. In the quietest voice he'd used yet, he said, "I missed them. I hate the silence."

She bowed her head, turning her hands in her lap. "Why can't you stay here, and—I don't know, take vacations? Why can't you experiment with form and place, the way Mandoran does?"

"I don't belong here anymore. I can't be part of them."

"Sedarias wants you to stay. I think she's most worried about you, out of all the cohort."

"She doesn't trust me. I mean—she doesn't trust me to survive. She trusts that I won't hurt them, of course. She doesn't believe I've changed that much. I don't think she believes I could."

"And if you had a name? You could hear them. You could speak with them. I don't understand why you couldn't just... do whatever you're doing now."

"No. You don't."

"So tell me."

"It's the name. It's the fact of the name. You have experience with the nameless—or those who've tried to escape the cage of their own names, right?"

She nodded.

"You thought it was stupid."

She nodded again.

"You would. You don't need the name."

"If it weren't for your names, you wouldn't awaken. You wouldn't be alive."

"Yes. As infants, we have no other options. But we don't

remain infants forever, and we have forever, if we're careful. But our names can be used against us."

"They can be used in other ways, as well—you should know this better than most of the Barrani out there."

He shrugged. "The name links us to this place. This state of being. It's where you and your kind live; you couldn't survive some of the places I've been. Or possibly you could, because of the marks of the Chosen—but not the rest of your kind. And not the rest of my kind, either."

She stood, slowly. "I don't want what you want." Her voice was soft; it was a statement of fact. "And I don't understand what you want. But... I understand the desire, the *need*, to be free. You think of Helen as a cage.

"I think of Helen as home. Not *a* home, but *my* home. I understand that this isn't the home you dreamed of, if you dreamed of one at all. I couldn't make the whole of Elantra my home—I can't imagine what your sense of home might be. Maybe home *is* a cage. I can still leave it. I can go to work—which is definitely *not* home—and come back. I need the work," she added. "I need to be a Hawk. If you asked me to choose between being a Hawk and having a home, I'm not sure what I would choose."

"Home," he said, no doubt in his voice.

"I am not at all certain that is true," Helen said, although her Avatar hadn't joined them in the room. "But I think it is the most apt metaphor for this discussion. Part of how Kaylin defines herself is her duties as a Hawk. They have been important to her for far longer than I."

"What if you had to choose between them?" Terrano then asked. Kaylin wasn't certain whether or not he was asking Helen or her. But Helen didn't have the choice to leave. If this was a cage, as Terrano implied, it was locked and barred. Helen could, and did, gain information from those who entered; she offered advice where it was wanted. Sometimes when it wasn't, as well—but everyone did that.

"I don't know," Kaylin finally said. "I could say I'd choose home, because I can always find another job. But…it's not just a job to me. And I could say I'd choose the job because I can always find another place to live—but that place would never be home. I don't know," she said again. "Because I love both. I can't imagine that I wouldn't miss one of them, if I chose the other. I couldn't imagine I wouldn't have regrets."

She slid her hand into the pocket of her bathrobe, and pulled out a small box. "When we were in the West March, Alsanis gave this to me. He said I'd know when to use it."

Terrano didn't even seem surprised.

"I think he thought you couldn't make a choice without understanding what it was you were choosing between. I mean—without having the experience. I think he's kept this for you, and honestly? If it returned to the West March, he'd continue to keep it. You did save him," she added softly. "And I think he'd return the favor if he thought that salvation—yours—was up to him. Maybe you could talk to him about it?"

Terrano shook his head. He held out a hand, and Kaylin set the box in his palm, where it trembled slightly. "I'm going to go take a walk. Alone," he added, not looking at Kaylin. Not speaking to her, either, if she had to guess.

"I will leave the back door open," Helen replied, confirming her suspicion.

Kaylin did not see Terrano the next day.

Or the one after.

Or the one after that.

She did get an invitation to a ceremony to be held at the High Halls, and she would have resented it more but every member of the cohort plus Tain had also received an invitation, as had Teela. It was, however, Sedarias who explained that the use of the word *invitation* was a polite fiction. It was a command, dressed in pretty paper with lovely handwriting.

Although the cohort had—demonstrably—passed the Test of Name, the High Lord considered the return of the lost children to be a moment of great import to the Barrani High Court. That celebration would occur in three days. All were expected to attend.

This had caused a welcome discussion over what had otherwise been a somber breakfast table, although there was some danger, given the color of Teela's and Sedarias's eyes, that it would spill into a less welcome argument. Perhaps because Bellusdeo was present, it didn't.

But on the fourth day after Terrano's departure breakfast was once again glum. Teela remained with Helen; Tain did the same. There were discussions about that, as well. Well, not exactly discussions; there was *gossip* about it, but Teela and Tain kept their disagreements to themselves. Teela was the only member of the cohort who could detach herself enough that she could maintain some semblance of privacy.

The cohort accepted this; if they'd grown into a hive mind over the centuries, they'd done so without Teela. Teela's absence, while it had been a cause for guilt and sadness, had not fundamentally changed their nature.

Terrano's absence, however, had left a hole in the group mind.

Four days became five; five became six. She guessed that Terrano had made his choice, and she understood, because everything she'd said had been truth.

Since the cohort had already accepted his decision, their continued gloom surprised Kaylin. But they hadn't had much time to make a choice, or accept a choice or discuss individual choices on that day in the green. They'd made their choices, and they accepted them. They could, once again, return home. The absence of Terrano had not yet become as real as it became in the months that followed.

His physical presence had been better than nothing, but...it was only his physical presence. It was why, Kaylin reflected, they pulled him into their group huddles, the physical piles that most resembled the Leontine family unit. If they couldn't hear him, they could still assure themselves of his presence.

That was gone. Apparently so was whatever it was that animated the cohort—or at least forced them to interact with words outsiders could hear. They were silent. Even Mandoran, whose idea of breakfast chat was admittedly tweaking the Dragon.

Bellusdeo asked Helen—before the cohort came down to breakfast on the seventh day—whether or not Terrano had even bothered to say goodbye.

"No, dear."

"I'm worried about Mandoran. He's been almost polite in the past week."

"I heard that. What do you mean, *almost?*"

"You kept your mouth shut," Bellusdeo replied without missing a beat. Any embarrassment at worry on her part was probably only in Kaylin's imagination.

Mandoran took a seat at the table directly opposite Bellusdeo's. "Perhaps I'm attempting to treat my title as Lord of the High Court with the dignity it deserves."

"Oh, please. I'm eating."

The rest of the cohort filed into the dining room. If Mandoran was up to his usual sparring with Bellusdeo, they weren't, although Annarion had a slight half grin on his face, which he wiped clean, figuratively speaking, as he sat.

"He is attempting to practice appropriate dignity," Sedarias said; she was the last to be seated. She wore a deep purple dress that accentuated her color. And her power. She looked like a storybook queen. "He will appear before the High Lord and the Consort as a Lord of the Court, and he will do so without fidgeting or attempting to pass through the nearest wall in boredom."

"I wish I could be there to see it," Bellusdeo said, golden-eyed.

"Given the difficulties your visit to the West March theoretically caused, that would usually be impossible," Sedarias replied.

Kaylin's ears twitched. She didn't say anything; Bellusdeo, however, did.

"Usually?"

Sedarias's smile deepened; Kaylin swore she could see exposed Barrani canines. "Were it not for your intervention in the West March, we would not have arrived in Elantra. We would not have taken the Test of Name. And Mellarionne would not now have a ruler." Definitely canines.

Tain's eyes were blue, although Kaylin didn't see much of them, as he covered his face with his hands.

For the first time in a week, Sedarias appeared to be enjoying herself. Kaylin decided that Sedarias and enjoyment should be kept a continent apart.

"Risky," Teela said, without any of Tain's obvious dismay.

"It is," Sedarias agreed, still smiling. "But Lord Bellusdeo would be an excellent emissary, and she has proved herself a valuable ally—a dependable ally—to Mellarionne. To me," she added, in case this wasn't obvious. "Mellarionne is not, despite my brother's best attempts to weaken it, a house without resources. I would, of course, extend an invitation. I would almost consider it a boon should you accept."

The Emperor wouldn't.

"You have a plan?" Bellusdeo asked, her eyes still golden.

"She always has a plan," Mandoran said. His eyes were now a blue-green, but he seemed resigned.

"If I am to play a part in it, I would like to hear it myself."

"Of course," Sedarias replied. She opened her mouth. Closed it.

Kaylin could see a wave of stillness hit the cohort at once; hands froze, cutlery held; cups stopped between table and mouth. Eyes widened, mouths remained closed—or open— as if movement itself had been denied all of them.

Mandoran was first to rise. Annarion was second. In a flowing stream, the rest of the cohort joined them, pushing chairs back from table, their eyes turned toward the open— and empty—doorway.

Sedarias remained seated. Sedarias and Teela. Severn was no longer at the breakfast table; he had returned both to the Halls of Law and his own home.

Sedarias's eyes were not a color that Barrani eyes normally adopted; they weren't a color ascribed to Barrani eyes at all. Nor, now that she was looking, were any of the cohort's eyes. They stayed the same shape, though.

Kaylin stayed where she was seated, as did Bellusdeo; Teela glanced at Tain, who had lowered his hands, where they rested, flat, against the tablecloth. Sedarias lowered her head; her chin almost touched the space between her collarbones.

Terrano walked into the dining room, his eyes the color of the cohort's eyes, his form Barrani. They moved toward him in a rush, as if they couldn't believe what Kaylin was almost certain they were hearing. But they paused without touch-ing him, and stepped back, stepped away, to give him room.

To give him a clear path to Sedarias, who remained seated at the end of the table, her back toward that door and its oc-cupant. He walked toward her and, to Kaylin's surprise, gently wrapped both arms around her shoulders. She stiffened.

Terrano said nothing—not out loud—but Sedarias lifted her head. She was crying.

Kaylin almost looked away. Almost. But Sedarias caught her gaze and, as always, held it.

"This isn't what I wanted for him," the Barrani woman considered the leader of the cohort said. "This isn't what he wanted." She closed her eyes.

Terrano, however, shook his head, and their hair, black and black, mingled, he was that close to her face.

"You made your choice—"

"Yes. I can tell you all about it now. I can *truly* tell you." He hugged her, his arms tightening before they fell away. He then turned to face the rest of the cohort. "They're really noisy, you know?" he said to the room that couldn't hear the internal voices of his friends. "I wanted freedom. You were all so much a part of me I didn't think about what freedom would mean.

"I loved the freedom. I did. I can't promise that I'll never regret it. But it was empty. It was empty without you. It wasn't the same. If you'd all come with me, it still wouldn't have been the same. You could see and hear what I saw and heard, but...not together."

The cohort converged then. Sedarias rose.

Her eyes were Barrani green; they were reddened, but if she cried, she didn't weep. "Are we his cage, then?" she asked Kaylin.

Kaylin shook her head. "Not his cage, but his home."

★ ★ ★ ★ ★